THE
EVER
AFTER
OF
ASHWIN
RAO

Library of Congress Cataloging-in-Publication Data.
Viswanathan, Padma, 1968-
The ever after of Ashwin Rao : a novel / Padma Viswanathan.
    pages ; cm
 ISBN 978-1-59376-613-9
 I. Title.
PR9199.4.V57E94 2015
813'.6--dc23
2015005832

Cover design: Leah Springate
Interior design: Tabitha Lahr

SOFT SKULL PRESS
An Imprint of COUNTERPOINT
2560 Ninth Street, Suite 318
Berkeley, CA 94710
www.softskull.com

Printed in the United States of America
Distributed by Publishers Group West

10 9 8 7 6 5 4 3 2 1

THE
EVER
AFTER
OF
ASHWIN
RAO

PADMA
VISWANATHAN

SOFT SKULL PRESS

For the lost,
And for the living.

I dont think it makes no diffrents where you start the telling of a thing. You never know where it begun really. No moren you know where you begun your own self.

—*Riddley Walker*, Russell Hoban

SUMMER 2004

All the new thinking is about loss.
In this it resembles all the old thinking.
                                        —Robert Hass

*A*t three in the morning, New Delhi's air is mostly remnants. This is its quietest hour, though the city is not still. The sounds of night business concluding, morning business being prepared, all sorts of shrouded transactions: these carry.

I locked my door and went upstairs to lay the key in its envelope on Vijaya's threshold. She was a widow I barely considered a friend, particularly since she wanted to be more than that, but I had to leave a key with someone. I would be away in Canada for a year. Fetching my bag from the landing, I trotted briskly down the stairs, across the courtyard and into the carport, clicking my tongue for the cat. Dirty-orange fur, three rickety legs, strangely swollen jowls; it slunk around as though hoping to be hit.

I put out last night's take-away, lamb biryani, at the usual spot. I had never wanted to keep a pet, but was overcome by the urge to feed the patchy creature. A memory knocked. My nephew, Anand, at six months maybe. When do they start with the pabulum? My sister, Kritika, was feeding him. She called me over—"Watch, Ashwin!"—as she lifted the little spoon toward his face and he opened his mouth, SO wide, his head bobbing a little, the eyes so serious, as though this were a contract he had agreed to fulfill: survival. My sister and I laughed until our sides hurt.

And two years after Anand came my niece, Asha.

Asha, my Asha. The child of my life. Sometimes I thought I recalled a whisper of her smell—green grapes and the pages of books; perhaps a hint of nutmeg?—but even the motion of my mind turning toward it fanned it away.

The cat still hadn't appeared and my auto-rickshaw was waiting. "Airport," I told the driver, no *good morning* necessary. He had been, for fifteen years, my favourite among those at the corner rank—almost surly, always prompt. He tossed his beedi and unthrottled his engine.

Two weeks from today, June 23, would be the nineteenth anniversary of a jet bombing that killed 326 people I didn't know, and three I did: Kritika, Anand, Asha. It had taken nearly eighteen years to drag two perpetrators into court. Last spring, April 2003, I had gone to Vancouver to witness the trial's start. My first time back in Canada since 1985. A Screaming Reluctance to See It had battled in me with a Driving Compulsion to See It. Guess which won?

Victims' families, along with various other concerned parties and/or gawkers, came from all over. They milled in the grand atrium at the provincial courthouse in Vancouver, their hot, thick optimism mingling with a slight steam from the bloodthirsty.

The atrium's high, glass walls gave the all-too-obvious image of transparency. Kafka's trial could never happen here. Glass houses: Canadians don't throw stones. On the government side, the excitement was both more stately and more tawdry: press releases, security expenditures, and a bullet- and bomb-proof courtroom custom-built several circles of hell underground, down where the sun don't shine.

Only two of the many hot-air buffoons allegedly involved in the bombing were standing trial. I would name them, but what's in a name? I try to block their faces, but they rise in my mind's eye. Specimens. Bad examples of their community, their race, their species. Bad men.

I felt the trial to be a sham and yet I had gone to see it. Why? And furthermore, Why?

Why a sham? Because it came so very late—and after so much had changed, from the political situations that fed the bomb plot to the security situations that permitted it—that it would do nothing to prevent future terrorist acts. The accused did not regret what they had done, but neither would they plant any other bombs.

But what of punishment? you might ask. I *hated* those men. I might gladly have punished them with my own hands, not that I have ever done such a thing. But for the government to mete out, what—justice? Hardly. No government in the world possessed a moral scepter weighty enough to flog these puny fellows.

So. Why had I gone? At the time, I didn't know why. In the courtroom, it wasn't the accused who interested me but the bereaved, the others like myself, those who had lost the people most important to them. Apart from my now-late parents, I had only ever spoken to one other living victim: my brother-in-law, Suresh, Kritika's husband. A good fellow, but we had not been in contact since a year or two after the disaster. I looked for him in the courthouse crowds, fruitlessly.

How is he? I thought, for the first time in years. Perhaps it was the first time I had ever thought that. When the bomb struck, my first thoughts were not for the suffering of others. Except my parents. Well, except my father.

How was Suresh? How were these people around me? These people *like* me?

In the therapeutic context, such a question would be no problem. I am a psychologist. Put me across from a client and I will ask, intuit, tease or ferret out everything either of us needs to know. Surrounded by the crowds at the trial, though, I didn't know where to start. Every two hours, after each break in the trial (lawyers need their Starbucks), I would have someone new next to me, such as the heavy woman in a *salwar kameez* whose aroma of frying dough couldn't quite cover an inky, pooling despair, or the tiny, twiggy-smelling couple in outdated business suits who sat without touching until, hearing some detail I didn't catch, they took each other's hands without meeting each other's eyes. Across the room, I saw a famous dancer whose husband and daughters had been killed. She had become active in the victims' advocacy group, and I had seen her name and photo in news reports. She had remarried, a gentleman whose wife and children had been on that same plane.

This was why I had come, I realized, to find out how these people had coped up. Not only *how* as in *how well*, but rather *by what means* did they go on?

There were so many of them there, but not a single one I could sit down with and ask. I should have contacted Suresh, I thought, then. Was he still in Montreal? Was he still alive? Who had he become in the years since losing his family—since losing my family?

✳ ✳ ✳

My auto slowed in the thickening traffic as we near Indira Gandhi International. Time can be defined by motion, I mused; the airport should be its own time zone. I wanted to be in bed, not assailed by people, vehicles, shouting, honking, business. Can one have jet lag in advance of a trip? I was hastily erecting a Potemkin village of mental activity, to let me get on the plane.

✳ ✳ ✳

Last spring, I had booked a month in Vancouver, but after only a few days attending the trial, I could take no more.. What to do with the three-plus weeks left to me? Try to answer my questions, perhaps. So instead of returning to India early, I retreated to my comfort zones: the university, the library.

Surely others had written about this, I was thinking. Over the years, in psychology journals, I had come across so many studies on victims of mass trauma. Longitudinal, informational, survey- or interview- or standardized-test-based. Beirut, Belfast, Kigali. I had never seen one on the Air India disaster, but then, I'd never properly searched.

After the World Trade Tower attacks, nearly half of all Americans showed PTSD symptoms. How did the researchers think to test for that? They must have observed the symptoms in others; they might have felt them themselves. Had Canadians suffered similarly, following the bombing? The U.S. has about ten times Canada's population. Three thousand plus people were killed in the September 11 attacks, three hundred plus in the Air India disaster. Do the math. It should add up, but it doesn't.

Canadians at large did not feel themselves to have been attacked, although nearly every passenger aboard that flight was a born or naturalized Canadian. Canada's prime minister infamously sent a telegram of condolences to the Indian government, who had lost what? A jet. Oh, and a couple of pilots. No wonder Canada failed to prevent the bombing in the first place. No wonder they had failed, for eighteen years, to bring it to trial.

And, I learned now, failed to take the bombing up in scholarship. I found no articles that addressed my questions. I looked, though it seemed even more improbable, for books. I found the same three I had read over fifteen years ago, one sensational, one implausible, and one by Bharati Mukherjee and Clark Blaise.

Mukherjee: tough broad. I loved her novels about the no-man's land—or, more often, no-woman's land—of the transplant. I might have felt nothing in common with her protagonists had I met them in life, but I identified with them as I never had with fictional characters before. Her book on the bombing was called *The Sorrow and the Terror*. (That title, in huge block letters and lurid flame-tones: really?) I sat with it in the reading room of the Vancouver public library. Much of it was good, far better than I had given it credit for the first time around, back when my pain was most acute.

Like all of us, Mukherjee and Blaise were appalled by the Canadian government's refusal for six months to acknowledge that the jet had been destroyed by a bomb, even given that another Air India jet, also originally departing from Vancouver, had blown up an hour earlier in Tokyo. Officials didn't want to admit their negligence. An FBI plant had met radical Sikhs who wanted to blow shit up in India, poison the water supply, disrupt the economy, kill thousands. The newly formed Canadian Security and Intelligence Service had tailed a motley crew of brown radicals who kept muttering to one another in secret code in Punjabi, a language none of CSIS's west coast agents spoke, despite five generations of Sikh settlement here. Phones were bugged, conversations were taped and sent back to Ottawa for transcription, all routine, no sense of urgency. After transcription, translation. After translation, decoding. ("Ready to write the book?" asked a pay phone caller. "Yes, let's write the book," responded the man who had picked up in some suburban home.) After decoding, perhaps alarm. (Wait a sec, is this—? *What* are they—?) But then, of course, it was too late.

And right after the tapes were transcribed, they were erased, per routine, leaving no original evidence to present at a future trial.

All that is laid out in the first part of Mukherjee–Blaise's book, a very serviceable catalogue of failures. Part two "honours" the victims, telling their stories in their voices, but framing and bending them so that this stream converges with the first to become a single roaring river of accusation: that the Canadian government failed to see this as a Canadian problem and a Canadian tragedy, even though it was a plot hatched by Canadians in Canada that resulted in hundreds of Canadian deaths.

"But it is never so simple!" I said, slapping the book's face, even though they were right. It was their methods and their tone that I disagreed with—but more on that in time.

Whatever I thought of the analysis, the interviews were a generation old. Had no one tried to learn what had happened to these people since? I hunted again for articles. I enlisted librarians to double-check my search terms. They were as puzzled as I—*What a good question*, they said. *I can't believe no one has asked it before.* "Sorry, sir. Looks like you're going to have to do a study," one gentleman in wire-rimmed glasses told me, glancing away from his screen to flash me a grin, then freezing when he saw my frozen face.

I had been in a thick, paralyzing fog, less and less able to work— I still believed in my work, but had lost faith in my ability to do it. I overcame this tower of self-doubt, this mountain of lassitude, to come to Canada, to witness the start of the trial. This decision, this trip, was the single meaningful thing I'd done in a year, which is not to say I had known what it meant. I had been suspicious, because it couldn't be the trial I was coming for. Rather, the trial led me to this: the subject of my next book. I should have known, as they say.

* * *

Fifteen months later, the trial was still dragging on, and I was returning to Canada to begin work on that book. I had avoided Air India on my last trip, but this time, I made myself fly Delhi–Heathrow–Montreal, reversing the route of all those dear departed and retracing my own of so many years ago.

At Indira Gandhi International's security gate, I slipped my bare feet back into my sandals and tried to see the X-ray of my single carry-on through a security guard's eyes.

I first left India in 1969, to attend medical school at McGill, but then abandoned that course of studies during my third year, in favour of a PhD in psychology. Then, as I was finishing my doctorate in 1975, I hit it off with a couple of Ottawa psychologists at a conference. We stayed in touch, and they eventually invited me to join their practice.

The conference was on Narrative Therapy, a term I heard for the first time that year, an idea that, at first, grasped me more than I grasped it.

Ever since I was very young, I've kept a journal. Not unusual, you might say. Lots of people do. True. My father kept a journal—he recorded in it the details of his days, where he went, whom he met, what he ate, what irritated my mother. My uncle kept a journal—he recorded each thing he bought and how much it cost. His entire life in purchases. He showed it to me once, with unreflexive pride. He thought everyone should keep such a book.

But I keep a journal differently. I note, on a left-hand page, an anecdote—something characteristic or outrageous a friend or family member said, or perhaps a confidence told to me. On the facing page, for as many pages as it takes, I properly tell the story: third-person, quasi-fictionalized, including matters not witnessed, details I can't really know; and so try to explain what I have seen or heard.

All my friends are in there. Everyone in my family, except my mother—I have often described the inexplicable things she says and does, but long ago bowed to their inexplicability. There was no sense in my trying to write fiction that explains them. I also make notes on my own life, though I have never tried to make fiction out of that.

When I was young, I hid the journal above a rafter in the room where my sister and I slept and studied. Kritika saw me writing in it, but I tried to keep it from her. It was a private endeavour. My countrymen don't believe in privacy, so I'm not sure how I got that idea. Perhaps some child in an English book kept a secret diary and the notion infected me.

My sister told my mother about the journal. They found it and read it, then my sister took it to show my friends.

Only one took it very badly, but that was because the passing around of the journal meant everyone knew about his incestuous relationship with his aunt, which I never would have divulged. He blamed Kritika, and rightly. She was a little like my mother, in her use of an imagined victimhood to justify morally dubious acts. Several others disliked one story about themselves, but found another story to redeem the first.

Kritika, by contrast, didn't like the way I wrote about her, ever. One story was based on a series of small lies she told when we were on holiday, staying with relatives. Each one cast her as disadvantaged or needy and told how she had gained something for herself: the final portion of a dessert, the window seat on the train. I wrote the story from her point of view, so it wasn't entirely unsympathetic, but as her fibs accumulated, it became clear they could be interpreted another way—my way. I may have been too close to her to get her right. Or it may have been my accuracy that offended her.

After I came to Canada, my journal-writing stopped. I seemed unable to represent Canadians on the page. I couldn't authentically write dialogue for them, for instance. I couldn't imagine details or deduce motivations. I could write about Indian acquaintances (dinner friends, I called them—Indian families who brought me home and fed me, out of some fellow feeling), but this was a lonely enterprise. They were not, generally, people who interested me very much.

Yet when, in my final year of grad school, I saw a notice for that conference, "Start Making Sense: the Uses of Narrative in Therapy," I felt an instinctive pull. I attended the conference and had some excellent conversations. One of them resulted in a job.

Four or five years after, I met Rosslyn. This was at another conference—"Mental Health Professionals in the Ottawa Public Schools." I never would have attended except that someone from our practice needed to go. Boring as hell. Rosslyn agreed, even as a newly minted guidance counsellor with much to learn.

There were many matters we agreed on, Rosslyn and I. It's nice to recall that, though my recollections depend on my moods. By the time we met, I was already feeling a kind of disaffection with my Canadian middle-class clientele. But *disaffection* is too strong. Boredom? Not quite that either, though it seemed that if I saw children, it was for tantrums and truancy; adolescents, anorexia and related rebellions. Adults? Marital woes, anxiety, depression.

I found my clientele homogeneous. Rosslyn thought my inability to distinguish them was a failure of imagination. At the time, her criticism annoyed me, but I might agree with her now. It wasn't so much that the clients and their problems were homogeneous, it was that I wasn't perceptive enough to differentiate them. My therapeutic interest is in framing individuals' maladies as stories within stories within stories, the way people themselves are nested within families and societies. Presenting problems may be superficially repetitive, but they will also contain many unique facets. My challenge is to tell the story on the individual's terms, giving a nuanced sense of his problems' origins—in himself, in his community, in societal expectations.

I came to attribute my blocks to my newness here. My clients' aims; their ideals; the things they felt they deserved in life—much of this did not make sense to me, even after long, hard thought. I could parrot their accounts of their family histories, homes, schools, but these places and people were not imaginatively available to me. In talk therapy, I would tell my clients versions of their stories, but these were so much narrower, shallower, than what I hoped for.

Rosslyn occasionally referred children to the practice where I worked. Anorexics or vandals she referred to whichever of the psychologists had a vacancy in our caseload. Native children and immigrants with adjustment troubles she tried to refer straight to me. I refused. She grew impatient trying to convince me. *She* was refusing, I thought, to see that, as hard as it was for me to help mainstream Canadians with their mainstream problems, the prospect of trying to address outsiders' problems was even further from my capacities. She thought I would identify with them, while I feared I wouldn't be able to tell their intrinsic psychological problems from the ones engendered more by societal demands. Which story nests and which is nested? I would be the blind leading the blind up and down Escher stairways.

The only exceptions were Indians. I saw two, in the four (or so) years that Rosslyn and I were together. One was—yet again!—an anorexic, a

wealthy Canadian-born teenybopper. The other was an engineering student who had attempted suicide after failing classes and admitting to a
friend that he was homosexual.

With them, I attempted the method I had mused on for so long
in the absence of opportunities to test it. They told me their stories;
I wrote my versions; I gave these back. We discussed, they corrected,
I revised, they revised; we worked, together, toward the future chapters, in which they became the people they envisioned—with increasing specificity, clarity, logic—themselves to be. The narratives broke up
their monolithic notions of their identities, their histories, and, most
importantly, their destinies.

These two early attempts were ridiculously successful. If Rosslyn
had thought me arrogant already (I was; I am), I must have become insuf-
ferable then. And yet these were the times she was at her most encouraging. She only wished I would find the confidence to use the method in the
rest of my practice. I believed I was not qualified and would not be for
many years, if ever. She thought me stubborn. Again, she was not wrong.

Then, in October of 1982, my father fell ill.

I arranged a leave to go back to New Delhi and spend time with
him. Kritika also came home, but only briefly: she was, by this time,
raising her own family in Montreal and couldn't stay long. While in
Delhi, I arranged to meet with a psychiatrist and a sociologist whose
collaborative work I had long admired. I spent a day with them at the
famous Institute for Research on Developing Societies (IRDS), looking in on meetings; even, when asked, offering an opinion. A week or
so later, the centre's resident Freudian, with a Jungian in tow, came to
see me at my parents' home. They proposed a collaboration to let me
further explore my theoretical model. They would give me an office at
IRDS, say, for three months or so, and resources to explore my ideas.
They suggested I see a couple of short-term clients. Their own client
bases included inmates from Delhi jails moving toward release, victims
of political violence or police brutality, police officers themselves, low-
caste university students, divorcées. India and Indians, they told me,
needed me more than did the West.

Psychologists know how to persuade. My practice in Ottawa granted me an extended leave, and I mentioned it to Rosslyn when we talked

by phone, as we did each Sunday evening. She was glad to hear me so excited, or I thought that's what I heard. It was hard to read her mood from half a world away, and I might not have been sufficiently attentive.

At the end of those three months, my work was barely starting to yield results. I had, perhaps rashly, taken on a few clients who needed more than three months' therapy. Perhaps I did it because I knew it would create an obligation in me to stay. I had begun again to write, for my practice and otherwise, in a way I had not for nearly fifteen years. Imagine how that felt. Like releasing a hand that had been tied behind my back—numbness, pins and needles, then a return of strength until it became as it once was, second nature.

I extended my leave for another three months. Rosslyn seemed to accept my motivations and voiced no objections. And yet our conversations grew tepid. It was hard for me to maintain interest in her professional activity, for the reasons I have mentioned. Talk of our days also felt remote, comparing her life in her nation's capital to mine in mine. She drove to work past tulips and the placid Rideau Canal. I saw from my bus window a crowd of newly minted Tibetan refugees; a protest, turned violent, against violence in Punjab; Indira Gandhi, with security agents and sons. What could she say? "Geez." "Wow." "Neat."

I wasn't telling her everything. Delhi was tense, and dangerous because of it. Indira Gandhi's Emergency was long over, but the sense of her reign as decadent and bloody remained. The optimism that had still tenuously prevailed when I'd left in '69 was in pieces, particularly in Punjab, our only Sikh-majority state, which was agitating for independence. Indira's response was to put the state under President's Rule. What's that old saw? To a lady with a hammer, every problem looks like a nail. Being at the Institute for Research on Developing Societies, though, felt like being part of the solution, while in Canada, I had felt like I was hiding my head in a hole. I met political scientists and sociologists who were studying our government, its problems, our people's response; I saw clients who personified, in many ways, our struggles.

At the expiry of my second leave, June 1, the IRDS offered me a permanent place. I thought about it, for an hour or so, and accepted.

Why did I not call Rosslyn that day? Why didn't I ask her to join me? How could I? I would have had to propose, but we hadn't quite got to that point before I left—or I hadn't—in part because of my problems with the marital institution. Our relationship had been largely static in the months since I left. She couldn't come to stay at my parents' house unless we were married, but it was unheard of in India at that time for a woman to live by herself, nor would I ask it of her. Would it be right to ask her to leave her family, friends, job, all that was familiar, to come and join me? What would she do with herself in India?

Really: did I think it all through like this, back then? No. I was revelling in the new force and clarity of my work. I had no wish to wade about in the marshes of my heart.

* * *

It was in exactly this time that the tension in Punjab became suddenly concentrated in the area around the Golden Temple, Sikhdom's holiest shrine, in Amritsar. The rebels' leader would roam the Punjabi country-side with his followers on missions of "purification"—violent confrontations with members of other sects, as well as acts of nationalist assertion—and then retreat, regroup and re-pray in the the Golden Temple complex, their safehouse and stronghold.

For as long as the renegades managed to survive in their bastion, they could continue to wage their war on the disagreeable sectarians and secularists. If, alternatively, by making Sikhdom's holiest place his fort, their leader was trying to tempt Indira Gandhi to make of him a martyr there—well, he succeeded in that.

June 3 was a holy day. The pathways and shrines of the temple were pilgrim-packed, as were the hostel, offices and library within the temple's grounds. That night, a curfew silenced the city streets as the militants shrank from the temple thoroughfares into the sanctum sanctorum.

June 4, the Dragon Lady's army began its assault, a seventeen-hour shooting day, with brief pauses for the army to invite pilgrims to exit the complex. Few dared. Reports leaked out: The army locked sixty pilgrims into a hostel room overnight—this was to protect them—but without water or fans, all but five were dead when the doors were unlocked the next morning. Crossfire wounded innocents as they drank from the gutters' blood-tainted water, all they could find.

We followed it all, at the office, blow by blow, shot by shot. We heard later that the generals had never imagined the fighters would be

so well armed or so persistent, but imagination is not, I suppose, a quality much cultivated in the army. Rebels popped out of manholes, shot
at the soldiers' knees, then disappeared again into the anthill that is
the temple complex. The generals admired their courage and cunning,
wished those Sikhs were on their side, as in days of yore. But the only
way to get rid of ants is to kill them all.

June 5, they brought in the tanks.

Rosslyn called that night, a Sunday.

"How are you?" I said. "Have you been following all this on the news?"

"All what?" she asked.

I was flummoxed.

"The Golden Temple stuff?" she asked.

"What did you think?"

"I was confused because you said, *How are you*, and . . . oh, never
mind. How are you, Ashwin?"

"Shocked. Appalled. So many dead who have no association with
the rebels." I sounded accusatory, to my own ear, and could feel I was
accusing her, though she didn't take it that way.

"Barbaric."

"Why can't we all just get along, eh?"

This time my tone penetrated. She took the bait. "I'm not saying
it's not complicated, Ashwin. I know it is. But it's not like you've told me
anything that's not on the news."

I waited. She waited.

"So are you going to tell me about it?" she asked. "The IRDS has
to be buzzing."

"It is."

"And so . . . you're still there? Your leave expired Tuesday. You're,
what—you're just hanging around?"

"They offered me a permanent place." So much had happened. I
hadn't told her already? "I took it." And then it occurred to me to ask,
"Are you considering coming here, to join me?"

"Should I be?"

I took a breath, which she interrupted, saying, "Don't answer that."
I didn't.

"I had better go," she said.

"That's fine." Did I really think it was? "We'll talk next week."

She didn't pick up the next week, when I called, or the week after. I was piqued. Why should I keep trying? A letter arrived the week after that.

It's not that I don't want to be in touch at all, Ashwin, but obviously I'm not part of your decisions any longer. I'm hurting. I didn't see this coming. It looks to me as if we've broken up just because you had to go back and not because of any problem in our relationship. Our relationship had no pull? I'm hurting badly.

She was right that I had seized on an opportunity and an excuse: the work, the illness. Though my father seemed largely to have recovered, there was also pressure from my mother that her only son should be closer than the very farthest point on the globe. I didn't fool myself that her complaints would lessen in proportion to my proximity, but my father also was glad to have me closer.

Rosslyn was also right that these were reasons to return to India but not reasons to break with her. I hadn't known, until she wrote, that I had broken with her. The shock of understanding also brought me to acknowledge the discomfort I had been denying, through these six months in India. While living in Canada, I had been able to avoid thinking of the many ways that I had always felt alienated from my native society. I am a naturally anti-social creature, born into the most social of places. Perhaps I had left India before I could articulate my own non-belonging. But then, the vocabulary of non-conformism was only coming into flower in the West when I arrived there, and it is only now, thirty years later, starting to gain a foothold in India. Spending nearly fifteen formative years in the West had, yes, formed me, in ways I had been denying. My thinking, my way of being, even my English, had changed. I could write about Indians, but perhaps I could have written about Canadians, as well, if I'd tried harder. I wrote to Rosslyn about these realizations, but didn't press her to come. I suppose I was still not sure of what I was doing. She didn't write back.

By October, I was ready to consider visiting Canada. I wrote to Rosslyn to suggest I return for the winter holidays, when she would have time off. I said that we should talk, in person, about the possibility of a shared future. I said, since I was finally starting truly to feel it, that I missed her. I was also very much missing Kritika's children, who I used to visit once a month.

I wasn't sure at all how the conversation with Rosslyn should go. I had recently made an offer on a flat. I wasn't entirely unhappy staying with my parents, but would be more content to live alone again—one of the ways I had become Western, or had always been different from my countrymen.

My stay with my parents had been congenial enough, though. They had a large house, which we had moved into some twenty-five years earlier. I had continued to attend high school across town and then left for university, so I never formed attachments to the place. My parents were by now quite settled here, however, and I had met a few neighbours through them.

My cousin, Vivek, his wife and their children were also staying with us. His parents, down south, were unhappy about his unemployability and his indifferent attempts to renounce alcoholism. They had appealed to my father, the family patriarch, who obliged by taking their son in and trying to find him a job. Vivek's wife had started vending saris and nightgowns out of the house, which brought in a little cash, though she also had to tolerate cracks from my mother about the hoi polloi tramping through the main hall. Vivek himself was forever running after pyramid schemes. He had recently cornered me in my room on his return from a revival meeting on expanding one's potential. I don't even think he had been drinking; he just had some questions.

"Where is mind?" he inquired, aflame with insight. "Is it here?" he wanted to know, pointing at his temple. He pointed at his chest. "Here?" At the heavens. "Here?" I resisted the urge to point at my elbow, my ass, my open door.

The best thing about the living arrangement was their children. Vivek and Jana had two, a boy and a girl a bit younger than Kritika's kids. Their presence attracted others into the house, which throbbed with slamming doors and bell-like shouts, with childish vitality itself.

Their favourite thing was to ask about Canada, and when they learned about Halloween, they begged for a dress-up party. They chattered all week about costumes; I was to provide sweets. I was thrilled about hosting a children's party, to a degree that (the IRDS secretaries informed me) compromised my dignity and my public image as a curmudgeon. I planned to dress up as a bad-tempered female vegetable-seller: I had cajoled an old sari out of my mother and fitted a wig with a wooden tray to fill with candy instead of peppers or eggplants. For days already I had shooed youngsters from my door as I transformed my bedroom into a haunted house.

The night before, I phoned Kritika and spoke to Asha. She and a gaggle of her friends were dressing up as characters from *The Wizard of Oz*. She would be the Tin Man. Anand got on the phone at his mother's behest, cool and laconic. I asked him if he was too old to dress up. He didn't answer, but seemed interested in my party plans.

I recall ticking off the final arrangements on my commute to work that morning. I had three clients to see that day and a meeting with a sub-set of my colleagues to discuss a multidisciplinary research initiative on the descendants of Partition. Though still in early stages, we were gaining momentum, and already had the sense the project would be massive.

When I think back now to the moment I entered the IRDS that morning, my memories are cinematically exaggerated. I could see no one, which was very unusual: the office was typically bustling by the time I got there, not with the senior fellows, who tended to keep later and more irregular hours the more senior they became, but with the office staff and junior academics, who were always ready to exchange a friendly word. Office doors were open as a policy: much of the point of the institute was to encourage dialogue and cross-fertilization. I only closed my door when seeing clients, and had been given a special room for this on a less-trafficked floor.

I was whistling as I entered. I am competent at whistling, perhaps more so than at conversation, and was feeling jaunty. The sound, in my recollection, was sucked away from me in the emptiness of the cor-ridors. I entered one of the conference rooms to find everyone huddled around a radio.

Indira Gandhi: shot.

Shot. The word in English is more onomatopoeic than ever we realize.

Shhh. The smooth sailing of bullet through barrel, fricting iron against iron, joined and separated by the hastening oil.

Ahhh. Iron against unresisting air, a fleshly sigh of admission.

T. The consonant finality of the bullet coming to rest.

We dispersed after some time and went about our business as

slightly conflicting reports trickled in by radio and telephone: two men with turbans had assassinated the prime minister. There had been an attempted assassination on the prime minister and she was being rushed to hospital. Mrs. Gandhi's Sikh bodyguards had shot and killed her in apparent retaliation for her having ordered the storming of the Golden Temple in June.

It was the last version that was borne out, exactly the sort of thing that many at the IRDS studied: communal conflict and cycles of revenge.

In my case, I saw therapeutic clients. All made reference to the news, but then turned to their own problems, the intimate narratives and narratives of intimacy that were more under their power to direct than ever they had thought.

Events in the democracy, however—the ones we as a nation had thought we had the power to direct—turned out to be beyond us.

Early that afternoon, when we convened our meeting to discuss the post-Partition project, we spoke only of the assassination and the events that had led up to it. There must have been seven or eight of us around the table, some talking with excitement; others, including the two Sikhs, more circumspect. Opinions varied, but people seemed too shocked to clash outright. India's current incarnation was less than forty years old. The assassination was a nadir in our young democracy's history. That any Sikhs, whose community was famously loyal to the multiplicitous notion of modern India, could feel so marginalized as to resort to this act seemed as tragic as the act itself. None of us was a fan of the prime minister, which fact also saddened us. She'd increasingly played the paranoid autocrat, rather than the freedom fighter and democracy defender she had been in her youth. But even through her various national and local suspensions of civil liberties, it had been possible to maintain the idea that civil society would ultimately triumph. Somehow, this violent end seemed the final shattering of that dream. I don't think any of us suspected that the final shattering was yet to come.

The head of the office staff, a former stenographer promoted repeatedly for her unusual acumen, looked in the open door. "I am sorry"— she frowned—"but I must advise you learned people to go home." She rarely encountered disobedience from those she supervised or those she served. We left.

My bus would take me right past the hospital where our prime minister lay dying. As we approached, government cars, with police motorcycles weaving and buzzing around them, overtook us. The crowds thickened—mourners, I supposed. The closer we got, however, the younger and more male the crowds appeared. Our bus slowed to walking pace, unable to get through; then a couple of young men stopped it, banging on the door until the driver opened it.

"Show me the Sikhs!" the first shouted as he leapt up the steps. He started down the aisle, checking the empty seats to make sure no turbaned head was ducked below, out of sight. Several of his fellows appeared behind him. Their eyes were red—not from crying, my guess. They wore half-unbuttoned shirts, moustaches, shaggy hair. Bollywood villains.

There were no Sikhs on our bus, but, as we arrived at the transit depot, I saw a tall gentleman dragged out of another bus by his shirt, spectacles askew. He was pushed down into the sweating, crushing sea of the crowd, where I lost him.

My second bus home contained a number of wary-looking Sikhs. I knew none of them. We reached my neighbourhood. They went to their homes, I to mine.

I found my father pacing in front of the radio. "Outrageous!" he said when he saw me, shaking his finger in the air. He had been a life-long civil servant, dedicated to civility and servility. He liked a pendulum best when it was still. He had been piously regretful at the Golden Temple invasion, but extremists must bend or be bent to the rule of law.

Vivek's children had come home early from school. They were mainly worried about whether our Halloween party that evening would be cancelled. I told them that although I wasn't much in a mood, I would go ahead with our plan if their friends showed up.

Three did, surprisingly. Although I couldn't bring myself to dress up, I gave them sweets and a tour of my Room of Doom, which included a disembodied hand that gripped their small necks and a ghost that popped out of my almirah. I had also strewn "poppers" on the floor so that their entry seemed to trigger gunfire. On other days, their screams would have been delightful.

Rumours floated in that I was not the only one distributing sweets: some Sikhs were celebrating the assassination. My sister phoned from

Canada to tell us they had seen images on TV of Sikhs in Vancouver and Toronto laughing, dancing bhangra, that Punjabi celebration dance made famous via Bollywood and weddings: arms aloft, shoulders shaking, wrists twisting to an infectious beat.

"It's just a handful behaving like this," she said, "but that's what makes the news, right? The rest of them are going about their daily business, but you can't show that on TV. I saw a bunch at a vigil downtown."

By the time the children finished their candy, their parents were at the door, anxious to get them home. We expected a curfew to be called, and one was. We expected, if we woke in the night, to hear the buzz and wail of police and army making smaller and larger loops through the city, lacing it tight with invisible cords, tying the city down as if it were a patient suffering a seizure, until tempers cooled and order restored itself. In some cities, this was what happened. In Delhi, things went differently.

The next morning, the air smelled of smoke. As I descended to take my coffee, there was a rattle at the back gate. My mother went out. It was the wife from the Sikh family who lived next door. The husband, in his fifties, was already a little higher in the civil service than my father had been by the time of his retirement, but the families were roughly social equals. Relations between them were cordial but not friendly, and I had wondered if the question of their equality might be the main source of the careful distance, along with the usual strangeness between members of different communities, a gap easily overcome when both sides so desire.

Now the wife was at the gate, pleading and sobbing. I went out into the garden but hung back to listen. Mrs. Singh was begging my mother to send my father to persuade her menfolk to come and hide in our house.

"They are killing Sikhs, you understand? They are going to each and every Sikh house, they are killing the men, they take the girls, they are setting the houses on fire."

Her Hindi was heavily accented and my mother's only functional, but still, my mother understood. She was hesitating to open the gate when the woman looked past her, and me. My father had come out to stand behind me.

"Please, sir. My husband, my sons. They will not go." Mrs. Singh's voice rose as she approached hysteria. "Sir, he says he is as loyal to India as the sun is loyal to the dawn. He won't believe they will attack our house."

"He must be right, of course," responded my father. He hadn't moved from his spot near the house.

Beyond the gate, Mrs. Singh stopped crying. She wiped her cheeks with her dupatta and turned to go.

"Please," I said. "Let me see what I can do."

She gave a slight nod but did not pause.

I went to our rooftop first and looked out across the colony. At its fringes, fires were burning, not a general conflagration but isolated posts of smoke rising around the periphery as though to make a fence. I descended to the front door and found Vivek on the street, talking with a neighbour. "It's true," said the man. He had one crossed eye, and it was difficult to tell what he thought about what he was saying. "There are mobs moving in from the Ring Road. They are going after Sikh homes and businesses, but they will destroy Hindu-Muslim too, anyone who hides Sikhs. No macho hero stuff, uh? Look after your family."

I went next door, but there was no answer when I rang, so I ran back through our house and shouted over their back gate. This time, Mr. Singh came out.

"My dear chap, why so distressed?" he asked in English. He was hale-looking, with a wide, sunny face and a tightly bound beard above a dress shirt and tie. "My wife has infected you with her anxiety!"

"Sir, I think you really would be very well advised to—that is, our doors are open to you and your family." I wanted to speak more force-fully (really, I wanted to drag him into our house just as those goons had dragged that poor gentleman down the bus steps), but could not make him seem subject to my instruction, or pity, or fear. *Singh* means "lion"; it is the name of the pride. "You are in grave danger."

"There are miscreants on both sides," said Mr. Singh. He patted my shoulder. "Everyone is in terrible shock. Let the police do their duty. I'm sure they will have matters well in hand very shortly."

I left him and began phoning friends and colleagues, who passed on to me still-tentative information, since confirmed. It appeared some-one, possibly in the ranks of the ruling party, had supplied lists—census? voters? ration cards?—of Sikh-occupied homes, Sikh-owned businesses. The mobs were not rampaging randomly; those batons of smoke were rising only from the addresses on the lists. The streets were unusually quiet, and when we heard any vehicle, we imagined it was one of these organizers, shaping and directing the mobs, avenging sheepdogs herding wolfish sheep. The rumour was that the Congress party had hired otherwise unemployed young men to enlarge the mobs, 500 rupees a pop. To employ professional mourners is no new thing; to direct them to express their grief for their dear, departed leader with gleeful barbarism—this we had not seen before.

And the police? The army? "Standing by the side of the road," one of my colleagues told me on the phone, choking on tears or indignation. "Fully complicit!" Later, I heard that Sikhs had called the police and found themselves arrested for actions they had taken in their own defence and that the few officers or commanders who protected citizens and property were reprimanded. Pogroms. State-sanctioned. Not officially, but.

The smell of smoke on our street was growing thicker, the fires visibly closer. I went again to the Singhs' back gate and this time was met by Mr. Singh with his wife, daughters-in-law, and a small horde of children.

"All right," he said, with the habitual optimist's stiffness in dire straits. "Let me deliver our womenfolk and children to you. I so hate them to be upset!" He seemed almost glad to be shed of his family's distress.

"Sir," I said, letting his family pass into our garden. "Please. If the crowd comes to your door, let me tell them you are not home. It will go easier for all of us. Please. For your family."

He drew a heavy breath. We could hear shouts now and guessed they must have reached our street. He inclined his head briefly and was gone. I went along between the houses, to the front, where Vivek met me, iron pot-tongs in one hand, paring knife in the other. I recall pausing briefly to wonder whether he was ridiculous.

The mob arrived, going straight to the Singhs' house. A number of them hopped the gate into the front garden and began to bang on the door.

"*Hai!*" I screamed from our own garden. "No one is home there! They heard about you lot. They left yesterday. Shoo!" I, too, was brandishing something—I remember the feel of it in my hand, along with the taste of acid in my throat—but I can no longer remember what it was.

Astonishingly, whatever we did was effective. The goons at the gate shouted to the goons at the door that there were other fish to fry, farther up the same road. Thankfully Mr. Singh and his sons were not tempted into confrontation.

Startled at how easy it had been to move the mob along, Vivek and I exited our garden into the road. My father followed us. There was a much bigger crowd at the end of the street, half-undone men in half-undone shirts. The smoke was thick and thicker, as were the crowds, but we caught a glimpse of a man being pulled from a house by his unbound hair, his turban also unbound and torn. We knew who lived there: two brothers, Singhs, no relation to those hiding in our house. They were about my age, owners of a motorcycle dealership a few blocks away, and lived with their father. Kritika and I used to joke about how we couldn't tell them apart. Singh and Singh. Singh and sons.

The crowd parted to reveal the man, now on fire. Oh God—which brother was it? Or was it the father? I couldn't tell. *I couldn't tell.*

He held his arms out, shaking, reaching, staggering. A whole man alight. We reached toward him, we froze. What can you do? These are the smells of a man burned alive: kerosene smoke, burning hair, roasting flesh, but also something else, something green and wet—a near-anonymous martyr tied to wood where the sap still ran.

"Bhangra!" someone shouted, seeing the man shake in his own flames, and others shouted too, even laughed. "He's dancing bhangra!"

In minutes, the street was empty. My father had run back to our house and fetched a quilt. He threw it over the now-fallen man and threw himself on top. The flames were doused, but there wasn't enough flesh for a pulse. I checked. Another body lay at the far end of the street.

After, my father tried to phone our local police deputation. He could reach no one. He was in favour of going in person, but I told him, "Appa, surely you can tell that the police must be permitting this to happen."

He looked insulted, angry. "Ridiculous. How dare you?"

"Then where are they? You think all this is somehow a secret from them?"

"Surely they are busy elsewhere—this must be happening all over the city."

"Yes, because they have failed and are failing to prevent it. There is collusion, Appa." I became more earnest as he stopped contradicting me, hopeful that I was wrong. "Come, I'll go with you to the police station, come." But now he sat, not meeting my eyes, looking drawn. I left him alone.

The next morning, a couple of my colleagues phoned to tell me of a protest meeting coming together in the compound of a relief agency. I was not inclined to go. I dreaded the rhetoric, the sense of mass action. I knew that it was necessary to show opposition, and that such protests might even succeed in dispersing a mob or two, but I have a near-pathological aversion to collectives. It goes against my grain to join any mob, even one forming to march and chant for something I believe in.

But Appa overheard the conversations. "This is it, Ashwin. We will make ourselves heard." Perhaps my resistance would have broken down even if he had not insisted we go.

It was a small group, perhaps 150 people. I think it could have been much larger if they had been able to spread the word more effectively. If I had not been staying with my father, he never would have known about that gathering of concerned fellow citizens. If I had been living in my own flat by then, they would not have been able to reach me, since it would be years before I got a telephone.

I remember very little of that day. Generic details, such as the detestable mass-shouting of slogans expressing admirable sentiments. We marched together to a neighbourhood that we had heard was among the most badly affected, a Sikh-majority enclave. We confronted mobs and were mostly successful, simply with shouting, in getting them to stop, if temporarily. I don't really remember. After the critical, desperate confrontations of the day prior, I think my brain's ability to form memories with any specificity was topped.

My father, however, would talk about it for years as a seminal moment in his life. He had awoken to a new reality. He wasn't sure whether it had been hidden from him or he had been hiding from it. Now that he had seen it, though, he would never turn away.

My mother's reaction would have been strange for anyone else, but was typical of her. She stayed in the house and, somehow, after the neighbours left, came to insist that practically none of what we had experienced had happened. She had seen nothing, she said. When we asked why she thought the neighbours were hiding in our house, she said it was because they were afraid, which proved nothing. When we asked if she didn't see what was happening on the street, she said we had told her to stay away from the windows. None of it was false, but all was incomplete, and inarguable. She objected to the protests, said we were agitators, that we should let the authorities handle it. My anger at her made it easier for me to stomach the marches, though I imagine her behaviour made it all harder for my father.

By the evening of November 3, the army and police had rediscovered their role as keepers of the peace. The mobs evaporated as quickly as they had formed. Official estimates range upward of 2,700 Sikhs killed; unofficial ones reach past five figures. Undisputed is that thousands more had lost their homes and livelihoods, were made instant refugees in their own city. Relief workers, sociologists, psychologists and lawyers dedicated themselves to the needs particularly of the women and children whose husbands and fathers had been killed.

I was not involved in the organization of tents and cooking pots. Making people comfortable? I wouldn't know where to start. But a former IRDS fellow contacted me to say that she would like to see whether my therapeutic skills could help these bereaved and traumatized women take up the work of heading their families.

I made no guarantees, but she took me on anyway. "I'm pretty sure you can do no harm," she said. I thanked her for the vote of confidence.

All in all, I saw a dozen or so families. I tried to help them in redefining and accepting their new circumstances, a task hundreds more managed without my help. They were usually referred to me because of some particular or extreme problem—guilt, debilitating anger, mental illness—that was preventing them from making the necessary adjustments and pursuing what little compensation was beginning to dribble forth from tightly shut government coffers.

The government claimed, much like my mother, that we had not seen what we saw. They set up "Commissions of Inquiry"—*omissions* of inquiry would have been more apt—whose main purpose seemed to be to shield those to blame for the atrocities. And our crown prince, Rajiv Gandhi, unexpectedly and uncomfortably inheriting the throne of what we had thought to be a democratic nation, passively voiced this summary of the three days of mayhem that his party had willed into being:

"Some riots took place in the country following the murder of Indiraji. We know the people were very angry and for a few days it seemed that India had been shaken. But when a mighty tree falls, it is only natural that the earth around it does shake a little."

He may not have been responsible for the violence, but he was grateful to those who did what he lacked the cojones to do. And after he washed into office a few months later on a tsunami of sympathy, he kept on protecting the perpetrators.

In addition to the victimized families, I saw people in the course of my regular therapeutic work who had been implicated in the violence, and were haunted. Three or four police officers, at least two of whom were on stress leave because they had been held back from acting as duty and morals demanded. Whether the leave was imposed by their superiors as punishment or given to them as time to accept the drowning of their innocence is not clear in my recollection; perhaps it is somewhere in my notes.

I saw a few of the relief workers, whose overexposure to others' grief was beginning to addle them. I saw some middle-class people from middle-class neighbourhoods, stalwarts like my father, whose guilt and disillusion were eating into their livelihoods and relationships, particularly in cases of obvious disparity between their feelings and those of their family members and colleagues.

I wrote the stories they told me. I gave them back. The stories intersected and informed one another. Seeing this, one family asked for a meeting. I put it to the others, most of whom accepted eagerly. Two Sikh families, all women; several Hindus from the affected areas; a single Muslim police officer; and my Appa, who, when I described the meeting, asked to attend. For several hours, they compared their experiences of betrayal and trauma and spoke to one another across religion and class. Our puny-yet-potent effort at truth and reconciliation.

Their individual narratives, and the story of their meeting, formed my first book. It is mostly about treating individual survivors of a sudden incident of extreme, state-sponsored violence, but it also provided me a chance to talk about secrecy and hypocrisy and the ways they wear on the psyche.

Who Are the Guilty? asks a well-known exposé on the riots produced by the People's Union of Civil Liberties, but the title is rhetorical. I called my little book *Who Are the Victims? Narrative Therapy in the Aftermath of the Delhi Riots*. I thought my question better than the one of the pamphlet on blaming, because mine could not so readily be answered.

My book included my father's experience, though I had half wanted to keep it out. His life had been premised on a sense of order and justice. Its course was altered by what he had seen, not just the violence but the failure of the state—his nation—to prevent it. I wanted to talk about all this, but not about my mother's denials, and yet these, too, were intrinsic to his difficulties. He was, by this time, working with victims, helping with paperwork and shopping and so on, over my mother's objections. He directed me to change his name, but put his story in. He had attended the meeting; he wanted his perceptions recorded. He was right, and I obeyed.

At the time, I couldn't bring myself to write my own story. Now, writing it here, finally, I am obliged to say that the pogroms had brought on in me a visceral, almost debilitating, longing for Rosslyn. When I closed the door on our burnt neighbour, I closed my eyes to see her sepia-smooth hair by the reading lamp, her look of irritation when I interrupted her. After each phone call urging me out to the demonstrations, I sat thinking of the faint blue veins in her breasts, the way a slim hand had so neatly fit around the back of my neck. The way I had failed to let myself know her, or failed to let myself believe I knew her.

When I recalled her lemon-leaf scent, I would also, inexplicably, think of a white-painted swing, dangling, empty, from a tree in a green meadow. Her hair was the colour of a chestnut horse I patted once, as a child, on a visit to an apple orchard in Kashmir.

When the streets began to calm, I wrote her a letter, telling her what had happened, saying again how I was missing her. I may have been more emphatic than before, though I did not press her to come—how could I, in the wake of these horrors?—nor did I pretend I could leave my work in Delhi to return to Ottawa in any permanent way.

The day I sent it, a letter arrived, her response to mine of a month earlier, when I had talked abstractly of restlessness and usefulness, of belonging and non-belonging, and asked when I might come see her to talk more concretely. Her letter was straightforward and firm. She understood how I felt, but said I had entirely failed to take account of her shock. She was involved with someone else now, someone who, like her, longed for stability; someone who, like her, had no reason to leave. She did not encourage me to come.

I didn't respond. A month later, I received her response to my letter about the pogroms, expressing regret at the violence—she had heard little about it—and sympathy for me.

How could I properly despair? I missed her bitterly by this time, but my loss was nothing compared to the losses of those around me. *Longing, we say, because desire is full of endless distances.*

When I finally wrote her back, in the spring, I spoke of my book-in-progess. She responded, saying it sounded like a book she would like to read. She further—farther—said that she was engaged, and expecting a child.

$\mathcal{H}$eathrow was much as I remembered it from the far-distant past, much as most airports have become. We had arrived in London two hours late—punctual, per Air India standard time—but the partner airline that took over from Heathrow was Air Canada, and so we departed on schedule at 3:15 P.M. The Potemkin screens of my mind got perilously shabby with the approach of the place where the bombed plane went down. Thankfully, cocktail hour coincided with it, right in the nick of Scotch o'clock.

* * *

When my colleagues at the Institute for Research on Developing Societies read my proposal to interview victim families in Canada, many were excited. They swallowed the 9/11 analogy, hook-line-sinker; they understood the question as I myself framed it.

> *. . . the effects, on the survivors, of a unique set of victimizations: First, the bomb, a relatively anonymous act of violence. Second, the adopted country's ascription of the conflict to the victims, purely on the basis of their country of origin. Third, Canada's failure to prevent the crime and its failure, for eighteen years, to prosecute it. In what ways are these victim families like and unlike those of other mass acts of terror?*

Few of them knew of my own losses in the Air India disaster and I did not mention them in the proposal. One who did, Aziz Ahmed, currently the institute's director, took me aside.

He asked to see the consent forms the subjects would sign, so that he could support my petition with the human subjects review boards. He also said, though I hadn't asked, that he didn't think the proposal needed to include my personal stake. I waited to see what else he would say, and he seemed to do the same for me, his fingers templed against his salt-and-pepper goatee, mine clutching the armrests. *A therapist walks into a bar*, I thought as I waited. Aziz said nothing further. He seemed disappointed that I didn't either.

The proposal received harsher treatment from a small flotilla of my colleagues. One was a political scientist who had resented my assessment of his most famous study: "Small questions, medium data, big conclusions." He said my method could not produce reliable results. Another, who called herself a Freudian economist and was working on some pea-brained notion that Bombay's slums were not only *anus mundi* but needed to progress out of an anal retentive phase to, to . . . never mind. She accused me of—what? Parasitism? The two others who didn't approve had been cold to me ever since I refused to attend their children's weddings. I sent gifts, wished them well. Why hide that I thought the marital institution wrong-headed? (Apart from my instinctual repulsion at any display of communal emotion, modern marriage seems to me the supreme expression of conformity.)

This small band attacked my methods, flinging the erroneous criticisms that hard scientists have levelled at social scientists since the dawn of our profession, and that we now throw at ourselves: sampling errors, lack of a concise hypothesis. In other words, no serious objections. It made me realize I no longer had anyone who could advise me in my research. My late mentor and analyst in Canada, Marie Chambord, had vetted my prior manuscripts long-distance, but she could not do that from the grave. I thought to ask Paromita, an eco-anthropologist and my erstwhile, occasional lover, but she had recently married. Anyway, we had not been close enough that I ever spoke to her about the bomb and my losses, those matters I most worried might blind me to some fault in my methods, and there no longer seemed to be an appropriate way to tell her. I had a psychiatrist friend, Sudhir, but we had such differing views on method that, though I respected him, I would dismiss his response. I had always trusted my father's advice. But Appa, like Marie Chambord, was dead.

I was flying blind. Perhaps any flaws or lacks would reveal themselves in the course of the work itself. I hoped they would do so in time for me to correct them.

✳ ✳ ✳

My brother-in-law Suresh met me at the gate in Montreal. He looked not much different from the last time I had seen him: a little greyer, but then, I wouldn't say nineteen years had done me any favours. We greeted each other awkwardly. He took my outstretched hand, clapped my back with the other, a symbolic hug, half open for easy escape. (Was he still my brother-in-law, even though my sister was dead?)

I had written to him, and to twenty other victim families, explaining my project. A dozen families from Montreal to Vancouver volunteered to participate; Suresh would be my first interviewee. I have tried to avoid the word *subject*, with its strange connotations: *subject* to another's caprices, *subjects* of some *ferenghi* monarch. In psychological research, *subject* seems oddly interchangeable with *object*—the thing observed, probed, dissected. Is this what I would be doing? Strictly speaking, perhaps, but strictness is not the same as accuracy.

Suresh had invited me to stay with him, and I accepted. Now, arriving at his home—a new address, not the one he had shared with my sister—I was surprised to be greeted also by his wife, Lisette. Platinum blond, mid-thirties, I guessed, though she already had a deeply lined face. She greeted me shyly in French-accented English.

Supper was quiet, but not awkwardly so. After, she went to watch TV in their bedroom and Suresh told me how they had met on the cancer ward of the Montreal Children's Hospital, where he had begun volunteering a couple of years after losing his own children. Hospice: that was where the thin wire of grief led him.

Lisette's son had died there, shortly after his fifth birthday. Suresh used to volunteer four nights a week and Saturdays; Friday night he went to the temple. Lisette invited him to the funeral. A single mother, a receptionist. They had married two years ago. He cut his volunteering down to Saturdays, came home for supper every night. She came to the temple with him on Fridays, and he took her to church and lunch on Sundays with her family in Trois-Rivières. Lying that night in their spare room, I wondered, would they fill it with another child? *They should*, I mused, surprising myself.

I thought back to his wedding with Kritika. He wasn't shorter than she, though he appeared so. PhD, employed in pharmaceuticals research, settled in Canada. I had recently started medical school at McGill, and my parents gambled on the likelihood that I would remain, so why not settle her here, also? It narrowed the groom search: there were only five Telegu bachelors of our caste and creed in Canada in 1970, one of whom was me. Suresh was the only one who could get home and get married that summer.

Kritika was a prize: curly hair, snapping eyes, educated, unambitious. Suresh adored her. I think he also liked me more than my sister did, and more than I liked him—he had a more generous spirit than either of us. Unpretentious chap, for all his aspirations; a much more patient parent than she (though she was warmer to the kids than I would have expected, given how much she was like our mother, no model of affection); a reader of poetry—obvious, sappy stuff, Tagore, Wordsworth, but still; and uxorious, which I admired, even more because I thought Kritika undeserving. Am I unkind? She would have said the same of me, were the roles reversed. The difference is that I would agree. In bleak moments—and most moments when I think of myself are bleak—I believe my solitary state confirms this. I am alone because I deserve to be. But then, wouldn't the reverse logic also apply to her?

She had her good points. Not least of which were Asha and Anand.

Suresh had taken the next morning off to talk with me, and after Lisette left for work, we sat in their small front room. I had never been to this neighbourhood: urban but aspiring middle-class, street upon street of duplexes. Francophones have a higher tolerance for shared walls than anglos, though if they hear anything through the walls, they prefer it to be in French. We sat with our backs to the window. Children shouted their way to school behind us, before the street fell silent. In Suresh's living room, a white sofa abutted blue recliners crowding houseplants from whose broad leaves dust motes floated into the morning sun. In lulls, we watched a patch of light creep along the back wall.

He told me of a tiff with Kritika on the way to the airport (she had forgotten to pack a small gift he had bought for his mother); the early-morning call from his sister in India, who somehow learned of the bomb before he did; his trip to India, afterwards, seeing my parents, seeing his own; his return home to his empty house, full of their things. He reminded me how I had come to Canada and helped him clean it out.

I listened and made notes on my steno pad; that afternoon, I transcribed into a composition notebook marked with his name; and, late that night, I wrote a few small stories about him. I didn't know yet whether I would show them to him. It was mostly that I couldn't help myself.

* * *

He started with the baby's room. He hadn't stopped calling her that until she was seven, and here it was, again. He stood in the doorway, his arms around an irregular stack of empty boxes. The room was crammed with doodads—a collection of miniature scented erasers; shiny purses hanging helter-skelter from a pink-painted rack; a makeup mirror, its pockets stuffed with Lip Smackers. Kritika would periodically go wild about the clutter, but continued buying the crap for Asha. How could he bear to clear it out? He had to. Much worse to pass by it each day.

Her clothes went into a garbage bag for donation, keeping aside only a silk maxi and bodice she had worn to her cousin's wedding in India three years ago, and a pink velour tracksuit that made her look sporty, sharp, ready for anything. On the floor beneath the bed, two lost teddy bears and a dustball made mostly of her hair. In one pocket of her school bag, the mush of a decomposed apple core in a tissue. In the other, a creased handful of notes, slips torn from notebooks, cryptic messages pencilled on both sides:

Mrs. G has abnormally long arms. Pass it on.

Kathy said she'll be your friend again if you'll take back what you said about her self-portrait.

Dana said she only said what she said because you said she said Valerie has hairy toes and she never.

I got my period!!!!!!

All the girls' handwriting looked alike. He tried to follow the strands of debate—was Asha mediating or instigating? Was she not paying attention in class? She got top marks in everything, both his children did.

None of it mattered.

Next, he dusted and vacuumed Anand's eminently tidy room. When he lifted the reading chair cushion to clean under it, he found a *Sports Illustrated* swimwear issue and a bra page from a Sears catalogue. He sat in the chair and wept at history's repetition, at the loss of so much of so little consequence. Under the mattress, though, were three ripped-from-a-magazine pages of women and men bound with black leather, hooded, orifices exposed. His mind briefly went blank, but then he thought, *curiosity*. Pictures, only.

In Suresh's own room, his and Kritika's, he expected to find a secret. He steeled himself for it: a diary full of complaints about him, or letters from an ex-lover, or expensive earrings she bought without telling him and only wore when she was alone. Nothing necessarily bad, merely secret. He had never assumed he truly knew her. That was okay. It was part of the deal.

But either she didn't have secrets, or he never found them.

He had kept nothing from her.

＊　＊　＊

Before I left the following day, we talked a bit further, about his work at the hospice, his meeting and marrying Lisette. I asked if they thought about having more children. He smiled and looked away—finally, I had asked a question he would not answer.

Changing tack, I asked whether he had attended any of the trial.

"I had no interest," he told me.

"None?"

"Not enough to buy a plane ticket, take time off work, leave Lisette."

"Why not?"

"Did you go?"

"Yes, for a day or two."

"Wasn't it a bit like entertainment, like those town square executions?"

"Not for those who lost their families."

"It won't bring them back," he said. I felt the droop of his face in my own, felt how grief compressed his lungs, made of his body a trap. "And why are you doing this, this study?" he asked, reversing the line of scrutiny. "This is what you do?"

I hesitated. "It's a bit of a departure. I assume you haven't read any of my books?" He hadn't. They were not widely distributed, and I didn't think him the type to Google a guy, though I have been surprised by others. I cleared my throat. "I'm doing the study because . . . for one thing, this tragedy was not owned"—I cringed at this word, but when speaking to people you must make yourself understood on their terms—"by Canadians at large. Emotionally, they did not feel themselves to be assaulted."

"It wasn't owned by the government either," said Suresh.

"No. That's one question, the isolation of the victim's families, though I don't know yet if it's the central one. The term I used in my letter, I hope you don't find it insulting, was a 'study of comparative grief.' I want to know: how have the families coped up? How have their lives progressed?"

"Surely that information must be out there, no? All the newspaper articles, pieces on TV?"

He had an intentness I didn't remember. He truly wanted to understand.

"There's media coverage, true, but no scholarship that I could find. Has anyone else talked to you?"

His expression suggested no one would want to. "I keep a low profile."

"So you see." I tried to sound convincing, but the more I talked, the less assured I felt.

"I don't see, Ashwin." He put his hand on my knee. "I'm happy to talk to you, if it's important, but why dredge this up? Let it lie."

It was only now that I realized: not only had I said nothing to my colleagues about my bereavement, I had said nothing about it in my letters to the victim families.

Okay, I thought, *that was wrong*. But I did nothing to correct it.

It wasn't only the need for scholarship that was motivating me. It wasn't only the desire to give the victims a voice. (As one grieving man had said to Mukherjee and Blaise, "'We are so wanting to talk! That wanting to talk is in all of us . . . we who have lost our entire families. We have nothing left except talk.'" That was eighteen years ago, but so many were still wanting to talk.)

It was, as much as anything, my desire to understand what had happened to me. I had not recovered. Did anyone, from so severe a blow? Perhaps not, but I had, in some way, stopped my life. This, I suspected, might be less true for the others. It didn't seem to be true of Suresh, or he didn't feel it to be. How or why did some absorb loss into life's floodplains, while others erected a dam?

JUNE 19, 2004

Lohikarma, B.C. Fourth town, seventh family.

I arose with the dawn, my habit. Canada was terrible for me that way: despite many years here, I never managed to wake long before first light in winter, long after in summer. I cracked a window to fan out the fug of night gas and snore breath. That smell, akin to stale popcorn, can linger, even in a large room. A faint priapism deflated as my pyjama and kurta cooled in the morning air. Twelve degrees Celsius perhaps? Like October in Delhi. I inspected my face in the bathroom mirror, the double-bagged eyes, the beginnings of jowls to rival the cat's. My cat. Had anyone—my widow, perhaps—taken over his feeding? I cranked the shower, pulled my kurta over my head, and was enveloped for a moment in the smell from my own pores, something dark and leafy, with the tang of iron. Cooked spinach? Lovely. I gagged a little, stepped into the coursing water, coated myself with strong soap, then antiperspirant, then aftershave. Sandalwood, bergamot, lime. By night the spinach would chew its way to the surface again, but then I would quell it with Scotch. The pleasures of a day fully lived.

I was accommodated in a self-contained suite at the top of a house. The owner rented it to holidayers, along with two suites on the ground floor; the middle was occupied by a dentist. At the back, where one entered my flat, off the fire escape, were two large windows. I took in the view before going out to find a newspaper: majestic mountains supporting an endless sky where the morning sun was carving mists away from the day's clean promise, everything any visitor to Canada and particularly the beautiful province of British Columbia could want, but also (eyes dropping to take in a sweeping palette of industrial greys) back-alley-

cum-parking-lot, chicken-wire fence, and dirt-dusted, supersized, aluminium Quonset. My guess: a curling rink. These ruddy northerners do
love to sport on ice.

I eased the morning stiffness from my knees, descending the stairs
of iron and air that climbed the back of the building. Walking around to
the front and through the garden in the moist morning, toward the rising
sun and the newspaper box across the street, I was entangled by a plague
of green worms descending on sticky filaments. I should have backed off
and found a way to bypass them, but instead I swore and flailed until all
the strings were broken, the caterpillars all over me, then I swore some
more and crushed and brushed them off.

Back in my room, I set the coffee to decoct, and opened the paper
to search for a mention of the trial.

Last spring, the prosecution had opened dramatically, broad hints
of intrigue and newly unearthed information setting the gathered families alight with speculation and hope. Then came weeks of hysterically
banal minutiae: ticket purchase, baggage checking, details nearly uni-
versally known. Some heartbreaking, if irrelevant, moments, such as
testimony from the stalwart Irish sailors who had fished bodies from
their seas; as well as misleading ones, such as a suggestion that the Canadian spy agency had had a mole inside the terrorist cell until shortly before the bombing occurred, a mystery never solved. Then came a long
summer break, occasioned by the prosecution's attempts to shorten the
process by presenting witness reports instead of witnesses. They could
have pressed on. Instead, they pissed off.

The fall brought more testimony, more research, more witnesses, a
growing weight of information. And so the trial sank down through the
newspapers, off the front pages, out of the public eye. I could go days
now and find not a mention in the press.

But look: this morning, Canada's National Newspaper *had* published an article on the trial, a moment that might prove crucial—
though who knew? A bookseller testified that he had given a book about
the bombing to a star witness for the prosecution, bolstering accusations
that the witness, "Ms. D," had repeated what she had read, not what
she had witnessed. As with all the trial news, I felt a detachment both
familiar and disturbing.

Ms. D's identity was masked by witness protection. She had been whisked away from her life years earlier. Death threats against those with inside information about the bombing were not uncommon. The publisher of a community newspaper, a man who had been part of the same Sikh-nationalist circles as the bombers but then began speaking out against them, had been killed.

In the courtroom, Ms. D's identity was no secret. Plenty of those present knew her as the former employee of one of the accused. She said they were in love, although the affair had remained nobly platonic, with both of them married. When she testified, on October 31, 2003, she started with a description, under duress, of the hold he had on her. She loved him still, she said, though he had fully confessed to her his role in the bombing.

Her challengers, in cross-examination, said she was making this up. Wanting revenge for losing her job. How could she love someone as evil as he sounded? She stuck to her guns, but now, ten months later, the defence brought a witness who claimed Ms. D owned a book about the bomb plot, *Soft Target*, which contained all the details she was now regurgitating, including errors of a sort she couldn't have made up on her own.

The sun was nearly above the horizon, and coffee was gargling up into the top of the mini-*macchinetta* I carried with me. I travel light, but this is one item I won't be caught without, anywhere in the world. I had bought eggs and onions on arrival in Lohikarma the night before. Now I scrambled them, squeezed on hot sauce—I always toss a few packets in with my toiletries—and scooped them with improvised chapatis a.k.a. store-bought tortillas warmed in the pan.

Done with breakfast, I readied for the day's interviews, taking out a fresh composition notebook and labelling it "Venkataraman," the name of a man here whose wife and son had gone down on the plane. I would not be meeting him until Monday. Today, Saturday, I would meet individually with his closest friend, one Professor Sethuratnam, and Sethuratnam's daughter, Brinda.

Dr. Sethuratnam seemed to be very involved in this Venkataraman's affairs, and had told me that it was he who had first noticed my letter and encouraged his friend to open it. Whenever possible, I was interviewing not only direct family members but also other relatives and friends, if they volunteered. It would let me investigate a theory, that loss radiates, and also paint a fuller portrait of the survivors. Also, for Indians in Canada, family friends become the equivalent of family. I was never like this, needless to say, but most seek out those who share their language and their recipes, and raise their children in proximity the way we grow up with cousins back home.

I swirled my second and final shot of espresso into a pan of hot milk, and took it to drink in the window seat. The view: let us edit out the pavement, chicken wire, Quonset. See instead soft, low mountains surrounding Kootenay Lake, which stretched fingers into the landscape's crevices and drew storms over the mountains as quickly as it drove them away. Three wispy clouds drifted against the black-green mountainside, as yet unlit by the rising sun. Two resolved into figures, so clearly that even I couldn't miss them. I'm not like Asha, for whom one thing always became another, some crumpled paper a rabbit, her bitten sandwich a ship. The two cloud-figures danced, while the third galloped past beneath them. The uppermost rose, feet in the air, like Chagall's wife in his paintings of the two of them, she upside-down, smiling, hands stretched toward him. Her limbs pulled apart and she vanished. The sun hit the top of the peak opposite and her partner, too, fled. The third figure ambled briskly forward, a buffalo from a cave-painting. Its hump grew as the sun crept down the mountain; it became a fish, a deer, five little v-sketched birds, then nothing. The sun shone as it had to.

I walked to the town centre, which lay between my apartment and the university. The Kootenay river valley descended to my right. To my left, High Street, where a stylish wine shoppe advertising B.C. vintages abutted a yoga studio with homemade beeswax candle displays that shared a wall with an upscale vintage furniture store. The air smelled as much of incense or baking as exhaust. Families of tourists occupied iron benches, unless they had been driven off by a homeless person parking a shopping cart in the curbside landscaping. There were a few of those, adding to the smells.

Brinda Sethuratnam had chosen a coffeehouse, Brewed Awakening, for our meeting. Tastefully restored art deco architecture; staff indistinguishable from patrons; lemon bars and Linzer squares baked in-house and cut to modestly sized portions suitable for modestly sized consumers—the type of place where Rosslyn and I used to pull apart the

Saturday books section before tackling whatever work we had brought home for the weekend. An hour remained until my appointment. I did some reading. I prepared.

And then there she was: an attractive girl, thirty-five, I learned, though she looked ten years younger. Longish hair, clear complexion, fit and fashionable, though with a twitchiness that undermined her looks.

"I'm very pleased that I got to Lohikarma in time to meet you," I told her as we sat. (I know how to make niceties, though I often don't bother.) "You must be leaving day after tomorrow, is it?"

"Actually," she said, "I've decided to stay on a few days longer." She chewed her lip.

"Good, then. You told me where you live, in our correspondence. Saskatoon, is it?"

"Edmonton. I moved there for grad school, ten years ago."

"Mm-hmm. In . . . ?"

"Epidemiology?" She pulled the cuffs of her jersey down over her palms and gripped her mug. "I went to do a PhD, but it never really took. I'm restarting, this fall, not a PhD, an MA in science writing, at Johns Hopkins, in Baltimore. I'm still fascinated by epidemiology, but I want to write about it more than I want to do it. Part of the reason I'm home—apart from that I always come back in the summer for a week or two—is that I'm interviewing a psychiatric epidemiologist at Harbord as part of my thesis. The MA programme's only a year long, so I thought it would be good to get started." Her manner had shifted decisively, as though she'd crossed the beam of a film projector. Now she projected confidence. "I want to take a magazine-feature approach, four profiles of epidemiologists, two Canadian, two American. They tend to be attached to universities, right, which are increasingly corporate funded, but many of these scientists, including the one I'll be talking to here, are effectively in the business of exposing corporate malpractice. Environmental cover-ups, for example. So I'm wanting to investigate some of those delicate balances in their work."

"I can tell you'll do well," I said.

She looked both pleased and offended—about right. I hate it when people say that sort of thing to me. Presumptuous, as though to flatter, or worse, condescend. Was I trying to sabotage myself?

"We should talk about your project," she said. "My dad showed me your letter."

"I had the impression that you were as close as family to Dr. Venkataraman and his late wife and son."

"It's true. Well, we are distantly related—Venkat Uncle is my mother's third cousin, or second cousin once removed. I never had a brother," she said, and cleared her throat. She wore a *mangal sutra*—a wedding chain—with a smaller than usual pendant that she would lift onto her chin when she was listening or thinking. "So Sundar was like that to us. We spent a lot of time at their house. When we were little, his mom would even invite me and my sister for sleepovers. I remember her brushing and braiding my hair in the morning. I think she enjoyed having girls around once in a while. And Sundar came on vacations with us a couple of times."

I was taking notes, and encouraged her to continue.

"We saw less of him once he got to high school. He wouldn't always come when his parents came over for dinner and what-not. I would see him around sometimes, though, and there was still something kind of special. Like, I remember once a picnic for the whole Indian community, at this lake. I must have been twelve or thirteen, and he brought his lunch over to where I was sitting and talked with me the whole time, about novels and music. I had just started junior high, and my friends weren't huge readers. I remember making some funny or sarcastic comment, making him laugh. I felt so proud, or included. Worthy. But maybe there was no one better than me to sit with!"

She laughed, then looked around the café self-consciously. "I had friends who were boys, but never a proper boyfriend, until I met the guy I married. I wasn't allowed to date when I was in high school, and by the time I got to university, it almost felt like I'd never learn how. Indian parents seem to think that's how it will work, that you'll meet someone when it's time to get married, and *boom*. My parents disapprove of dating different people. But where are you supposed to get the life experience to make a good choice?"

"Did you think Sundar might have advised you on this, or been a model in some way?"

"Hard to imagine, but he's frozen in time, right?" She had a distinctive way of working her brow. Her expression often seemed at odds with what she would say. "Our relationship never evolved. I always felt I had a lot in common with him, and looked up to him. After he left to go to UBC, we only saw him a few times. Like my sister, I think he really wanted to get out of here."

"You didn't feel that way?"

She shook her head. "Sundar . . . I like to think he wanted to be . . . not famous, he wasn't crass, but something huge. Real but huge. I think he could have done it." She had become hunched, her torso concave. "It seems like an important drive, to want to leave. I don't have it. Do you think it could be because of the crash?"

That seemed pat, and unexpected. I thought to flip the question back: How had the crash affected her? How might it have been different for her sister? But before I could, her eye was caught.

I looked where she was looking: at a young man of about her age, black hair flopping into his eyes. I looked back at her. Her face was suffused, some soft burst of oxygen radiating from her. He came over to say hello. They chitchatted, gym or shopping or coffee-to-go, and she introduced us: Adrian, an old school chum, now in medical school in Toronto but home for a month or so to help his parents on the farm while his father underwent cancer treatment.

"A good friend?" I asked after he left.

"An old friend." The tremulousness returned and she began steering our meeting toward the exit. "So you're meeting my dad and Venkat Uncle today?"

"Your father this afternoon, and Dr. Venkataraman day after tomorrow, Monday morning. They both asked me to come to their offices."

"What about my mom and my sister?"

"Ranjani, your sister, she's in Vancouver, yes? I haven't had a confirmation from her. Your mother hasn't responded yet either." I waited a moment and then said, hesitantly, "I would like to talk further, if you have time in your remaining days here." She had withdrawn so dramatically that I felt aggressive. "Perhaps if you don't know your schedule yet, you could call me? I am quite open."

She agreed, but I watched her with a kind of fear as she left. Not that I wouldn't see her again—if I wanted another interview, I would get it. She hadn't the strength to decide against me. No—I was fearful for her. Was she ill? The therapy room is better for detecting nuances in tone of voice, or scent. Fever, for instance, hits me in the back of my sinuses, fur-like, medicinal in its own distorted way. Emotional states alter body chemistry, and so alter a person's smell. Although I'm most acute with people I already know, there are patterns, and I have been doing this a long time.

I stayed and transcribed as I always did, immediately and exhaustively, expanding on my scribbled notes while her words, inflections and pauses were still fresh in my mind, and then began to annotate: her clothing, her posture, my speculations on her state of mind. She was charming to talk to, but an image came to mind: a piece of paper that could eternally be folded, to become a SWAN! fold-fold-fold; BOAT! fold-fold-fold; ORCHID! while only ever showing its outside. I could see the hands doing the folding, but not the person they belonged to.

Looking up in the midst of this, I noticed a woman of indeterminate age in a purple wool coat lumber in to take a stool at the counter. She lifted the veil of her hat to order an apple juice, and opened her beaded clutch. Gazing with childlike pleasure at her image in a small mirror, she retraced and reinforced her already racoonish kohl with a stubby eye pencil. Thirsty work. She ordered another juice, rummaged again in the purse and took out a pair of tweezers.

It was both performance and not. She would look around from time to time, as though pleased to be seen. But where did she imagine herself to be, as she began plucking her chin and upper lip, wiping the tweezers on her napkin, leaving little orange stripes of makeup?

Lohikarma, I would learn, held a special attraction for eccentrics. Its founder, John Harbord, was a remittance man and visionary who arrived in the Kootenay mountains in 1895 after seven years of travel from west to east to west again. His diaries zigzag the landscapes! ceremonies! hallucinogens! of the Urals! Orissa! Ürümqi! as he speculates on entomology, etymologies, and other subjects he had no real means to penetrate. While sojourning among Finnish utopians on an island off North America's northwest coast, Harbord had chosen a name for the place he sensed he would shortly discover: *Lohikarma*, his pronunciation of the Finnish word for "dragon." He cites the word as final proof of his theory of the Finnish language's Sanskritic origins. Many cultures compose their dragons from the parts of other animals, reincarnating them: the dragon's karma is to inherit their qualities. Harbord's mission was to found a New World university on the traditions of "the many cultures the tides of history had washed up on these verdant shores." The town was named for the dragon. The university was named for him.

In the hundred years since, Lohikarma had grown, mostly in the usual ways. Gold had brought the first white men here, but lead, silver and zinc attracted further waves of entrepreneurs. Mines, mills and money fertilized an ecosystem of hotels, transport, provisioners and traders. But the town also attracted three other populations in greater concentrations than any other place I'd been. One was renegade or persecuted religious and ethnic groups, fleeing czars, dukes, generals. But while conservative and conformist Hutterites and Mennonites can be found in various places, the anarchist Doukhobors—a.k.a. Sons of Freedom, a.k.a. Spirit Wrestlers, setting fires to protest personal property and shedding their clothes to protest war—are found only here. A second was the followers of various spiritual leaders who had chosen this area for their ashrams, attracted by energy centres or some such, in the rocks and earth. Funny how such vibrations are rarely discovered in the wastelands of northern Saskatchewan, say, but rather only in the prettiest areas of the continent. The Kootenays ranked—rolling hills and rocky outcrops, flowering meadows and sparkling lakes. And that was likely what attracted the third group of note, much smaller, but one that had influenced the landscape and culture of the town as much as any other: wealthy eccentrics who chose Lohikarma as the place where they would build their follies and live their visible or invisible lives. I would come to like best the French-Spanish fop who built here a miniature replica of his family's castle and the lesbian heiress who serially seduced rich and famous daughters from Victoria to Regina, assisted by her boat-driver, a Marseillaise dwarf.

A barista pled in undertones with the Tweezer, who stood, declaring, in a flat Canadian accent, "Bug off. I'm not your stepping-stone!" As she made her way regally out into a hard rain, I imagined how her wool coat must have smelled, the rain releasing odours of a domestic menagerie: guinea pigs and rabbits, urine and wood shavings, and the oddly fresh scent of fur itself.

I finished my notes, and ate a ciabatta sandwich as the rain eased. I walked on damp but warming sidewalks toward the university to meet Brinda's father, Professor S. P. "Seth" Sethuratnam. I followed High Street from its lowest point, in the centre of town, straight up toward the university, which is on a rise of its own. The sidewalks dried as I dampened. Pale clouds lifted and dissolved off the tops of the purple mountains. If ever you visit Lohikarma, huff and puff up to one of the many high points to take in the vista of the lake accompanied by the sound of your own laboured breath. I should not assume you and I are alike in this, dear reader: I am a grizzled old fart and perhaps you could run circles around me. Still, allow me to press my point: while Lohikarma gives a marvellous view of the mountains from almost anywhere, for no work at all, only when you climb do you get the full effect. Trismegistus, I came to call it: lake, mountains, and long, low sky.

I was grateful to stop a hundred metres or so from High Street's summit. I could see it ahead: the quad, with its eight or ten neo-classical, Canadian-Edwardian facades, always featured on the covers of Harbord U.'s brochures, as if to demonstrate that the colonies' inferiority complex was far from resolved. Physics was in a newer science facility closer to downtown, a modernist structure typical of the early seventies building boom in Canada, unfortunate materials but lots of light.

In the atrium, I detected an organic chemistry lab by its unnatural, tart-and-sweet smell, chemical (I suppose it goes without saying) and burnt, but not in the comforting way of woodsmoke. It was a smell I had not encountered since leaving medical school, but the olfactory cortex is well-protected from the ravages of time, unlike, for example, the knees: my own, already complaining about the climb, confronted a wide brick staircase with anticipatory discomfort before I spied the elevator behind it.

I found Dr. Sethuratnam's name on his third-floor office door and knocked.

* * *

I liked him from the very first. He was a small man, though not so much so by the standards of his origins. I, too, am South Indian, though of taller stock. In a gathering of our fellows, I, not he, would have stood out. And I am only five-foot-ten.

I held out my hand. "Ashwin Rao."

He shook it and gestured me in, lifting some papers off a chair that faced his overflowing desk. "No student came to office hours today. My desk starts to colonize my chairs if they're unoccupied."

"The impulse of empire," I said, as he tried to find somewhere for the papers, ultimately stowing them on top of some others on a low shelf.

He laughed. "I know it! At home, my wife confines my mess." He found his way back into his desk chair. The spot on the green plush where his head rested was shiny and worn. As it was a Saturday, I had been surprised that he was teaching, but he explained that summer school ran six days a week.

He wore a new-looking suit, conservative but not unfashionable. Chartreuse silk tie dotted with tiny purple fish. A hint of cologne and Wrigley's Doublemint gum. He was clean-shaven, with hair thinning on top to expand a forehead dominated by a pair of remarkable eyebrows. If they were still, they might not have been so notable. But they were never still. His voice was pleasant, his face well-shaped, but his eyebrows were his defining feature. (These were also Brinda's eyebrows, though she used them so differently that further comparisons were useless.) Seth's brows spoke as he spoke; gestured when he did. They made me think that this man could never lie: his eyebrows, shooting like arrows from his third eye, would shout the truth even if he fought to suppress it.

"Rao?" he asked. "Telegu?" It was the usual first question, sprung from that human desire to identify one another by clan. *What is your place, your people?*

"*Hah*, originally, yes. My father was from Nellore, and we spent holidays there, though I was raised first in Hyderabad and then New Delhi. I did graduate studies at McGill, though, and lived in Ottawa for some years."

I imagine he might have liked to know my caste, to add that stamp to my resumé. But such questions are no longer the done thing among the educated classes.

"And you live in Delhi now?"

"That's right," I said. There was a slight brightness to his eyes that conveyed genuine, relatively untainted interest. He struck me as a man concerned with bonds of affection and community. He might like you; he might even, somehow, someday, help you.

"And you would like to hear about our involvement with Venkat?"

"If that is what you want to talk about. Also your own experience of the disaster."

He sat with elbows on the armrests, hands in his lap. I waited for him to ask more about the focus of the study, as others of my interviewees had. *Why are you doing this?* Or, as Suresh had: *Why dredge this up?*

"And your experience?" he asked instead.

"I, mine?"

He cleared his throat. "Did you not lose loved ones in the disaster?"

To this point, none of my other subjects had asked me this, and I can tell you now that none but Seth ever did. They were caught up their own grief and their own stories; they must have figured they would have known my name if my wife or children had died.

Since this was not a therapeutic relationship, and since I had withheld that information for no reason I could name, it seemed wrong to deflect. "My sister and her children."

I watched Seth's face. Not much changed, except for a shift of those eyebrows. And yet I distinctly felt that my pain was filtering through him, and that he had no sense of how vulnerable this made him.

I elaborated, my mouth dry. "My brother-in-law, who still lives in Montreal, was my first interviewee. His wife, my sister, Kritika, and my nephew and niece were coming to India for their summer holidays."

His eyes looked steadily into mine. "Your parents are still alive?"

"No, not anymore."

He hadn't moved, nor had I, and yet it was as though some column connecting our chests was collapsing, drawing us toward an unseen centre.

"And your own family, is anyone travelling with you?"

"I don't have a family. I . . ." This, too, is always an awkward thing to say, particularly to men of my own age and station in life. "I chose to remain unmarried." I broke his gaze. Too much. I was short of breath. Looking around the office, I saw a PhD from Indiana State University, framed on the wall, together with several teaching awards. Jumbled into the shelves, physics toys: a drinking bird, a Newton's cradle, wooden blocks in a Roman arch.

Seth looked out his window. "The sun is out! Perhaps let's go sit in the, what do you call it, gazebo sort of thing, in the garden. There are comfortable chairs that stay dry."

"That rainstorm was quite something." I don't make small talk. It really was quite something.

He swept some untidy stacks of papers into a briefcase and closed his door behind us. "It's the lake. Pulls the freak rainstorms in."

"You are a professor of physics?" I asked as we descended.

"Everyone has to profess something. I profess physics and God." Sly and harmless delight.

"Ah?" I said. The G-word raised my arm hairs a little.

"Associate Professor only," he said.

He was approaching retirement, not as a full professor but one rank below. Some halt in his career? "What is your specialty?"

"I don't specialize, as such. I like to think my specialty is making people love this subject." He cleared his throat. "Let me put it to you this way. Every scientist sees the world through his discipline's teachings. When people learn about physics, the world expands for them. The Big Bang, I like to call it: if a man continues to learn, his universe will be constantly expanding, isn't it? So I teach Introductory Physics, Physics of Chemistry, Physics of Biology, Physics for Non-Majors. Courses that might typically rotate among faculty, but I like to teach them. I have never gone in much for research."

"And yet . . . teaching here?" We found seats in the garden, very nice, an outdoor student lounge. "Harbord is a research institution, isn't it?"

He cleared his throat again. "When I first came to Harbord, the physics department was not the best in the country. If it was, they wouldn't have hired me! Maybe they didn't know that, then. Not much resources. Very little equipment, not too many graduate students. My area of research was elementary particles. I worked on muons, for my dissertation. You know much about . . . ?"

I'm sure I looked quite blank.

"Doesn't matter. Anyway, I got married in the summer between completing my PhD and coming to Lohikarma. After I arrived, and got settled, I started to see how competitive it could be to get research funding. Such a big part of your time, competing for grants and prizes and publications. Competing, competition . . . it's not really my thing."

Seth used his hands when he talked—we all do that, Indians—but in concert with his eyebrows, as though one pair were conducting the other.

"My wife, Lakshmi, arrived about six months later, in the middle of a Canadian winter, poor girl. I had to get her settled. I was the junior man on the totem pole that year, so I taught all the introductory classes. And I very much enjoyed it. Especially the classes for non-majors. I enjoy the feeling of bringing them into the field. Initially, students are fearful. They think they will be bored; they think they might feel unintelligent. But they come to love physics! It's truly satisfying, truly so.

"So. There was no real opportunity for me to continue my research that first year, and without my dissertation director, I felt a bit lost. I had enjoyed my research, but I didn't kid myself into thinking I was the most brilliant physicist that ever walked the earth. Have you read any Richard Feynman? Now there's a brilliant fellow. A very dedicated teacher, also. He used to say that if we can't explain it to an undergraduate, we don't know enough about it. I try to keep up. I read the journals, try to incorporate the new research into my courses. Keeps it interesting. You know? So many people out there are driven to do research, to write. I ride on their backs!"

I smiled, still waiting for an answer to my question.

"But, back then, my old mentor was writing a book, using the research I had conducted under his supervision. I read the book as he was writing, offered some suggestions. He invited me back to Indiana one summer, to work with him. And when the book was published, he gave me co-author credit. This was some four years after I was hired here. I had published two other papers in the meantime, also co-authored with him. Anyway, it was unusual, for a young physicist to have co-authorship on a book. I had good teaching reports. My colleagues liked me. I got tenure.

"My children came along, and I kept on teaching—but research?" He shook his head. "Not for me. I never tried to advance beyond Associate level."

I would learn, in time, what a popular teacher he was, both among undergraduates and with his students in an adult education course, which he taught almost entirely using examples in nature and real-world experiments, rather than in a lab. He was beloved as a teacher, even while remaining a figure of some ridicule among his more ambitious colleagues. I was struck, then and later, by Seth's having shaped his seeming lack of ambition into a professional niche, justifying his tenure by being both popular and indispensable: teaching courses that higher-reaching professors might feel were beneath them while also providing them with a gratifying sense of superiority.

"I talked about it with Brinda, my eldest, when she was deciding whether to quit her PhD." He leaned back in the lawn chair, put a hand in his blazer pocket as if to reach for cigarettes. I made a little note: *smoker?* Former, maybe. I would have smelled it. No one in Canada smokes anymore. "She did Biochem here, then took a break, a year or two off, then joined the epidemiology programme at the University of Alberta. An excellent programme, and I think she could have done very well, but the drive wasn't there. She's a brilliant girl. You are meeting her, this week?"

"I met her this morning," I said.

He smiled as if to say, *So then you know.* "She seemed to think it wasn't what she was meant to do. She stopped, took a job with the alumni magazine. Within a year, she was writing half of the articles. No training! Now she wants to take it further, so she is entering this master's course, at Johns Hopkins: Science Writing." He looked off at groups of students dotted in the half-sun. "She would have made an excellent prof."

"She might yet become one," I interjected. Was I reassuring or challenging him? "In writing or journalism or some such."

"Yes, yes," he agreed so fast it was as though he were contradicting me. "How many jobs of that sort are out there?"

I didn't respond.

"Writing these articles about others . . . She has been married six, seven years, but still they don't seem settled. No children. And now she's off to Baltimore." He brightened, falsely: the eyebrows stayed low. "Questions, questions!"

"What does her husband do?" I asked.

"Dev? He is a Chemistry PhD, but he works as a lab technician. I don't know what happened. His father teaches at the University of Alberta." Seth leaned back to pull a peony toward his nose, from a bush that spread behind him. He indicated the flower with his eyebrows. "Very nice." He resettled in his chair, the hand back in his sport coat pocket, fingers working at something in there. "Dev is a bit of a funny guy. Doctorate. Employed at a university. But he puts down academia, acts as though it is beneath him somehow. It's not for everyone, as I well know." He seemed now to regret his candour. "But what does all this have to do with the bombing? What am I talking about?"

I offered a hook. "Brinda talked to me a little about Dr. Venkataraman's family."

"Yes." He met my eyes, giving me, again, that strange feeling of collapsing toward him. "My wife and I, and Dr. Venkataraman and his wife, when we were all young, we used to get together every weekend. A small group of us, young academics, from all over India, but Venkat and Sita were the only Tamilians so we saw them even a bit more. He is my wife's relation. You have seen him yet?"

The question was not merely casual, but I couldn't say why. "We have an appointment, Monday morning."

Seth nodded. He spoke slowly. "I have two girls, no complaints, but I was very attached to Sundar. Different, you know, a boy. Even before I had my daughters, I used to play with him. Venkat is not so much the type to give horsey rides, that kind of thing. I enjoyed that. When we went to their house, I would be on my hands and knees the whole time!

"The children grew up together. Once, Sita and Sundar joined us on our holiday, at a cabin, for a week or two. We had never done that before, and this place was a bit remote—Malcolm Island, off the west coast. Can't remember how we chose it. Venkat didn't want to come. Not his cup of tea. So Sita brought the boy. We had an excellent time. Board games, swimming. Absolutely relaxing. We still talk about it. A beer on the . . ."—he waved his hand horizontally—"the veranda, in the evening. Sita and Lakshmi used to get along very well also, a bit like sisters. Sita was a quiet type, but that week she talked and laughed. Venkat had, well, you'll see—he used to have a bit of a temper. And Sita, just as we were attached to Sundar, she doted on our daughters." His eyes went a bit glassy. He paused. Sniffed. Went on.

"One day, Sundar and I went fishing. I wanted to try it, but my daughters were still too small, and they were never the type to fish. We're Tamil Brahmin, raised strictly vegetarian, but we started eating meat when we came to Canada. It was hard to be vegetarian here, back then, not like now. But both my daughters turned vegetarian again when they found out where meat came from! Soft-hearted girls.

"Sundar was very eager to go fishing. He must have been eight or nine. We got the poles and bait from a shop in town, and they told us a good spot to go to, a kind of fishing hole, a dock area, where you could sit. We had a bucket, in case we caught something. We had packed sandwiches, candy bars. We sat around with the other fishermen. I didn't know what the hell I was doing! But Sundar didn't get bored, all day. And he caught one fish, a little thing." He held up one hand, putting his other pointer finger to the wrist. "One of the fishermen told me I shouldn't keep it, so I said to the guy I would throw it back, but I was afraid Sundar would be disappointed. We took it home, kept it alive in water in the bucket. But then I didn't know what to do with it—kill it? Take out the bones? He had been talking all the way home about frying it or roasting it, but Lakshmi and Sita had made supper, and by the time we took baths and ate, he was tired, and forgot about it. After he went to bed, I checked on it, but it had died. I threw it out in the woods."

Again he stopped, rubbed his forehead with his fingertips. A vein throbbed on his temple. He worked his mouth, swallowed, put his hand back in his pocket.

"A couple of years later, Sundar came to Disneyland with us. Once more, Venkat didn't want to do it. He only ever shelled out for trips back home to see his mother. Sita had just begun a part-time job at the bank, so I think maybe she didn't have holiday time yet. So we asked, could Sundar come with us? Venkat and Sita insisted on paying his portion. I think Sita must have put pressure on, and Venkat didn't like to be seen as cheap. Sundar was very excited. Our daughters must have been, perhaps, six and eight? And he is about four years older than Brinda. We drove. It was a bit awkward. Motel rooms are made for four, but we would get him a cot, and he behaved perfectly, an angel, the whole trip. He was old enough to even help with the kids. One night after our daughters were in bed, Lakshmi and I went out, to the restaurant attached to the motel. We could see our room from our table, but still, we would not have done it without him there.

"But there was one thing that happened on that trip. Sundar was old enough for some ride, I don't remember what it was, but our kids weren't big enough. I can see now, one of us should have gone on it with

him. I don't know what we were thinking. Probably we were tired, and
he said he could do it by himself. We agreed to wait for him, but the
kids were restless, that must have been it, end of the day, so we told him
we would get a snack and meet him, right at the exit to the ride. Well,
we came back and he wasn't there. We thought we were early, he hadn't
come out yet, but we waited, twenty minutes, half an hour, and then we
started to panic. There wasn't anywhere for the kids to sit, so they were
whining. Lakshmi and I were sweating, let me tell you. So finally I left
to find an information kiosk.

"They put out an all-points bulletin and finally, maybe an hour or
two after that, some person in a Donald Duck costume brings him. Disneyland. It's huge. Thousands of people. Sundar couldn't tell us how we
missed each other. But, really. What would be worse, losing your own
kid or losing someone else's? Oh God."

He had noticed me watching his pocket, and now pulled his hand
out a little to show me what occupied it in there. No ancient cigarette
pack, but a *japa mala*, a rosary of *rudraksha* beads, each wrinkled, tobac-
co-coloured seed like a dwarfish pocket idol presenting in a queue for
worship. "I am a devotee of Shivashakti. Heard of him?"

Said with a straight face: my introduction to Seth's deadpan humour.
No Indian could avoid Shivashakti, a "spiritual leader" of tremendous
fame and, dare I say it, fortune. Shivashakti's cult was massive and international, as with Rajneesh and his ilk, nearly on a par with Satya Sai Baba's.

I do not like godmen, and reserve my greatest dislike for those
with the wealth and adulation it seems to me should belong only to rock
stars. My attitude, common enough among self-styled intellectuals, is
to see religion as infantilism, unwillingness to take responsibility for
one's own decisions. True, certain thinkers I admire intensely, including Erich Fromm, have thought differently, but I had never gotten far
with these ideas myself, not least because meeting a devotee shuts me
up tight, their fawning and mindlessness. I had vowed, as a therapist, to
help people to think for themselves.

What to do? Religion has hobbled my countrymen. It has poi-
soned my country.

And yet. "I've heard of him," I said to Seth. None of my usual
bile, despite the japa mala snaking out of his pocket, despite the lack of

a therapeutic frame—historically the only harness that can restrain me from telling someone what I think. I wasn't thinking it. I wasn't even feeling it! What strange spell had this man cast?

Many people who know me imagine I must be a cruel sort of therapist, an old-fashioned abusive Freudian, hastening transference by becoming the problem itself. Not at all. I'm not a misanthrope, even if I don't like most people. I am indescribably touched by anyone who has been moved to dig in the embers of his life and find what glows there. I stoke, blow, add wood or dung chips as needed . . . the metaphor founders, but I think you understand. Seth provoked in me a glow: credulity. He had started to break my longstanding habit of skepticism. It felt good and strange. I wanted to see what he saw, or, no, not that. I wanted to be seen by him? It wasn't only that. He had guessed, about me. He *had* seen.

"You must come home," he said, still using that expression after how many years in Canada? I, too, live between my Englishes, and claim them all. "On the anniversary, we typically have an evening at our place, a remembrance, short prayer, a meal."

I said I would see, yes, perhaps, my heart dropping a little. Such gatherings are not my thing.

"No need to confirm. Just come." He wrote his address on a card. "Can I give you a ride back to your hotel, or . . . where are you staying?"

"No, no, it's very close." I gestured behind me, toward town. "I walked. Less than twenty minutes."

"I live even closer, but walking? Bad enough to have to work!" The habitual deadpan. "I do a forced march along the lake each evening in summer." Eyebrows up, tilted asymmetrically. "My wife."

His wife. I was curious about her, about his home, his other daughter. Curious about the daughter I had already met. Also his friend, the excuse for our meeting: Venkat. Also to see Seth again.

I took a long-cut home and was on a bench by the lake, watching the geese, someone diving off the opposite bank, white legs disappearing into the green water, when I looked up to see thunderclouds running in again from the horizon, dangling sheets of rain that darkened the shining town against the sun, until everything was rainbow, rainbow, rainbow!

I don't like to get wet, and so did my best to defy my knees, going up, up, up the side of the town, so steep that sidewalks alone cannot cut it. Rather, the sidewalks have been cut into steps, several flights per block. (A "flight" of stairs—that's a good one.) I only made it a third of the way before the rain hit. Torrential. Lashings. My notepads would be soaked. I was trying to cross a wide thoroughfare when I saw two punks huddled with their dog under a dry cleaner's awning, who waved me in. They told me they were from Montreal, hitchhiking west, where berries, they said earnestly, were bursting to be picked. Their German shepherd wore the standard-issue homeless-dog bandana, a splash of purple amongst punk-black clothes and punk-white faces. We peered out into the rain, avoiding leaky spots and eye contact, at least on my part. I didn't want more conversation. I wanted to think.

I hadn't needed to explain to Seth that someone who had not lost immediate family in the crash could still be intimately affected by it. He, like his daughter Brinda, was self-effacing, but in a way that had nothing to do with self-hatred. I couldn't name it, but it was powerfully attractive. Gracious forbearance. His admiration for his daughter. His bemusement at her life-course. I remembered a book by someone who taught in that science writing programme at Johns Hopkins. Perhaps she was still there. Ann Finkbeiner. *After the Death of a Child: Living with Loss Through the Years*. An unexpectedly good book, one of the few I had returned to out of the dozens on the subject that I had picked up and, mostly, dismissed.

For many years, researchers searched and researched for proof of "recovery" from bereavement, the very term suggesting that a person could return to fully robust being by accepting that "dead is dead" and letting go. Freud himself appeared to believe this, until he lost his own child. I remembered this: therapists I knew, in Canada, shepherding bereaved persons through identifiable stages toward recovery. Rosslyn argued this with me at some point, or, at least, that was what I thought she was arguing. She seemed sometimes to think I was misrepresenting her positions. No doubt she was sometimes right.

Finkbeiner says that researchers finally are starting to admit that we perhaps never recover. They still look at stages in grief. Not the old, hard-and-fast ones: Denial: ✔ Anger: ✔ Bargaining: ✔ Depression: ✔ Acceptance? Check. But changes of some sort—erosion, shape-shifting. Grief is as subject to the forces of time as every other real thing, from love to trees to stones. Finkbeiner matter-of-factly says that

". . . letting go of a child is impossible." And yet, with time, the great sloth heart may move.

The storm began to thin and dissolve, and the Montrealers moved out toward the road. I gave them some money, enough for a couple of bowls of noodles at the Chinese restaurant, if they could get in the door smelling as they did. Before going home to make my notes, I bought a rainproof jacket at a second-hand store on High Street. Black, urban-looking, nothing I would wear back home, but it cost less than my recent investment in the Youth of Canada and rolled up neatly into a little packet that I swore never again to be caught without in this volatile little town.

※ ※ ※

I had it with me the next day, Sunday, when I went, as I have every Sunday of my adult life, to find a novel. I had spotted the bookstores downtown, and already decided where I would go, a cavernous store stacked with books organized according to mysterious rules, and attached to a vegetarian café.

Rosslyn and I had loved Sunday, loved our system, both profligate and restrained. You buy only one book, and sometimes not even that; sometimes the other already owns the book you most want to read, but if you want a book, you buy it. Only one. You spend the whole day reading it. It keeps you from worrying, the rest of the week, over whether you'll ever get to read fiction again. It keeps you from being acquisitive. It is calm, measured, stately.

Although I always have several titles in mind, I also like to browse. Today: CanLit. Had to be. What a plethora of books I'd not heard of! Canadians do love their authors. This was coming, when I left, with the Mordecai Richler this and the Margaret Atwood that, but it hadn't achieved anything like these proportions. I'd read the *Globe and Mail* Saturday books section yesterday, over (and under) my solitary meal, but it only brought home that I was Out of Touch.

This week's winner: Wayne Johnston's *The Colony of Unrequited Dreams*, nosing out Anne Carson's *Autobiography of Red*. I paid the chatty, bearded fellow at the cash and went through a set of aquamarine-painted doors to order a breakfast burrito at the café. The book's cover bored me but I wouldn't hold it against the novel. Our era in book design is dominated by photos-from-behind.

Earlier this year, back in Delhi, Vijaya, my upstairs neighbour, the widow, had begun inviting me to meals. Somehow she learned about my Sunday routine and somehow I invited her to join me. She was an MA in literature, after all, teaching at the college level. Perhaps she had seen me leaving one Sunday or another for Chandni Chowk, Oxford Books, Bahrisons? I sometimes thought she conspired casually to run into me in our stairwell—evidence not of my allure, but rather of her desperation.

So one morning we went to look at books together. I was sweating lightly and already regretting it. So self-conscious! We had no idea how to behave. There is no template, back home, for middle-aged dating. Others out and about were mostly younger, students, bachelor profs. Occasionally a middle-aged couple, but terrifyingly chic; women with short hair, men with long. It was Sunday: anyone who looked like us was at home, the men lounging on divans, the women cooking.

Vijaya chose a Jane Austen reissue, one of the few, she said, that she hadn't read. I hate Austen. Artificial, sentimental claptrap. I chose Bruce Chatwin's *On the Black Hill*. She peered politely at the blurbs.

Impossible to think of going to a coffeehouse, sitting among shouting, pretentious would-be poets. It would have compounded the awkwardness unbearably. As I hesitated, she invited me home for lunch. We entered her flat and followed the script: I lounged on the divan with Chatwin while she cooked. Her children telephoned: chatter-chatter-chatter. She switched on the television or radio, the blare of Bollywood. We ate and made small talk in Telegu. A hot midday meal induces a siesta, so I made my farewells. It was late afternoon by the time I woke. I never finished the book. I doubt she even opened hers. What piercing solitude. I recalled it now, here in the Big Bean Café. I was alone with my book and my meal, but it was that day with my widow that I felt in full my loneliness. How the other half lives, the variety, the social engagement: would this have been my life if I had succeeded in having a family? How would I have coped up with all that?

The breakfast burrito was passable, despite hard-core vegetarian ingredients requiring long mastication. The coffee was better than expected. And the book was excellent—Highly Recommended for All Collections. Indelible characters, and a view on a corner of Canadian history. I wondered if Seth or Brinda had read it. I was feeling very warm toward Canadians just now.

I remembered, randomly, as always, my parking-garage cat. Would Vijaya give it some yogourt rice to keep it going?

It probably had run away or been struck by a car.

* * *

At eleven o'clock on Monday morning, the longest day of the year (sun-up at 4:42! Rise aaand shine!), I was walking from one greystone building to the next in Harbord's lush quad, looking for Sonnet Hall, where, funnily, the department of math and statistics did its thing. Professor Venkataraman's office was on the second floor. He seemed to be on the same teaching schedule as his friend Seth, and had asked me to come immediately after his class.

His door remained closed to my knock, so I sat on one of several smallish wooden chairs in the hall. They were scattered, like hard, uncomfortable throw pillows, for use by anyone waiting for tardy profs. Several were decorated with angry words, deeply inscribed. I waited nearly an hour, but refrained from deepening any of the inscriptions. I called his office number and listened to it ring; I called his home number and left a message saying I would try again the next day at the same time, and could he please confirm?

He didn't, but I returned the next day in any case and waited fifteen or twenty minutes before giving up once more. As I pushed the elevator button (going down stairs is often harder on knees than going up) a man of about my age emerged from the stairwell. He was unlocking his door as I caught him.

"Professor Venkataraman?" He looked at me blankly. "Ashwin Rao. I'm conducting the, er, doing the study. I sent a letter and we spoke by phone last week . . ." His face seemed to harden but he nodded.

I followed him into his office, breathing his trailing scent: dusty, ammoniac, faint but distinct, perhaps intensified by raised body temperature because he had walked up the stairs. I couldn't identify it and wondered if it might be a drug I didn't know. Anti-anxiety medications alter body chemistry in specific ways, common enough that I often can distinguish them. The skin of his face and hands was flaccid, as if from sudden weight loss.

He pulled a visitor's chair out from his desk and gestured me into it, then sat on a sagging sofa, as though we were therapist and client. I reminded myself that this was something else.

"Rao?" he asked. "Telegu?"

There was an odd immobility to his face, not severe but noticeable. It wasn't the slackness of stroke, but rather a rigidity that could almost have been conscious or, if not, then otherwise psychological in its origins. He also had a noticeable facial discolouration, not uncommon in Indians with a particular type of skin, which gave a bluish shading to his features. He was quite bald on top, the fringe behind his ears neatly combed. His pants and shirt were of the sort not to wrinkle, but he was not dressed with care.

I gave him the same answer I had given Seth. He asked where I was based, my academic history. I had the clear sensation that I was being ranked.

"So you are interested in what?" he said, at last. "How I have got on since the bombing, is it? The trial has stirred up all the old emotions. Now we are waiting, again, for it all to be over."

I nodded and waited. One of the victims' fathers had been quoted in the papers, on the trial, saying, "It is like somebody putting a needle in a wound that has formed a crust. It was probably bleeding on the inside, but you couldn't see it. Now it is bleeding on the outside." Freud felt this himself, when his own child died, "a deep, narcissistic hurt that is not to be healed."

Venkat cocked his head coldly. "You want to ask some questions?"

I sniffed and swallowed, and rubbed my nose, which was itching. "We can start wherever you like. People often want to talk first about the early days, when you found out about the bomb. I would like to know that, as a sort of baseline. And more about your family."

"*Accha*, is that so? And how will this help, *who* will this help? I didn't want to do this, you understand." He gestured in my direction, as if toward something unpleasant. "Sethu's idea." He sighed. "He and Lakshmi are good people. But how, what is the model for this research? Someone will publish this? You travel around and ask questions of any-one who will answer? Journalism, then? Maybe made for TV?"

Despair filled me, a chilly blue liquid, seeping in from the ground. My feet grew cold, my fingers numb.

Why are you dredging all this up?

"I hadn't realized Dr. Sethuratnam had put you up to this. Please. You don't have to." But if he didn't talk with me, I would have no reason to meet Seth again, and all the unfamiliar, perhaps groundless optimism of the last couple of days would be snatched away.

"No," he barked. "That would not be right. Let us talk."

I stayed more than two hours. Don't think this means things got more pleasant. It was simply that once he started, he did not stop.

* * *

On my way back to my apartment, I bought two mickeys of Canadian whisky. For after I finished my notes. My steno pad, in my shirt pocket, thwapped my heart in time with my steps.

The composition notebook marked "Venkataraman" was on my dining-table-desk. I made a sandwich, then found the first blank page after my notes on Seth. I pulled a fresh pen from the package and my steno pad from my pocket, and began to write.

Dr. Venkataraman's monologue (monolong?) had often seemed virtually incoherent, but I did my best to record it the way he had told it, to try to follow the lines of his thought. He began with the accused, those in the dock and the ones who seemed to have gotten away. He ranted about governmental incompetence. Air India had been threatened, don't forget. Planes were going to be bombed, that's what they said, payback for decades of atrocities. Air India let the Canadian Aviation Security folks know, but, as happens, the white people thought the brown people were merely asking for a handout. Extra security? Make 'em pay for it. Next! Same with the Canadian Security and Intelligence Service—insecurity and stupidity service was more like it! And whatever information they could get, they refused to share with the RCMP, who were working blind, not that they would admit it! He told me in nauseating detail, much of it redundant to me—we had read the same sources—how the bomb was made, how it was planted, right under the noses of everyone whose job it was to prevent such things. The RCMP made him fill out forms, then lost them. The Canadians didn't bother sending anyone to Ireland to help with logistics—that fell to an Indian diplomat and the Irish themselves. Over and through he cycled—details, details, details—hardly mentioning his wife or child or how he lived his wreck of a life. I was unable to interrupt, to guide him or ask questions.

Transcription took six hours. I permitted myself coffee at the three-hour mark, while my whisky stood like a Buckingham Palace guard beside the hot plate.

Ann Finkbeiner said that the parents she interviewed had found "subtle and often unconscious ways of preserving the bond" with their children. I had begun to see this in many of my interviewees' stories. It sometimes took hours of talking for the subject to reveal the ways they had found, and I often didn't recognize these until I transcribed the interview, even if it seemed obvious in retrospect. My brother-in-law, Suresh, had gravitated to hospice work, comforting other grieving parents and departing kids. Another man I talked to had given up his career as a research scientist to found a charity in India, its various branches named for his late wife and children, providing schooling and medical care for needy kids there. The dancer I had seen at the trial last year famously emerged from several years of debilitating grief to found what has become the premier academy of Indian classical dance in Canada. Eventually, she created and performed a choreography inspired by her horrendous losses.

I couldn't tell, with Venkataraman, how, if at all, he had "changed his life to preserve the bond." He was the only person I interviewed who hadn't wanted to talk to me. Finkbeiner, like me, interviewed volunteers only. Perhaps people who found a way to "preserve the bond" were more willing to talk about the course of their lives following bereavement? Would Venkat be the exception that proved the rule, the one who had felt his family float away, leaving him grasping at ether?

Shortly after nine, I finished. Full stop. I creaked my back upright and tried to straighten my neck. I massaged my right hand with my left, then sat on it to undo the kinks. The goiter-like callus on my bird-finger's first knuckle was throbbing. The sky was starting to pink.

It had been good to discharge him onto the page, but the feel of him lingered in me—his quaking inadequacy in the face of the disaster; his loneliness, for how could someone like him find anyone else to be with? I had let his emptiness pass through mine onto the page but still it blew about in me, its cold surfaces shifting and tumbling freely.

I should have boiled up some rice and dal and delivered myself early to bed with some poetry to read upon the pillow. I was carrying a leafing-apart copy of Robert Hass's *Praise*, left by some tourist at a Delhi bookstall, just as I would leave it here for some other tourist, or maybe even the same one, on the same circuit as I, some invisible doppelgänger I was unwittingly trailing around the world, and who was trailing me . . .

Instead, I cracked open the whisky. An aluminium cap, perforations tearing as you twist, perhaps not as satisfying as magazine-subscription-card-tearing, or bubble-wrap-popping (this latter delight has come lately to India thanks to online booksellers), but quite good in its own special way, the brief cracking of something made to be torn.

It was 22nd June, the eve of the anniversary. All over Canada, we were in our rooms, alone or with others, readying ourselves for the onslaught of memory. I took up a small tumbler. I poured a shot. *Shhh. Ahhh. T.*

I would never have volunteered to be interviewed in such a study as mine. And now, I could not think of a way I had kept my bond with Asha. I never properly even had a bond with Anand. Let alone Kritika. Who were they? I would never know. No one would ever know. (Rosslyn. Thoughts of her lurked continuously since my return to her country.)

My glass was already empty. I poured a second shot. Remember the Mukherjee and Blaise book? I fetched my copy, wanting to hurt myself. Now let me tell you why it infuriated me. Not the polemics—those were merely inadequate. It was the way they talked about the dead.

They did interviews with the victim families. Suburban Indian parents, who tell their moving stories themselves, while the novelists describe them, and the scene around them, with only occasional lapses into the ridiculous: "The winding streets of middle-class Toronto suburbs, bearing names like 'Brendangate,' 'Wildfern' and 'Morningstar,' should never have known such tragedy." What? Tragedy belongs to places with ugly names? "Schillong," perhaps? "Ouagadougou?"

But here is the offensive part. Here is how they describe the children who died:

> . . . *truly bicultural children. They were bright synthesizers, not iconoclasts and rebels. Every day at school, where mainstream kids chatted around them about drugs and dates and at home where parents*

pressured them to study hard and not let go their Indianness, they negotiated the tricky spaces of acculturation. These were children with the drive and curiosity of pioneers, but they were also children who took family love, family support and family dependence for granted. They switched with ease from Calvin Klein and Jordache to saris or salwar-kameezes brought over by doting grandparents, aunts and uncles. They ate pizzas with friends in shopping malls, and curries with rice or unleavened breads at home. They were smart, ambitious children who won spelling bees in a language that their parents spoke with heavy accents; they were children who filled high school chess clubs and debate clubs, who aced math tests and science tests, who wrote poems and gave classical dance recitals while they waited to go into en-gineering, medical or law school; they were children who pleased their old-country parents by avoiding school proms and dances where kids misbehaved, and above all, they were newly affluent children with purpose and mission, who organized benefits for Ethiopia and Bhopal and projects closer to home.

These were *our children*, reduced to some majority opinion of what they *should* have been, perfect little conformists, the best of both worlds, untouched by darkness or dirt or curiosity. No iconoclasts. No rebels. No thinkers. No individuals. Stiff little brown Barbies and Kens.

Tch-tch, Canada, your loss, not India's. Is that right? Get this: their chastity-obedience-intelligence had nothing to do with whether they deserved to be acknowledged as Canadians. Those children weren't de-serving of investigative attention because of their virtues. They deserved to live because they were alive. They were Canadian because they were born or raised here.

Besides, Mukherjee and Blaise are novelists. They should have known better.

I hate the sentimentalizing. I hate the saint-making. I hate that I hate. I threw the book down, poured another shot and raised it. A toast! Congrats, bombers! Conviction or no conviction, you did it.

On a wrought-iron chair on my balcony, I watched the Quonset's aluminium roof grow roseate. My whisky blazed in the syrupy sunset. A memory blazed in my mind: a man—*which man, which?*—dying on my family's street. The bombers took *his* revenge. The government would take ours. And then? What next? It was absurd! To "prove" these men's individual culpability would change nothing.

Was this why I was so violently uninterested in who the accused bombers were, as men, as individuals? Alone in a room with them, what would I do? Anyway, I was not alone with them. They were off limits to me, with good reason. I was alone with myself, about whom I have mixed feelings. The whisky wobbled a little in my glass, but I steadied it, and drank.

* * *

Nineteen eighty-five: a year and a half since I'd moved back to India. The unforeseen bloody horrors of the past year—the Golden Temple invasion, assassination, pogroms—had made me go over and over my list of reasons for coming back, had seen them diminish as personal motivations even as their intrinsic importance increased. And Rosslyn's news—engagement and pregnancy!—increased my self-doubt to the point of vertigo, even as I knew that my work was more meaningful than ever.

So as June approached, and with it the North American school holidays, when Kritika and the children would visit, when, with my parents, we would all take the train together to a hill station where my parents had taken Kritika and me as children, I dreamed increasingly of my niece. The child of my life. I hadn't seen them since I left Canada, nearly two years back, and she already looked different in the Christmas pictures my sister had sent, skinnier, the teeth that seem so large in late childhood shrinking within the proportions of an almost-adolescent smile; that smile still, always, the focal point of the family composition.

I tried to incorporate that new face—surely it would be different again by the time they arrived—into hazy daydreams of us playing Snakes and Ladders, or reading novels in cots set at right angles so we would lie with our feet making an arrowhead and chat over the tops of our books, she perhaps enjoying one of my childhood favourites, which still fed worms on a couple of shelves in the upper reaches of my parents' home.

Sometimes I pictured all of us together, my sister, nephew, parents, but those thoughts were more obligatory, more effortful. Images of time to be spent with Asha, in contrast, were like the japa mala Seth carried in his pocket. A particularly obnoxious colleague, a boring meeting, even a less than fully sympathetic client, and suddenly I was off in the clouds, quite literally: thinking of the hill station, where, if one were an early riser, one would take coffee on the veranda amidst the low cloudsthat settled onto the hilltops each night. I imagined Asha, wandering out to find me, trailing a quilt. She would nestle against my shoulder, watching the mist snake through the bushes, wrinkling her nose at the smell of my coffee, or perhaps asking for a contraband sip, as the rest of the house slept on.

In steadier moments, I gave thought to Anand. He was fond of baseball, and I wanted to take him to a cricket game. He also loved books, though I had been stung by his rebuffing my suggestions, or, worse, his starting a book I had loved only to rubbish it with a few choice descriptors. Of course I had had some successes, and his expression, when something intrigued him, was particularly pleasing to me. I should have found his inability to fake interest disarming, but we were too much alike, particularly in this way. Even my sister could see it and said so. She said it was her karma: she had done so badly on her first attempt to live with me that she was being made to try it again. Except, as I would point out, I wasn't dead yet. Kritika would roll her eyes and say, "One of God's karmic accountants is scratching his head. Or rubbing his hands in glee." She had her moments.

She would tell me that I should have given her children cousins to play with. I would counter that I should then have been deprived of her children's company. "Selfish," she said, "as always," though I didn't see it that way. Of course, had I had children of my own, I suppose my craving for hers would not have been so fierce.

* * *

The liquor was giving me courage. I would apply myself to the problem that had vexed me to nightmare for so long: discerning the moral source of the disaster.

I went inside the apartment to fetch my journal and my still-warm pen. I saw the notebook marked "Venkataraman," and picked it up as well. And, why not, the second bottle.

A mechanic, Inderjit Singh Reyat, had been serving time in England for building the bomb that went off in Tokyo. The Brits agreed to send him back to Canada to face the music for building the other one. Once he arrived, though, he struck a bargain to testify in his old buddies' trial instead of standing his own. His testimony could and should have been a bomb indeed, but at the trial he developed sudden-onset amnesia, an unfortunate disability that later resulted in (hooray!) a perjury conviction.

In the dock, then, two men.

1. Ajaib Singh Bagri, the Sidekick. Big family. Received welfare payments with one hand, paid for expensive cars with the other, openly preached violence against Indira Gandhi and India as a nation.

2. Ripudaman Singh Malik, the Millionaire. Charismatic as far as these types go. Rabble-roused in the temples, kept bad company, and ran the Khalsa School, Sikh education for the chosen ones. Ms. D's love, the unconsummated affair. He had told her that the second bomb should have gone off at Heathrow, should have killed many more than 329.

The Canadian Security and Intelligence Service had made tapes of phone conversations, mostly coded, between the suspects prior to the bombing, but then erased them. The erasure was routine, procedure. Somehow, no one plucked these particular conversations from the conveyor belt. ("Ready to write the book?" "Ready to write the book.")

Imagine the lad who did the erasing. I'm fairly sure it was that, and not recording over. He loads the massive disk of tape onto the axle, threads its end onto an empty, waiting spool. He adjusts the alignment and flips the lever for the sixth time that day, the forty-fourth time that month, the two hundred-and-nth time since he got his job. Then he sits, one lightly fuzzed cheek cupped in a rubber-gloved hand. The rubber glove seems redundant, since the only evidence he is handling is to be destroyed, but protocols and procedures must be observed. He lets his eyes blur as he watches the spools go round and round . . .

I threw down my pen. My brain was full of the details, but I couldn't stick with them, the bombers, the investigators—banal, not evil. Where was the evil that wrecked my life? What happened, and how did it kill my child?

I will tell you now, dear reader, because I want to tell you everything: I heard voices. Yes, they roiled in on the whisky, the sunset, my unselfconscious grief, my uncontrollable self-pity, loud, undeniable and loud: a multitude of tiny, tinny voices in chorus. I picked up the pen again and turned the page and pinned them down into my journal, out of my head.

We were mere bits and bobs quivering undetectably on separate shelves in a store where motes danced on breath soured on deprivation and depredation, wafted promises that we would be united in good time—in bad time!—to fulfill our Daddies' purposes. Other components dreamt of coming together as stereos ... TVs ... clock radios, for gods' sake. Conduits to false hope. When we were chosen, we knew what for. We were going to give them what-for.

The gods create the parts, but components are not born until they are united in a function. The Daddies conceived us, conceived of us, birthed and rebirthed us out of hateful innocence.

There were Others, before us. We could feel them in their elemental state, their components sundered, atomized, quivering undetectably in the old, old woods of the island where the Daddies had gone to blow them up, our prototypes, progenitors, predecessors. They predeceased us so that we could decease others—cease them, that is.

Acronyms—FBI, CSIS, RCMP—would bumble after the Daddies at a distance, getting stopped at traffic lights, missing ferries, looking through binocular lenses, or bifocal glasses, or fickle eyeballs, that made the Daddies all look alike, those Sick Sikhs: turbans or no turbans, beards or no beards, but all with handsome brown faces—how do their gods make them so alike? Gotta be a conspiracy! Police Agents tripped through the woods, close enough to hear a big explosion, whereupon they thought ... "Gun!"

Gun!

Even so, Officers in the one Agency didn't tell Agents in the other Office. Sometimes they didn't even tell their own. They might have thought a thought or two but didn't think to mention what they were thinking, and then said later that they thought it better not to mention their thoughts when really they weren't thinking much at all.

* * *

In hindsight, everyone had premonitions, if you believe the accounts. One man, a Sikh but no extremist, leaving on business, leaving his family behind, saw a man he knew to be an extremist at the airport. They exchanged pleasantries, after which the departing man went straightaway to a kiosk where he bought a hundred thousand dollars' worth of life insurance before getting on board the jet.

Another man, after seeing his family off, noticed the British Airways line was full of observant Sikhs while the Air India line had almost none. "What's going on?" he asked a friend. "Hadn't you heard?" the friend replied. "Sikhs are warning each other: avoid Air India." The man tried to go after his wife and kids, but was stopped.

Suresh fought with Kritika on the way to the airport. "Did I do that to make it easier to say goodbye?" he asked me. I didn't answer, that people often pick fights with loved ones on the eve of a separation, because I didn't know what he most wanted to believe.

Planes would fall from skies, some Agents heard our Daddies say.

Planes flying. Planes falling. What goes between?

Mechanic Daddy bought us on plastic. We: Sony. We: Sanyo. He: Reyat. He: *IDIOT!*

But even an idiot can assemble a bomb, blow it up in the woods, assemble another, blow it up, assemble us and . . .

We were in the bag!

Bag Daddy closed the zipper over Us. His hands were sweating. We were covered in clothes. Toothpaste. Deodorant. Aftershave—a joke? Well, this was one of those handsome Daddies without a beard. He was nervous, shaking and grinning. Scared! Of us!

Oh. The Twin. Our Double.

Grrr. We were jealous. Our Twin was on its way to Japan. We wanted Japan. Like Hiroshima-Bomb and Nagasaki-Bomb. They WERE The Bomb. The H-Bomb and the N-Bomb dancing A-rings and O-rings around the other bombs, Alpha and Omega. That was Us now.

Us going West. The Twin going East. Going, but not to arrive. To go.

Daaaaa BOOOOOOMMMMBBBB!

Bag Daddy stops at the airport, but his ticket doesn't go past the next stop. He's checking us, so we won't be checked. He's not checking himself—he's letting the counter gal have it, and she's got a line full of people all craning their necks to give her the stink-eye. What's the holdup? He hasn't got a gun!

She's giving in, "Okay, okay," agreeing to Check Us Through.

We are in like Flynn, checked in because she checked out, into the hold, interlined because Daddy was out of line in the line.

Who's your Daddy? He's gone. And the line is moving again.

* * *

I phoned as they were getting ready to go to the airport. Some small thing, an excuse. I had no premonition. I only wanted to hear their voices. My sister was stressed: in a hurry. My nephew was curt: mono-syllabic. My brother-in-law was out getting gas. My niece—my niece was all ready, her knapsack packed. She told me which books she was bringing, what games, stuffed animal, candy.

On the conveyor belt, on our way, we hear, behind us, kerfuf-fling. The detection equipment has gone haywire, awry, kaput!

Security folks call for dogs, but all the dogs—yes, ALL THE DOGS—are at a training session. Every wet black nose off who-knows-where.

A wand! That's what they come up with. Hocus-pocus! The trained wand-bearer demonstrates: Hold wand by handle. Wave wand over bags. Say a magic word under your breath, under the roses, nobody knowses, so they supposes, but they supposes erroneously.

What? They found something! Another bomb? Some oth-er bags are being pulled aside. The wand quivered and beeped over them like a terrier, a Ouija board, a crystal on a string. Dowsed!

Kikikiki. Hahahaha.

They pulled the wrong bags.

They let the flight close. We roll away, quivering undetect-ably, as they search the magicked bags, the conjured problem that vanishes as they search, poking with left hand, tossing with right hand. What do they find? Clothes. Toothpaste. Aftershave. Curry powder—ah. That must have been what the wand sniffed. Spicy like dynamite. Asian hot.

Thank gods, think the pokers and tossers, *we didn't delay the flight for this.*

* * *

For a long time after, I couldn't remember any of it, though I remembered now that I pictured her, leaving the security cage, hoisting her small, stuffed tote onto her shoulder, pulling a ponytail from under the strap, her shoes slipping on the newly waxed floor, Sikh women cleaners looking past her impassively. Unless I'm making that up.

A buzz and a hum and a click-tick-click. We are aloft, alone, all on our own. Daddies left behind. Cut from our origins, we become one with the plane. Its components become us. Buzz, hum, and click-tick-click goes the timer, under people (subhuman). Our clock's on, our coxswain, synchronizing the plane's components, now marching with us in lockstep, marching in time to stop time. To disappear it. The horizon approaches, the vanishing point.

Ah! The Twin has gone and done it!

It was supposed to run in time with us but it ran out of time. Jumped the gun.

Hahahaha! We are delighted. No—we are lighted! We are THE BOMB.

* * *

For a long time, I thought that all I had heard, over the line, was pure sound: her voice. Her voice, the sound of which I will not try to describe, the sound of which had no precedent in history; the sound of which will never be heard again.

She was sweet beyond sweetness. She was not a saint. She was not a future unrecognized Canadian asset. She was beautiful and peculiar and still-unknown. She was just a child.

Oh, her voice! What sound fell into the sea? My child, oh, my child, oh, my lost, my smiling child.

JUNE 23, 2004

J woke on the floor beside the bed instead of in it, not with the
sun, which was above and beyond me, but to my phone's jangling.
My mouth was glued shut and my knees, old unreliable knees, were not
bending. The floor. I want to say this is not as sordid as it seems. My own
mother only moved to a bed late in her life, and her mother never used
one. When we holidayed at relatives' homes, we all sacked out on bamboo
mats on the floor, wherever we found a free spot.

I wished I had made it to the bed. My brain had swollen so that
I couldn't open my eyes, but the floor stayed still as long as I didn't
move. The phone beeped a voice-mail alert as I pulled myself to sitting,
grasping the bedclothes on one side and the dresser on the other. The
wrought-iron balcony chair had left a legacy, I discovered, as I stood,
breathing shallowly: hemorrhoid. Blood feels the pull of cold iron.

My own iron smell of unappetizing leafy greens filled the space
around me as I shuffled miserably toward the shower, disrobing as I went.
The steam drew out the alcohol as well. I smelled *pickled*. Kimchee, that
was me, with a thousand-year-egg in my ass. What a wreck.

As the coffee decocted, I tried to figure out who had called me. Not
a number my phone or I recognized, but there was a message: Brinda.

I perked up a little.

Her voice was breathless and uncertain on the message, thin and
small when I reached her on the phone. She wanted to meet.

"But yes, I would be happy to . . ." The throbbing had returned.
"Tomorrow? The same café?"

"Um . . ." I heard her swallow, and grew concerned that if she had
to wait, she might not show up.

"Or now?" I could pick up Tylenol on the way and surely the coffee would help.

She exhaled. "Now would be great, but, I don't suppose you have an office or anywhere, that— I would really prefer somewhere private?" She had tears in her voice. The bombing anniversary, perhaps? My mind was working slowly. More privacy—why?

"I'm so sorry. I don't have an office." The dentist started his drill downstairs. I felt it in my molars, loosened by the drink. "I suppose, if you don't mind, you could come here. It's a studio apartment, but it has a sitting area. There is a dentist's office beneath, but the place itself is quite private. Come, why don't you?"

We agreed that she would, within the hour. I opened a window, cleared an empty bottle off the balcony table and scouted for further signs of my binge. A burst of laughter from downstairs. Elsewhere, people were eating or opening a window or just walking dully along. Not everyone re-died each June 23.

I lay down on the bed with a cool washcloth over my eyes, then drank my coffee, but the fog was only starting to recede when Brinda tapped on the window of the door.

"You found it," I said to her. She, too, was newly showered, hair wet. Eyes also wet? "I feared it would be tricky." She seemed unsure whether to enter. "Please." I indicated the sofa. "Take a seat."

She stepped over the threshold, but stopped, one elbow in a hand, painful indecision. "I shouldn't have come."

"Not at all. A cup of—"

"I really should . . ." She was turning again toward the door. But then, with a shuddering breath, she let her hands and head drop.

I touched her back lightly, moving her toward the sofa. She sat and I brought her a glass of water and a kitchen chair for myself. Then I waited.

She sipped and began. "I'm sorry for coming, but I'm in such a bind. I need so badly to talk to someone and I don't really want to talk to my friends, because, well, I guess you'll understand once I tell you the whole thing, that is, if you're all right with hearing it. It's a long story, and I've never told anyone, and . . ." Finally, the tears arrived.

I put the box of tissues near her, small tidal waves assaulting my cranium as I stood, as I bent. Despite this, the ol'factory wheels were turning: shampoo, clean clothes, and something peppery. Fenugreek? Nothing unhealthy. I sat and squeezed my eyes closed for a second. Massaged my temples. Brinda's hairline, her eyes, something about her features reminded me of Asha. Nearly the same age, they would have been. It could so easily have been Asha, coming to me for a word of comfort. Or perhaps she would have been hit by a car, or overdosed, or come to mistrust me. This was an old game, alternative misfortunes, and I'd exhausted its philosophic compensations. No. Asha would be like this: healthy, accomplished, stretches of contentment, hard work and love, occasionally troubled by matters where my help was useful. But then, I should never have moved back to India. The loose skin of my forehead slid easily over my skull. I pulled it taut. The kettle rang. I opened my eyes. Brinda was looking at me.

"Are you feeling okay?" She wiped her nose.

"Yes, fine," I said, blinking. I stood up to fill a teapot. "Tell me."

"I need to see a therapist, badly, but I'm not in town for very long, or I don't know how long I'll be here, and since you and I already met, I thought perhaps I could— I'm obviously willing to pay."

This was sticky. "I'm sorry. I'm no longer licensed here in Canada. But I'm sure I can help you find someone. There must be many therapists in Lohikarma."

"No, no, no—please?" Her eyes and nose were red and her shirt looked too big for her. "I don't want to deal with trying to find someone I connect with, all that. Is there any way you— We could do it informally, or—I . . ." She blew her nose assertively. "Never mind. I'll figure it out. I never should have come."

I poured a cup of tea for her. Milk. Sugar. I had no biscuits; what's a cup of tea without biscuits? "No—let's talk. Informally, as you say. No payment, no . . . promises. This is not therapy. It is merely talking. Is that all right?"

"I need one promise, though. You can't breathe a word of this to my parents."

"Tch. I wouldn't dream of it."

"Well, not to anyone. Like, I don't want this in your book. It's not related, anyway."

"So, not therapy, but therapeutic confidentiality."

She nodded through the tea-steam. "I kind of have two problems. The first one, maybe it's the biggest one . . . maybe they're the same problem."

I waited.

"Let me back up." She took a big breath, sipped her tea and smiled at it. I do make a good cup of tea. "As I told you yesterday, I wasn't allowed to date in high school. I had crushes, fooled around a tiny bit in secret, but never a proper relationship."

This was the preface: no intimate relationships while she was in university, such that this fact itself became something of a burden. After undergrad, a terminated relationship with a slightly older fellow who didn't feel comfortable taking her virginity. A year working for a London NGO that included an affair with a married doctor—he was her first lover, though she hid that from him—and a fling with some young man on holiday in France. I imagine her story's start was different from those of most young Canadians, though perhaps it became more like theirs at the end? She stated that she hadn't rebelled much, and she did seem more attached to her parents, more concerned for their approval, than I recalled was the case with those young Canadians I saw all those years ago. But here I am, generalizing about them.

"After my year abroad, I headed to Edmonton to start my PhD, lonely all over again. I wasn't totally pathetic. I lived in a house owned by a co-op, with six others, which gave me a built-in social life. And grad school was better than undergrad. I met people from all over, people who were passionate about what they were doing. But I was conscious of residual pain and insecurity. I thought I didn't know how to have a normal relationship." She frowned, deeply. "I still have no reason to believe I can." She had confirmed my guess: Problem #1 was Dev. "All I wanted was a regular boyfriend, someone who lived where I lived, a normal, routine relationship. Was that too much to ask? I didn't think so.

"There was a video store, a few blocks south of my house. The Film Wagon, specializing in old films, foreign films. That's where I met Dev. We had tons in common. We're both science people who aren't fundamentally science people. We both have Indian parents, but grew up here. I'd never met anyone like him. It felt so easy." She slowed as she sounded her thoughts out. "For all our problems, it's so painful to think of not having him to talk to." A possible separation? "At first, it wasn't a big bang of attraction. But that was fine. He was a buddy—encouraging, funny. It was so comfortable that when I realized I was developing a crush on him, I resisted the feeling. Until it became clear he felt the same. But when he finally spoke up, he didn't, really. He gestured toward his feelings without making a real declaration. Now, looking back on it, I have to wonder if there was something he couldn't bring himself to say."

I asked her to clarify.

"Most men would have been all over me. Right? Dev seemed overcome with embarrassment or shyness. He spent the night, but we didn't have sex, because he said he wasn't ready, which I thought was sweet. Like I said, our histories seemed similar, though he said he'd had steady girlfriends, even lived with one during grad school in New Brunswick. He never told his parents they lived together.

"He had moved back to Edmonton maybe a year before we met, but was living with his parents in the suburbs. He'd crash at friends' places when he stayed late in the city. It was easy for him to switch to staying over with me. That fall, maybe six months after we started dating, I got a place of my own. I wanted to see what that would be like. I think the relationship had given me a bit more confidence or security. He was getting tired of going back and forth. And we didn't really want to deal with how our parents would react to our living together without being married: when I brought Dev home to meet them, he stayed in the basement, which was especially silly because we weren't having sex anyhow!"

She reacted to something in my face by raising her hands, palms up, and dropping them.

"It just never happened. I would get frustrated, and try to talk about it, but nothing ever changed. He gave me excuses, got defensive. But everything else was still, I thought—this was a year or so in—great." She lifted the pendant of her mangal sutra onto her chin, looking mournful. "He was my best friend." Past tense. "As I said, though, he was getting tired of commuting from his folks' place and didn't see why he should get his own place in the city if he was spending four nights a week with me, anyhow. Somewhere in there—I'm not really sure how—we agreed that maybe it would be best if we got married. Big weddings have always made me a little squeamish, but—compromise: that's adulthood, right?

The parents were all thrilled. We had a proper Hindu wedding in Lo-hikarma and a Christian one in Edmonton—his mom is Christian, pretty religious, but his dad is Hindu. And even on our wedding night—no sex. And still, no sex."

"Never?" I paused in my note-taking to ponder this.

"Not one time." She was looking at my steno pad. "Sexual-type activities, up to a point, but, no, our marriage is unconsummated."

We were interrupted by the screaming of cats, seemingly on my roof. It was a metal roof, slippery and overhung with a great many branches, so that there seemed always to be creatures falling onto it or off it or trying to scramble across it. Sometimes I would glimpse a crow or a squirrel through one of the three (three!) skylights. And where there are birds and rodents, naturally there occur cats, and where there are cats, catfights. The yowling was heavily disturbing, particularly since they came on that ominous note in Brinda's narrative. Unless they didn't and I'm putting them there for dramatic effect.

Brinda blinked and checked the time. "Maybe we should break there for today? Listen, are you really sure this is okay? I'm in town such a short time, but I . . ."

"No, I had no plans for today, nothing at all. I'm quite available." My stomach growled—bodily functions resuming. I took a sip of tea.

"I can't tell you how I appreciate it." She stopped, breathed. "The chance to sort it out."

"The obvious question I must ask is whether he isn't homosexual."

"Naturally." Slight impatience. "He has rare moments of candour, when he'll admit he might have a problem, but he has never thought he was gay. He says he has never been conscious of an attraction to men. I believe it."

"Has he ever said what he thinks the problem might be?"

"No. He seems mystified."

"Has he seen a doctor?"

"I begged him until he finally went." She rolled her eyes. "He came back and told me he'd been given a clean bill of health. The doc had sug-gested a tensor bandage for his trick ankle. I asked, *Did you tell him why you made the appointment? Did you ask him about our problem?* No straight answer. More often, he blames the situation on me. He says he never had this problem with his previous girlfriend, implying I somehow make him impotent." She crunched her pretty brows. "All the evasions, the contradictions. He's got to be lying about something, but I can't tell what, and it's like with a child: I think he won't confess unless he's caught and I'm getting tired of trying to figure it out. He is a child in lots of ways, actually. I have to beg him to cook. He's gotten competent with laundry and dishes, but acts so bewildered and is so inefficient that I feel almost guilty. Can't drive, which made the commute from his parents' place particularly tedious. So I do the errands, shopping. I pay all the bills. Every single time he has to write a cheque, he asks me how. Every. Single. Time. It's like a campaign to demonstrate his need. And his devotion to a life of thought.

"That's the thing. He's always interesting to be around. Always reading some great-sounding book or tracking down some long-lost classic film. That's what his mind is filled with, while the rest of us have to think about cleaning the toilet and making supper.

"I admired that. I want to live a life of the mind, too. Except that life has necessities, and, because we live together, I do more than my share. Years ago, I made my peace with the daily, regular incompetence. But there were still all the problems in bed.

"Finally, toward the end of last year, I realized that to stop feeling tortured, I had to renounce *any* hope of change. I love him. He understands me in a way no one ever has before. This is who he is. This is what I've got. I stopped trying to ferret out the problem, stopped putting pressure on him. I didn't say anything about it, though, and neither did he. I couldn't tell if he noticed, but I thought I sensed some relief. It had to be a relief, right? Not to have that expectation from me.

"That was December or so, when I was applying to grad school for writing programmes, and my view shifted again. It was like a Rubik's Cube. You know that stage lots of people get to, one side of the cube all nice and uniform and all the other sides a scramble? That's what it's like: I'm finally totally clear what I want to do professionally, but nothing else in my life is coherent. It was easier not to think about, though, while everything was unresolved."

Pitch the yahoo! I thought. *He doesn't deserve you!*

Her face—I hadn't said anything, I swear—changed. Back to something like the haunted little thing who had first come to see me. "The big elephant in the room, of course, is babies." Her eyes were large and dark. "I've always wanted children. Dev knows. But anytime I've brought it up recently, he's balked. I'm thirty-five! The window is nearly closed, but now Dev says he's inspired by my example, that maybe he wants a change, too. You know he's a lab technician. Lab director, now. The job's beneath him, and he doesn't love it. I kept thinking, in the early years, that he was getting ready to move on. It seemed normal: he took this job his dad got him because he was getting ready to apply for academic jobs or whatever, maybe private industry. But he never got around to applying for anything else. He hangs out with his friends from undergrad. One works at the Film Wagon, and he and Dev started a film series at the public library. They have a little following. Now Dev says maybe he'll write a book about film music. Maybe he'll start playing music. Can't think about kids when he might make this huge life change. But he hasn't done anything about it."

A lull. I had been distracted from my headache, but now it began to distract me in turn.

Brinda must have seen. "I should go." She rose. "You must have tons of work. You've been so kind to see me."

"Talking can help." I pressed my forehead. "Come again. You still have more, is that right? The other problem?"

She pursed those Sethuratnam brows, as if in apology. "Yes."

"The day after tomorrow? We may not have the chance to meet again after this week—you are going to Baltimore straight from Edmonton, is that correct?"

It was.

"After you go," I told her, "I will try to put together your narrative and send it to you. Ideally, we would meet to talk it through and revise it together."

This time, her brows went up. "Ideally, you would be licensed in Canada and I could pay you for all this."

"Ideally, we would both be different people than we are," I responded, and we laughed. "But perhaps I can at least give you an external record of your story, help you to see it a bit more objectively. Let me try."

"That's how you work?" she asked. "You write your client's story, and then work from what you write?"

"Essentially, yes. It seems likely I will make similar narratives from the stories I am collecting for this book, the one about the bombing. I haven't quite determined how it will work."

"Day after tomorrow, then. Here?"

"Yes. Very good. Oh, and I may see you tonight." I had forgotten this when she came, and was still ambivalent, but now thought it prudent to mention it.

"The memorial?" She looked wary. "My dad invited you?"

"I repeat: I will say nothing. Your parents don't even need to know we met today." I mimed zipping my lips. She didn't look happy, which made me sad, but how many ways could I promise not to talk?

As she descended my fire-escape stairs, a blur of two cats in a chase rounded the end of the alley. I thought of Old Mangy in my parking garage and wondered if he was dead yet. Why did I cultivate his trust knowing I was likely to leave so soon? I needed the guilt. I hoarded and treasured it. It had been so long since I had been close enough to anyone to cause pain.

I raised a hand and smiled at Brinda as she looked back up at me and waved.

I wanted nothing so much as to go back to bed—or *to* bed, since I never reached it the night before—but my method is too ingrained: I went across the street to buy Tylenol, then returned, made more coffee, and transcribed.

What is one girl's love life against terror, mayhem, massive governmental cock-ups? "First-world problems"—a phrase I heard recently, the sort of assessment I would have agreed with when I left Canada, twenty years ago. But I thought differently now.

Brinda's worries, my own worries—that we might never have the chance truly to love, or to love again—these are the ways we best understand the effects of terror: someone's father killed in a falling Twin Tower, someone's fiancé blown up at a checkpoint in Afghanistan. First-world problems? Statistics are well and good, but names, faces, stories make us understand, pay attention. *Who are the victims?*

Transcription took no more than two or three hours. The best thing for pain is work. It settles me. The lives of others.

I ate half a cold rotisserie chicken with leftover naan, and followed it with a three-hour siesta and another shower, during which I considered the gathering at the Sethuratnams' house that evening, which I wanted badly to attend and was simultaneously dreading. Reading this over, now, I see this is identical to what I said about the trial. It seems I learn as much about myself through my writing as I do about anyone else.

The memorial would be as valuable to my book as it would be painful, no doubt. *Observe it,* I advised myself, *and write an account of it in your journal. Make yourself an actor in your own life, see yourself as you see the others.* It was enough to get me out the door. Seth lived about a half-hour on foot from where I was staying.

The streets grew slightly wider toward the lake, and evinced a beach town's smugness and desolation. It reminded me of San Francisco. There was a bridge across the lake's narrow western arm, literally a pale imitation of the Golden Gate: a crooked little thing painted two shades of rusty apricot. There was even a tram, just one, retained for tourists after the rest of the circuit was replaced by buses.

In the months I would eventually spend here, I never tired of trolling the residential districts, where each house differed markedly from the next, evidence of the personalities within. Several blocks from where I was staying, for example, was a house whose deck resolved into the prow of a ship. A mast rose to hoist a Jolly Roger, watched over by a gargoyle rusting contentedly on a peak in the roof. Another shabby housefront had balconies in which each vertical rail was half a bright-coloured fibreglass ski. In another garden, a shop mannequin dressed like Dorothy of Oz served as a scarecrow.

Seth's house did not stand out among these: a modestly pretty pale-grey facade, dark-grey shingles, and a patio with pillars and red-painted concrete, curiously like verandas in our villages back home. The single exceptional detail was a multicoloured mosaic tile abstract that formed the walk from garden gate to front door, a project of one of the children perhaps, or of Lakshmi.

As I approached the door, I felt myself fill with a dark heavy slowness that made it difficult to continue. There were cars parked in the driveway, and I had turned to go back when one more pulled up to the curb. Seth got out on the driver's side, Venkat on the other. Seth came around to greet me, and took me by the arm to lead me again up the path. No turning back now.

Venkat followed a little behind: he lifted a large covered birdcage out of the back seat, which he carried to the door. He said nothing to me. If he looked at me, I didn't catch the glance. No question of rudeness: on this day, anything could be forgiven. Still, I doubted whether he would meet with me again. I had shuddered on seeing him emerge from the car, and so thought I might be glad if that was what he decided.

Brinda herself came to the door. I gave her the grocery-store bouquet I had picked up on the way. I could hear bhajan songs already underway, and she led me to the family room, where a small group of people, more than half of them white, sat in a semicircle facing a shrine. It occupied one side of a gas fireplace hearth, and crept up the wall: pictures of Rama, Sita, Krishna, Durga, and Lakshmi, the goddess of prosperity and namesake of my hostess, as well as a large portrait of Shivashakti, Seth's guru, saffron-robed and hooked-nosed, with his famous signature hairstyle, a long, silvering pageboy, taking up much of the picture. A sandalwood garland was hung on the frame.

Incense had burned already to the stub and its faint remnants were being overtaken by smells from the kitchen: basmati rice, mustard seed, cumin and coriander. I don't cook, but the nose knows.

Seth brought his wife over and we made our introductions, palms together. The devotees' strident singing made conversation with them impossible—a relief I appreciated even as I forcibly lowered my hackles at the God-glorifying. Venkat had already slid onto the floor to join in and Seth did likewise, while Lakshmi gestured that I should follow her.

Seth's cologne and Lakshmi's perfume curled away from each other against what I recognized as a whiff of recent sex. Seth, you devil! She wore a white sari with a tangle of flowers along the hem. Some fluttery fabric—not silk. Kritika would have known what it was called.

In the kitchen, Lakshmi gave me a glass of savoury lassi.

"So you met with my husband and daughter this week?" Her tone put me on my guard.

"I did," I answered. The lassi was lemony and cool, made from homemade yogourt, just the thing after a hilly walk under the still-high sun.

"Collecting our stories." There was something girlish in the way she looked down at her hands, spread on the counter, but nothing timid in her tone, which had an edge. Skepticism? She looked up again.

"I am . . ." I wanted to add something but not to give her anything more to react to until I knew where she stood. And in this pause, each gazing at the other, locked in mutual expectancy, I was further disconcerted by the realization that Lakshmi was beautiful. And in that moment she, too, either felt some current between us or realized that I had noticed her. She looked away.

I plunged ahead, foolhardy perhaps. "Would you like to meet with me?"

She narrowed her eyes a little; her lips tightened. "I'm not sure I will have much to add."

"Does it bother you that Seth and Brinda have been talking to me?"

She raised her chin slightly. She was in her late fifties, with some lines around her eyes to prove this, and perhaps a softening of the skin around a high forehead and pronounced cheekbones. Full lips, curving nostrils: classical Dravidian features. Large eyes, in a defiant mood. She was curvaceous, a woman who had borne children, but with a self-containment, something like pride, evident in her figure. I suppose there was nothing inappropriate in my noticing her attractiveness, though the force of this noticing was unusual, at least for me. I have never been a great pursuer of women.

"I'm so sorry if you feel I have imposed . . ." I really was.

My apology softened her, or perhaps she felt sorry for me.

She waved a hand as if to restart. "It's simply that I am not comfortable talking to anyone outside the family about our private matters."

"You understand that I will not quote you without your permission?" I asked.

"I understand that, but it doesn't seem to make a difference." She smiled. (A first!)

I smiled back. "I appreciate what you are saying."

"Seth wants me to help you."

Ah. "You really have no obligation." But I was curious to hear what she would have to say.

She looked over at the devotees, her husband among them, and then indicated the living room, in the opposite corner of the house. I followed. She waved me toward the sofa and took a chair herself.

"I don't want to seem ungenerous," she said, playing with her *pallu,* which was wrapped around her back and pulled across her hip. "I recall trying to find some books on grief, back when it happened, when we were trying to help Venkat and to deal with our own shock, and there weren't any, really, that applied to the situation. A book like yours could help people, I suppose."

"Did you seek the advice of a counsellor, back then?"

She looked mildly appalled. "No, I, we were fine. Venkat, of course . . . well, but I'll let him tell you about that, if he chooses."

"May I ask, how did you cope up? I don't mean how well or poorly. I mean, what means did you use?"

"For my own sadness?"

"You have also mentioned shock."

"Yes. It was all of that. The fear." She leaned forward. Her eyes, as I have said, were large and liquid, kohl-lined on the inner lower lids. "Because, to us, it came out of nowhere. A bomb. A plane exploding! How, how do you even start to think about that? I was very concerned about Venkat. He is my relative. He's not . . . strong. And poor Sita and Sundar. They were some of our oldest friends here."

"You were close?"

"Oh, yes." She hesitated. "Well, Sita confided in me occasionally. I think you could say we were close. She knew she could talk to me."

I could imagine that a friendship with Lakshmi might be one-sided, that she would be firm and loyal, a good listener, but not a person to reveal much. It could leave a friend wondering how close they really were, if the friend paid attention.

"It was hard, for her, being in Canada. She had miscarriages, one before and one after Sundar. She was always very quiet, especially at gatherings, but every once in a while, she would say she wanted to talk to me, and she would tell me things. Like after the second miscarriage. Venkat didn't seem to understand at all what she was going through. And then, much later, when Sundar was a teenager, he and Venkat had some very bad fights. Sundar came to Seth for help, once or twice. But he went into engineering, in the end, the way Venkat wanted him to. He was a super kid. Always good to my daughters. I worried most about the effect on them. They were adolescents, not babies, but still. Or maybe I knew it would have more of an effect because they weren't babies."

"What effect do you think it had on them?"

"It . . ." She angled her shoulders, crossed her legs, a defensive posture. Her collarbones stood out from her sari blouse like a boomerang, an accidental elegance. Admiring the smooth expanse of her décolletage, I noticed what must have been her mangal sutra, a thick gold chain, the pendant hidden in her blouse. "They managed. I always made a point of talking to them about their feelings. But there's no way to make sense of it."

"You are all Shivashakti devotees?"

A quick shake of the head. "No, not at all." She seemed puzzled that I had presumed.

"I'm sorry. You're not religious?"

She looked away, toward the window, which framed none of the stunning vistas I associated with this town, but simply the house across the street. "If you had asked me back then, I might have said I was. I believe in God, in some way. But I have no patience anymore with rituals, with any organized religion. I still meditate, but I believe that if there is a higher power, it is within us. Self-knowledge. That's what I'm seeking. Of course, Shivashakti's followers say he is helping them to find God within themselves. Our tradition says a guru is a guide like that." She had included me in that "our." "But I feel uncomfortable with putting that much trust in someone else, to lead you. Especially after nine–eleven, I . . ." At this point, I think she noticed my extreme and genuine interest and realized she had said more than she had planned to say. She snapped shut. Would she resent me for having gained her confidence?

But then she smiled a little. I wondered at the possible relief to her: being pushed to confide in someone, being given the means safely, harmlessly, to betray the iron-clad unity of her family. "Seth, as you can see, is a devotee. That came out of the crash." She spoke slowly. "The rest of us, my daughters and myself, we let the deaths become part of who we were. We . . . grew around the losses, maybe? I'm not quite sure how to explain. Maybe it has something to do with being a woman. Others' emotions are not so shattering to us. We're taught, even while young, to deal with others on an emotional level. Seth needed something more, to be able to cope. He was so shaken at the idea of losing one's family that we, his family, we weren't enough to help him through it." Her tone implied she still felt this inadequacy. "I couldn't comfort him."

She was ravishing. Crushes on both Seth and Lakshmi? What was wrong with me? No, I knew what was wrong with me; I thought about that all the time. This required a different question. What was the question?

In the other room, the singing-masters of the soul had finished. We rose to meet them.

Seth was struggling to straighten his legs, and making some joke about it, though the mood was sombre. Warm, though. I liked the faces, particularly, of two of the older, white devotees, men whom Seth brought forward to meet me as Lakshmi tried to usher us toward the buffet, handing each person a plate. One was a school principal, Kaj; the other was Nick, whose profession I didn't catch. Nick was quiet and reticent, though with an air of leading from behind, as though he would not permit stragglers. Kaj had a loud, red face and bluff manner, and so generated in me some early suspicion, a bull in the china shop of sadness. As we served ourselves, though, he said to me, his Delft-blue eyes vulnerable beneath brushy blond eyebrows, "Seth told me about your project. Good for you. Must be wrenching, talking to people. It's needed, though, with what Indo-Canadians here have gone through with that. It needs to be acknowledged."

Lakshmi brushed away compliments on the food as we found places around the kitchen table or on the family room sofa, where I found a spot to eat, plate on my lap. On Seth and Lakshmi's mantel, there was a clutter of family photos. I rose again to take a closer look. Seth and his siblings in formal portraits. Seth as a sturdy, handsome preschooler in short pants. Such earnest faces. Seth and Lakshmi's wedding pictures, mid-sixties, to judge by his black-framed eyeglasses, her bejewelled ones. Flash exposure and tension made Lakshmi's face look like a fawn's in headlights. Barely out of her teens, my guess. A California sun bleached a seventies-hued shot of the Sethuratnam family group. Brinda's little sister Ranjani held the hand of an outsized Mickey Mouse. Ah: and here was Sundar. Darker than the others, hair in his eyes, standing a little apart from Seth, whose arm was extended to include him. Graduation photos of the girls, and wedding pictures for Brinda: the couple framed proudly by parents; Brinda laughing with Ranjani; and Brinda and Dev alone, a casual, friendly pose, charged with meaning now that I knew their story. What would I see if I hadn't? I glanced over at Brinda herself now, and she caught and returned my look, but sat on the steps leading down into the sunken family room from the kitchen instead of joining me.

You must change your life, I thought, telling her telepathically what I doubted I would have the courage to tell her in person. Rosslyn used to love Rilke's poem on Apollo's partial perfection. She was a much better reader of Rilke than I was or ever will be. A little preachy, to my taste. The poem's ultimate exhortation rang in my head—*You must change your life!*—as Venkat's gruff, indignant voice rose above the dinner chat.

"Let me put it to you this way," he was saying, loudly. It was difficult to watch him talk, with that unsettling stillness in his face. I wondered how his students managed. He taught a dry subject, though, statistics. Maybe they didn't pay too much attention. His voice rose. "What did the Americans do after nine–eleven? Leapt to the chase. Even Canada closed borders! Sent troops! All-out war! Do we not deserve this treatment? My son was born here and raised here, never lived anywhere else. My wife and I, citizens. Through and through. Not one phone call from them. No condolence visit. Nothing."

Seth patted him nervously on the arm. "But now things are different, aren't they?" he murmured. "Look at how much effort and money, this most expensive courtroom ever, bulletproof—"

"Sure, in case those guys' thug friends try to shoot them out," Brinda said, not seeming to address anyone in particular.

"Progress can be slow," Seth said, ambiguously. Was he admitting this or making excuses for it? "Canada is timid. They did finally ban the Sikh Youth Federation and the Babbar Khalsa last year."

"Under the post–nine–eleven anti-terrorist legislation, right?" A smack of mockery sounded in Brinda's tone. "Convenient: the Americans want laws pushed through, and suddenly Canadians realized that the Air India bombers *were* targeting Canadians after all."

"These things take time." The stubborn cast of Seth's jaw was animalistic and noble at once. "The wheels of justice turn slowly."

Venkat raised a fist. "And now that the wheels have begun to turn, the deserving will be crushed beneath them."

His declaration reminded me of the line . . . from *Stray Birds*?

I think so. Tagore, not someone I am in the habit of quoting: *I thank Thee that I am none of the wheels of power, but am one with the living creatures crushed beneath it.* Venkat seemed to feel differently.

"I guess," said Brinda, without looking over. "What about that bookseller, a few days ago, undermining Ms. D's testimony?"

"Miss D-for-divorcée," Venkat spat.

Brinda flinched.

"No morals. Attention-grabbing. Why did she wait until the trial to come forward, if she knew all this?" Venkat sneered.

She must have come forward before, I thought. Otherwise, why would she have been in witness protection?

No one was stopping Venkat and so he went on. "Trying to take her revenge on them. Those Sikhs always stick together except when they are fighting each other. A pathological liar. How stupid must she be, to be strung along by a married terrorist? Pathetic." A light shone through his unfocused eyes. "Unless she came forward with the information in order that she could be discredited, and so support her lover's cause."

There is a particular sinking nausea I feel when confronted with conspiracy theorists, whether clients or taxi drivers. It triggers my flight response. I stood, took my leave of Brinda as I passed her, put my plate in the sink, pressed grateful farewells on my hosts, and in moments was out the door, inhaling sweet, fresh Canadian air. I steadied myself on the Sethuratnams' veranda, looking down at the walkway. The mosaic tile-work was meant to be abstract, but as I stood there staring at it and breathing perhaps a little too deeply the rarified mountain air, images resolved out of the chips and chunks: a grouping of three hearts, a pink-eyed rabbit, some long-snouted creature with a voracious toothy grin.

Did they always simply let Venkat say whatever he wanted? Did they agree with him? Poor Ms. D. The truth of her life was probably unimaginably small, but now it—she—was magnified by mystery. The accused bombers, also, were subject to this: they had opted not to testify, not to tell their own versions, and their silence made them larger than life.

Gaps. Voids. Each track, each trail, yielded nothing. It was driving Venkat nuts. Not that he would have believed the truth, necessarily. Not that any of us was equipped to discern it.

But there was something else. Venkat doth protest too much, I thought. The way he spoke at dinner was the way he had spoken to me in our meeting: obsessively tracking command chains, purse strings, the accused not the dead. He thought about what happened in ways that allowed him to not think about what happened.

*　*　*

I met Seth for lunch in the Student Union the next day.

"I'm sorry for my hasty departure last night," I said as we stood in line at a food kiosk.

"Did you feel unwell?" he asked.

"A little."

"Lakshmi was concerned."

"Not the food! It was wonderful. Hit the spot. A difficult occasion, simply. I suddenly felt I needed to be alone."

"Can I ask you something?" Seth chose a table amid the clatter of brightly flashing youth, between industrial lighting and shiny brick floors, small matching tables joined by bent and painted steel pipes that also supported small matching chairs. "What are your impressions of Venkat?"

I used the business of unwrapping my sandwich to gain some time. "How do you mean?"

"I mean, as a professional," he said. "You met with him?"

I waved my head, *yes*, still very busy with sugar, cream, the stirring of coffee.

"And then you saw him at our house, last night." His tone was that of someone acknowledging the obvious.

I inclined my head again, but more cautiously.

"Does he give you the impression that he is stable?"

My neck stiffened.

"I'm not looking for guarantees," Seth said, rushing into my silence. "You understand me? But he had seemed to have stabilized, over so many years. Now the trial . . ." He slurped his coffee. "He has us worried. I pulled strings to get him a summer teaching session this year. Get him out of the house, some structure, distraction. I was trying to make him see someone, a psychologist, you know? He's very resistant. So when your letter arrived, I told him, if you don't think you need help, at least you can perhaps help others."

I felt a flush of annoyance creep up my face.

"At least he would be seeing a psychologist, right?" Seth seemed satisfied with this. "An eminent one."

What is it with these people, waiting for a therapist to come from India and find them? Even I could tell, after less than a week, that Lohikarma was a hot spot for narcissistic mindfulness and spiritual questing, as well as uncertain self-employment. Therapists here probably outnumbered potential clients.

"I'm sorry," I said, "but I'm not in a position to give an evaluation."

"Even an informal one?"

A very strange position, all around. How resentful could I be? Seth, Brinda—they were grasping me, pulling me into their midst, across clinical distances. Even here, Seth seemed so at home in himself. Every line of his face and his body sloped outward, giving that sense of ready embrace:

OPEN!

I wanted to walk into his arms. I wanted to give him what he wanted. If Seth wanted to help Venkat, I wanted to help him.

But it wouldn't do to respond rashly. "Last night was a very particular occasion," I said. "It is not surprising that Venkat would be emotional. As for my meeting with him, I didn't have diagnosis as an objective, and if I had, it would be a breach of confidentiality for me to tell you . . ." A thought occurred to me. "Do you have any medical power of attorney, for him?"

Seth's eyebrows preceded his answer: "Perhaps I should back up."

*S*unday, June 23, 1985, Seth mowed the lawn as the morning turned hot. He retreated to his recliner to catch up on recent issues of the *American Journal of Physics*. His children's school had let out recently, and though he was teaching an adult education class, it was a lazy time. The house was quiet, kids gone off with friends. He found a response to an article that had intrigued him, "Rumors of Transcendence in Physics," on "intimations of a real world beyond the natural order." Seth never got to talk about this stuff as much as he would like. Students had enough trouble with the concrete.

As he read "We can never know more than the mind can assimilate and process, nor can we discuss any aspect of the world for which there is no language," Seth nodded off. The line must have repeated in his dreams; he still remembered it twenty years later, though he had never made it to the end of the short letter.

The phone interrupted his nap. When he picked up, he might have thought it would be one of the children, asking to bring a friend for lunch. That part, he didn't remember. He remembered the strangeness of the sound at the other end, and repeating, once, "Hello?" before making out what it was: someone's sobbing, but not one of his daughters', and his wife was at home.

"What?" he asked. "*Enna'idhu*? What is it?"

"It's gone down." Venkat's voice, or some version of it. "Crashed." And in Tamil, as he began again to cry, "Ayoh! My son! Sita!"

Venkat's son and wife had left day before yesterday, for India. They had driven to Vancouver and their plane would have departed, what, last night?

"Lakshmi and I will be right there. Venkat? Venkat! We're coming. Wait for us."

There was no reply, but the sobbing receded as though Venkat had wandered away from the phone. Seth, too, left his phone receiver on the counter at first, not wanting to hang up, and then realized he had to try to locate his daughters.

He shouted for Lakshmi, trusting that she was within earshot. She came running at the emotion in his voice, saw the phone off the hook. Horror filled her eyes, and Seth had to say, "No, no. It's Sita and Sundar. Their plane has crashed." He saw two quick ripples, each effacing the expression that went before: relief that it was not one of their daughters, then horror again.

Ten minutes later, they were in the car. They had asked Ranjani's friend's mother to keep her there until they came to pick her up, but they hadn't been able to find Brinda, who might have been at the pool or ice cream parlour. They left a note on the front door telling her to wait at the neighbour's until they came home. Lakshmi had snatched their list of phone numbers from the telephone table in the hall as they left and now clutched it in the passenger seat, the names of everyone they were connected to.

Venkat's front door was locked and he didn't come when they rang the bell. After several tries, Seth went around to the patio doors and peered in. Venkat was sitting on the floor in the family room, his back against the sofa, not crying, after all, but staring as though being spoken to by an authority expressing grave disappointment and possibly anger. His was the look of a man accepting judgement. Seth never saw such a look on his face again.

The news was on, loud enough for Seth to hear it through the glass doors. He knocked twice, hard, before Venkat started and stood.

Reports from Cork, where rescue efforts were fully underway, squawked from both televisions as well as from the radio. Lakshmi took Venkat's hands and his sobbing resumed. He withdrew his hands to put them over his face.

An Air India plane, which had left Vancouver Saturday afternoon, picking up more passengers in Toronto and Montreal before heading for Heathrow, had disappeared off Irish radar at quarter after eight Irish time, a little after seven GMT, round about midnight for Canadians. It had simply vanished: no panicked messages, no blinking diamond wandering off the screen. Even a plane that passed through the same airspace shortly after saw nothing. In place of more than three hundred people, *the void.*

As Lakshmi led Venkat back to the family room, Seth turned off the radio and the kitchen TV, replaced the beeping phone in its cradle. He wanted so badly to see his daughters that he was tickled by a shard of resentment for Venkat, whose need was holding Seth here. *Venkat's need*: first thing was how to find the survivors. The news from the TV sounded bad. He had to call Air India, but didn't have a Vancouver phone book and they wouldn't be listed in Lohikarma's. Travel agencies here would be closed on Sunday. He settled on calling a friend in Vancouver, an Assamese chemist who had left Harbord for Simon Fraser University. He occupied a line on their list with three previous phone numbers scratched out, an immigrant academic's history.

"Mukund? Seth here."

"Seth. Are you . . . Were Lakshmi or the children . . . ?"

"We're all fine. So you have heard?"

"Oh, yes, yes."

"Your wife?" Seth asked. Mukund had brought a young bride over a few years back.

"No, we are fine, but one of my colleagues, his whole family was on the flight: wife, children, mother-in-law."

Was? "Mukund, I need a contact number for Air India. It's Sita and Sundar." He heard his own voice crack a little, saying their names.

"Oh, no, no."

"Can you get the number for me?"

Seth was writing it down when Venkat jumped over to wrench the receiver out of his hand. "Sundar might be trying to call. He always calls." He choked, pressing the receiver to the cradle so hard that his palm looked waxen while the dark brown skin on the back of his hand crinkled. Lakshmi had had a Benares silk sari exactly that colour that tore on a door hook, once, before she even realized she was caught. Seth put his hand on Venkat's back and looked over at her.

She came and guided Venkat once more toward the family room, but Venkat peeled away, toward the stairs. "I'm going to pack a few things. It's good you're here, to stay by the phone. They'll be in shock. I must go and bring them home."

This, at least, made sense to Seth. It was what he would do. They let Venkat go. "Lakshmi, *kanna*, maybe I should go call Air India from home, find out what is happening and also find out about flights to Ireland. I'll pick up Ranjani on the way." Though she was fourteen, Ranjani's baby fragrance, like sweetened milk, had never changed. He still smelled it when he hugged her, especially where her neck met her ear. He wanted—needed—to hold her.

Lakshmi wiped her cheeks, hard. "Maybe you should go with him, Seth. To Ireland."

She was right. He would have to go.

He fetched Ranjani from her friend's house, and found Brinda sitting on the doorstep with her friend Jenny when they pulled into the driveway. "Did you hear about the Air India crash?" she asked. "Jenny's dad had the radio on in the garage. What's going on?"

He told Jenny she perhaps should go home.

Inside, he looked at his daughters and quaked.

"We went to Venkat Uncle's house. Sweethearts." He felt his face crumple and was filled with shame at seeing his daughters grow afraid, but he couldn't stop his tears, not even for them. More shame: he may have been carrying Venkat's pain, but he was crying for himself. It could have been his family. He told his daughters, "Oh, sweethearts. Sita Aunty and Sundar were on that plane."

The girls started crying.

"We don't know, whether they are alive or . . ." He could see they were crying as much out of fear as anything—fear of the possible impending grief, or of whatever else would come. He, too, had never faced such a thing, didn't even know yet what they were facing.

The girls wanted their mother. He told them Lakshmi had stayed with Venkat Uncle, and that they would go there as soon as he got through to the airline. He turned on the news. There was no way to protect them from this. Brinda comforted her younger sister on the sofa. He watched them, so glad to have two, and both girls. You can't expect that kind of affection from boys, and affection is what counts in a family. He had thought this many times, but now his mind fled guiltily toward Sundar, such a good boy, very affectionate toward his mother. Where was he now?

* * *

It took him hours to get through to Air India: an hour on hold, before he was cut off, another hour back on hold to learn that they had already called Venkat, though he couldn't make them clarify whether they had called before Seth got to Venkat's or after he had left. While he sat on the phone, Brinda made and brought him cups of instant coffee.

The airline agent informed Seth that Venkat had been told he would be couriered a ticket to Ireland as soon as there was a compelling reason for him to come. When Seth pressed, they explained that "compelling reason" essentially meant if or when there was a body to be identified. There were not thought to be any survivors, but many bodies—and parts, the agent stammered, in a brief departure from his script—had already been retrieved from the sea. This Seth knew from the news anchors, who also kept mentioning the danger that sharks might get to the victims first. The agent also said that they would prefer no one come until all the bodies had been retrieved and identified. "You don't want anyone sitting over there, sir, simply waiting . . ."

The other big news that day was that there were not just one but two Air India bombs. A bag, from another plane originating in Vancouver, had exploded at the Tokyo airport, an hour before the jet flying the Atlantic route was blown apart. That bag was being taken off the plane, which was on the ground and empty by then, but it killed a couple of baggage handlers. What was going on? Would there be other bombs? Who was doing this, and who were their targets?

After he hung up, he returned to Venkat's house with the children. As they walked in the front door, they heard him shouting. "Goddamn Paks!" Lakshmi cowered against the kitchen counter while Venkat roared at her. "Since day one they've had it for us. Show India who's who. Let us give them jihad!"

"Venkat. Venkat!" Seth got between them and gestured behind his back for Lakshmi to go to their daughters, who were frozen at the front door. "That makes no sense. Pakistan could have bombed India if they wanted: why bomb a jet flying from Canada?"

"We are chosen ones, Sethu. We made it out. Jealousy." Venkat patted Seth's cheek, a little hard. "Pakistan is a poor nation, because . . . ? Their nation itself was born in a deal with the white devil. They are paying for it ever since." This was a familiar rant. Pakistan was one of Venkat's stock monologues. Daily life depended on the suppression of a person's worst fears. Bereavement kicked open the doors to let the demons swell, stretch their tongues, show their fiery eyes.

"Whoever it was, we'll find out soon. Venkat, did the airline call you?"

"I'm all packed. Let's go." Venkat moved toward the front door, where his suitcase sat.

Seth went after him. Lakshmi still stood there, arms around the weeping children, clearly tempted to open the door and run away, dragging her kids with her.

"Air India said they would send you a ticket," Seth said after him. "If necessary."

"You think I'll get on one of *their* goddamn planes?" Venkat picked up the suitcase. "So you have not made any arrangements?"

"I think you should wait a bit longer." Seth thumbed sweat from his eyebrows, wiped his forehead and upper lip. "Wait for a call. It's not as if we can go, what, on the rescue boats ourselves."

Venkat's brow folded. "Are you going home?"

Seth looked at Lakshmi, who telegraphed her desperation to get the kids out of this house. Venkat's grief put him in mind of that turning-point passage in the Gita, when Krishna, a little reluctantly, takes his true form for Arjuna. Divinity revealed. The mortal quakes. Here, they were being shown the infinite depths of human vulnerability. *The void.* No need to dangle the children above it.

"No," he said.

"Seth will drop us at home and come back to spend the night with you." Lakshmi let go of one of her daughters and patted Venkat's arm. "You should stay here in case of a call, but Seth will be right back." She let go the other girl, took hold of Venkat's shoulders, and then hugged him, a gesture permitted, even mandated, by their life in Canada. She never would have done that in India.

Seth and Lakshmi didn't talk much on the drive home, except for agreeing that she would call their circle of friends. Others would want to help, and they had to arrange a substitute for Venkat's summer session, and for Seth to have the next few days off. More, if he were to go with Venkat to Ireland. They were thinking of the five other Indian families who had been in Lohikarma as long as they, families from Bengal, Punjab and Maharashtra, as well as a man from Kerala with a white Canadian wife he had met in graduate school.

The Sethuratnams had multiple bonds with Venkat, little as they fundamentally liked him. Sita had clung to Lakshmi on the younger woman's arrival in Canada. Venkat insisted on speaking English to her during the day to help her learn—puzzling, because while she was perfectly fluent in English she had never in her life used it at home. Lakshmi had been taken aback at first by the intensity of Sita's need, but soon came to understand, even as she and Seth fell in love in a way that she thought Sita and Venkat must not have done.

Seth packed an overnight bag and containers of frozen *sambar* and *rasam* to defrost for their supper, although, as he did so, he realized Sita likely had filled the deep freezer before she left, to cover her three-week trip. He and Lakshmi parked the children in front of a VHS movie. Out of sight of their daughters, finally, they embraced.

Seth's arms closed around Lakshmi's body, whose shape was starting to change, the upper back curving slightly into what might someday be a stoop, her waist growing broader. Her breasts pressed against him through his thin summer shirt. She had cut her hair off when she went back to school, a couple of years ago, but it still reached her shoulders. Seemed it got shorter every year, though, and his view of her, his bride, his love, the only woman whose bare skin he had ever caressed, whose body he had ever entered, was changing too. Their marriage was comfortable, and not infrequently romantic, but distant now from the raw obsession of those first years, when he would unthread her plait, her hair fanning down to brush her bottom, when they would make love every afternoon when he got home from teaching, and sometimes again before sleep. The tresses would wind around her as she sat naked on the bed, afterward, talking, singing a bit of a movie song they both knew, and he would run his fingers through its silken lengths. He had thought her a goddess. It did seem that assimilation, or perhaps merely time, had made her less divine, even a bit mannish in the way of many western women.

He had an uncle who had once spent a couple of weeks in the U.S. and felt, on the basis of that visit, qualified to make all sorts of pronouncements on western culture. "American love marriages are a hot pot on a cold stove," he would declare. "These Americans, they get bored. They divorce. But our Indian marriages"—a finger held aloft, lips smacking—"a cold pot on a hot stove."

Seth was not so sure, not that he needed or wanted, in his forties, the intensity he and Lakshmi had enjoyed before having kids. But what would he do without her? It was one of his few certainties: he would be lost.

* * *

Lohikarma's chill, closed beauty spread below him. He drove down into it, toward Harbord Avenue, a wide cut alongside the narrow arm of the lake. He could have taken the residential streets, each tilting at an angle to the next; anywhere in Lohikarma could be reached by multiple means. But the avenue, practically a highway, was the most efficient, the most impersonal.

He didn't think the Pakistanis were behind the bomb; that made no sense. White supremacists, that was his guess, lowlifes like the ones who had recently attacked a couple of Sikh kids in a Vancouver suburb—Surrey, was it? The Sikhs, who had been the earliest Indian arrivals in Canada after the Ice Age, actually might be competing for jobs with those undereducated, under-motivated types. Fourth-generation lumberjacks and farmers, that early brown sub-population now also mixing uneasily with the wave of Indian post-grads and post-docs that had washed Seth up on these shores. The late sixties had seen quota restrictions on non-white immigration replaced by a "point system" to let Canada skim the cream off the post-colonial churn. The previous policy reluctantly allowed a small, set number of "undesirables"—i.e., Asians—to squeeze in each year; now, the professionally assimilable were separated from the horde.

There was racism everywhere, wasn't there? It was just more elegantly masked in educated or moneyed circles, say the upper echelons of the university's administration. Seth pictured Harbord's Dean of Science. He wouldn't be one to bomb an airplane. He just wrinkled his nose in amusement at the curry smell coming off your suit, and made his jokes and other derogations later, when he was alone with his cronies, all of them pink, pink, pink with rosacea and drink. No, it would have been a mechanic, someone good with his hands, in the thrall of some evil mastermind.

He held the wheel tightly as he passed the buttery, benign facades of the houses on these long-familiar streets, their inhabitants locked away in unconfessed murderous fantasies. The parents of his children's friends—who knows? Hate was illegal here, not to mention frowned upon, so people hid it. That was why you didn't see it coming. That was why Venkat didn't fit in: he'd never learned to hide it.

When Seth came in the front door of Venkat's house, the smell hit him—grey, fuggy, miserable—the afternoon's dread giving way to the decay of grief. Seth realized that Venkat understood now that his family was dead, whether or not he was ready to admit it.

The phone rang as he was walking down the hallway. Venkat, running to answer it, bumped into him.

"Sundar?" Venkat's look of anticipatory relief, which didn't contain any hope—he was faking it—shut down and he hung up.

"But who was it?" Seth asked, leaping to pick it up again, uselessly.

"Singh."

"You cut him off?"

Venkat was returning to the family room, but the phone rang again and he came back at a run. Seth intercepted.

"Venkat. It's just Singh calling back."

"Make it quick, man," Venkat said as he turned away.

"Jaskaran?" Seth said into the receiver.

"Ah, Seth. You're there. Lakshmi just called. Did he hang up on me?" Professor Jaskaran Singh was the most cosmopolitan among them, graduated from Delhi and Edinburgh; stint in Halifax before being hired at full prof standing into Harbord's economics department, of whose inadequacy he never ceased to complain. He was brisk and snobbish, but not unkind. Seth speculated on Singh's inferiority complex—even joked that Jaskaran had fabricated his British accent—but that didn't dent his own slight deference to the man.

"He's convinced Sundar is trying to call," Seth said.

"Ach, poor fellow."

As Seth talked to him about arrangements to be made with the university, Venkat returned to the kitchen, where he opened the doors on a closet that would have been, for a western family, the pantry. Here it was a shrine. The shelves had been removed and pictures of the gods hung on the walls. The accoutrements of prayer—beads, incense, holy ash, coconuts—were strewn on and around a pretty *kolam* of a lotus that Sita had painted onto a board and lain on the closet floor. Pride of place was given to a large photo of Shivashakti, Venkat's guru, whose eyes crinkled humour and benevolence from beneath thick bangs.

Venkat seated himself before his gods, crossing his legs and laying his wrists on his knees. "Om . . ." His voice, quavering but insistent, rose into the air.

Seth's attention was pulled entirely away from Singh.

Practical matters, logistics: these were Seth's way of keeping chaos at bay. When he prayed, it was in the orderly, formal way he had been taught as a child. The beliefs he had formed then, vague and therefore unchallengeable, had changed little.

"Om . . ." The immortal syllable expanded, bubble-like, to fill the room.

Venkat began chanting the Gayatri Mantra, his voice gaining sonority as he completed the first iteration, sounding markedly clearer as he began a second.

"*Om bhur bhuvah suvahah. Tat savitur varenyam. Bhargo devasya dhimahi. Diyo yo nah prachodayat . . .*"

Seth extricated himself from the phone call.

Gayatri Mantra, the Sun Invocation, whispered into the ear of a Brahmin child at his second birth—the ceremonial induction into caste and scholarship. Seth had not heard it spoken aloud in years. He took his place by Venkat's side and began to chant with him, their distinct tenors blending and bringing back the lost years, of priests fogged in aromatic smoke, of funerals, of weddings, of long-dead fathers and grieving mothers left far behind.

"*Om bhur bhuvah suvahah. Tat savitur varenyam. Bhargo devasya dhimahi. Diyo yo nah prachodayat . . .*"

Oh, universe, with your heaven, your earth, and all the unknowable, unseeable realms surrounding them; and, oh, that sun . . . lost! The sun-filled mangoes, sun-baked streets, sun-burnt skins, lost! But still . . . *we sit* as our fathers taught us, *seeking illumination . . . hear us, especially, in this hour of need. We are opening ourselves to your radiance, God, with expectant and willing minds.*

The sound did not hide the void, but it filled it with a kind of light: nothing that would stop you from falling, but maybe stop you from being so afraid.

Venkat faltered, felled, he told Seth, by a recollection of Sundar receiving his holy thread in Shivashaktipurum, the ashram his guru had founded in India. Venkat and Sita had taken Sundar back home for his coming-of-age ceremony. In the land of his ancestors, surrounded by his relatives, their beautiful boy slouched between them, covered by a silk cloth, cowed by the grandeur of the ritual, his rebellions still incipient. Seth felt the knife in Venkat's ribs at the memory of that adolescent cheek slightly glowing, his lips brushing his son's ear as he whispered these words.

A *poonal* ceremony back home. Venkat was that kind of Hindu, full of orthodoxy and energy, sincere in devotion both to the old gods and this new guru who had revivified and reinvented the ways Hindus practised their faith, the ways they believed.

He and Sita conducted a special puja on Sundar's birthday each year until he left for university, at the Shivashakti Centre downtown. Seth recalled the last one, Sundar's seventeenth perhaps. He had started shaving the peach fuzz from his cheeks and lips. It made him look younger. He had come to Seth for help around then: he wanted to go on a school ski trip, and had had a massive fight with Venkat over it. Seth talked to Venkat, who said that skiing was dangerous and that he had heard from a colleague about kids on such trips drinking, doing drugs. Seth couldn't, in good conscience, push. Sundar stayed home.

The episode now clouded Seth's consciousness in a single black burst—no start, no finish, self-contained and sodden with loss. Why not let Sundar go, be with his friends? So he might have drunk alcohol, maybe even been tempted into s-e-x. But probably not: he was a sensible boy. You have to trust them at a certain point.

He looked over at Venkat, whose mouth hung open, almost panting, and who was swaying a little, at least in Seth's strained vision. He himself was only functioning for Venkat's sake. Otherwise, grief could easily have unhinged him.

Seth resumed chanting, and Venkat, when he regained his breath, did too.

A half-hour later, the doorbell rang: it was a group of other Shivashakti devotees, mostly strangers to Seth, a mix of whites and Indians. Venkat didn't rise, nor pause in his chanting. The devotees greeted

Seth at the door with their customary phrase, "*Jai Shivashakti*" ("What's wrong with them?" he had joked to Lakshmi, once, at an ashram event. "They can't say 'hi'?"). Here, they seemed to show, in contrast with what he had seen in devotional sessions, far *less* emotion than was appropriate. Moving with clear purpose toward the kitchen, they sat in a circle around Venkat and joined the chant. Then, as if they had received a cue from some distant conductor (all their eyes were shut), they began to sing together, a Shivashakti bhajan. Westerners' Sanskrit pronunciation always grated on Lakshmi like nails on a chalkboard. But she wasn't here.

Its tune was one Seth knew well, from the traditional repertoire, but just as Gandhi had rewritten religious lyrics to deliver pacifist messages, Shivashakti's people had turned songs for other gods into songs for him. But really—and this was their point—all gods are One. It's simply easier, especially if a god has been so kind as to manifest in your lifetime, to conceive of the Ultimate Reality as embodied in a particular man.

Seth stood and watched them from the kitchen entrance. The devotees' faces radiated a confidence and certainty he had never felt. They had wordlessly enclosed Venkat in their protective circle. No sobbing, no chatter. It was as though each had carried here a piece of a one-person-size geodesic dome, and they unanimously and simultaneously put their pieces in place with the first note of their song, enclosing Venkat, along with his grief, his regrets, his love and hate. They didn't pretend to share what he was feeling. They didn't try to relieve him. They just reminded him, as if by prescription, that there was something more.

Something more. Seth stood on the outside, watching a moment longer, and then began to sing. No eyes opened. Nothing changed. He seated himself amongst them, and he sang. He felt a sensation akin to what he had felt while praying with Venkat, but greater and clearer. The words and whatever they signified dissolved in their own sound, each syllable striking at that rigid cloud of grief that kept blowing up and obscuring Seth's vision. The relief, sitting shoulder to shoulder, a sense of warmth and solidity from sacrum to sternum, his own voice only as audible as all the others, no more no less, but made greater by the joining—it wasn't joy, don't think that, but it shrank the pain of grief.

Among their friends in Lohikarma and Vancouver, one in ten was a Shivashakti devotee, as were half their relatives in India, to some degree. But then, for Indians, and Indo-Canadians, religion was more general and informal than it was for whites. Hinduism was full of options—which god? which form? pick a favourite—and the finding of a guru a respected, even mandated, path. In this way, to attach to Shivashakti was no radical act. He was a teacher in all the old ways, though he also brought something new—a greater comfort with modernity, internationalism, a disregard for barriers between cultures and belief systems. The fervent light in the devotees' eyes, also, was new. None of the anonymous, itinerant teachers of Seth's childhood had had the charisma to attract such a following. He and Lakshmi had visited the Shivashakti ashram when it first opened here. Lakshmi, both a skeptic and a seeker, found it lacking, as she had all the local ashrams. Seth wanted a temple: formal prayer followed by food. He had been hopeful about Shivashakti's establishment, but its new style of worship didn't fit his bill, and the fervency had made them both uncomfortable.

Seth felt its draw, now, though, a craving answered.

When the phone rang, as it did every fifteen minutes or so, he would answer it. Other families and other friends came, with or without notice, most bearing food. They would sit for a time, and Seth would talk with them, while Venkat would not. The Shivashakti devotees continued to sing throughout, keeping Venkat under their protection, for some three or four hours.

Each time Seth was interrupted, the spell broke a little. He thought that if Lakshmi had been here with him, he never would have joined the circle, and when friends came to call, the devotees' behaviour seemed a little rude to him—they were keeping Venkat apart from his closest friends in Canada, his surrogate family, those who had known Sita and Sundar the way Lakshmi and Seth had. Calling Lakshmi to check in, he mentioned this, wanting to criticize them to her, unable to tell her how moved he had been in the singing-circle, or even that he had joined in at all.

"Venkat shouldn't have to play the host," she said. "Everyone will understand. He is doing what he needs to do."

Seth felt bad. "It's true. That's not exactly what I meant." She waited for him to explain. "I suppose that's why I'm here."

"Yes." She was quiet, and he wondered if she was crying. "Though I think we were closer to them than anyone else."

That evening, after everyone else had gone, Seth heated some food. He and Venkat ate in a vast and liquid silence. He didn't know when the TV news had been turned off, but they turned it on again at eleven. The second day of the search was beginning in Cork. There were still no survivors, and every reporter, every report, repeated the unlikelihood of finding any.

Seth made Venkat go to bed, actually tucked him into the bed he had shared with his wife, pulled the covers up to his chest in the bluish heavy air of the room. The slack of Venkat's neck against the pillow, the thin hairs spread on his large, bald head, his bulgy reptilian eyes with their yellowish whites—all were grotesque and made it seem as if his body was some discarded casing with a small creature hiding inside. Seth was glad to leave the man.

He thought of calling Lakshmi again, but it was past midnight. He fixed himself a cup of instant coffee and walked out into Venkat's backyard. This close to the solstice, the northern sky retained some hint of light just gone or light soon to come. *Tat savitur varenyam.* The familiar silhouettes of fence and trees projected a sinister air.

In India, people died easily and without much fanfare. Canada had so many resources dedicated to keeping every single person alive. And yet, in India, even on their visit last year, Seth felt safe, irrationally so, in the bosom of country and family. *Home* as he might never be here. He pictured his loved ones in their beds. He always felt nervous away from them. Was this because he thought he could keep them safe? That was part of it. He was a man, after all, and they were his charges. Or was it that in such a time of separation, something might happen to them and not to him, so that he could be left, alone, with nothing?

Nothing.

Bomb. Terms and facts associated with explosions cascaded in sheets through his thinking, his physics mind activating in self-protection. Detonation: a supersonic, exothermic shock front accelerating through a medium, solid or liquid. Dynamite: composed of nitroglycerine and . . .

He saw a plane breaking apart over the ocean, bodies and people flying out, sailing away into nothing, children falling down through clouds, lungs collapsing, passing out from oxygen deprivation or fright before hitting the steel grey water—or worse: seeing the water ascend, as ungiving at that speed as steel itself, who knew what awaited you at the bottom, flying out and falling, falling, flying out and falling.

The chanting, and the visitors, had crowded out the images that the mild, chill night now sent at him, as though these peaceful heavens, the sky he could see, were discharging legs, heads, pregnant bellies. Is that what Venkat saw, circling in his hollow eyes, as soon as the chanting stopped? Nothing and no one could survive what they knew had happened.

No one.

He sat on a bench enclosed by Sita's rose bushes, breathed in their scent and felt his body heave and sob, at last. Sundar: a funny, sunny child, curious about Seth's own babies when they came along. He had continued to be one of the few kids in their circle of friends whom his daughters genuinely liked: not square, nor pretentious. He had developed a brooding side as he got older. Once or twice Seth's girls had been hurt by his seeming standoffishness. But then he would make it up, once letting Brinda help him build one of his model airplanes. (Oh God.) Some of them flew: he used to fly them in Willard Park.

Sundar was now between his third and fourth years of engineering at UBC. He hated engineering, which they guessed from the way he refused to talk about it when they saw him, but Sita had also confided to Lakshmi that it was Venkat's insistence that kept him there. He was doing well despite devoting an inordinate amount of time to outside interests, particularly improv comedy and friends' films.

Seth, Lakshmi and the children had gone to Vancouver for spring break, just a few months ago. They had taken Sundar out for dinner at a vegetarian place near the water. He seemed excited to show them around the city, his city, and was open and candid in his dad's absence. Slightly self-centred perhaps—he was only twenty-one—but he did talk to the girls. He had had the same Grade 8 Language Arts teacher that Ranjani had now; they agreed that she was very cool. He asked Brinda how she was liking high school. She said anything was an improvement on junior high.

Afterward, Sundar took them to a rinky-dink theatre, a black-painted box off a back alley—not a place Seth ever would have sought out, but Brinda thought it was "so cool" and Ranjani echoed her, faintly and perfectly.

The actors would shout questions to the audience, and improvise sketches based on the answers: "A fruit?" "Pomegranate!" "An animal?" "Gila monster!" "An illness?" "Kwashiorkor!" Kwashiorkor? It seemed nothing was off limits. Sundar and the others would leap onto the stage, already speaking, competing to see who could get funniest fastest.

When Sundar had come home to Lohikarma—only a week ago, could it be?—for a quick holiday and to drive his mother back to the coast with him to get their flight, the girls had repeated back to him some of the lines from the show. He had already forgotten, having done so many shows since, while the jokes were now part of their private repertoire. "Crazy!" Sundar had laughed. "I'm sure it wasn't as good as you're making it seem."

Earlier memories began to surface. One of their basement dance parties of the late seventies. Sundar was holding Ranjani's hands—she must have been, what, five? He would have been eleven or so. He was clowning, and she was hanging off him, laughing so hard the gums shone above her baby teeth. He whirled her in circles, her feet rose, and Jaskaran Singh's disco ball glittered over them as the grown-ups backed off the dance floor and watched. With all their degrees and their accomplishments, the families they had abandoned to seek their fortunes and send money home, these kids, with their shiny hair, their wisecracking English, and all their other mysteries, these kids were the best they had to offer. To offer . . . offer to whom, to what?

Seth wiped his eyes and stared past the blurry stars. What had Sundar seen, felt, thought as the plane cast him out, up, down into the Irish dawn?

An earlier memory still: Sundar at four, playing Hanuman, kitchen towel for a tail, jumping off sofas, inspired by the Amar Chitra Katha comic books that taught all their kids the Hindu myths. Seth's own kids were yet to be born then, so he was fully available for Sundar to monopolize. Seth felt again the restless pressure of those small bones bundled against his arm as Sundar crouched on the sofa beside him, holding his breath for the story to start, but maybe he was remembering his own girls, their own little ghosts. How many times had he read the opening page of Hanuman's story to that little boy? It held a single image, Hanuman as a child, and the text: *Hanuman, thinking the sun was an apple, leapt toward it.*

Tat savitur varenyam.

Did death interrupt some banality? *When on* earth *is the bathroom going to free up* . . . then nothing. Or was it gradual—an explosion—*what the hell?*—and the plane opening in parts to the sea, the sun, the thin, thin air?

Seth began praying, in the old, familiar way of his childhood, praying for Sita's and Sundar's souls to be sped on their journey, praying that they had no fear nor pain, even as part of him thought *as if.* He realized, with a prick of self-hatred, that he was praying to comfort himself.

* * *

Seth dozed on the family room couch and rose to broad daylight at six thirty. He went to get the paper: the crash was all over the front page but the headlines only repeated what they had heard on the late news. When he turned on the CBC morning show, though, he learned that people were starting to say this was the work of Khalistani nationalists: radical Sikhs, terrorists. Ah. He cast back in his mind, the *gurudhwara* politics, the celebrations after Indira Gandhi's assassination. The assassination itself. Savages. Hypocrites.

On TV, they were interviewing a reporter who said she had been following this movement's Canadian adherents for years, and that she and many others, including police, had suspected that the separatists would try something this summer, on the first anniversary of Indira Gandhi's assault on the Golden Temple. Rumours, she said, had been afloat for months that Air India was not safe. Obviously the rumours weren't that widespread or the plane wouldn't have been full. But what would the Sikh community—which was, the talking heads hastened to say, predominantly peaceful—say now that their self-appointed representatives had taken their ire out on 329 innocent bystanders?

Professor and Mrs. Arora, the only observant Sikhs in Venkat and Seth's immediate social circle, had come to the house last night. Amandeep Arora was six-foot-three, but stooped humbly under his royal purple turban. He liked to say that his passions were physics and metaphysics. His wife, whose eyes lined up with his solar plexus, would giggle. They were devout, private people. Unassuming. Vegetarian. Seth couldn't recall Amandeep ever having expressed a political view. It would be awkward when next they met.

At eight o'clock, the Shivashakti devotees returned. Venkat still had not risen. One of the men offered to help Seth check on him, but Seth waved him off, knocking and entering the bedroom to find Venkat just as he had left him, on his back, eyes open. Seth pictured, for an instant, closing them with a hand, as one would those of a corpse. Venkat's chest rose, then sank in a long shudder and he got up and went into the bathroom. Five minutes later, he emerged, dressed, from the bedroom. He sat again in front of the kitchen shrine and his fellow devotees took up their song.

Seth made a percolator of coffee and put bananas, boxes of cereal and a carton of milk on the table. He tapped on the back of a fortyish white man who seemed like a leader. When the man stopped singing, Seth whispered, "I have breakfast for all of you. Perhaps you could get Venkat to eat something?" The man rose and put a gentle hand on Venkat's shoulder, another on one of his companions, and urged the group toward the food.

Seth was about to check on Lakshmi when she called to say she would be over shortly. By the time she arrived, the devotees had resumed their singing. After taking in the scene for a few moments, she went to the living room to sit with a Tamil Brahmin family who had arrived a few minutes earlier.

When friends were present, Seth would always sit with them, away from the singing. Mere manners, yes, but it was also that he would have felt embarrassed to have witnesses beyond the circle itself, whose members seemed reassuringly indifferent to whether he stayed or went.

When the family left, Seth gestured toward the singers with his head and asked Lakshmi, "Do you want to sit with them?"

She shook her head quickly, and he didn't press. She could be so obnoxiously non-traditional, he felt, and yet when he asked her later why she wouldn't consider singing, she said it felt contrary to their tradition. "I know what you mean now, what you said yesterday. I was expecting, you know, to sit around and talk, talk about Sundar and Sita, and console Venkat. The singing, by these people, who—how well do they even know him? Or Sundar and Sita?"

Seth shrugged. "It seems to calm him down."

She nodded. "I am not saying it's wrong, but it—it's not what we are used to."

She asked him to go home for lunch, check on the girls. He went but returned in early afternoon. By then, all the Shivashakti devotees were gone. Lakshmi said most of them had jobs or families they had to get to, but that they had said they would return each evening until Venkat was up to coming to the ashram.

Seth asked, "Do you still think I should go to Ireland with him?" There had been no call from Air India and he had done nothing about booking a flight.

"I don't know," she said, frowning.

He watched her eyes, which were large and a little bloodshot, beautiful the way courtesans' eyes were in poems. She still lined her inner lower lids with kohl; at least she hadn't given that up. She looked around Seth, as though checking for Venkat.

"I think you should go if he does, but if there was reason for him to go, they would have called, wouldn't they?"

Seth nodded.

Venkat's packed suitcase still stood by the door. And when Seth walked back into the kitchen after saying goodbye to his wife, Venkat asked him, "When are we going?" Venkat's jaw was set and his eyes narrowed.

"I think we have to wait to hear from them, Venkat. They're not going to let us anywhere near the site unless they have asked us to come."

"My son was on that plane! My wife!" Venkat came close to Seth, gesticulating, his breath smelling of yogourt, coffee, plaque, his teeth betel-rusted, his pores large. He was not beautiful, but he had loved, and Seth saw himself in the other man as he never had before.

"I know it," Seth said. "But there are procedures."

Venkat narrowed his eyes and walked to the kitchen. "I'm going to book the tickets. What kind of a man sits at home like this? I don't need your help."

"Venkat, Venkat, let me do it. I'll call now."

"Ha."

"I'll do it. Now. See, here's the number." Seth took it from his breast pocket. "But stay with me. I'm sure they'll want to talk with you."

"You're calling Air India?"

"Sure. There could be no safer time to fly with them, you know. They would provide us with tickets. I would come with you. No other airline would do that. And it would give you a—a legitimacy." Seth was making this up as he went. "We should co-operate with them, for now."

He dialled. Venkat looked expectant in the way of a child waiting for a dentist, or a teacher, to administer an exam: passive but ready.

Air India asked if they could wait a few days. "Retrieval of bodies has slowed considerably, sir," the agent told Seth. "They should be finished processing the remains by the end of the week. It would make it much easier if families would come when there is the greatest chance of taking the loved ones with them." Seth put a hand over the receiver.

"They think we should wait another day or two, Venkat."

Venkat leapt to his feet. "They are behind this in some way." He wrested the phone from Seth. "You nincompoops! What are you hiding?"

Seth couldn't completely disagree: Air India had messed up in some serious way. If it was a bomb, as everyone was saying, they and no one else had let it on the plane. He listened to the squicks and squawks from the phone, the agent likely explaining that there was not much point in Venkat going before the coroner was ready to release the bodies.

The agent eventually said that they could pick up their tickets the morning after next at the Vancouver airport and depart the same afternoon. Air India agents would assist them in making a transfer at Heathrow, and the Irish police would meet them at the airport in Cork.

* * *

Shortly after they hung up, two RCMP officers arrived at the door. One, beefy with a pale moustache, introduced himself as McMurphy; his partner was White. They held their hats in their hands.

Venkat came from the kitchen, where he had remained to pray, straightening his shirt above his dhoti. "It's about time," he said, gesturing toward the living room. The men thanked him and entered, their enormous black boots leaving pale impressions on the rose-pink carpet. "So who's responsible?" Venkat asked, as the officers took seats on the sofa. He leaned over the back of an armchair like a lawyer at a lectern. "You know, in India, the police would be paid off, simply turn a blind eye."

"Ah, um." McMurphy swallowed air and coughed a little.

"I'm Seth Sethuratnam, a family friend and relative." Seth guided Venkat around and into the armchair, torn between wanting to hear how the cops would answer and wanting to ease their discomfort. "I'm stay-ing with Dr. Venkataraman, to help. Can I get you some water, coffee?"

"Love some water, thank you," McMurphy said, and White nodded. "Warm day out there." He began again. "I'm very sorry for this tragedy, sir. We are, I can assure you, doing absolutely whatever we can to find the guys that did this. Interpol's involved," he said, seeming impressed by this, "because of the international nature of the, the incident, but our guys here are heading up the investigation. I wanna start out by getting a few details about your loved ones, the last time you saw them, and all that."

Seth brought water, the glasses beading in the gathering warmth.

"The last time I saw my family," Venkat said slowly. "Last Friday. I was leaving the house to teach, they were in the kitchen. Sundar woke late, a bad habit." Seth saw vestiges of the expression Venkat wore when he criticized his son. He'd never need that look again. "I hugged him. He's taller than me, now, you know?" Venkat's eyes welled, and he re-peated, breathing through his nose, his voice cracking, "I hugged him. He wore a T-shirt, and pyjama." He pronounced it "pie-jama" as per the Hindustani, but they knew what he meant. "I said, 'Drive slowly. No rush.' But I didn't worry. My wife was going with him. She would never let him do anything unsafe. Then I left, to teach. I left them there—" He stood and gestured toward the kitchen and the figures shimmered there a moment: a slight woman in ivory pants and a modest blouse purpled in flowers, leaning against the counter, her waist-length braid come over her shoulder to the front, and a young man, seated at the table, warming his hands on a mug.

"They called me that evening, from our friend's house in Vancou-ver. They said they would call again from India. How will I face my mother," he asked, as though he would value the policemen's advice, "without my son?

To lose your wife, Seth imagined his mother saying, *is a misfortune. To lose your entire family looks like carelessness.*

"Sir, we hope you'll bear with us while we ask," McMurphy said, "what state of mind was your son in? Did you get along?"

"Did we get along? This is not a question we ask in Indian families." Seth felt relief to see the old Venkat resurface, even as he marvelled at the artifice of his certainty.

"I see, sir," the Mountie responded. "Was he unhappy in any way, though? Doing all right at school?"

"Wonderfully."

They waited a second for him to respond to the other part of the question, but Venkat was brooding again.

"And your wife, sir? Again, I apologize for the insensitivity of the question. But were there any problems between you?"

"What the hell is this, I want to know? You think my wife blew up this plane? Because, what, because she was unhappy in marriage?"

It struck Seth that Venkat's response made Sita's unhappiness sound like a given.

"No, sir. No, of course not. These are routine questions. Your loved ones are—they're missing persons right now, and we need to know as much as possible about them so we can find them for you." McMurphy unzipped a document case and pulled from it some yellow forms. "That's fine, anyway. We have some paperwork that we need you to fill out in as much detail as you can." McMurphy's sweating fingertips frilled the forms' edges. "We're also"—he indicated a large briefcase that White had set down beside the sofa"—going to take some finger-prints and other evidentiary, um, evidence, from their rooms, if that's all right . . ."

Venkat began another outburst but Seth went to him. "Venkat, come." He guided Venkat by the elbow to the dining table, which was covered with a rose-pink tablecloth, overlaid in crochet-lace, itself pro-tected in clear plastic. He drew a Cross pen from his breast pocket, one his daughters had given him for Father's Day, a week ago Sunday—was it so recent? "Fill them out however you can." He beckoned to the of-ficers, and showed them the way upstairs.

The doorbell rang again. Seth, looking through the peephole, sighed: Mohan "Moe" Iyer. He opened the door.

"Seth," Moe said, removing his shoes and walking past him. Mo-han's wife Sarojini, overdressed, as usual, in a starched gold-plaid sari and a sapphire jewellery set, greeted him as she and their kids slipped off their sandals as well.

Mohan went straight to Venkat, who was slumped over the yellow forms, the dome of his forehead resting in a palm, pen lying on the page.

Mohan squeezed his shoulder. "Bastard Sikhs, eh, man?" He spoke in a broad, Western-Canadian drawl, buttoned tight over his native accent like a loud shirt across a midlife gut. "We'll break 'em, I swear to God."

Seth saw Venkat's breath cease, his veins pulse. Then he nodded. "The Sikhs. Ah, okay." He rose, fiery and fearsome. "Yes, that makes sense."

"Oh, you hadn't heard, yet?" Mohan turned his palms up. "Sorry, man."

"The damn Sikhs," Venkat muttered, fists clenched at his waist. "Should have thrown them out of Punjab with the Paks."

"Well, that's exactly what they want. Khalistan Zindabad! Eh? I say give them to Pakistan, why should they get any Indian turf? Hope baby Gandhi doesn't give in now. No good comes of dealing with terrorists," Mohan ended with a growl, wandering away from Venkat, each man too consumed with his own thoughts to feel slighted by the other. "Seth." Mohan gestured at him with a help-me-out-here squint. "Coffee?"

The officers lumbered down the stairs. "How're you doing with those forms, sir?" McMurphy asked.

Venkat leaned in to McMurphy. "It was the Sikhs!" He hit the policeman's chest conspiratorially and Seth poised to pounce in case the cop drew his gun, but the mountainous man only winced. "Go get them!" Venkat waved at the door. "Hang them high! Sikhs," he repeated, frustrated by the officer's paralysis. "You know, turbans!"

"We have, um—that's what they're saying on the news, sir." McMurphy nodded gravely. "RCMP in Vancouver, they're following up every possible lead."

"What is this?" Venkat asked, still standing close enough to the officer that they must have felt each other's warmth. "Ask anyone, they'll tell you who did it."

McMurphy looked at him strangely and asked, *sotto voce*, "Do you, sir, have any knowledge of identity of the individuals that might have done this?"

Venkat snarled. "I told you—the Sikhs." He gestured, toward himself, toward some vague entity beyond. "I look like one of them to you?"

Mohan stepped forward holding a business card, like a cigarette, between two fingers. "Iyer," he said, the *r* unrolled, the *y* disappeared, so he might have been trying to say 'ire.' "I'm a developer here in Lo-hikarma. West Wind Condos? Terrible shame, terrible, terrible."

The officer stood and fished out a few cards of his own.

"Any and all information would be welcome," he said, passing them out, and then addressed himself to Venkat, trying to regain focus. "Could I ask you to fill out those forms, sir?" McMurphy looked at Seth. "Vancouver wanted them back by the end of the day. They've gotta get them out to Ireland, eh."

Half an hour later, the RCMP left with their paperwork.

The Iyers hovered an hour longer, talking nonsense, thought Seth. Three years ago, Mohan had hit him up for an investment in that condo project. Seth and Lakshmi had fought: she didn't trust Mohan. Finally she had thrown up her hands. "Don't talk to me about this, Seth. I don't want to be involved."

When, a week later, the cancelled cheque drawn on their capital improvement account came back, she confronted him. "What have you done?" He reminded her that she had told him to go ahead and do what he wanted, but that wasn't how she remembered it.

Now, Mohan had promised investors dividends by the end of the year. Lakshmi was impressed that the condos had been built, but still found Mohan slick and shady in ways she couldn't quite name. He was a big Social Credit party supporter; went to Vancouver and Victoria for parties in politicians' mansions. Seth had no talent for power, but he admired it. Confronted with Mohan himself, though, the hennaed hair, the pinky ring . . . it was nice, occasionally, to see things as Lakshmi saw them.

* * *

The next morning, Seth went home to pack a bag and, by ten thirty or so, he and Venkat were on the road. Seth drove Venkat's car, a Honda sedan he had bought in Vancouver the previous year. He had driven Sundar out to the coast for the start of school, left the old car with him, and drove home in the new one. Every little thing, Seth thought, gripping the caramel-coloured steering wheel cover, was bound up with their families.

He breathed hard against the fear and sadness, and the fear of sadness, and leaned over the wheel, willing himself to focus on the road.

They exited Lohikarma into the verdant countryside, the mountains sometimes close, sometimes far; clumps of lupins in lavender and rose dying out against the roadside green, making way for thimbleberries, chicory, glorious pink paintbrush. Past the Doukhobor lumber mill. Past Glade, Thrums, Brilliant—towns whose names bespoke the shining optimism they all had brought here, the vitality and beauty they saw here, in the beginning.

Venkat was staring out the window, hunched and small-looking. It was strange to see him reduced to infantilism by loss, needing to be told to eat and bathe, and occasionally making demands he knew everyone would run to fulfill. Maybe the adult Venkat would return when they hit the Irish shore; with his family in the vicinity, perhaps he would be restored to his old bossiness, which Seth was almost starting to miss.

* * *

From Vancouver, Seth and Venkat flew the same route the dead had flown, bouncing from Toronto to Montreal, and out over the Atlantic. The jet was nearly empty, holidays cancelled, relatives in India saying, "It's not worth it. Stay back." Seth looked around the cabin, repopulating it with the passengers of the lost plane, eating breakfast, watching TV. How long till the vanished became invisible?

A little under an hour from Heathrow, he tried to look down, through the clouds, but his forehead rapped the invisible inner layer of the acrylic window. Beside him, Venkat sat the way he'd laid in bed, straight, staring, unresponsive, only his knuckles, white on the armrests, suggesting tension rather than catatonia. But as they passed through the airplane-shaped void where Air India 182 had exploded, nothing happened.

They landed in London, where beautifully groomed Air India employees came forward solicitously to escort them to their connection gate. They were trailed by a white Canadian in a suit with a maple-leaf pin on his lapel. He seemed relieved to have delivered them.

They realized, in the queue to board the small plane headed for County Cork airport, that there were at least eight other families going the same way for the same reason. They made eye contact, acknowledging that they, too, had been singled out by history, tapped on the shoulder and asked to step out of the long file of people shuffling obliviously forward into an unknown future of children, grandchildren, spouses with whom to grow old. With them were a few hand-holders, like Seth, bereaved but not shattered; in shock, but, by the grace of God, still in that other line.

In Cork, each family was met by its own cop, sent by the Irish Gardai, and its own grief counsellor, usually a nun. Venkat's was Sister Bernadette. She introduced herself first to Seth, who explained his own role as she continued to hold the hand she had shaken. Then she took Venkat's unresisting arm, murmuring some words Seth couldn't hear in a brogue he barely understood, not that it mattered. She was a guiding spirit in a cloud-grey cardigan and Seth, as he followed her, felt something inside him, twisted tight all week, release a little. Sister Bernadette sat them down and explained they would go straight away to Cork Regional Hospital.

"The coroner is still working with the bodies. As soon as they are finished, then families can start identifying their loved ones," she said. "We're told it may take another day or so. Folks are disturbed that they're not yet permitted to claim their own, but, I must tell you, only perhaps a third of the lost have been brought back. Still, it's something." There was in her voice a greater comprehension of disaster than Seth himself felt. In the days following, it seemed all of County Cork was working to provide some comfort to the families and see the bodies recovered and returned. Their only piece of luck, the families would say later. In a bigger place, it wouldn't have been like that. In London, they would have been ignored, milling about—another few hundred Indians, give or take, *what could they want?* In a more insular place, no one would have known what to do with them. But in a place where everyone had tragedy mapped on the palms of their hands, where every family tree was torn by civil war or emigration, famine or sudden squalls at sea, here, they knew how to address themselves to death.

On the way to the hospital, Sister Bernadette asked Venkat if he had brought pictures of his family. He had tucked two small albums in his shoulder bag, and took them out to show her now. "I have dry clothes for them, in my suitcase."

At the hospital, they were led into a large assembly hall, where a Gardai detective addressed them. "We can't tell you how sorry we are for your losses. Our hearts, every one, go out to you. Our mission is to make sure that each and everybody recovered goes back to his or her loving family."

A young officer passed out forms, identical to the ones Venkat had filled out at home a couple of days prior, except that these were pink where the others had been yellow.

"I did this already," Venkat said, pushing the papers away, but the police officer gently handed them back.

"Sir, I've heard that the Canadian police had you do something similar, but we think there's been some breakdown of communication. Could you jot it down again, sir? If it's no trouble . . ."

Again, this unawkward recognition, these officers so unlike the Mounties, who gave the impression they had never heard of death until they arrived at Venkat's door. How many generations does it take to achieve fluency in the language of grief? Venkat filled out the forms and handed over a family picture, he and the young officer holding it between them a moment, as though it were a diploma or some other certificate of achievement, while the Gardai promised Venkat that it would be returned to him.

And then, the waiting.

Sister Bernadette asked their preference: a nearby hotel had been found for them. They could eat here at the hospital if they were hungry. The food, she said, was not as bad as it might be. And a coach trip had been arranged for the next morning: to Bantry Bay, the closest point on land to where the plane had last signalled its existence, to the point in the water where, two days ago, two sharks were added to the body count, killed by their mates in a feeding frenzy.

Venkat seemed without opinion, but Seth found his limbs were waterlogged with a drastic, irresistible fatigue and asked whether, yes, they could be taken to their hotel. At a small, family-run place about ten miles from the hospital, they were shown to their room, two double beds on a carpet the same rose tint of Venkat's at home in Lohikarma. Sister Bernadette said she would be back for them in the morning.

Venkat set his bags down and took the albums out again, minus the snap he had entrusted to the Gardai: one of him and Sita on either side of Sundar, who wore his high school graduation cap-and-tassel. Venkat sat on one bed while Seth lay down on the other and watched him take a school portrait of Sundar and his own wedding photo out of one album to prop upright on the bedside table.

They were all fond of Sita: she was sensitive and conversational—at least when spoken to; she didn't initiate social contact much—such a contrast to Venkat's humourlessness and bombast that it was often painful to see them together in a room. Sita, whose every fibre tensed visibly when he got started, had only ever managed to influence him a little. Lakshmi, who had her own battles with Seth, said she couldn't imagine how on earth one would approach Venkat on the subject of his stone-set views and the ways he embarrassed himself. Perhaps that was the angle. Someone with so much pride surely couldn't be immune to embarrassment.

Poor man. Seth looked over at him, now paging through the albums. He must always have known, in some inadmissible corner of his psyche, that she really was his better half.

Was.

The digital clock at his bedside glowed 3 A.M. when Seth woke. He didn't see Venkat at first and sat up, afraid he might have gone out. His eyes, adjusting, lit on an empty, chintz-covered armchair in a corner. Venkat was seated on the floor in front of it. Seth stood and breathed in the air of the room, which could have been that of any hotel room, anywhere: vacuum cleaner, tinted with the faintly chemical scent of roses. Their expedition, the reason for it, the sea-water slicked bodies, the shards of aircraft corkscrewed to the white breast of the dim sea, all felt less and less real—farther away, not closer.

"It will mean much to Sita that you have come." Venkat spoke, their eyes, in the dark, unmeeting. "She's not the type to chatter, you know, it's hard on her. She can feel very alone, at gatherings, everyone else making small talk. But with you and Lakshmi, she relaxes."

Seth moved to sit on the corner of Venkat's unmussed bed, across from him, and then slipped to the floor to join him.

Venkat's voice sounded small and private in the gloom. "Her own parents died before she ever had a chance to go back to see them."

Seth had known this: Sita was the only daughter of elderly parents, in their sixties when they married her off to Venkat, then a promising postdoc at the University of Victoria. It was six years before they could save enough money to go back, taking their toddler son, not an unusual length of time, but by then the only close relatives they had were all Venkat's.

Seth saw, in Venkat's hands, a mala of rudraksha beads, the sort prescribed by Shivashakti for his followers. Rudraksha: eye-of-Shiva. The story, in Seth's vague recollection, was that the rudraksha tree sprang from the earth wherever Shiva's tears watered it—what was he crying about? Seth had forgotten, if he ever knew. It suggested watchfulness, though, *eye of Shiva*, and Seth somehow recalled that was why Shivashakti came to adopt it as his emblem, enjoining his worshippers to carry with them the eyes of lord Shiva's incarnation, their god, so that he might always be watching over them. "You are like my eyes to me," Seth recalled one of the devotees reading from a speech at the ashram, out of one of many such compendia Shivashakti published to be read to his followers worldwide. "So dear to me you are."

Onne, onnu; kanne, kannu. The Tamil proverb popped into Seth's head now: when had he last heard it spoken? Possibly by his mother's sister; she had a proverb for everything, though this one was common: *an only son is as precious as an eye.*

He and Venkat meditated on the name of the god who rules the realms of destruction, until it was time to prepare the way for the light of day, when they started praying to the sun. Sister Bernadette had set their alarm before she left them, and when it rang, at six thirty, they had been chanting the Gayatri Mantra for over an hour.

Seth showered first, then Venkat. Dressed, they went down to the breakfast room, where they had beans on toast, oatmeal and strong, scalding tea. At seven thirty, while they were waiting outside for the coach, a young woman with short brown hair exited the garden of the house beside them, pushing a pram and holding the hand of a small boy. As she turned toward Seth and Venkat, her pretty mouth froze and she yanked her son back. Seth, without turning, saw this from the corner of his eye. He felt the familiar pinch of shame and rage that the few instances of overt racism he had faced in Canada had brought on. His children had had it worse: for several months, there was a little gang of older kids who harassed Brinda and Ranjani as they walked to school. Once the kids threw eggs. "Pakis, go home!" they would shout.

The woman reversed back through her gate and Seth wondered what she found threatening about two middle-aged men in neatly pressed trousers. Accompanied by a nun, no less! He had heard about the U.K., riots in London, a racism entrenched, practically institutionalized, by a hundred years of colonial migration. In Canada, it was rare and random, as though they hadn't figured out yet how to do it properly. Seth had found some older children to walk to school with his own; identified the culprits; met with appalled parents who assured him that they would discipline their children. The bullying stopped after that. Clearly, even Canadian parents had some control over their kids, if they chose to exercise it.

Then the Irish mother emerged again from her front door, biting the insides of her pink cheeks. Her son gripped a plastic bag encasing a wad of wet newspaper wrapped around half a dozen bent and thorny stems of fat pink roses. They came up to Seth and Venkat, and the woman said, "We're all so very sorry for your loss. Please, can we give you these?" The little boy held the bouquet out to them with stiff arms.

Venkat took the roses and wrapped the boy in a hug, which he accepted for a moment before wiggling free. A little sister with her mother's eyes watched, unsmiling, from the pram.

* * *

In the coach, Seth stared out the window at a landscape he couldn't decipher, though the rocks, water, rolling hills reminded him more than a little of Canada.

Ireland. *That is no country for old men*, he heard ring out in childish voices from his mind's past. Seth and his classmates, ten years old, shouting Yeats's lines back at Father O'Sullivan, to see the joy come upon his sweet face, he the ringer, they the bells. *An aged man is but a paltry thing / A tattered coat upon a stick, unless / Soul clap its hands and sing, and louder sing.* Seth had understood almost nothing of the poem and so learned that he could love what made no sense to him. The sounds, *Of what is past, or passing, or to come.*

Father O'Sullivan, past. Childhood, past. Sita and Sundar, past. What was passing now? What was to come?

He dozed, his forehead smudging the window, and woke as the bus eased to a stop and the families aboard rustled their belongings together, so many Venkats with so many duffle bags pressed to their laps. Several carried roses. Seth stood, head bowed under the luggage rack, as the others filed off. He followed them out and over grass and rocky shore toward the water.

Because he didn't really know what they were doing there—scanning for injured swimmers the sharks and rescue boats had missed? Sifting for bracelets and comic books?—Seth's mind divided between its two most familiar paths: physics and his family. He re-saw Bantry Bay, even as he saw it for the first time. Not only the water molecules, but the forces holding their atoms in formation, and within the atoms, the subatomic particles in their inviolable, preordained roles. Zoom out again: NaCl, N2, crude oil and C6H6. Zoom out further, again, to see other creatures and refuse, sinking and floating, life and the detritus of life, ambergris, algae, sand and stone. Boats. Swimmers. (Sharks. No.) See now the waves and tides, note the position of the moon, see its gravitational pull; see water reflect sun, moon, sky; now see those light rays reach your eye.

As a scientist, he fully accepted the indifference of nature. Did that mean he had also to believe that God was impassive, impartial, impersonal? He wasn't sure his religious upbringing had a good answer for that one. Karma: we make our fate and God helps us execute it—is that impartiality? But any observer of fate and nature could tell that it made practically no difference in a given life whether a person was good or bad: bad things happened to good people; bad people were only rarely punished. Where did God enter? Was His only role that of observer, the only observer between one life and then next?

Seth looked down the row of them on the beach, dots and dashes, a telegraph to that indifferently watching God—*Distress! Distress!*—and then back out to the massive bay, where he saw, bobbing in the surf, a head. He looked at the others, pointed, gasped, his jet lag amplified, it seemed, by his snooze aboard the bus. He tore off his jacket and waded out into the surf.

"What is he—?" someone asked behind him.

"The rock!" another shouted. "He's . . ."

"Sir! What is his name? Sir!"

"It's a rock!"

Merely a rock. Seth could see it before he was twenty feet out, the waves having wet him to the crotch. He receded, to shore; the waves receded, to sea.

"It's okay," said one gentleman, who grabbed his sleeve, needlessly, tugging Seth toward shore as he waded back. "Good man."

"I thought the same thing," said a woman in a pink sari, "when I first got here—two days ago it was."

Someone wrapped his jacket around his shoulders and his hand around a Thermos-top cup of steaming tea. Venkat stood back from the ranks of the hovering solicitous. He glanced at Seth, and Seth at him, impersonal and sombre as the sea.

He sat on the shore. The woman who gave him the tea crouched beside him. "You think, why would God have brought you so far unless it was to give you a chance to bring them back?" Her face crumpled and Seth reached toward her, but she rose quickly and walked away, holding her sari end to her mouth.

For the same reason God would let your family be killed, Seth thought, his brain kick-started by the water and her tears. Then someone else shouted. There really was a head progressing steadily through the surf at a much greater distance than that rock that had tricked his foolish heart.

Seth himself was not a terribly good swimmer, none of them was, but their kids were and that was why they hoped. The husbands and wives wouldn't have made it, but there were life jackets, seat cushion flotation devices, all the things the attendants pointed out at the start of a flight. Who was that and how would they reach him? He didn't seem to be headed for shore—disoriented? He wasn't shouting for help—good sign or bad?—and he was moving pretty fast.

A man had binoculars. "A seal," he told the rest. "It's a seal."

Each pair of hands took up the binoculars to spy the seal, traversing the bay at what may have been, for him, a leisurely pace. And when he was nearly out of sight, there came two more. Seth looked last and looked longest. Even Venkat had looked, and why shouldn't he; was he any different from the others? That was the thing, Seth thought. Each of them bore a loss every bit as enormous as Venkat's, one that might expand or contract with time, change shape depending on occasion and mood. Three-hundred-and-twenty-nine times infinity—that was the magnitude of what had happened, that was the size of it. Seth started to feel dizzy. He handed the binoculars back and sat down again.

The man, after unstringing the top of his knapsack and re-inserting the field glasses, sat beside him. He wore a utility vest and khaki hat, not a get-up Seth had ever before seen on an Indian man. "These people here, we have come to know each other a little, these last few days," he said, and cleared his throat. "They say they were good mothers, good fathers, husbands. It should be true. But the Hindus believe, don't we, that we deserve this, it is our karma, all of us—we did something in a past life?"

He turned toward the water again, and Seth felt him groping around in his mind, coming up empty, watched his mouth twist.

Venkat stood on the beach in the spot where he had stood since they arrived. He held the duffle bag tightly to his chest and seemed to be speaking, though Seth could hear nothing above the surf and the persistent winds whistling at his ears. All around him, others observed rituals of their own making, or clustered to compare notes of grief. Eventually, more than half left things for the water to take, keepsakes, offerings, roses.

* * *

They got back from Bantry Bay to find a cautious message: *Come to the hospital, please.* They believed one of the recovered bodies to be Sundar's.

Three other families were also summoned. They all sat on melamine chairs at the morgue, waiting to be called, a father–daughter, a husband–wife, and a man, a man, and another man.

"Mr. Venkataraman?"

Venkat stood but didn't look at the coroner's assistant. Seth, beside him, put a hand on his back. They followed the assistant into a ward and behind a drawn curtain. There, he gestured at a wall of death-mask Polaroids, faces, swollen, cut, bruised, all eyes closed. "Mr. Venkataraman. Could you tell me, please, if you see your son here?"

Venkat was standing with his eyes closed, fingers pinching the bridge of his nose. Now he walked up close to the wall, and began looking down, up, left, right, in a staggering figure-eight that irritated Seth, who came up beside him and began searching, too, his eyes starting at the top left corner and travelling methodically down each column. At the end of the second queue, in a miasma of creeping nausea, he realized that he was forcing himself to look into every dead, broken face, while Venkat skimmed haphazardly over others' pain, only searching to confront his own.

They found Sundar at the same moment. His face, or a version of it. They had been warned of the possibility that all the bones were shattered beneath the skin. They searched the small picture. There was swelling, and stitching, but no one else so closely resembled their boy. The coroner's assistant took a note, perhaps the number of the picture, or the fact that they had affirmed it, and they followed him into a room where the body was already waiting.

They knew it was Sundar from the tattoo. No one knew when he had gotten it. Apparently, he had already had it so long that he had forgotten about it by the time of the Indians' Canada Day picnic on Kootenay Lake when he was nineteen. The kids all stripped to bathing suits and took turns swinging out over the lake on a tire. A tire could have no better purpose, the adults thought, as they watched their children flash and drop, sunlit, into water that seemed their natural home. They would emerge, giggling gods, to take their places again in line. At some point, someone exclaimed and reached to touch Sundar on the shoulder and he turned, alarmed, but couldn't keep his back to everyone at once. His father ran over to see: a slim dagger that seemed to enter the shoulder blade from above and emerge again beneath it, a cunning trompe l'oeil and wonderfully executed. Venkat was predictably livid.

Now that one pinned wing brought his angel back. In time, they would match the dental records. Now, they left the men alone with Venkat's dead child.

Venkat lay across the body and began to sob as Seth looked at Sundar's face. He saw, in his mind's unwilling eye, sound-wave patterns of the blast, fall time in relation to distance:

$$t = \sqrt{\frac{2d}{g}}$$

Decomposition slowed to a halt by saline immersion. Then the physics melted away and Seth saw only the terror, Sundar going to the cremation fire with a look on his face that showed he knew his life was ending in horror and unfulfillment.

He felt himself shot through with that horror, as though he were a conduit for lightning. He also felt the desire to pray. But to whom? For whom? Later, he would be able to recall all this, in sequence, in detail, though it likely took no more than a second or two. He felt as though he were searching, looking up into a vast nothingness, and then he felt what he would call a cosmic wind around his ankles. In the moment he began to fall, he woke with a violent start in the coroner's arms.

Venkat raised himself from the body to take his son's face in his hands. Seth, still steadying himself, drew a breath of pity for what Sundar's father would see.

"So peaceful!" Venkat cried. "Look, look. So peaceful, just as he looked in life. He is sleeping, merely sleeping."

Was Venkat seeing Sundar as he remembered him rather than as he now was? But when did Sundar ever look peaceful? Perhaps when he slept, his daylight restlessness rubbed out by dreams of stillness. Seth had seen him sleeping, a few times. The night of that day when they nearly lost him at Disneyland, Seth had kissed Sundar's forehead as he slept. He was old enough that Seth couldn't do that anymore when he was awake. That childish face came back now, hovering, transparent, over this one.

"Sundar." Seth's voice cracked as he said it, and he said it again, and his voice cracked again. "Sundar." It meant "beautiful"—the perfect name for him—how could they have known? One of many names used to call Krishna, the beautiful boy-god, valiant, mischievous, lordly.

Perhaps terror and peace became the same thing when life's mysteries were unveiled. In the Bhagavad Gita, when Krishna reveals his divine form at Arjuna's request, Arjuna is terrified at seeing what no mortal can stand to see. But the end to human doubt surely must also bring with it a definite, final peace. Maybe Venkat, with his greater knowledge both of God and of his son, could see that grace, while unenlightened Seth saw only fear.

✳ ✳ ✳

Back out in the foyer, they accepted the other families' weird congratulations on their dubious good fortune—finding a body, the best they could hope for, now. Only one other family present had also positively identified a loved one. The others would continue to wait. "What a world," Venkat told Seth in that night's rare moment of speech, "when I fear the evil eye from congratulations on having my son's dead body. Reflex, eh? What could *drishti* do to me now?"

Sita, too, had an identifying mark: her mangal sutra, her wedding necklace, unique in the world. Venkat had no close picture of the pendant, but told the police he would know it when he saw it. They didn't discuss the possibility that it had separated from her through some dismemberment. He was shown two mangal-sutraed necks, both wrong.

Sundar knew how to swim. Sita did not.

Venkat and Seth went back to Bantry Bay three more times, each time superstitiously hoping that on their return they might get a message about Sita's body. On the fourth night, Venkat confided to Seth that he had known, when he saw his son's body, that he would not receive his wife's. "I don't deserve that much," he said, and Seth thought how losses might differ in their sharpness, how pain's varied qualities might relate to varieties of guilt or forgiveness. It was not a fruitful train of thought.

Venkat flew to India, with Sundar's ashes, destined for the Kaveri River. Seth, from Ireland, returned home.

Seth drove Venkat's car from Vancouver to Lohikarma, seeing now
the rolling hills and rocky shores of B.C. as though through the
Irish coach window. Lakshmi radiated relief at the door. He knew she
would ask him later about what he had seen and what happened, but she
seemed uncharacteristically glad to defer her questions. Brinda brought
him a cup of instant coffee and she and Ranjani crowded him on the sofa.

"What was it like, Dad?" Brinda asked first, attempting to mask
the extent of her curiosity, making him wonder if she would repeat what
he said to her friends. "Mom said they found Sundar's body but not Sita
Aunty's. What's happening now?"

Seth looked into his coffee and crossed his legs. The sight of the
morgue rose in his head, with its smell, medicinal and sweaty, of a damp
mop never properly dried. He put his nose to his coffee and patted Ranjani's knee. "I don't know what's happening now. Only about a third of
the bodies were recovered." He checked their faces. Were they upset?
Brinda, the clinical one, was frowning and listening. If ever she became
upset, she would tell you. Ranjani was harder to read. She was frowning
too, but not looking at him.

"Many never will be found. But some still might surface. I convinced
Venkat that he should go on to India with Sundar's ashes, that the chances
of finding Sita's body were too small. The Irish police would be in touch if
they found anyone that looked like her. They seemed very sincere."

Lakshmi came in, wiping her hands on a towel, and Seth felt sickened by the sense that perhaps he had not yet arrived home, that there
was a gulf between him and his family that he hadn't yet crossed. His
mind was filled with impressions he couldn't properly share: He had
seen a boy they loved, puffed and mutilated and dead. He had slept in
the bed next to that boy's father, prayed with him and heard him weep
at night. He didn't want to cross the gulf, didn't want to share what he
had gone through. He even thought Lakshmi might prefer to be spared
that burden.

The void: he couldn't seem to retreat from the verge, from staring down into it, even when he and Lakshmi made love that night. He was desperate to return to her, and she pretended that he was merely ardent and tried to respond, but it didn't work and they stopped, unsatisfied. She held his face in her hands and looked at him hard. He permitted himself to be scrutinized. He wondered if she was annoyed and whether they might fight, and he had started to think—think!—that he might welcome the distracting anguish—there was nothing worse than fighting with his wife—when she patted his shoulder. "You need to rest."

She kissed him, and they lay back in the midsummer half-dark, her head sliding from his shoulder to the pillow beside him, though she still held his hand. He felt angry, a bit, at her easy abandonment, at how she sighed and drifted away.

* * *

The next night, he and Lakshmi resumed their customary after-dinner walk. The tradition had started years earlier, when their children became old enough that they could be left alone for an hour in the evening. When summer began, either Seth reminded Lakshmi, or, according to her, they both remembered at the same time, and they resumed. Eight months of the year, they trod the treadmill and cycled the bike in front of the basement TV, but in this brief warm time, they strolled, conversationally or in silence. That evening, silence prevailed.

As they left the house, Lakshmi checked her peonies. One bush showed half a dozen open blooms in a cheerful if unexceptional middle-pink, but filled the air with a delicious fragrance, oddly reminiscent of tea. The two other bushes bloomed later, their tightly wrapped globes barely starting to open into a deep, meditative red. They gave off no smell—worse, when Seth stuck his face in deep, he got a whiff of dead fish. Her irises were finished but the lilies were about to arrive. In the yard's coldest corner, a last stand of poppies wobbled to the breeze from the lake, their frothy heads dropping a few petals. It was a competent garden, nothing compared to Sita's grand passion. As Seth retied a shoe and frowned at their lawn—unmowed for weeks now, glorified by an ambush of orange hawkweed—Lakshmi snapped off a few dandelions puffs and slipped them under the lid of their garbage bin at the curb without disturbing the seeds. What would become of Sita's heirloom

roses, her perennial beds with their precisely timed bloomings, her in-
comparable herbs and tomatoes, which each friend received, at the end
of the season, essentialized into a gift-pack of homemade chutneys?

They headed down a set of concrete steps at the end of their street,
crossed a road to another set of steps, and repeated this until they landed
up at a small street that led directly to the walking path along the lake.
Ten days since the solstice, and still hours to dusk. Sailboats, kids playing along the shore, a couple of evening swimmers though the water was
always a bit chilly. On the opposite bank, a familiar mountain stretched,
low and passive, reminding Seth, as always, of a book he used to read
his kids: *Danny and the Dinosaur.* Its shape resembled nothing so much
as the dinosaur, head lowered, like a dog's, for a nice scratch behind the
ears. As they walked, Lakshmi told him about a drama that seemed to be
developing around her new supervisor. Seth lost the thread. She accused
him, half joking, of not paying attention, but didn't try to go on.

These things kept happening, for days. Seth felt depressed and uncomfortably distant from his family; every time his heart leapt toward
them it was backhanded by a racket of fear.

Finally, Lakshmi erupted. "I'm thankful you were available to help
Venkat, I am. But Venkat has gone to be with his own family now. You
have to come back to yours."

Where was her terror—of grief, of death, of the risk of love itself?
He had wondered that even before going to Ireland to confront death in
person, its putrid colours and livid smells. Why was she not paralyzed?
He didn't know how to ask her—it would sound like an accusation, as
though he thought her unfeeling. He didn't: it was the opposite. She
knew how to feel. He didn't. No one had taught him how to live with
these emotions. Who could teach him now? The only time he had felt
at peace in these last two weeks was when he was praying.

✳ ✳ ✳

Lakshmi accompanied him to a satsang the next night at the Shivashakti
Centre. It was on the second floor of a two-storey building on High
Street, above a yoga studio and an office of three accountants, one of
whom, Seth would learn, was a Shivashakti devotee. When they arrived,
at 6:20, a white woman dressed in a salwar kameez was unlocking the
doors; Seth recognized her from Venkat's house. He could almost feel

the hairs on the back of Lakshmi's neck rising. Perhaps he should have come alone, but he had felt compelled to ask his wife. Perhaps she had felt compelled to agree.

Daisy—that was the name of the devotee who let them in. She bade them sit while she lit incense in the largest of the three rooms. Several other acolytes arrived while she was doing this, one carrying plates of snacks to the kitchen. Others took places on the carpet, facing the shrine. By six thirty, some fifteen people were assembled in a state of cross-legged readiness, filling perhaps a quarter of the space. Most of the devotees from Venkat's house were among them, and a few nodded at Seth in recognition.

A young, ginger-bearded man stood at the front and did a short puja to the large photo of Shivashakti on the shrine: illuminating the picture by moving a ghee lamp before it in circles and then offering the flame to each of the assembled devotees, who waved hands over it and took its blessing by covering their eyes and gesturing over their heads with warmed hands.

The young man set the lamp on the shrine and took the blessing himself, running his hand through his long, orange-marmalade curls and adjusting Shivashakti's sandalwood garland, which had gone slightly askew. He pressed a button on a tape player: Shivashakti's weekly lecture, delivered in person each Sunday afternoon in India, in the Great Hall of Assembly at Shivashaktipurum, then transcribed and sent out to every Shivashakti centre in the world, along with an audiotape of the original and a spoken translation.

The theme this evening, Seth would never forget, was "Confession."

Confession: You may wonder, why do I need to speak my doubts? God knows all—so why must I put my guilty things into words, the devotee asks, if God understands? Yes, God understands, but do you? It is through speaking that you come to know your own doubts and the sorrows of your life. You must do the work of understanding. God knows you, fine, but do you know yourself?

He felt the guru—God—was speaking directly to him.

It is the same for the Christian man, the Hindu man, the Mussulman— "Listen to my soul and hear it crying from the depth!" This is what the great Christian sant *Augustine, he said. "Listen to my soul and hear it crying from the depth. For if your ears are not present in the depth, where shall we go? To whom shall we cry?"*

"The night is yours and the day is yours."

Seth felt small and safe, a child in a parent's arms. *The night is yours and the day is yours.*

The congregation sang bhajans, followed by Shivashakti's mandatory acknowledgement of non-dualism: each person present turned to another to say, "If you are God, so I am God," a reminder of the light their guru shone at the end of the tunnel of ignorance.

A chanting meditation emerged naturally out of this ritual, then faded into a silent meditation, out of which people retired subtly to the kitchen where coffee had begun to perk.

Seth loved the sedate procession from each level to a deeper one, as though from one subterranean pool down to another, no stop too long or too short. He loved how he and Lakshmi, nearly complete newcomers, could so easily fit in and follow along. And the snacks and coffee were tasty, especially following the rigours of spiritual exercise.

Afterwards, he felt calm and uplifted. How had he never seen how this would suit him? He supposed he had never attended a normal satsang, only the special occasions, and he recalled having been a little turned off by the fervency.

But now that the blood-dimmed tide was loosed, and the ceremony of innocence drowned, Shivashakti's method was a rope to take hold of and follow, hand over hand, toward introspection and faith—it was just the thing. He found a schedule and other information on a table by a bulletin board. Satsangs were Monday and Thursday nights at six thirty. There were quarterly sign-up sheets for various duties and details. There was a phone tree for such matters as the volunteer and charitable activities that Shivashakti prescribed for his followers.

As Seth and Lakshmi ate pastries, some of the others introduced themselves. The young man who read the lecture was called Carsten. He asked what had brought Seth to the centre, the question proving mainly to be an opening for Carsten's own story: he was a ski instructor, who first came with a friend. He was saving for a one-way ticket to India, which seemed synonymous for him with "Shivashaktipurum."

Daisy, who had let them in, was in her fifties. She wore a crystal over her unfashionable salwar kameez, and her speech was larded with the language of healing and non-denominational spirituality that marked the town's New Age Tribes. She introduced a friend, Irene, younger, in her thirties, perhaps. Seth noticed Lakshmi had disappeared from his side. Irene was small and bubbly—they were talking about a visiting lecturer and volunteer opportunities, unfunny topics, but she laughed after each thing she said. Her cheeks looked painfully red and flaky. She kept pushing thick bangs ever-so-slightly out of her eyes; they would immediately fall back in.

"I remember now," said Daisy. One woman was at each of Seth's elbows, while Lakshmi, across the room, was talking to an Indian couple. "You were at Venkat's house, when we came there, on the grief vigil. How is he?"

They listened with interest to how Venkat had taken Sundar's ashes back to India, and would stay some weeks in Shivashaktipurum. Other devotees gathered in. Nick was one, a man of about Seth's age who ran a copy shop and stationery business, not talkative, but with a warm and ready smile. And Kaj Halonen, the principal of a junior high school, big, balding, a bit hearty in conversation, so you weren't sure how closely he was listening when you talked. But Seth had looked at the other devotees while they were praying, and thought he had glimpsed on Kaj's face a true loss of self in the divine, depths of peace beneath the bluster, exactly what he himself desired.

* * *

He surged home, enclouded, almost inappropriately buoyant. Success! He had found his guru—so quickly! Who knew it could happen like this? Never mind that Seth had known about him for years. It was a common story, and an old one, that God could only be seen when the mind of the devotee was ready and open.

As they were getting into bed, Lakshmi asked him, with careful neutrality, "You liked the satsang? You thought it was good?"

He hadn't given a thought to what his wife had felt since the first word of the lecture. *Confession.* He almost drifted back, but, instead, forced himself toward her. "It was just what I needed."

She nodded and they said nothing more, spooning into sleep.

* * *

He resumed summer teaching the following Monday, and went to the satsang that night. Lakshmi went with him, but then declined to come on Thursday, and the week after, and the week after that.

Seth was enveloped by a quality of ecstatic awareness, a sense of pure feeling—what feeling? Feeling itself. How long had it been since he had really *felt* in this way? A long time.

Was it like this when he and Lakshmi were first married? He'd been consumed by her presence, their communion, all that was so surprising and delightful. It was spurred by erotic discovery but reached quick tendrils into every part of his being.

His children, also, provoked surges of emotion. His family's beauty still made him heady at times. But ecstasy? No. Not after years of chores, bills, backtalk. His love had deepened—it underlay all he did—but he was not, usually, aware of it.

So, now: not only had he found his guru, he'd become infatuated.

He felt more energetic, and more attentive to the small charms of life than he had in years, yet when he cut himself on the screen door, he didn't notice until Ranjani pointed out that he was bleeding. The colours of sky, sunset, trees and stones were intensified, but also appeared distant, as though seen through a veil: devotion. He lost weight—food held no interest for him—and had difficulty focusing on teaching and remembering such mundane matters as groceries. Yet he had the sense of being hyper-alert, flooded with lost memories and exhilarated by insights.

One evening, as he was singing with the other devotees, some with finger cymbals, others, like Seth, clapping hands, he had the feeling that he was walking back from the market with his mother, stopping by a roadside shrine, where one would clap hands to call out the god. *An aged man is but a paltry thing / A tattered coat upon a stick, unless / Soul clap its hands and sing, and louder sing / For every tatter in its mortal dress . . .* He was back in the classroom with dear Father O'Sullivan, his bulby red nose, his joy at his students' voices. So many dead.

Seth wrote poems, something he had not done since writing one for Lakshmi in the first weeks of their marriage. It seemed there was no other action adequate to all he needed to express, as he immersed himself in Shivashakti's writings, and stories by fellow devotees. He learned that Shivashakti sometimes appeared as a woman, sometimes as a snake, embodying both the male and female energies, which is why he had the names both of Shiva and of Shakti, the god's wife. He was a man first, and claimed that the male power was superior. (Seth was aware this would rankle Lakshmi deeply if she learned of it, but she was not asking too many questions and he found it easy not to talk to her about all he was learning.) Yet he encouraged his followers to call him MataPita—mother and father.

Shivashakti was born Shanmugham, a Kannada Brahmin boy of some intelligence and secular promise. When he was in his early twenties, just finished engineering college, he went on a trip with friends to the western ghats. They had taken their morning bath in a waterfall and had plans to go to a cave temple in the afternoon. Shanmugham was a small distance away from his friends, drying off, when he saw, on the path, a cobra. Its head was raised, its hood open, but for some reason, he was compelled to go toward it. The cobra slithered through the woods and he followed, until suddenly he saw, on a rock, an old woman. The cobra was on her lap, her hand raised and slightly cupped, much like the snake's hood, as though they both were blessing him. The snake spoke: "There is no more man or woman. Shiva and Shakti are one." The snake slithered up through folds of the woman's sari and around her neck to enter her chest through the dip of her clavicle. The old woman opened her mouth to speak. A snake's tongue darted forth. "There is no more man or snake," she hissed. "I am the cobra." She bent into a circle and he saw she had no feet, but rather a snake's tail. She began to swallow herself.

Shanmugham felt dizzy and fell to the ground. His friends found him there, weak and barely sentient. He had a snake bite, but recovered, took his new name and began the life of an ascetic. He was married but now took a vow of celibacy. (He did not cast out his wife; she became his first devotee.) After travelling the "length and breadth" of India, garnering knowledge of its peoples, languages and holy men, he started an ashram close to Mangalore, in 1973. His intention was never to promote himself as a God—"I am not here to say I am God—Aham Brahmasmi. I am here to prove that you are God—Tat Tvam Asi," he famously said. But he had achieved samadhi, a conscious union with the divine, and could not deny the many who hungered to feed from his light.

Seth consumed this information, though there was also a part of him that knew the history and testimonials were irrelevant. He remembered, early in his marriage, playing with Lakshmi's fingers while she talked to him about her childhood, when suddenly she pulled her hand away to slap his. "You're not even listening!" she had said, but it wasn't true. He hadn't registered the words, but he was listening with every atom of his being to the sound of her voice. Like that, he now wanted to know everything about his guru, but not for what he learned. It was simply another way of basking in his presence. *Bhakti*—love of God as though he were a lover. This is what it was, for Seth: honeyed wonder. He was drenched in it.

* * *

While he was caught in the beam of a personal sun, though, Lakshmi grew more sombre with each passing week. They acted normal—meals with the children and rides to the pool–library–mall, along with discussions of Venkat's fast-approaching return at the start of the academic year. But on the nights when he went to satsang, he would return to find his wife quiet.

On one of those nights, perhaps in the fourth week, he came home with Shivashakti's 1984 lecture compendium and lay reading it in bed.

She came into the room with a basket of folded laundry, paused, and put the basket down to open the closet. "So that's it. You're a Shivashakti devotee now?"

He closed the book on a thumb. "I, uh, it looks that way, doesn't it."

"Yes, that's how it looks," she said, putting the clothes away, her face to the closet.

"You go to the Vedanta Centre," he reminded her.

"But I'm not a devotee." She sat on the bed, the basket dangling from her hand.

"No," he agreed.

Lakshmi had, more than once, questioned the value of gurus, which were fundamental in their tradition. Before the bomb, he had thought, in some vague way, of trying to find a guru someday, when he was in his sixties, maybe post-retirement, some proper age for renunciation and seeking. Lakshmi was more of a true seeker than he was, so he had thought, but repeated disillusionment or her native non-conformity seemed to have turned her off the quest. He realized now that she believed that the two of them had rejected Shivashakti bilaterally, years ago, she in her typically intense way and he in his typically joking one. Now, she felt betrayed. Perhaps even jealous. She had been waiting for an explanation of some sort. He, too, felt he owed it to her, and so he tried.

"It . . . it was so scary, Lakshmi," he began. "Terrifying, the idea, losing your family. I realized . . ." Was he making sense? "I realized I would have nothing, if that were to happen to me, to all of you."

"It's not going to happen," she said, putting a hand on his leg.

He didn't mean to, but he gave her a look. She took her hand away.

"The fear, Lakshmi, what I saw there, the broken hearts. You'll understand, maybe, when you see Venkat again. Horrible."

Lakshmi was silent.

"You want to love us less?" she asked, finally, with a detectable note of what sounded to Seth like ridicule.

"The opposite," he said. "Devotion to God would mean I can also be devoted to you."

Had he detached from them? Not exactly. He had pulled back, but that didn't mean he loved them less. The scriptures preached love without attachment but didn't that ultimately mean detaching from those you loved? His love for his wife didn't lessen when he had his first daughter nor did his love for his first child dim when the second was born. In fact, his attachment to his family increased. He had to admit that his devotion to Shivashakti hadn't had the same effect, so far. And yet, he still felt it was what might enable him to love without fear of being destroyed.

"That's like having an affair to save a marriage!" Lakshmi said.

Seth laughed.

"No, it is!" she said. "You might feel more content at first, maybe even more loving toward your spouse, maybe because of guilt. But then eventually that other love eats into you and makes you discontent or the lover becomes more demanding, and then you have to choose."

"You've thought about this a lot, *kanna*!" How was it he had been given this excellent girl? "Are you sure you're only making a comparison and not really thinking I am having an affair?"

"You would be if it were up to that Irene woman." Lakshmi sniffed. Irene, Seth's fellow-devotee, worked in the municipal government building, as did Lakshmi. That week, she had come up to Lakshmi in the cafeteria and talked at inappropriate length about what a wonderful man Seth was. "*So gentle*, she said. *And brilliant. Oh, and handsome? My, my!*" Lakshmi, impersonating Irene, emitted a vacuous yet evil giggle.

Seth covered his blushing ears with his hands, laughing harder. "Oh, Lakshmi. The poor woman."

Lakshmi, too, laughed. "It's her own fault, don't pity her. Pity me, having to listen to her. And what's all that flaking and cracking on her cheeks? She needs to see a doctor."

They laughed and laughed and laughed. They went to bed in a peace that was not uneasy, the air cleared. Still, each also knew the other would prefer a closer agreement, and that neither would budge.

I didn't exactly get all of this from Seth in that one afternoon. True, we talked for some hours. True, he covered much of this period of time. I went back to my apartment and transcribed—that, dear reader, you've heard before. But I waited to write. Seth was not strictly linear when he talked; more a charming digressor. The information filled in, the narrative filled out, over the course of this year. The writing came, in time.

I, too, may have a linearity problem, and must admit now to a small detail I have so far failed to include in this narrative:

Ottawa. En route east from Montreal, I interviewed a family there. I stayed three days, in a hotel, with a phone book. Where Rosslyn was listed.

Thank goodness for Maureen McTeer, the anodyne P.M. Joe Clark's feisty First Madam, who refused to change her name upon marriage or even, à-la-Hillary-used-to-be-Rodham, upon ascension to Official Helpmeet. Thanks to her, a whole generation of Canadian girls, Tory, Liberal or NDP, were inspired to remain Ms. from birth to death. Rosslyn was listed under her own name.

I Googled her: still with Ottawa public schools, but also teaching in the College of Social Work. She had published a few papers, co-written. I drove past her house, barely able to bring myself to look, but in any case, I saw nothing of note and drove away not quite understanding what I had done.

I had seen her shortly after the bombing, but not since.

* * *

June 1985. After the bomb took my sister and her children, I went on an indefinite leave from IRDS and, though I had finally got my own apartment, went back to stay awhile with my parents.

I was at work on my book about the pogroms, but the bombing stopped it cold. *Who Are the Victims?* I thought, in the sleepless nights I spent pacing, hearing my mother wail, sensing my father's cavernous grief from the chair in his room where I knew he sat, awake, too. Could I now count Kritika, Anand and Asha among the victims of the Delhi riots?

Suresh, my brother-in-law, came to India a couple of weeks after the bombing. He stayed with his own parents, and would come to pay his respects to mine. You can imagine the scene. The magnitude of grief in our house. Once or twice I went out when Suresh was expected. My father looked disappointed, but didn't stop me. I couldn't tell that my mother even noticed.

Back in Canada, Rosslyn saw Kritika's name on a list of the dead. She called me at my parents' home. She got the time wrong and the phone rang at two in the morning. In normal circumstances, the household would have been thrown into alarm. Now that the worst had already happened, no one blinked an eye. Her voice was like warm sand, and yet I felt pierced, all over, with shards of longing—endless distances—and regret.

She asked if I might come to Canada, if there wouldn't be a funeral. It hadn't occurred to me until she asked, but when she did, I said yes.

After Suresh returned to Montreal, I came to visit him. He and I had never established much more than a formal warmth, so I didn't pretend I was going to comfort him. I hadn't known if there would be a funeral— there was, though I never would have attended it if my father hadn't asked me to do so on his behalf. My mother asked me to bring back keepsakes from Kritika's home, although Suresh would have been a more reliable person to ask to choose something. I'm too unsentimental about objects to be counted on for such a wish. But my mother had a stubborn, tribal quality that meant she would never ask an in-law, no matter how devoted, but only a blood relative, no matter how dismissive.

In any case, Suresh seemed genuinely glad for my company and my help in reorganizing the house. Despite his sappy taste in poetry, he was not one of those who clung to material reminders of the departed.

He sorted through their things methodically, using the process to work through his grief. I came to admire him, in those days, more deeply than I had before. He kept only what was of genuine value to him, and asked me to help him get rid of the rest.

He never went to Ireland: he waited for the official word, but said he felt in his blood that his family were gone. He didn't know how or why he was better able to recognize this than so many others.

I would have met him there, but my sister's remains, and Asha's and Anand's, were never found.

* * *

One day, I went to Ottawa to see Rosslyn. Hazel eyes flecked with concern. Gilded brown hair in a style slightly different from before. Freckles accentuated by the sun. Pregnant, she looked curvier, and happier, than she had with me. She had walked to our rendezvous, and now fanned her blouse and blew down her neckline, glowing faintly as we waited for a table.

"Marriage, is it?" I asked, once we were seated. She had suggested one of our favourite old places: informal, but with heavy wood tables and big windows; all original recipes, several named for regulars.

"The wedding's in a little under a month."

She wore an aquamarine stone on her left hand. I remarked that her nails, while short, were not ragged.

"I've been using something to help me stop biting them."

"While planning your wedding? Don't tell me you've started smoking?"

A smirk. "Yeah, yeah."

She was marrying a teacher, someone she had known for years. He must have made his move as soon as I left—and why not?

"Ashwin, I'm so sorry." She put her hand over mine. "I don't know what else to say."

The sensation of her hand was softly electric: it had been so long since I had been touched. I had never been so intimate with anyone, and I wanted so much to talk to her, about the bombings, the pogroms, my confusion, my book-in-progress. I tried a little, but like most Canadians of her age—generations away from the old countries; never seen war or riots; barely seen poverty outside of native reserves—she couldn't hold the personal and the political together for too long. That really is a first-world problem. Her concern was for me, as an individual, a friend, and she couldn't fully fathom the bigger picture.

I let it go, but there was nothing further I could say about my own emotional condition. I could see she was perhaps hurt by this, as well as a little frustrated by her own inability to ask the right questions or offer me comfort. She was in love with another and her life was a far country.

I asked what she was reading and she told me, and said how our favourite bookstore had changed owners, and how the school where she used to work was being torn down. I told her about my new apartment, and she noted down the address. It was a decent, easy means of paving the way to goodbye.

✳ ✳ ✳

Back in Montreal, I asked my old mentor and analyst, Marie Chambord, for her thoughts on my book. That was to be the last time I saw her, though she continued to advise me on my work until her death in 2002.

"My anger will show," I told her.

"It won't," she replied, and pursed her narrow lips at me. She picked up one of the many small steel sculptures she kept, brightly polished and randomly arranged, on a low table between her chair and the client's. "You did your project with those families, those people. You wrote their stories. Now, a year later, you are injured by a revenge. Would you sit and tell such things to your patient? *Je pense que non*. You tell your analyst. This is why every analyst has an analyst."

I, too, palmed one of the figures—weighty, cool, Brancusi-esque. The metal absorbed the warmth from my hand.

"*Bon*. Write the book." She opened her hand, balancing the thing, shaped like an Egyptian cat, on her palm. "Your opinions go in. Your story, it stays out." Though her hand seemed not to move, the little figure rocked and rocked, merry-seeming at first, and then increasingly autonomic, back and forth without ceasing.

✳ ✳ ✳

When I returned to India, I had a vasectomy. In Canada, if you say "never before," they won't let you say "never again." This is the difference between a staid young country with an aging population of 3.2 persons per square kilometre and an old one careering toward the billion-person mark and trying to find the brakes. If you so much as mention the v-snip in India, they clap a sweet-air mask on your face and scalpel-pop your scrotum before you can change your mind. There may be monetary incentives, for doctors and patients. I've had no reason to regret it.

I brought my mother back a bag of doodads—a jewellery set she had given Kritika, some crafts the children had made. A few photos. She was not content—had I chosen wrong? Was it too little? I don't know. I hadn't expected her to be pleased, so I hadn't tried very hard.

Rosslyn sent me a birth announcement for her son. I threw it away without responding. Were there subsequent children? If so, I wasn't notified. There may have been a Christmas card. We had no contact after that.

But—I wrote the book.

*I*t was, what, my fourth or fifth day in Lohikarma. Only that? All I say in my journal of that morning is how deeply I had fallen into this place, these people. Brinda would come to see me again, late that morning.

True confessions: the more I thought of her, the more I saw her as some sort of reincarnation of my niece. Nothing literal! But Brinda appeared to me as Asha's figurative re-embodiment, and the prospect of listening to her, helping however I could, my undeniable small tender wellings of paternal feeling, these were in some way serving my lost little girl.

Did I let Brinda in as a way of *changing my life to preserve the bond*? I wasn't so articulate about it at the time. We never act authentically if we have this level of self-consciousness. And yet, looking back, that doesn't seem too far off the mark.

When she arrived, there was a short, quiet interlude, but as though under pressure. My guess was that she felt that she should show some interest in me and my project, out of politeness, rather than plunge straight away into her own story, even if that was what she was most eager to do.

"I can't remember," she said, gathering her hair back off her shoulders, "was the other night the first time you met Venkat Uncle?"

"I had a long interview with him, on Monday." I didn't want to think about Venkat.

"Was he like he was the night of the memorial?"

"He seems to need to follow a train of thought without interruption."

"He spends a lot of time alone."

That could also be said of me. I needed to move the focus to her. "Are you anxious, about the trial outcome?"

She chewed her lower lip, though her nervous mannerisms had decreased slightly. She emanated a thoughtfulness, now, more than anxiety. She wore a purple summer dress, pretty on her.

"I probably was, right at the start. Excited, maybe, more than anxious. I thought it was an open-and-shut case! So naive: nearly twenty years to come to this point—it's got to be complicated. I'm not sure the outcome will prove much. But they have to convict them, right? After all this time, why would they bring it to trial unless conviction was a sure thing? How would the government live it down?"

I nodded. This was how most of us felt.

"And I think it might help people like Venkat Uncle to feel some small measure of resolution." Her eyes suddenly looked huge and strange. "I feel bad saying this. He lost everything. But he's a pathetically sad person."

"We should talk about you," I said, bluntly, but it was what both of us wanted.

"I suppose, eh? I leave day after tomorrow." She smiled and sighed. "So problem numero uno is Dev, everything we were going through. And then I came to that resolution, this spring, told myself to stop hoping against hope that anything about him would change." She bit a cuticle, looked at it, sat on her hand. "And then, last week, here in Lohikarma, I ran into an old friend. Adrian. You met him, remember?"

The young man at the coffee shop.

* * *

A high school buddy from the smart kids' crowd: school newspaper, chemistry club, skinny wiseacres, quasi-misfits. Adrian had gone west, after high school, apprenticed as a boat builder while ambling through an undergraduate degree. Now he was finishing medical school in Toronto. He was to have spent this summer in Europe with his girlfriend—he referred to the girlfriend at their first meeting, while Brinda somehow didn't manage to mention Dev—but now she had gone on the trip without him while he came back to Lohikarma to help his parents. His father, a fruit farmer, was dying of cancer.

It had been ten years since he and Brinda had last seen each other. He had the same curly hair and green eyes, but the solidity of adulthood suited his frame, which had been gangly and awkward when they were teens. She recalled a little crush on him back then, but she had little crushes on lots of boys. Doubtful that many turned out as nice as this.

Initial conversation was easy, bridging topics old and new, and he asked if they might get together sometime. He had left Lohikarma so young that he had only a few friends still in town.

The next night, they met at an old drinkers' haven that Brinda had frequented in university, The Minter's Arms, one of the last High Street strongholds. The bar was brightly lit; the carpet red and gold with themes of empire.

Adrian looked across the room as he sipped his beer. "Play pool, by any chance?"

"I have done," Brinda said with a note of calculation.

"You're probably really good," Adrian said.

"That wasn't what I meant," she said, and *thump-tha-thump* she felt she had to wreck this, now, *wreck it!*—at least a little. "My—my husband and I play sometimes." Her mouth felt tense and she folded her lips in and pursed them. "I really am not very good at all. But then, he's a bit of a sore loser." She breathed through her nose.

Adrian lifted his beer glass to look through it. They were in their thirties. Everyone had a history. Friends had died. Others had had babies early and divorced. Others had ended up happy—fancy that. Life was approaching its midpoint and not becoming any more transparent with the years.

"And what does he do?"

"Lab tech. University of Alberta."

He nodded, she nodded.

"Let's play," she said. "Table just came free."

"I'll get quarters. You go stake it out." They got up and went in opposite directions.

* * *

"Will your husband come to Baltimore with you?" he asked, later, in the car. She had walked downtown to meet him and now he was dropping her at home. His parents still lived out on the farm, a twenty-minute drive from town.

"Nope."

He waited a sec. "Separation's no fun."

"I guess not."

She asked nothing about his girlfriend, and chided herself for this later as she replayed the evening, chin on her knees in the window seat of her childhood room.

✳ ✳ ✳

The next night, the phone rang. Because she was in the kitchen, she answered it and was already walking into the family room to hand it to her parents when she realized it was Adrian, calling for her.

"I took my dad to chemo today," he told her as she mounted the stairs to her room. "Awful, you know? But the alternative, dying of the thing, quick and hard, you have to assume that would be worse. I don't know."

"It must be so difficult."

"My mother looks almost as broken down as he does."

"Are you thinking about staying on?" She adjusted the window seat cushions as she sat.

"They haven't asked me to." He sighed. "It would be such a huge shift. Maybe if I were done med school, but now, and with my girl-friend . . ."

Was Brinda supposed to ask about her now? Her cheeks burned and she lifted the phone away a little to lay her face against the window glass. "Is she in med school too?"

"No. She teaches at U of T. Art history."

"Ah." Power duo. "Nice."

"I guess."

Where was he? She wanted to ask, but thought it would sound as though she were asking what he was wearing. She wondered what he was wearing. She pictured him in boxer shorts, absent-mindedly rubbing his chest. She pictured herself running a finger along the waist of the shorts.

"How are your parents?" he asked.

"So far so good." She got up to turn out the light so that she could see the night sky instead of her own reflection. "I don't know what I would do if they had a crisis."

"You have a sister, right?"

"In Vancouver."

"Does she have kids or anything?"

"No. I don't have the sense that she wants kids." Ranjani had al-ways seemed above that. Children, children . . . the thought made Brin-da salivate. "She's been living with someone for five years or so."

Brinda heard a fridge door open and shut. He was in forest-green boxer shorts and bare feet, she thought, getting a beer, the dark of the house growing stale around him, his exhausted parents in separate beds.

"My parents have been in a situation for years where they sort of look after a family friend," she told him.

"Oh?"

She heard what sounded like a beer cap and something in her surged, thinking she must also be right about the shorts.

"You remember the Air India crash? 1985. The trial's . . ."

"Yeah, hell, yeah."

"The wife and son of one of our closest family friends were killed. Did you know that? We were in high school."

"Oh, yeah. It was . . . Sundar, right? I remember, I asked you about it."

"Did you?"

"Didn't you tell me you were related?"

"Distantly, to Sundar's dad. He's a stats prof. He's kind of a tough person to be around, I suppose it's not nice to say, but he's always been a bit of a boor, self-righteous. Though it's a bit different since he lost his family."

"How old was Sundar?"

"Twenty-one. Five years older than me. He would have been forty this year. Funny to think."

"Were you close with him?"

"Yes. I don't know. Close? We grew up with him."

"Hmm. And so your parents look after his dad? How's he doing?"

"I can't really tell. He still comes over for dinner once a week and my parents look in on him."

"How's he feeling about the trial?"

"Obsessed with it. Can't eat, can't work. My dad's thinking he should apply to the U for more stress leave. Harbord's been super indulgent: the benefits of tenure, as your girlfriend might learn." She realized how that sounded. "Not that, I mean . . ."

"No, don't worry about it."

"Sorry." She thought it his privilege to determine where the conversation would go next.

"It's nice to have you here to talk to," he said. His voice made her think of unvarnished pine. She imagined he might smell like that, too, early in the morning. "I hope you don't mind."

"Of course not. Suppose it's a bit late to call Europe." That sounded sarcastic and she didn't think that was what she intended, but it couldn't hurt to put up a bit of a barrier. Last time she checked, they had phones in Europe. And why wasn't she talking to Dev? Because she couldn't think of anything to tell him.

"Too late to call Edmonton too?" he asked.

"It is," she said gravely. "Yes."

She sat in the window seat long after they had said good night. *Just one kiss*. That's all she wanted. Dev's farewell pecks were always exactly that, no more: his lips pushed out into a beak as though to peck her away. Brinda's deprivation was abhorrent; her need so undignified. *Why can't I get just one kiss?* The Violent Femmes song from long ago thrashed merrily into her head. One slow kiss. She sat by the window imagining Adrian's light, piney smell, his slim, happy-sad looks, his intelligent Azorean mouth.

✳ ✳ ✳

The next night, June 21, there was a solstice concert in Willard Park, a musician both Brinda and Adrian liked and neither paid attention to once they were there. They had agreed to a picnic and each brought wine in a Thermos as a surprise, and they laughed without saying what was making them laugh, their potluck public seduction, nowhere to go from there but childhood rooms in houses where aging parents drew aging breaths.

They drank the white first, fast, from cups, amid the crowds, then walked around the lake with the red, trading the Thermos back and forth in the indulgent dusk. The longest day of the year. They found a place to watch the sun go down. The sun rested on the horizon a moment for a joke. Brinda laughed, again, and Adrian kissed her. One. Slow. Kiss.

Which was so nice it made her giddy, and they kissed some more, until the dark was complete and they couldn't quite see the other's eyes and one said, *Perhaps we should go*, and the other said, *Yes, perhaps we should.* When he dropped her at home, she felt him waiting for her to speak, and in fact she wanted to speak but couldn't figure out what to say.

✳ ✳ ✳

Tuesday, June 22, they went out for dinner. They dressed up a bit, and drove up along the lake to a well-known restaurant a ways out of town, where they sat at an outdoor table on the waterfront.

Brinda thought of her affair with the married Englishman. While it lasted, it had generated its own justifications, their attraction sparking off his marital unhappiness. Months later, when Brinda was back in Canada, his wife had phoned her, wanting to "ask some questions." Her husband was in the room, she said, presumably not answering to her satisfaction. *What a debacle!* she thought, recalling it now.

Adrian looked at her. "Hello?"

She smiled but didn't know how to restart the conversation, which had been halting and superficial, though not uncomfortably so, all evening.

"I don't want you to feel guilty, about what happened," he said at last. A pelican flew along the lake behind him and landed on a pier.

Was she glad he was talking about it? She had thought so many things since last night that she no longer had anything to say. How to choose?

"I don't think we've done anything wrong. Not yet, anyway," he said, smiling. Oh God, that mouth! "It's totally natural you would feel uncertain, this huge change coming up." Was he even talking to her? "Kirsten and I, we've had some rough patches lately too, so I admit to feeling not entirely stable either, as you might have guessed."

It would not have been hard, that night, to grab a blanket from the trunk of the car and spread it in some isolated spot along the lake, or even stop in at one of the many cabin motels that they passed. They both had known this when they decided to leave town for dinner: a step in the direction of full flight. Who suggested it? Each might have thought it was the other.

But the night-before giddiness did not prevail. Brinda said only, "In my defence, all I can say is that Dev and I have a big problem." She stopped there. That was all she had rehearsed as an outlet to her guilt. It was the first time she had so much as alluded to their problem, to anyone. Her tongue tasted rusty.

Adrian waited, and as her silence congealed to a full stop, they finished their meal and drove back, not-home, not-not-home.

✳ ✳ ✳

"Why did you never tell anyone?" I asked.

"I thought it was between Dev and me, I suppose," she said. "It never occurred to me to tell. Maybe out of loyalty to him. Maybe because it was humiliating. Does it matter why? I called you the morning after Adrian and I had dinner. I hadn't been able to sleep all night, and I was having weird physical symptoms, stress, I guess."

"Do you still? Do you need to see a doctor?"

"I don't think so. I'm already feeling a bit better, just talking about it."

"Have you seen him since the night before the memorial?"

"Yes. He called me yesterday."

"I can't stop thinking about you," he told her, "as nervous as I am about seeing you. Can we meet up?"

Brinda was far from certain she wanted an affair—she still felt she owed it to Dev to give him an ultimatum, a last chance to shape up—but she lacked the willpower to deny herself the pleasures of Adrian's company.

They met beside the lake.

"Do you have sex with him?" Adrian asked.

There was a bench beside her and she sat on it as though she had been pushed.

"How did you know?" she asked. *Who else knows? Is it so obvious?*

"I never would have guessed if you hadn't—well, aren't sexual problems the most common marital issue?"

She buried her face in her hands, then looked up at the sky, breathing the lake air. "No, it's money, isn't it? I was hoping you'd think compulsive gambling. Really? The most common problem?"

"I had a little fling, shortly before I met Kirsten, with a woman who had been married twenty years. She and her husband had had sex four times. No kidding. Or that's what she told me. She didn't seem unreliable. They conceived two of those four times."

"Quite the success rate. Maybe he was scared to have any more kids."

"I think he just didn't like sex. Some people don't. Physical intimacy isn't for everyone."

"Sure, but then he should say that, right, own up to it?"

Adrian nodded, cautious. "I suspect he likes being married."

"Nice deal for him."

"And maybe he doesn't really know what the problem is."

"Hard to find out if you don't want to know. Dev implies, most of the time, that it's me," she said, checking Adrian's reaction.

He nuzzled her forehead. "Dubious."

"D'you think I should have an affair?"

He winced. "Not without me."

She glared into his eyes, her nose nearly touching his, and frowned. "You're not available."

He kissed her and shivered. "If you say so."

They behaved toward one another, that afternoon, as though they were lovers out in public, exhibiting a restrained show of physical affection that looked like evidence of a deeper, stronger, private love but was in fact the barest venting of the tension between them, as of a tiny train whistle atop a steam engine. On parting, they made no further plans.

That night, Brinda went out to hear a band. A friend of hers owned a ski shop, and a clique of Québecois ski bums, recognizing him, joined them at the bar. One caught Brinda's eye with his blue eyes and biceps. Could he refill her glass? When he stretched out his arm to take it, she shocked herself by tucking a finger under his T-shirt sleeve, lifting it to check out his tattoo. His date appeared out of nowhere, at his other side. They didn't talk again, until he sought Brinda out to say goodbye, kissing her on both cheeks and saying, "The summer is young. We will see each other again."

The summer is young? He couldn't have been out of his twenties. Men never flirted with her. She snorted with laughter as she returned to the dance floor.

* * *

"It's like something has broken open," she told me.

I had already noticed. A *shekina* curled around her, a mystic breeze. Her hair fell over her bare shoulders; her brow was full and light, her lips full and dark. I was surprised she didn't have to beat men, and—why not—women too, away on the street.

How quickly she was progressing! I should have known to distrust that rapidity, but instead unwisely believed it to be evidence that she knew what she must do.

There is a reason doctors are not supposed to treat their own loved ones: if there is a problem, they will not see it because they don't want to believe it is there (unless they conjure non-existent problems out of worry). I had told her I wasn't doing therapy with her, that she should see me as an older friend without a social stake in her situation. I never told her how she reminded me of Asha, though that, too, was already changing. The better I got to know B, the more distinct she seemed from A.

Was I finding a new, real attachment to overwrite the morbid, old one? A better way to *change my life*?

"I'm seeing Adrian tonight, to say goodbye," she told me. "The worst choice I've ever had to make."

"But it is not your choice alone," I told her. I felt certain she would leave Dev, though she wasn't ready to admit it. She would return to Edmonton and confront him first. I had to think whether to ask her about that the next day, our final session.

She noticed a book in my window seat: Yann Martel's *Self*, the Sunday book of a couple of weeks prior. "Are you liking it?" In the novel, a boy in late adolescence spontaneously transforms into a female. "I love how he makes the impossible seem plausible."

"You yourself hid such a big secret for so long." I opened the door. "Maybe one of your friends was born as a mermaid, or an alien."

"Yeah. Maybe Dev was born a woman."

"Women like sex," I reminded her.

She laughed. "You're right, he's an alien."

"Aliens don't like sex?" I asked.

"Only with mermaids," she said, and trotted down the stairs.

$\mathcal{B}$y the time I finished my notes on our session, I was itching to leave my stuffy, thought-filled apartment. It was the time of evening when slats of sun blasted through my picture windows, when there was no comfortable place to sit. The air in my flat was burning and dancing with dust.

I opened the door, inhaled—air crisp and dry. Checked the sky—blue and clear. Twice now, I had toted my rain jacket up and down town only to carry it home again, dry. I left it on its peg.

I had a craving to walk at the lakeshore. This was yet another way that Lohikarma might have been good or bad for me, I couldn't decide: I loved walking in the town so much that I did it every day, sneezing at my knees' insistent protests. It was slightly easier to descend the slope of the road and ascend via the stairs. I kept my eyes down as I descended—the only thing worse for my knees than climbing is falling, and one excellent way to fall is looking up while walking down.

I was thinking about a bench I liked to sit on. Painted red, facing west, toward the bend in the lake where the mountains hid it, with a little plaque that read "A Place of Tranquility Dedicated to Victims of Crime and Tragedy." Maudlin. Obvious. Exactly what one wants, sometimes, when no one is looking.

Snow on a far peak. Goose turds on the lawn. Wild rose bush at the water's edge. Child on a blow-up alligator. Birds in the trees, those dying generations at their song.

Turgid, clay-coloured clouds—here they came. Their unpredictability was the most predictable thing about them. I rose and turned my back on the lake. Behind me, a splash, as of a boy falling out of the sky. The rain began.

The weather was as crazy as everyone else in this town. I exaggerate, but truly I'm like a cat, I hate getting wet, and I was so looking forward to this stroll.

As I steamed, I saw a couple hurrying through the downpour. Seth and Lakshmi, with two umbrellas.

"Here," Seth said, holding his out over my head. "Take it. You haven't learned yet, eh?"

I opened my mouth to blast him, but who could do that to Seth? I was happy to see him, and his beautiful wife.

"We were on our way home," he said. "Do you want to come?"

I looked at Lakshmi. She wasn't repeating the invitation, as custom dictated. Should I have said I was busy? But I wasn't. I wanted to go home with them.

Seth insisted I keep his green plaid umbrella while he and Lakshmi huddled in lockstep under her bell-shaped, floral one. It hid their heads, making conversation difficult, so while Seth and I shouted at each other as we went up the municipally maintained stairs—"Careful," he warned, "slippery when wet!"—Lakshmi had an excuse to say little.

As we arrived at their gate, the rain frazzled to a stop and the sun re-emerged. We all smiled at each other and shook out the brollies.

Seth ferreted out that I had not yet eaten, and Lakshmi started pulling containers out of the fridge to fix me a plate: rice, *kootu kozhambu*, cabbage curry with coconut.

"A pukka Tam-Brahm thali!" I exclaimed. They looked uncertain. "It's become fashionable, Tamil Brahmin cookery. Kids sent from Chennai to work in Delhi and Bombay banks imported their *pattis* and *mamis* to make the food they missed. When they invited their friends, it caught on."

"It's very healthy," Seth said modestly. "Vegetarian and so on." He fetched me a glass of water, then asked his wife, "Is Brinda home?"

Lakshmi widened her eyes, shrugged one shoulder. Preoccupation tensed her face as Seth went to the bottom of the stairs to call up, "Brinda?"

"She must have gone out while we were walking," Lakshmi said to him as she put my plate in the microwave. Not surprising that she was attuned to Brinda's distress, even if the girl wasn't giving her parents any details.

"And how goes your work?" Seth asked, putting the plate in front of me.

Lakshmi added, "I imagine it's tough going."

I had to agree. "And tough to assess, at this stage."

"Have you met with Venkat again?" Seth asked.

The food was delicious and I wished they would hush and let me eat.

"I haven't," I told him. "He was very forthcoming, that one time, but I'd be surprised if he'll see me again."

"I'll arrange it," Seth assured me.

I didn't respond.

It was a nice opportunity, me, at their table, with the both of them. Lakshmi, like Venkat, had not volunteered to be interviewed, but here I was again, in her house at Seth's invitation, and she was not acting terribly guarded. Perhaps I could draw Seth out on the remainder of the story. We had left off, I reminded him now, on the verge of Venkat's return to Canada, after spreading Sundar's ashes in the Kaveri River.

Seth and Lakshmi nodded. "He spent a few weeks at the Shivashakti ashram, I think, and then maybe a month or so with his mother," Seth began.

"Yes, he came back to Canada mid-August or so," Lakshmi confirmed.

"Bala, that Vancouver friend Sita and Sundar stayed with before they left, drove him back."

"Long drive," I said, thinking that I would be making it at the end of this week.

"Yes, and it would seem even longer given the company," said Seth. Lakshmi scolded him with a gasp, but didn't disagree.

* * *

The Sethuratnams had gotten ready to host both men that night, and assumed they might be putting Venkat up for some time, but when Seth greeted them and asked to carry their bags in, they told him no.

"Venkat has said he wants to go stay in his own house," Bala explained, jogging in place to wake his cramped body, flinging arms out to crack his elbows in the mountain air. "One is not used to sitting so long! I will take him after the meal and sleep there tonight." He was tall, lean, exacting. And a Shivashakti devotee, which might have been how he and Venkat met.

As Venkat and Bala entered ahead of him, Seth murmured the news to Lakshmi. She was skeptical, as was he: Venkat's house had been left exactly as it was before the crash. How could it be healthy for him to go back to it?

Lakshmi had laid out an *idli* buffet, and as Bala headed to the dining table, Seth approached Venkat. "Why on earth do you want to go back home already?" he said softly. "Take it easy, stay here for awhile. I'll take you there when you're ready and we'll . . ." He had to stop here because, as he and Lakshmi had discussed, they had no idea what Venkat's plans were.

"I want to stay at my house, Seth," Venkat replied. "All I have now are their memories."

* * *

"You could see he was a man who had been crushed, emptied," Lakshmi said now. "It struck us even more, after not having seen him for a couple of months. We were already starting to get on with life, a little. We had our kids and work, and so on. Isn't that right?"

Seth nodded.

"But Venkat returned here to nothing. Worse than nothing, I suppose."

"All those reminders," Seth said, "but he wanted to be back among them."

I imagined him saying that to Lakshmi that night, on Venkat's return, as he watched his wife get ready for bed, her nightgown frill scooping the smooth expanse of her sternum.

The scent of Nivea cream crossed to him from her cheekbones, knuckles, elbows: all her sharp points. Seth thought of Venkat, in his own bedroom, which would be cold and unanimated by any feminine spirit. Would he turn on Sita's bedside lamp, open a jar of cold cream and hold it under his nose, maybe even leave it open in the bathroom, along with her jewellery box? Would he put his nose among the hangers, drizzle a little of her shampoo on the pillow?

How long would Venkat be able to recall Sita's own scent? Had he already forgotten it?

Seth felt enveloped as his wife got under the covers. He put his arms around her waist, his unshaven muzzle in her neck. He trailed his nose down between her breasts; the nightgown pulled down easily to let him kiss them. It pulled up easily to let him kiss her belly. Those other scents carry you to this one; you fall to your knees before its regal advance, its crazy-making, uncatchable variety.

Erotic reverie: I was tingling lightly. It had been a long time. I shifted in my chair, swallowed hard, uncrossed and recrossed my legs.

Seth and Lakshmi were talking, not to me, to each other, about how their daughters confided in Lakshmi (but not everything, as I knew), about how women are trained for empathy. While I saw in my mind's eye Seth watching Lakshmi as she curved, sleeping, through the dark. The mood of terror had subsided and yet his need for Shivashakti remained as pressing as ever. He had not missed a satsang all summer.

"I have a recurring nightmare," Seth admitted to me now.

It went like this: He fell asleep, almost. He wakened, falling, *gasp*, *thump*, on the pillow. Not uncommon. Happened to him all his life, as it did to others. Except that, since the bomb, it always came with the same nightmare: he was naked on a clifftop. Dark night, rubble beneath his toes, arms outstretched, a breeze in his face, on his back. Pushed or lifted, he toppled into the void.

"I get it once every year or so," he said.

"Really?" Lakshmi asked. "You never told me."

"I did," Seth answered.

"You never," she said.

"I did," he said. "Years ago. You forgot."

"Maybe, if you only told me years ago."

"I assumed you would remember, so why would I tell you again?"

* * *

Seth felt a keen disappointment in Venkat and Bala's early departure that night: he had been anticipating, more than he wanted to admit even to himself, conversation on the subject of their now-shared God. He had left the latest lecture compendium on the coffee table, but the men never made it into the living room.

Still, he couldn't completely restrain himself, and had asked Bala, over dinner, "I recently acquired Shivashakti's lectures from last year. Have you read it yet?"

"No, no," said Bala. "But of course we attend satsang every week, so we never miss a lecture. When did you become interested?"

Lakshmi glared across the food at Seth.

"I'm not sure when . . ." Seth kept his gaze averted from his wife, on Bala. "Well, was there any one address or topic that you specially liked?

I'm very taken with his ideas on family and community life. To think he could have such wisdom on both though he himself has neither!"

"You could as well say he has both." Bala prissily dabbed small bites of idli in ghee and melagaipodi, making Seth feel bizarrely compelled to stuff himself. "His devotees are family and community."

"*Ahmama.* True." Seth wagged his head in agreement with Bala, and wagged it again in appreciation of his wife. "Lakshmi: *mallipoo* idlis. Wonderful." They were. Nothing like Lakshmi's idlis, particularly with eggplant *sambar*. He addressed Bala with renewed cheer. "And the best part is that it is eternal, isn't it? There is no death, in his family. Because it is not the individual who loves or is loved by him. It is the mind of God."

"I think it is correct to say the individual devotee is loving him." Bala tossed bites of banana into his mouth without touching his lips, Brahmin-style, and folded the peel neatly onto his plate. "But we are also part and parcel of his makeup."

"Yes, yes." Seth licked his fingers, then his whole palm, as noisily as he could. What did Venkat make of this? Was he even listening?

* * *

It was Seth who took the lead in the work of assisting Venkat to re-enter his former life. He asked a hundred questions about his routine in the morning: What time did he get up on weekdays? How did he get up? What did he do first? What did he do next? And together, step by step, they worked out a new routine, without the sounds of Sita first readying the puja corner for his prayers and then preparing his breakfast. Venkat would set his alarm clock. He would mix an oatmeal packet into a bowl of water and put it in the microwave before sitting to pray, so that it would be ready when he was done.

Did Venkat say, *Seth, I'm not a baby*? No. As an Indian man and a psychologist, I will attest that there are very few useful generalizations to be made about the Indian male psyche, but this may be one: Indian men are raised to be cared for. An Indian woman might have told such a friend as Seth to back off, but Venkat meekly accepted this instruction and Seth's monitoring, in the first few weeks of the semester, to make sure that he was following the routines Seth had devised. In those weeks, everyone wanted to visit and bring food. Venkat's already-full freezer was packed to the hinges until the Sethuratnams, the unofficial but undisputed organizers of his life, asked friends if they could hold off, please, until the stores were depleted.

One other generalization to be made about Indians—they don't tiptoe around death. You could even say that about me, as hyper-perceptive and socially hapless as I am. This is not to say that Indians' ways of coping up are better. There are the hysterics, who will fall down and thrash for you so that you are numbed, the depths of your own emotion unable to compete with the heights of theirs. There are whole communities that insist on immediate remarriage. Many of the women bereaved in the Sikh pogroms complained of being remarried to a relative of their late husband's in such rapid order they felt they were supposed to throw their love and grief out the window on the way to the wedding. But to the extent that Indians have failed fully to progress into secular modernism, we understand that death is part of life, while books about Westerners and grief all talk of people who stayed away from the bereaved, possibly out of fear of becoming sad, possibly because they don't know what to say and fear saying the wrong thing.

Lakshmi also raised the question I had been waiting to ask the families on my next round of interviews: their thoughts on the bombing as an act of brown-on-brown terrorism that a (nearly) white government failed to prevent or even properly to investigate.

"I wondered at the time if *that* was why the white-Canadian colleagues avoided Venkat," she said, her elbows on the glass-top table. "Maybe they were afraid, if they talked to him, he would blame them."

"Some Indians also felt ashamed that the conflict in India had spilled over here," Seth said. "You can feel you're all being lumped together."

"You felt isolated?" I asked.

I remembered this myself—I had lived in Canada from 1969 to 1983, and every new person I met asked where I was from and whether I agreed with his assessment of some Indian restaurant's authenticity. To Rosslyn's family, I was always intractably foreign. Her mother was shocked that I ate meat; her father asked me about suttee. He asked her, in private, how she could be sure I didn't have another wife and family back home. When she told me, we laughed, but he must have read a news story that frightened him. Poor man: he was concerned for his daughter. And they were never unkind to me.

Seth nodded slowly. "I haven't felt like that, for a long time."

"Is that so?" I hadn't been back long enough to tell what had changed.

"Yes, I think I mentioned. You raise your kids here, they feel more Canadian than Indian, they marry Canadians, or . . ."

His voice faded there, quickly and strangely, and I was convinced that he had somehow sniffed out what was happening with Brinda. My best guess, in retrospect, was that his faltering was related in fact to his *other* daughter, who had called that afternoon with unsettling news.

"For me, it has been Shivashakti," he went on, his voice strengthening, his back straightening, "more than anything, who has helped me feel at home here. Our centre has members from all over—Indian, not Indian, it makes no difference—and the community service means you reach out, you get to know people in a way that is impossible otherwise. My guru gave me the way to see and feel how I belong here."

Lakshmi had straightened too. "But even those of us who are not devotees have found a way to feel that we belong too."

I mentioned her eyes, right? They blazed.

I helped them remember what they had been speaking of when I had diverted them: settling Venkat back into his life.

* * *

The only subject of disagreement (on this, they could agree) had been his house. Seth tried to suggest that Venkat come to stay at their house while he and Lakshmi packed away Sundar and Sita's things and shifted the rooms around a little. But Venkat was categorical. The house stayed as it was.

Venkat's courses that fall were ones he had taught before, Statistical Methods, an intro course that rotated among faculty members, and Theory of Experiment Design. Neither was particularly challenging.

Lakshmi and Seth asked him to come every Friday night to dinner. He complied, though Seth usually had to remind him, either catching him at the office before he left or, on a couple of occasions, phoning him when, after waiting some time, they realized he had forgotten.

Also, at least one night a week, Seth would take Venkat to a Shivashakti satsang. It was odd to feel that he was guiding Venkat back into his own fold. Seth was also uncomfortably aware of having ranked the rest of his fellow devotees according to his own arbitrary standards of temperament and authenticity.

Daisy and Irene were in the middle somewhere. "Where's your pretty wife?" one or the other would often ask. Maybe if he told Lakshmi they made him uncomfortable, she would come with him more often. Carsten, the leonine young man who read the lecture the first time Seth came, was on the lower end. Seth sensed his ambition and didn't much like the way Carsten talked down to him. Very near the bottom was the Reverend Jonathan Dunn, a Unitarian pastor whom Seth found suspicious for no good reason. One night, he had persuaded Lakshmi and his daughters to come to satsang. On the drive home, he wondered aloud whether Dunn attended every kind of service in town. "Is he hoping to get people to come to his church?" Lakshmi and the girls replied that the Unitarian philosophy might be closer to their own even than Shivashakti's.

"What?" He turned around to look at them, three captivating, dusk-lit strangers. "You would go to that guy's church but I have to beg you to come to satsang with me?"

"It's nothing personal, Dad," Brinda said.

He would think about this exchange for years. *Nothing personal? What the hell did that mean? How could it not be personal?*

It was an irony of the worst sort that those devotees most visibly buoyed by a surging elation in their Lord were the ones Seth least liked to talk to. The ones he liked best—Nick Copeland and Kaj Halonen—for all their steadiness and dedication, tended not to effuse in the way Seth himself wanted and needed. He had pinned some hopes on the Indian families. Maybe, he thought, he needed people who knew what his ideas of God had been before. But they, too, disappointed him.

Unlikely as it seemed, he wondered now if Venkat might understand. Venkat so often came across as insensitive, mostly because he was preoccupied with his own moral agendas. But he had also, occasionally, surprised Seth with an insight, proving not so absent as Seth's women tended to think. And Venkat had travelled to Shivashaktipurum, many times, had sprinkled Sundar's ashes there and prayed and meditated at the lotus feet of his Lord. What did he find there? What did he feel? Seth asked him one night on their way home, trying not to sound too eager, nor merely curious.

"Did you have an audience with Him?"

"I did," Venkat said, glancing at him, then back out the window at the purpling dusk, perhaps smelling the approach of autumn. His face in the half-light seemed illuminated in pixels, shifting dots that emphasized, if anything, the rigidity of his features.

Seth waited. It seemed rude to ask what Shivashakti had said, though he wished Venkat would volunteer it. *What was it like to meet your God in person?*

"You should go, Seth," Venkat said. Insight or prescription? It didn't make a difference. It was what Seth wanted to hear.

"I will," Seth said, leaning over the steering wheel to release a sudden stiffness in his back. He had to go. There was no other way. He was expecting from his fellow devotees what could only be found in himself and in his God. He would go. The only question was when.

It was nearly dark outside, that's how long I stayed: much longer than I had intended. Such a strange bubblement of feelings, to be with them— I was stung by the fullness and inviolability of their love, but wasn't it exactly that which made them so satisfying to be with?

Still, I could stand it no longer, and they had work in the morning.

Seth wanted to drive me home—he seemed to spend half of his time ferrying people about town or trying to—but I refused in favour of a starlit stroll. I stumbled only twice, unable to look away from the inner dome of heaven.

$\mathcal{I}$ had already stayed in Lohikarma several days longer than planned and would leave the following afternoon for Vancouver, with less than twenty-four hours until my first appointment there. But what could I do? Brinda needed to see me once more before she left.

"You said goodbye to Adrian last night?" I asked her gently.

She thumbed a tear from the corner of her eye and twitched unhappily. "Guess what else? My younger sister, Ranjani, called yesterday afternoon, to tell us she's pregnant." Her voice tore a little on the word. "We had no idea she wanted babies. She never gave in to a big wedding, the way I did. She does what she wants—she *knows* what she wants—and it turns out fine!" Urgency entered her face. "Tell me what's wrong with me."

I felt a tremor of caution. "There's nothing wrong with you!" I had no real way of knowing this, but I was now her friend, or hoped I was. This is the sort of thing friends say, isn't it?

"I've been with Dev for ten years. Why did I put up with it? Did I want it this way?"

"You and I have known each other such a short time . . ." I was hedging, as surely she could tell.

"Give me something."

When the child asks, it is hard not to give, even against one's better instincts. I had so little practice resisting.

"Okay," I said. "I have known you only a week. You understand?" She nodded. "You must take whatever I say with great skepticism. This is going to sound simplistic."

She tried to appear circumspect, though her eagerness was clear.

"Dev, as you already know, may be in many ways the more vexing and intriguing case." Now she looked hurt. "Not a more interesting person! You seem to be the better thinker, more gracious, more complex."

"You only have my side."

"Indeed. His problem sounds more complicated and more difficult to unravel."

"One of the reasons I thought to talk to you is that you're Indian. Although Dev grew up here. Do you think that being Indian has anything to do with it?"

"I can hardly begin to guess. I have never encountered another case like this. Homosexuals married to women, yes—but you're quite sure that's not his problem?"

She scratched her head. "I caught him." She looked away. "Masturbating. Once. With a lingerie catalogue that had randomly come in the mail."

This seemed convincing. Unless he had been trying to convince himself. "How did you react?"

"He was embarrassed, but I was relieved. Evidence of interest in sex! I tried to talk to him, but it never really went anywhere."

"You mentioned some immaturity, in other areas?" She affirmed this, but I raised my hands—I could say little more about Dev. "I would have been curious to talk to him."

"What about couples therapy?" she asked.

"Have you tried this?"

"I could never get him to go."

"It could be good."

"I'll try again when I get home. But you were going to tell me why you think I stuck with him."

I was. "With a grain of salt, yes? Your first and most significant erotic attachment—after the parents, of course, but we're not speaking in those terms—was to Sundar. His death, at the moment when you were coming into a sense of yourself as a maturing sexual being, at sixteen, a rich age, in more ways than I need to enumerate—his death made you terrified of forming a similar sexual attachment to anyone else. You idealized Sundar. How could you possibly find a replacement? You can't, and perhaps you weren't sure you wanted to. You stumbled into this relationship that was structured, by Dev's inadequacy, to hold you back from the deepest levels of attachment and intimacy. But now time itself has worked on you, through your frustration, through these years of giving love. Now you want, you are ready for, a full sexual relationship, for babies, with all the emotional risk that entails, terrifying as it may be." I wasn't positive of that last. I wasn't positive of any of it. I just wanted to give her what she wanted. I changed tack. "So much in our lives is governed by strange forms of luck—how on earth did you happen to find this puzzling man, Dev, among so many others who surely would have been happy to find themselves in his place? Adrian, to name one?"

"Adrian was doing his own thing, then."

"He was. Again, luck, destiny—we cannot make choices until life presents them to us. And this level of pathology, yours, what I have described, this is not at all unusual. It doesn't need to hold you back. Whatever the sources—here, we depart from orthodoxies—they needn't govern your behaviour from here forward. And perhaps I'm entirely wrong in my hasty, forced"—I raised my eyebrows at her and she smiled—"'diagnosis' of your problems. Perhaps there are myriad, small, forgotten factors in your history, too many and too minute to be retained, much less recounted, and these are what made you vulnerable to such a marriage. I don't know you well enough to know.

"The reasons you stayed were also good ones. Loyalty. Hope. Dev's own virtues, the way you enjoyed one another's company, the way he made you feel comfortable until you were—as I think you are now— able to feel comfortable without him." I winced. I had gone too far.

She jumped at the opening. "You think I should leave him?"

I looked at her reproachfully, and she apologized.

"My parents will be heartbroken," Brinda said. "They thought this marriage was perfect for me. What if he can still change?"

"That would be wonderful," I said. I reached to take her extended hands—a gesture foreign to me, nearly artificial—yet I did it.

"It's been so useful talking to you," she said, and I was deeply discomfited, then, by a sexual buzz. Something like transference, but disturbing and hateful in a way it never was in therapy, where it was natural, expected, contained.

I took a little breath, acknowledging now the degree of denial I had invoked to get me through these intense days. A blooming rose such as Brinda, baring herself—figuratively—and I, racked with deprivation and longing—could I admit it now? Desire was felt. Nothing to fret over.

I shook it off. Withdrew my hands.

"I admire your loyalty," I told her. Her eyes were burning and impenetrable. Was she angry? At me? "The love you have given him

sounds like the sort you might give a child, the indulgence, the patience.
You are very strong."

"Maybe someday I'll have a child to love like that."

There was something fierce in her. I longed to know the particular
brightness of her future, to be in it. As an uncle, only that.

"Will you keep in touch with me?" I asked her.

We stood and embraced, but it was not so fraught, so ambiguous,
now. The moment had cooled and this was a simpler affection, easier on
an old man's nerves.

FALL 2004

Death will come and will have your eyes.
—Cesare Pavese

*F*rom Lohikarma, I continued on to the west coast, did my interviews there, and made another attempt to drop in on the trial. It had vanished entirely from the "Glib and Stale," as Brinda called the *Globe and Mail*. "Canada's National Newspaper," the masthead declared, but everyone knew it would be better called "Toronto's National Newspaper." The *Globe*'s coverage of the trial confirmed—and cultivated—a national indifference to the events transpiring in the Vancouver courtroom.

I admit that I had been craving information. But after only a day back in that courtroom, I started to fear both saturation and addiction. A team of defence lawyers was working to seed doubts about whether the accused could have been in Vancouver at the time the plot was being hatched. The witnesses—drug dealers, thugs, informants, FBI agents, illicit lovers—were both banal and fascinating to me. But did I need to know what was happening in the courtroom? I went back the next day, feeding my rage and helplessness, and also my desire to hear more, more, more. This time, when I left, I resolved not to return.

The bombers' code phrase for the plot still echoed in my head, as it had for years now. "Ready to write the book?"

"Ready to write the book."

I stayed in Vancouver and started drafting *The Art of Losing: Narratives of the Air India Disaster*. I also wrote up Brinda's story, fretting over it much more than I would have if she were a client I would see again and work with. But perhaps I thought I might draw her back to me, that way. The glow I had felt in her presence, the warmth of her parents, the spell of Lohikarma, it was starting to fade. Work was going well, but as the weeks passed I felt increasingly unmoored. Grey. Static. A drift back to the way I had felt in the year before I began this project.

Brinda's thanks, when I finally sent her the document, were brief and uninformative. Had she moved on? Was she in the throes of a decision? I didn't want to ask, not by e-mail. I wished her well, and again encouraged her to call on me if ever there was anything I could do.

I wanted to go back to Lohikarma. Why? I had done interviews in eight cities, all rich and emotional, but only in Lohikarma did I feel that other spark. *You must change your life.* People went west to change their lives. *Go west, old man!* I was even farther west now, but in Vancouver—a big city, where I was anonymous, alone, and life was little different from my life back in India. I wanted to change my life. I could do that only near Seth. There—I wrote that down.

Nonsense, I thought, reading it in my journal immediately after writing it. What did Seth have that could make me feel that way? *Gracious forbearance*. It didn't matter what. It would give me courage.

I would go back. He and I would meet, regularly. Coffee, lunch. We would become friends—real friends. Over time, his daughters would be like nieces to me.

And Lohikarma made sense—it was a place many people went to change their lives. It was a good place to do that.

* * *

I arrived back in October. I called Seth and we met, putatively in order for me to ask questions that had arisen in transcription, clarify a few points. He asked how long I would be staying this time. I said I wasn't sure, perhaps a month. A week later, he invited me to have a coffee. He invited me.

* * *

We met at the mall, where we were surrounded by Halloween paraphernalia. I mentioned that, although I love to see the children dressed up, my apartment in Lohikarma had no front entrance, so that I could not distribute candy. I further broadly hinted—okay, I said bluntly—that October 31 had unpleasant associations for me.

He asked if I wouldn't rather spend the evening with him and Lakshmi. So it was that at 5:30 P.M., October 31, 2004—the twentieth anniversary of Indira Gandhi's assassination—I was traversing Lohikarma's scenic avenues in a multicoloured afro and a red rubber nose, carrying a bag of lollipops, thinking, *Indira G.: R.I.P.*, with uncharacteristic lightness.

Lakshmi was holding the screen door open when I arrived.

"Two-by-twos," I said to her, indicating the crowd pushing past me down her walk.

She looked at me quizzically.

"Two years old by two feet tall," I explained. It was not quite dark, still the hour of Baby's First Halloween, children *knee-high-to-a-grasshopper*, as Rosslyn's mother used to say, bumble bees and Ninja turtles.

Lakshmi looked as though she still didn't understand, but it wasn't that; she didn't recognize me. I pulled my nose out by its elastic band; it made a wet, sucking noise as its interior humidity released.

"Ashwin?" I said over it. I proffered the sucker sack, wishing I had that hand to pull off the wig. Lakshmi was not in costume. "Seth invited me to . . ."

She gave a quick sigh, and blinked her eyes wide open as though to keep from rolling them. I looked past her, trying not to seem rude: Where was Seth?

She had a chair set up in their foyer and brought another from the dining room for me. She had left her paperback open and face down on her chair seat: Rohinton Mistry. The cover: a photo of a man facing away. See? I gave my own quick sigh.

"Seth is staying with Venkat tonight," she told me as she went to give more candy to children too young to eat it.

"Don't choke on that!" I told one, and popped my nose at him.

I wiggled my wig by working my eyebrows, and glanced sideways at Lakshmi. Disapproval or amusement? Her face was not nearly so expressive as Seth's.

"What happened to Venkat?" I didn't really want to know.

"He had an outburst of some sort." There was a lull in the trick-or-treaters and she sat with a sharp outtake of breath.

"Bad?"

"He's been put on leave. Perhaps permanently."

Another crowd, old enough to know what they were doing, shouted, "Halloween apples!" from outside. I waved at her to stay in her chair while I did candy duty. "You didn't know I was coming?"

"Seth didn't come home from the office today. We talked, but it must have slipped his mind." She was rubbing her forehead. "It's fine. Stay."

I kept her company for an hour or two. She told me what little she knew, or perhaps less, about the incident in the classroom, and then, as the Hallow-baloo decreased, I excused myself.

* * *

The next day, at a downtown diner, Seth filled me in. "I suppose it was only a matter of time, with the trial, the trial, the trial. It's been going on so long, it's become a trial for everyone."

"What happened?"

"He was teaching a class. The economics professor who teaches in the same room, next period, was waiting outside but it was getting late, the door wasn't opening, and then she realized she was hearing something that didn't sound quite right. Finally, she peeked in. Venkat was shouting at the top of his lungs, all kinds of nonsense. The kids were too scared to move. Then he starts insulting this professor. There might be a lawsuit." He rubbed his neck, looking tired.

As Venkat had ranted on about betrayal and misplaced faith, his colleague waved his students out and went to find help. By the time she returned, he had gone.

What was the trigger? It was not clear. His students were interviewed by the university's counsellors, but most gave the impression that they had, for all practical purposes, been drowsing in their chairs. They woke to find him in full flight.

The colleague, who talked to everyone about it, thought Venkat was a step away from bringing a gun into the hallowed halls of academe. While I saw Venkat as too harmless a fellow for that, it did not escape me that this incident came one year to the day from Ms. D's testimony, and twenty years after Indira Gandhi's death. I never would have put much stock in this sort of thing—surely the date could not consciously be meaningful to Venkat; he wasn't even in India at the time of the assassination—if I hadn't seen the workings of such seemingly distant associations in the lives of my clients.

"It would be such a favour to us if you would talk to him, Ashwin," Seth said.

I had seen this coming, and dreaded it. "Yes," I said. "I will. But I have questions. Last time I was in Lohikarma, I asked you if you had any legal status in his medical care. You never answered. Is there anything I should know?"

Seth hesitated.

"If he were referred by his employer, his doctor, I would receive a file," I insisted. "I don't like to feel I am going in blind."

He took a breath and let it out heavily. "Okay. After Venkat got home from his time in India," he began, "all seemed to be going fine, as far as I could tell."

"You had set him up, his routines, his teaching."

"Exactly." Seth had a mannerism sometimes, small, jerking motions of his neck, as though the weight of his jacket on his shoulders was too much. "Venkat was distant, but otherwise normal. Uh, except . . ." He digressed. "Except sometimes, when we were on campus, or once when I took him shopping, he would think he saw one of them."

"One of them?"

"Sita or Sundar. He would become lively. All of a sudden. A startling kind of change. He would stop and stare, at the campus, or the mall, looking very happy." Seth showed me, half standing, agape. "And then, *phoosh*, he would deflate again, his cheeks sinking, his shoulders going down. Once he explained it to me, so then I understood the other times. He was thinking he saw one of them."

"Not uncommon."

"Oh?" The eyebrows went up, the shoulders down. "You have heard this from other family members, research subjects?"

"Well, yes," I said. "And also clients, in my therapeutic practice. Although they know, intellectually, that their loved one is dead, they will go on for years thinking they spot them, here and there."

"But he, he got Sundar's body. With Sita, I could have understood more. No closure, and all."

"I've seen it in cases where the death was unambiguous, not even sudden." Seth seemed to accept this. "But he appeared to be adjusting?"

"I suppose. I was worried. Every once in awhile, I would wake up in the night and be so worried, and I would go and see him."

"Worried? Had he said something to worry you?"

"No. Well, I don't think so. One thing he said, but I don't really remember if this was before or after . . ."

"Before or after . . . ?"

"I'm getting to it. He told me he could still remember the sound of Sundar's voice, but he couldn't think of what Sundar would have said." Seth looked at me, questioning, I think, whether I understood. "I knew exactly what he meant. It was because he lost Sita too. When our daughters were small, I would come home from work and my wife would tell me the things they said. I would make her repeat them; I could never remember exactly how they went. Even when I was there, with the children, she would repeat to me what they had just said. You're not trained to notice those things, as a man, or to remember them. So I knew what Venkat meant."

"And so you would go to see him, in the night?"

"The door was never locked. He was always awake, often sitting on the family room sofa. Most often, we would pray. And then I would make him go to bed, and I would sleep on his sofa, go home in the morning." Seth swallowed. "On this night—I guess it was late October? There was a bit of snow already. I woke up, like I said. Cold chills. I had been feeling fine, but now, it was like a fever. A fever of dread. I rushed into his house but he wasn't on the sofa, not in the bedroom, bathrooms. I ran through the house, calling his name, but I didn't hear anything. I thought, *He went somewhere? In the middle of the night? He didn't come home from the office?* I had this fear. I knew I had to keep looking. I opened the front door, but there were no footprints in the snow. Suddenly, it hit me. I rushed to the garage. He was sitting in the car."

He put his hand in his jacket pocket, as he always did at his narrative's worst moments. "Thank God I thought to press the button, open the garage door, before I went to get him out. I don't know how I thought to do that. I could have died too, passed out. I was holding my scarf over my mouth but the carbon monoxide made me sleepy even when I was turning the car off. I ran and took a breath of fresh air, or I think I did, then I dragged him out of the garage, around the front, so the carbon monoxide wouldn't get in the house, and pulled him up the stairs. Concrete stairs, and it was snowing, wet snow. I was worried I'd slip, kill both of us." His tension made him laugh at his inadvertent joke. He rubbed his eyes, then continued. "I think I laid him on the rug in the hall with door still open. He had begun to regain consciousness by the time the ambulance arrived. He must have started his car just about the time I started my car, at home."

"Do you think Venkat wanted to be rescued?"

Seth looked appalled, as though this had never occurred to him. "No. I don't think so."

"Was he angry with you?"

"How could he be angry at me? I saved his life! I saved his life." His tone was insistent. "He told me, much later, when he was in the hospital, that he had wanted to hurt himself but didn't have the courage. He was afraid to use a razor, so he did this instead. 'Totally Canadian, eh?' he said. 'No garages back home so we have to use more primitive methods!' I'll never forget it. The guy has never made a joke in his life, and when he finally jokes, it's about this! I was so relieved when he went into the hospital, and then, after that, to India for a few months. We were scared when he came back to Canada again, the next year. Geez."

"Truly, you felt him to be your responsibility."

"Who else does he have? Someone has to look after him. Poor guy. We felt terrible: we should have insisted he would stay with us. We should have insisted." He ran his hand from pate to nape and made the shrug, his tic, twice.

"If I can ask, did his suicide attempt affect your feeling that Shivashakti had saved his life, after the crash? Didn't you believe, to that point, that his faith in Shivashakti was giving him something to live for?"

"Well, I should have said Shivashakti saved his life by getting me up in the night and making me go over there."

I didn't ask if Shivashakti got him up every time or only the one time it mattered. "Let me just—you said, if I'm not mistaken, about your own devotion to Shivashakti, which started that summer, you said you came to God because God is eternal, and would survive anything and so help you survive anything. Clearly, Venkat's faith was not enough to sustain him through the loss of his family."

"He was in shock," said Seth.

He wanted me to drop it, but I waited. And in time, perhaps because he was not accustomed to shutting people off, he resumed.

"In fact," he said, "I asked him about that, when he was in the hospital."

* * *

Venkat spent several days in the ICU before being transferred to the hospital's psychiatric ward. His doctors were hopeful of a full physical recovery.

Seth and Lakshmi were permitted to visit him but had no legal status to influence his care and Venkat had no immediate family in Canada. Even in India, he had only his widowed mother and three sisters, two of whom had families of their own. When his elder brother died six years earlier, Venkat had brought his mother and youngest sister to live with him, but the experiment ended when winter began. His mother begged to go back to her home and friends; his brother's widow in India said she needed the help. Venkat's sister had no choice in the matter, and Sita, to put it mildly, didn't object. Now there was no one who could come to be with him. The doctors listened to Seth, however, on what Venkat had gone through, and when they asked where he would go when he was released, Seth told them he had written to Venkat's family in India to tell them what had happened and suggest that Venkat return home for a time.

He visited Venkat several times a week in hospital and tried to stay off heavy topics. If Venkat occasionally made reference to the suicide attempt or its precipitating causes, Seth typically would do nothing more than listen, although, once or twice, early on, when he himself was still too shaken, he changed the topic. Then, six weeks after the ambulance ride, shortly before he was due to be released straight onto a plane to India, Venkat mentioned he was planning on visiting Shivashaktipurum again with his sister. Before Seth realized it, he had asked the question that had been troubling him.

"I know you still pray," he had said. "You still have Shivashakti. So how, why, could you try to take your life? Is his love, and your love for him, not enough?"

Venkat frowned and looked away. "I am paying, Sethu, for some sins of a past life. And worse than this, my wife and child paid also for my sins. They died to punish me. My mother has written to remind me that if I had succeeded in killing myself, my spirit would anyway have wandered on earth until my destiny said I should die. But I don't know. What if it was my destiny that I should die by my own hand? And then how much better to come back as some unfeeling animal . . ."

"No. It is a betrayal of your God." Seth was livid. "Shivashakti says be humble. It is your egotism letting you think you are to blame when all of this is God's will. The fact that you lived . . ." He held up a hand to stop Venkat, who was attempting to interrupt. "No. The fact that you lived is proof that you were not meant to die. Come back as an animal—*pah*. These matters are not in your hands. Go to Shivashaktipurum. Go and pray. You cannot know the mind of God. Your part now is to love him."

"All right, Seth. I understand." Venkat nodded. "You are a good friend." He patted Seth's hand, and Seth shook his head, *no, no thank-yous, please*. Venkat went on. "But don't forget that Shivashakti is both a God and a path to God. Even this guru-attachment—you will need to renounce it someday. Attachment is pain. Our guru says that, too."

Venkat lay his head back on the cushions of the sofa where he sat, and closed his eyes. Seth looked around at the rest of the crazy people in their hospital-issue pyjamas—watching *Dallas*; being talked to in stern tones by their families; trying to extract a candy bar from the vending machine with a fat hand that couldn't fit through the flap, so that the inmate was forced to drop his prize, over and over. Seth tried to summon again the anger that had made it so neatly clear how wrong Venkat was, but found himself, instead, close to tears. He went to help the large man get his Kit Kat out of the machine.

* * *

After his two months' recovery in hospital, Venkat went to India, to stay with his mother. That was right before the winter holidays. Lakshmi said something to Seth about her surprise that he continued attending satsang so faithfully. Seth didn't respond. His desire to visit Shivashakti-purum, to experience his God as a corporeal reality, had become fierce. He saw no need to detail for Lakshmi this burning, but told her simply, in spring 1986, that he needed to go.

"So what is this about?" Lakshmi asked, the question that forced him to try to explain.

"I think a pilgrimage would somehow . . ." He wanted to say that it would formalize his commitment in some way, make his relationship to Shivashakti more real in his own eyes and in the eyes of the world, much as marriage does. But he wasn't sure Lakshmi would take that very well. "Somehow it would make things clearer for me."

She didn't look as though this made anything clearer for her.

"Besides, listen. I'm due for a trip." This was true: Seth had been the only one of his siblings to leave India and so was obliged to visit his widowed mother at decent intervals. Lakshmi had not gone the last time: her mother had come to live with her only brother in Toronto and so she had no pressing reason. "And I'll check in on Venkat." It was a question they had already discussed: what risk, or responsibility for his safety, Seth and Lakshmi would be put to if Venkat returned.

They agreed that he would go when their daughters' school let out.

He wanted to take both girls, but Ranjani didn't want to go without her mother. India was never an easy trip for the girls. Last time, Seth had persuaded them to come, but it had been even harder managing in relatives' homes without Lakshmi to anticipate the compulsory cultural adjustments and mediate their missteps. Brinda, by contrast, felt ready to try it. They decided it would be her high-school graduation present.

They flew Air India, whose ticket prices had gone down and security practices tightened up to the point where most people thought they were the safest airline going. It had been a full year. He'd flown Air India himself less than a week after the . . . *bombing*—the word he was trying not even to let himself think. But still, it was quite another thing to bring his child aboard with him, and Seth was aware of holding a lid down tight on his anxiety.

The flight was two hours late departing. They received meals within ten minutes of takeoff—although the airline rarely ran on time, they always had lots of food. Their flight attendants were gorgeous and snooty, as always, and Brinda and Seth in a mood to make fun of them.

"They all look like sari models," Brinda said. "But mean ones."

"Yes, I'm scared to even ask for a glass of water," Seth murmured.

"Don't even think of asking for an airsick bag." Brinda poked him with her elbow. "Vomit in your coffee cup, if you need to."

He hadn't said anything about his nauseating nervousness. Had he? "So." It seemed a good time to talk about their plans. "I was thinking we would recover from jet lag in Bangalore, spend time with your grandmother, maybe five days or so, and then head to the ashram after that." He had failed to specify veg or non-veg, and was tucking into a chicken tikka. "Does that sound all right to you?"

Brinda had not specifically said she was planning to accompany him to Shivashaktipurum, but he wanted her to come; he thought it might be good for her; he thought she might finally understand why this was important to him. He didn't want to force her, though.

She stirred her dal and *mutter paneer*. "Okay, but so, when would we go to Mysore? From the ashram?"

"We could do that. The last week or so. Three days there should do it."

"Three days at the ashram, so how many days in Mysore?"

"No, three days in Mysore: one day for the city, one day for Sri-rangapatna, maybe a day at the bird sanctuary. I was thinking ten days, maybe two weeks, at the ashram."

"Are you kidding?" That look, of North American teenagers. Do they teach it to one another? Learn it from TV?

"Why don't you wait and see how you like it, and . . . really, why are you deciding in advance? We're only talking."

"That's what I thought," she said, looking at him as though he had been the one to get exasperated, when it had been the other way around, entirely.

The flight attendants were marching through the cabin, reaching across passengers without a word to slam down their blinds. The first movie was *Shanghai Surprise*, which turned out to be good for almost as many laughs as *Three Amigos*, the movie that followed right after. By the time their third dinner was sullenly popped in front of them ("Shut up and eat," Seth said, channelling the air hostess), they were happy to com-pare the relative comedic merits of Martin Short and Madonna and to worry about crossing the Shivashaktipurum bridge when they came to it.

✳ ✳ ✳

"You want to leave?" Seth asked. "We just now arrived, only yesterday!"

"I know." Brinda was leaning on the wall by the window and now turned to look out. Their room was no more than seven feet wide. He stood in the corridor between the cots, befuddled. They had attended their first satsang that morning. Brinda had seemed willing enough.

"Why don't you give it a few more days, at least? I really . . ." He was the father here; he was within his rights, even his responsibilities, to guide her. "This could be a very good thing for you. I think you need this."

"I'm not comfortable here." Her arms were crossed and brow knit-ted, everything hunched toward her centre.

"You won't even tell me what the problem is?"

"Part of the problem is that I don't feel comfortable talking about it," she stormed, but then, when he sighed, she softened. "I think faith is, like, one of the most private things there is. I hate all these people coming at you, presuming you believe. You can't seek; if you're here, you're sup-posed to have already found what you're looking for, and I haven't. Oh, and it's totally creepy the way they use his name as a substitute for other words. Like when those bossy, usher types were trying to get us to move over, instead of "excuse me" or "thank you," they went '*Jai Shivashakti? Jai Shivashakti.*'"

Seth smiled a little at her imitation.

"I know you love it, you really feel it," she said, sounding more cautious now. "But I don't. And it's suffocating to be surrounded by people who do."

He sat on a cot and reached awkwardly to stroke her hair. "You are young, still, Brinda. I wish I had, at your age, been guided in this way."

"That's condescending." She pushed herself away from him to lean back on the wall. "I said I respect your feelings. You should respect mine."

Where do they come up with these things? She's seventeen! An Indian child couldn't imagine saying something like this. But Lakshmi had set the path and he had gone along with it.

"You always do this," Brinda went on. "You don't ask how I feel or what I can handle, but just decide, as though I'm a baby. I'm leaving for Bangalore tomorrow. I know how to get to the train. I'll call Periappa to come and get me from the station. I'll see you there when you're finished here."

He'd never figured out how the more authoritarian—the more authoritative—parents did it, made their kids obey. He looked at the stubby fingers of his clasped hands, and reclasped them so that his fingers were shut inside. "I'll take you back to Bangalore tomorrow."

"I don't want you to have to give up your dream for me. I'll be fine."

"That's enough, all right?" He stood. "I'll go with you and come back. It's only a couple of hours each way."

"Then why can't I do it by myself?"

"It's not a good idea," he said, his speech slowing—a sign that trouble was afoot if she pushed further. She didn't.

* * *

He had been so proud and happy to have her with him. Walking out of the dorm, yesterday morning, down the ashram's shady lanes, he had imagined the four of them coming someday. And beyond—retirement, maybe here; grandchildren, maybe here.

And then, this morning, the excitement of seeing his God. Shivashakti had entered the arena at a point unseen, but Seth could tell, everyone could, it was as though a current had run through them. He himself felt faint, until God entered his view.

Shivashakti seemed to him less distinct, more mutable, than in pictures he had seen, as though his outlines were drawn in shifting light. The sunlight in the outer court seemed to blend into his features, as though He were continuous with it, instead of reflecting it as did every mortal creature on God's earth.

But others, he came to realize, saw something—someone—different.

One devotee later made reference to the benevolence of his aspect. "What do I see when I look at him? I see goodness. He shines it. Out of his eyes."

Another seemed to find him simultaneously unreachable and omnipresent: "He is, for me, like the sun, moon and planets. He governs my life's motion, the rhythm of my days. So when I meet him, it is like he is always with me, anyway."

After seeing him, that first time, Seth rubbed his eyes the rest of the day. They felt warm and tired. He didn't want to sleep, though; he wanted to meditate, to contemplate that which is without form.

Every August, before beginning teaching, he reread Richard Feynman's *Lectures on Physics*. For him, Feynman was the greatest, his model, the scientist and theorist Seth would never be, but a teacher in Seth's own mold. He thought now of Feynman's lecture on Brownian motion, and his citation from biology, since, for Feynman, all sciences were connected, and the connections were love and physics: *Everything that animals do, atoms do.*

Seth knew this to be true, but had not *felt*, before, his own atoms animalized. Here he felt not simply at peace, but somehow beyond the knowledge that he was a mortal composed of immortal particles, which, after him, would recombine in infinite ways determined by the universe and the laws that he had been made to preach. *Felt* there was no separation between being and truth.

Even the fight with Brinda left only a mild residue of discomfort, easily washed away in a satsang he attended that afternoon, while Brinda explored the ashram grounds and read. He took comfort in her seeming strength and confidence—surely these would serve her? He did feel detached from conflict, he thought. Such a disagreement, *before*, would have shattered him. That night, he lay spinning in his cot, skewered on an axis that also pierced the earth's centre and the ever-living heart of the cosmos.

* * *

The train for Bangalore left in the morning at ten, but Seth wasn't able to catch another back the same day and by the time he arrived back in Shivashaktipurum, he had missed two *darshans*. He wasn't happy about that, but was coming to recognize that his dream of worshipping in happy communion with his family was unrealistic, and, in light of that, felt a dawning relief on arriving back in Shivashaktipurum alone.

That afternoon, as he sat reading in the shade of a margosa, he was approached by a severe-looking young woman in a dark red cotton sari, the uniform worn by acolytes living at the ashram.

"*Jai Shivashakti*," she saluted him. "You are Sri Sethuratnam?"

Seth had grown irresistibly drowsy, bent over his book in the still and fragrant shade, and had been wondering if he could succumb right there on the grass or haul himself back to his cot. As he rose to face the woman, he wondered if she had, in fact, awakened him. He brushed at his face: *neem* pollen or the cotton wool of sleep?

"Sri Swamiji wishes to speak to you. You will come, today at 6 o'clock P.M.," she said, in the dice-tumbler accent of south Indians to whom English doesn't come easy. "You know where it is?"

He tilted his head in the affirmative. "I know, yes."

He had asked for a tour, the first day, and had seen the bungalow that had recently replaced the thatched-roof huts of the original ashram. The house was set in a garden, the garden within a grove, so that the impression one had, viewing it from a distance of fifty metres, was that it must be a very inviting place, if one were so lucky as to be invited.

No one knew the process by which visitors to the ashram were asked to come to the bungalow for a personal audience with their guru, but everyone heard about these encounters, and everyone hoped. Last year, Venkat had been granted a semi-private audience, together with another family who had lost relatives in the Air India bombing. Shivashakti had materialized *vibhuti*, holy ash, from the heads of the children there, and given it to them all to take home.

There were other stories, from other visits, other devotees. Venkat had told him that his first time there, he had been waiting to see Shivashakti when a man emerged, weeping, from the inner sanctum. He was from Finland or Sweden, Venkat hadn't been sure, and grew up speaking a language now known by fewer than a hundred people. Shivashakti had spoken to him *in his mother tongue*.

Why was Seth being called? Perhaps he already knew. When he needed a guru, Shivashakti had come to him. Now he needed to meet Shivashakti in person, although he hadn't recognized it until now— there it was, a gnawing hunger. And he had been called to satisfy this, as well.

Any remaining mental mistiness had been burned off by the invitation, which seemed to issue directly from the sun. *Tat savitur varenyam.* He walked out of the shade into its warmth and paced the grounds, a walking meditation that took him, three times, past the evening's destination, before he returned to his dorm to bathe and dress.

* * *

By five thirty, he was walking toward the western end of the compound, and the house of his Lord. He realized he was thinking of the bungalow and garden as though they were a temple complex and wondered whether Shivashakti's acolytes performed for him similar rituals to those done for deities in the usual temples, where the gods were represented in wood or bronze instead of taking the form of living beings.

Seth had loved, as a little boy, to visit the Krishna temple when the priests were getting the deity ready for bed. He and his mother would watch them give the idol his dinner of yogourt, milk, ghee, all those rich foods beloved of the child-God and of all children, then bathe the small figure and dress him in silk garments before parading him around the temple and singing him to sleep. Seth's mother donated such a garment once a year.

Seth once told his mother that he wanted to come and look after baby Krishna when he grew up and his mother had shushed him— "Become a priest with your marks?"—as though the priests were grown men playing with dolls, rather than men invested with the holy offices of worship.

The density of margosas increased around the path, absorbing the heat of the day and releasing a slight, oily pungency into their shade.

Sound, dust, the enmity of the common world, all seemed held at bay as Seth climbed the steps. A veranda, terra-cotta roof tiles, rooms and people, as with a temple or a home. One or two muttered *"Jai, Shivashakti"* toward him, and understanding both Seth's purpose and his uncertainty, pointed him ever farther into the interior of the house. He saw a bench, finally, outside a closed door, where a middle-aged white couple sat.

"*Jai Shivashakti,*" he greeted them. "You are waiting to see Swamiji?"

"*Jai Shivashakti,*" they answered.

He sat and waited.

Shortly before six, the door opened and a family exited, a frolicky little girl, a sombre adolescent boy, and a man and woman—Indian but prosperous and progressive, to all appearances: she with bobbed hair, he a gold watch—who leaned into each other. He wiped tears from his eyes and cheeks as her manicured fingernails dug into his starched shirt sleeve.

From behind them, an acolyte beckoned the white couple. The Indian family shifted to let them pass. When the white couple exited some twenty minutes later, looking brave and buoyed, Seth thought of *The Wizard of Oz*, which Ranjani loved and had made him watch every time it came on TV. The Wizard, we were to believe, possessed no special powers other than making people (or lions, or scarecrows) see what strengths were already within them.

"*Jai Shivashakti,*" the usher said now to Seth. *We're off to see the Wizard!* Seth's mind sang—not what he wanted to be thinking.

"*Jai Shivashakti,*" he said, feeling one part of his mind quiver in readiness, a blossom in the wind, while another part raced, a greyhound of analysis: *The Wizard lets us see what is already in us, but, as with Krishna to Arjuna, his powers also reveal his divinity to us . . .* The two parts joined in silence as he entered the chamber and his God came forward to greet him. Seth bowed, palms together.

"If you are God, so I am God," Shivashakti said to him, and Seth repeated it back to his god.

"Your daughter has gone," his guru said. "But you remain."

Seth flailed briefly in panic and incipient grief. His daughter had died? Which one? Was this an instruction? Then he grasped, easy as snatching a firefly out of dark air, the obvious meaning. "Yes, yes," he said.

"You feel somehow alone."

How did he know? Seth could not recall later whether they spoke in Tamil or English, or in words at all.

Remember that I am always with you and within you. Think on my name, you will feel my presence.

Close up, Shivashakti radiated a hypnotic stillness. He had wide black eyebrows above a strong nose and below the silvering bangs of his still-thick pageboy. He was a small man with large features, something like a big-boned bird, feathers fluffed into a saffron robe. His keen eyes, too, had something of a bird's intense attention.

In his presence, Seth was, almost against his will, more aware of his God's humanity than his divinity. His divinity inheres in his humanity, he reasoned afterward, savouring the experience. At close range, then, you must feel less God-warmth, and more person-warmth. Else, how could you approach him? At such close quarters, you would be burned.

Seth felt himself surrender, felt love surround him, absorb him, perfect him.

"I am here, Swamiji," he said, and fell at the feet of his lord.

* * *

During his weeks at the ashram, Seth called his brother's place in Bangalore every few days to speak to Brinda. Or rather, he would go to the Shivashaktipurum Post Office and place a call to his brother's neighbour, hang up, wait ten minutes, then call again to find Brinda there or to be told a time to call back. His brother had applied twenty years ago for a phone line, but claimed he hadn't gotten it yet because he refused to pay bribes.

These things—India!—increasingly drove Seth nuts: corruption, congestion, poverty, dust. To his daughters, he defended the conservatism, the rituals, the sex-segregation, but inarticulately, and with decreasing conviction. It had long been a reflex for him, in his adopted country, to imagine that there was another place where he felt at home as he never had in the Great White North. Returning to India, though, he learned, over and over again, that the country of his birth was no longer his to claim. He was suspended, as if in mid-bound, between two shifting-drifting continents whose appearance, texture, even location, changed even as he watched them from his great-seeming distance. That was the other problem: he couldn't fully know either country because both were transforming, not even glacially. India was visibly more urban and modern than when he first left; Canada, too, was more cosmopolitan and open than when he first arrived. So maybe that problem would turn out to be the solution.

These were his thoughts as he rode the train out of Shivashakti-purum, on his way to his sister's place in Chennai. His brother would bring Brinda from Bangalore to meet him there. Before they arrived, Seth planned to pop in on Venkat.

The agrarian landscape of his boyhood scrolled past. The exposed dirt, in mounds beside rice paddies, in furrows beneath bullock hooves, was a different shade of red or brown every half hour. The air, too, would smell different for brief periods, though this was not all natural: sometimes he would smell manure, or dampness, the smells of child-hood rambles; sometimes a putrid, nose-burning smell of chemical exhaust, some factory, plastics or fertilizer, employing an entire village and likely giving everyone cancer and holes in the heart. It happened in Canada—Lohikarma, the environmentalists liked to remind them, was downstream from the pulp mill, and who knew what they were getting in their water? But Seth was sure more precautions were being taken there than here. Canadians would insist.

He was in a third-class compartment, which he had always enjoyed, even in his youth, when his school performance and the Brahmin ethos (*Brahmins are under siege*, he heard his uncles saying, *our advantages are disadvantages*) meant he was far snobbier than he was now. A third-class carriage was a place between places, and within an hour, he had gotten to know his neighbours: the cringing Tata Company peon with his wife and three crusty kids; the Marwari trader, with waxed moustache points that stuck out past his earrings, who was no doubt toting gold or diamonds; the retired Tamil Brahmin couple who, on learning they shared Seth's sub-caste, talked doggedly through their entire family tree until they figured out how they were related to him—by marriage, at a distance of more than six degrees.

They all then drowsed in the rocking carriage, as Seth's thoughts drifted sleepily back to Canada. A few weeks before he left, he had run into Kaj Halonen, with his family, at the mall food court. As Kaj chatted, his wife left them without smile or excuse. Their children were waiting: a sullen-looking dark-haired boy, and a blond girl with long, misshapen limbs, flailing in some kind of kitted-out wheelchair. Kaj had never made reference to his kids before and didn't now. Seth was left thinking about children—or adults—who never fully grow up.

Sundar would always be twenty-one to them, floating, in his own way, in some Neverland. If and when Venkat returned to Canada, he and Lakshmi might forever be responsible for him. Was that what terror did—give us unwanted family, weird and delicate alliances; did it drive us into the arms of people who were then forced to embrace us? Did Venkat see it that way? He had turned to Seth and Lakshmi, but then Seth had turned to God.

Venkat's house, in a Chennai suburb, had been built by his late brother, whose widow and children still lived on the second floor, in a roomy three-bedroom flat identical to the one on the ground floor where Venkat's mother and sister had long been installed. Venkat met him at the door with a handshake and some back-patting and his sister Parvati appeared immediately behind him with a stainless steel tumbler of lime-water balanced, reflected, on a stainless steel plate. They gestured him to a sofa.

Parvati had been widowed at nineteen, weeks after her marriage, and her in-laws hadn't tried to keep her with them. She wore a silk nine-yard sari and a fleet look of cunning desperation that Seth recognized from others who had lived their whole lives with overbearing parents.

Venkat's mother, lurking noisily in the kitchen, called out, "*Enna*, Sethu? *Sowkyumaa*?" She too, wore the traditional nine-yard, which accented her broad middle, and she had her daughter's thick hair, parted and combed severely over a wide head. Their silhouettes were almost identical, the mother's only a bit wider and taller. *Self-similarity*, Seth thought, *fractals, infinite regress.*

Venkat was dressed neatly, in a white dhoti and pressed mauve kurta. He didn't appear to have gained weight, but didn't look any thinner either. There was an alteration, though—what? Seth sensed, not calm (that would be asking too much), but less bewilderment in Venkat than he had become used to.

"You're looking well," Seth told him. He would have said this either way, but how nice that it was true.

"I've heard back from Jerry Czaplinski," Venkat said. The statistics department head.

"Ah?" Venkat had told Seth he was thinking of returning to work in the fall. The university would be virtually obliged to comply if he did.

They both reached out to receive saucers of fresh-hot onion *bajjis* from Parvati.

"So you are coming back?" Seth wanted to know.

"Very much coming back, Sethu. Very much coming back."

"We think it's a bad idea," Parvati said from the kitchen entrance at the other end of the living room, not precisely observing the customary rules against women mingling with outside males, but, by staying in the doorway, not exactly violating them either.

Seth remembered Lakshmi telling him once that Sita complained a little about Parvati, who had worshipped Venkat and his wife and the now-deceased elder brother who used to live on the top floor. Parvati would stifle them with attentions, insist on carrying Sundar everywhere, even when he was so old as to feel uncomfortable with it. She wanted to comb Sita's hair, make Venkat's coffee; she became a Shivashakti devotee when they did and came with them whenever they went to Shivashakti-purum. Sita pitied her and tried to be kind, unlike the other sister-in-law, who lived upstairs and spoke sharply to Parvati. Venkat, too, indulged her: the youngest, their father's pet, a widow. Now Parvati had fixed all the largesse of her immature affection on Venkat.

Seth looked at her with polite bemusement. Could Parvati sway him?

Their mother passed another plate of *bajjis* through the kitchen doorway to her daughter. "*Chi!* He's a man. He needs to work. Is he going to sit around the house with you, reading *Stardust* magazine?"

Seth sneaked a look at Venkat, whose face was a mask of bizarre, unreadable neutrality. Was it his mother who convinced him to return? But that wouldn't quite account for the sense of energy behind his declaration, a rumbling of determination greater than any he had felt from Venkat since before the disaster.

* * *

When Seth called Lakshmi later that day, he tried to give an account of Venkat's mood. "I suspect that being home with his mother and sister has reminded him of his obligations. Who else can support the family now, with his brother gone? I don't think his mother would put up with him quitting his job and moping around the house." There was some-

186 ✳ THE EVER AFTER OF ASHWIN RAO

thing else Seth was grasping for, something he himself had been cheated of. "I think it's been healthy for him to be back where he truly feels at home. He even seems to have made some new friends."

"Then why is he coming back?" Brinda asked later. "Isn't he going to get sad and lonely, and, you know"—she didn't say "suicidal" but the word puppeted, herky-jerky, between them—"all over again?"

Lakshmi had asked the same thing. Seth said, "He didn't tell me why, exactly. He probably needs to feel more productive and important than he can here. And he will earn enough to support his mother and sister and come back every summer if he wants."

* * *

In August 1986, Venkat came back to Canada. He flew in to Vancouver, as before, but this time Seth drove out to pick him up.

Venkat was thinner, which almost never happens on a trip home. He sat with his shoulder bag clutched in his lap, the same one he had in Ireland, filled, back then, with the photo albums and his family's clothes. Seth wondered what it had in it now.

They were on their way to stay with Bala. Seth had been to the house two or three times, but the suburb was dramatically altered every time. New residential roads, first with nothing at all around them, then with new cul-de-sacs tacked at intervals by spindly trees; new mini-malls, their exterior decor meant to evoke Switzerland or California; new houses of worship: a Pentecostal church; and, now, a Chinese temple in red and gold, rising up from the wayside earth.

Bala's wife Vasu answered the door with a smile, then stood aside for them to enter as Bala came to greet them. His starched short-sleeved button-down looked like a packing box, thought Seth. If he lay on his back, his torso would be perfectly flat. What was that book Brinda had liked so much? About the boy squashed flat one day who mailed himself to a friend for vacation. *Flat Stanley*, that was it. Flat Bala.

He smelled sandalwood incense, coconut rice. The Balakrishnans' daughter was reading on the sofa. She would start Grade 12 in a few weeks, a girl in her parents' mould: A for academics, A for athletics, All About Achievement. Their son, Sudhir, not at home, a different story, as they say. Pudgy, shortish, darkish, sweet. Daddy's pet. They kept Sara Lee brownies in the freezer for him, even while Bala—who strode laps around his little street each morning before staging a grand finale on his lawn, bopping bony knees to palms, jumping his jacks, pushing his ups—made subtle cracks whenever anyone hoisted a samosa at a party.

Bala offered Seth a Johnnie Walker, a gesture that Seth, as the only drinker in the room, felt was laden with moral condescension. He accepted. It was good, that caramel burn, after the long drive. He looked forward to an oversoft bed. He wondered if he and Venkat would be sharing a room, as they had in Cork.

"Our Mahalakshmi temple?" Bala was responding to a question Venkat had asked. "Coming along, coming along. We think we'll have the groundbreaking within the year. All of us out here are exceptionally committed." Bala handed plates to the men and began murmuring insistently that they should help themselves to the buffet Vasu had laid out.

"Is that so? Excellent," Seth said, making reciprocal gestures that Venkat or Vasu should really go first. Venkat, with an absent air, began, and Seth followed.

Bala took a linked set of measuring cups from a drawer to serve himself, three-quarters of a cup of vegetable *kootu* atop a half-cup of rice. "Even some of our white Canadian friends from the Shivashakti Centre, they have made contributions to the temple fund. They think it can only be good."

They moved to sit at the table.

"This is good," said Venkat. "From the British and the Portuguese converting the Hindu man to Christianity now they want to know the greatness of our ancient scriptures. The Muslims are not so open. And the . . ." Venkat's voice shook a little. "Not the Sikhs."

"We don't see them at the temple, no." Bala spoke with uncharacteristic caution; no idiot he. "But they come to Shivasakti satsang. Even now. Some have specially made a point of coming. Some Sikhs."

"Gandhiji said it: 'There is in Hinduism room enough for Jesus, as there is for Mohammed, Zoroaster and Moses,'" said Venkat. "Most of the Indian Muslims converted from Hinduism. Right? Yes? The father of our nation, he said, 'in a free, prosperous, progressive India, they would find it the most natural thing in the world to revert to their ancient faith and ways of life.' India is a Hindu nation and these others, these others, these—we must make the circumstances for them to revert." He finished his minuscule portions. "India could be a superpower now, but for this *vazha-vazha, kozha-kozha*"—his gestures illustrated: namby-pamby, wishy-washy—"multi-religious nonsense. You see what comes of that!"

The Balakrishnans had stiffened and Seth was looking at his plate.

"Everybody wants his own country," Venkat went on. "We too need to keep up our homeland. India—what does this name mean except 'country of Hindus'? These others, the defectors, they want to fight. Okay, I say, let us fight!"

Seth had heard such things from him before, but, of course, that was before.

There was a deadness to Venkat's face as he spoke. His lips barely moved; his voice was a monotone. It had begun the week after the bomb, but back then it seemed no more than appropriate, the numbing effect of horror. Had it continued through last fall? Or had it returned or worsened? Perhaps a very minor stroke? There was also some discolouration, on the skin of his face. Looking at it distracted Seth from what Venkat was saying. It happened to Indians, unlucky ones: light-skinned ones got dark pouches under their eyes; dark-skinned ones a spooky frame edging the hairline. Venkat's was something else, a visage-haunting.

Vasu diverted them by rising to offer fruits, giving Bala a chance to switch onto the evils of sugar, more comfortable territory for all of them. Venkat had no chance or, perhaps, inclination to return to his topic that evening, but whatever held him back, decorum or fatigue, was absent the next day in the car. He monologued without restraint on the Sikhs: on forcible reconversion, mass expulsion, jail.

Occasionally, when he stopped for breath, Seth tried to challenge his logic. "But Sikhism was an attempt to reform Hinduism because it had become corrupt," he said.

Venkat had a response to everything. You cannot reform from without, only within. The caste system was morally neutral—a way to divide labour, as in any society. You think we don't have caste in Canada? And the Sikhs kept it, as did the Muslims, as did the Christians, whatever their leaders said. They don't forget their heritage so easily but they want to pretend. A return to the fold! And so on.

Perhaps Venkat had spent his entire time in India working up these speeches, discharging them on his mother and other relatives. Perhaps they thought as he did. But whether any of this was a solution to terrorism, Seth wasn't sure. After all, Sikh separatists themselves agreed that India was a Hindu nation. That was why they wanted their own country. He let Venkat go on, and, at times when he couldn't stand it any longer, hummed a bhajan to himself and focused on the road.

* * *

On their return, Seth helped Venkat to settle again in his own house, and again was unsuccessful in removing any of Sita's or Sundar's belongings. Venkat returned to teaching. Though he seemed perhaps slightly more energized than he had the previous fall, his features never regained a normal level of animation.

"It's like his face is a kind of screen," Lakshmi said. "A blank screen with some pattern projected on it." She frowned. "Though I couldn't say what kind of pattern, exactly."

One Saturday night early that October, the Sethuratnams had a dinner party. Moe Iyer came with his family and talked a lot about the grand opening of West Wind Condos, the following week. "People are moving in. From all over. Some from Toronto!"

Lakshmi rolled her eyes at Seth. He had been feeling impressed with Mohan but could also see she was right.

"We're having a ribbon-cutting ceremony on Saturday. In the grand atrium. Cookies, everything. And I will be giving each resident a bird."

A bird?

"Indian ring-necked parakeet. Beautiful bird. A bird in every condo! The finishing touch!" He kissed his fingertips. "I have extra, actually." Slurped his whisky, clacked his rings. "You wanna bird?" he asked Seth.

"No!" said Lakshmi.

Ranjani had overheard. "I want a bird!"

"No," said Lakshmi, who had been stuck with cleaning their cat's litter box, despite everyone's promises.

Moe tipped his drink at Venkat. "You, Venkat? I'm going to bring you a bird. Really, I have extra. I wanted forty-two, one per condo. The guy said cheaper to take fifty. You know, wholesale. Very nice birds. Not too big, not too small. And they can talk! Or learn to talk. Very intelligent."

Venkat: "Indian, you say?"

Moe wagged his head. "Beautiful birds."

Lakshmi pulled off her apron and announced the meal.

✳ ✳ ✳

At the end of the evening, the Iyers were the last to leave. Lakshmi cut into Mohan before Seth heard his car door slam.

"You have to tell him not to give Venkat a bird, Seth. What if it dies? That's all he needs! What kind of nut . . . All those people just moving into new homes, the last thing they need is to look after a bird. It's going to be such a mess. You have to talk to him tomorrow."

Seth was, from a prone position, working on his recliner's sticky point. David Letterman was goading an actor in black leather. Familiar, but Seth couldn't place him. He yawned.

Lakshmi tucked dirty napkins into glasses, used a clean one to wipe crumbs off the coffee table. "Can Brahmins even give animals as gifts?"

"Sure: *godanam*?" The traditional *gift of a cow*—not something he had seen, but they all knew about it.

She huffed a little and carted away the party debris.

He called after her. "Better than him giving *kanyadanam*, eh?" *Gift of a virgin*—this was still a term of currency: giving a daughter, in marriage: a good work, an act of dharma.

Her answer carried in from the kitchen. "That's enough out of you, buddy." He could tell from her voice that she was smiling.

✳ ✳ ✳

The following Friday, they got a busy signal when they tried to call Venkat to remind him to come for supper. After fifteen minutes of this, Seth got in his car and peeled out of the driveway in a panic, wondering if it would be preferable to find Venkat had had a heart attack or fallen in the tub.

At Venkat's, he went straight through the sliding door at the back. Called, "Hello?" and was headed for the back door into the garage when Venkat popped his head into the kitchen and caught him.

"Ah, Seth!" Venkat beckoned. Seth followed him into the dining room.

In a cage on the dining room table, an unexpectedly large bird rocked from leg to leg like a toddler needing to pee.

"Look! This is Mandarin. I thought his eyes have that—see, the colour of orange peel—and then I remembered that the word *mandarin* has its roots in Sanskrit. *Man. Mantri.* Mandarin."

Seth took a breath, pulled out a chair, sat. The bird looked at him from one of two orange-ringed eyes set in a turquoise head. Its beak was a deep rose-pink that brightened to a gold blotch, though the underbeak was black, as if lined in kohl. The black continued from the lower lip around the neck to form a narrow band. Below the collar, the bird's body was powder blue, several shades lighter than its luminous head. Was there a feathering of lavender in among the cyan?

Seth had never been so close to such a beautiful bird, and, as Venkat chirped at it, "Hello, Mandy! Hello, Mandy!" he wondered how he was going to explain to his wife his failure to forestall this infatuation. He had to figure it out quickly. Venkat refused to leave the bird alone so soon after its arrival and Seth had no power to change his mind.

On returning home alone, he described the scene as he had found it. For a minute or two, Lakshmi didn't say anything. Their daughters were already eating. Seth had been hoping the fight wouldn't happen in front of them, but now his own irritation rose.

"What was I supposed to do, take it away?" he asked his wife. "He's not my child." Not that he could do much with his children, either. He started to help himself to food.

Lakshmi was quiet for a few moments, then asked, "Do you think he needs help, making arrangements? Bird food? What—parrot food? Did Mohan give him any of that? Those things make a mess, you know."

Not my problem, he thought. "I'll take him some old newspapers when I see him tomorrow."

"It's not your problem." Said with a conciliatory smile.

Seth snorted. "Damn right."

* * *

The next day, he picked Venkat up and took him to the condo opening. He was curious, he told Lakshmi.

"Sure, go," she said, "but don't even think I'm coming with you."

Even Venkat would not have come except that he wanted another bird.

"Have you done research?" Seth asked him en route. "How to care for it? What does it eat?"

"Birdseed. Fully vegetarian! There is a dish, it was full when he brought Mandy to me. It's still half full. But I gave him some mango this morning. That was a hit!"

"Find out before you start feeding him all sorts of stuff. You don't want to give him gas or diarrhea or anything." Venkat said nothing, and Seth felt bad for being negative. "Call the pet store. That's all I'm saying."

Venkat looked at him, surprised, as though he hadn't been listening. "*Seri, seri*," he said, wagging his head. "Don't worry."

The condo atrium was hexagonal, crowned by a glass vault. Moe back-clapped them, his eyes hidden by an enormous smile. "Like being inside a diamond, isn't it? That's what my architect said and he speaks no lies. Let me introduce you." He pulled on their jacket elbows but then released them in the direction of some modular sofas when an elderly white couple returned from the show-home suite.

Seth had heard that some units hadn't yet sold—rumours ranged from five to twenty. He had toured the model unit the year prior, when the condos first went up for sale, but it was more fully furnished now. There was a ring-necked parakeet on the glass-top table in the kitchen, and another by the French doors to the balcony.

"Let me go ask," Venkat said, and went toward the office. When Seth found him, he was holding a cage with two birds inside.

Moe's assistant, a woman whose face was shiny and pink, asked Seth, "Would you like some birds too?" Her eyes showed whites all the way around blue irises and she smelled of cosmetics and peculiarly female sweat.

"No, no," he said, waving at her.

"You sure?" she asked, wringing her hands. "We've got a lot."

Seth thought, as he often did when he was away from his wife, that Lakshmi was exactly right. *What a terrible idea!* But watching Venkat settle the new birds in the back of his car with anxious absorption, like the father of a newborn, he refrained from saying anything. So many ideas were terrible, if you let yourself think about them.

S eth had nothing more illuminating to say about Venkat's state of mind. I wondered if the birds worked against my thesis, Finkbeiner's assertion. In fact, Venkat had found a way to love again. But had he *changed his life to preserve the bond* with his late family? I motivated myself with this research question as, against my better judgement, I went to visit Venkat at home. I had phoned him, to set a time, but when he did not pick up or call back, Seth told me when and where to go.

I had to drive. His house was farther out than the Sethuratnams' and the north winds of November were making the streets hostile to strolling. Even from within a car, though, little of Lohikarma is unattractive. Nervous and reluctant as I was, I was still cheered by the views.

Venkat's street was drabber than most here and his house looked extremely shabby in comparison to his neighbours' stalwart facades. A pocked lawn, flowerbeds littered with toppled, half-frozen weeds, cracked concrete steps. I rang the bell, heard it bong, waited.

I girded myself against the chill and rang again, opened the torn screen door and knocked. Lightning has to strike somewhere, I was thinking—a storm builds: friction, release. (My version of Seth's physics mind.) Nothing personal. Right? Lockerbie. The Twin Towers. I needed to stop thinking of myself as some special victim—

My freshly impersonal thinking fled as the dead bolt shunted and a vast image troubled my sight: Venkat and me, matched at the threshold, then folding away from each other in a chain of men like us, paper men, arms outstretched across this too-wide country, ready for uncoming embraces.

Count on a therapist for a fancy prose style. Venkat opened the door, but he wasn't even looking at me. He had eyes only for the bird perched on his cuff.

"Come, come in," he said, pointing his chin toward me, no eye contact. My shoes might have made it into the frame of his peripheral vision. "This is Mandy." He stroked the bird's head and neck with a finger, and it gave a little shake and fluff. "Mandy, *namaste*."

"*Namaste*," said the bird.

Venkat threw me a look of pride. "*Howd'youdo*, Mandy, *Howd'youdo*?"

Mandy squawked. "*Howd'youdo!*"

"Intelligent bird," I grunted. This was, to judge by Venkat's expression, what he wanted to hear. Was that why I said it? I followed him down a hallway, his smell, like gunpowder traces, in my nostrils. *Ah, the birds*, I thought, but that was wrong. I got close to the other two, as he took them out of their cages to change their newspaper. The smell came from him.

The birds had the run of the house. The flight of the house? They hopped along the backs of the chairs, a game. They appeared to live on the dining table, which was covered in a scratched plastic protector. There was a doily-ish thing under the plastic and a tablecloth beneath that, in a pink that matched the carpet.

I fed Mandy some pieces of apple.

"*Tasty*, Mandy?" Venkat asked.

"*Tasty!*" said Mandy.

"*Mandy is a good boy?*"

The parrot repeated that he was.

The cages were cleaner than the house, but the house was not as dirty as I expected. I watched one bird drop its business from a sideboard onto the pile carpet. Seth, I learned later, had arranged for a cleaner. I thought such a person would have to be paid well.

"Seth told me he likes to repeat "E equals mc squared," I said, by way of bolstering our strange sense of rapport.

Mandy flapped to a trapeze in the doorway. "*E equals emcee squared!*" He somersaulted, once, twice.

Venkat glanced slyly at me. "'*Bande Mataram*'?" he asked his bird.

"*Bande-e-e Mataram!*" Mandy willingly sang, and nipped a pineapple chunk from Venkat's fingers.

This, the chorus of a de facto Indian national anthem, raised my hackles—I hate anthems, all anthems. Drivel and dreck. When I hear schoolchildren sing it, I wanted to snatch them and run; when Lata Mangeshkar does it, she despoils the films of my youth. "Perfect," I said, "coming from a parrot." Venkat showed no reaction.

I was being drawn toward my reason for coming here. To Canada, and now, to Venkat's house. It wasn't to do what Seth had asked, though I hadn't admitted that to him, and possibly not to myself, but I must have known I could not be this man's therapist, help ease his pain, soothe his demons. He was too far gone. He didn't want to be helped. And, most of all, I feared him too much. Not him, exactly. My similarity to him. I was here to get to know him, because only then would I be fully convinced that we were different. The superficialities of his barren life were so close to my own that they brought all my despair to the surface. But I would change my life.

So much for my reasons for coming—why was he acting so differently toward me? He wasn't resisting me as before. He had opened the door.

"A noble bird," he told me, "beloved of ancient Greek emperors, because they would cry, 'Hail, Caesar!'"

"*Hail, Caesar!*" agreed Mandy.

"The other ones don't talk?" I asked. Venkat's breath smelled dead, but in the way of many people's breath, extruding as something grey, lumpy.

"They may still learn." He helped one of the others down from the chandelier, from where it had shat onto the clean cage, and caressed its apple-green nape, eliciting chuckles and trills. "But Mandy is the brightest." He looked up toward his favourite again. "Mandy! *Bharat Mata ki Jai!*"

This second praise-phrase for Mother India pulled a shudder up through my body from soles to scalp. Mandy parroted it, as Venkat continued speaking.

"You never said, when you came to my office last summer, that you are here because those same bastards killed your family too. Once Seth told me, I wanted you to know: don't think that, because I stayed in Canada, I have forgotten our motherland. I returned to Canada to better support our struggle."

My mind ticked forward through the implications. I had heard that ashrams, in India and abroad, were a favoured fishing-ground for Hindu nationalists looking to snag homesick *desis* with cash jangling in their pants. "Which struggle?" I asked, even though I was suddenly, irrationally sure that I knew. "What kind of support?"

"My good man." He gave me a complicit smile and rubbed his thumb and forefingers together. Venkat drew a full professor's salary. The money didn't go to the house, nor to the birds. A small portion alone would support his mother and sister. He had selected me of all people to tell: he was sending his money to—

"Mandy!" he said, still looking at me. "Khalistan or Kabristan?"

"*Kabristan!*" Mandy gaily responded, swinging on the trapeze.

"I must go," I said, and left him, letting myself out and tripping down his cracked steps to his yellow lawn, where I loved the bitter wind blowing away his thick smells.

I walked around the block, not ready to get back in my car. I pictured the scene: seventeen years ago, Venkat, fresh from his suicide attempt, is at Shivashakti's ashram. Perhaps with his younger sister. He is ashamed. He is at loose ends. His mother is urging him to return to Canada and his job, but he is nervous. Perhaps sub-nervous. Numb.

His life back there is meaningless: Sita and Sundar were not merely his reasons for living. They were his reasons for earning. Now he has no one to feed and no one to come home to—no reasons to go home and no reasons ever to leave the house. He knows, in some inchoate way, that if he returns to Canada, he will attempt suicide again. It's the only logical response to the conditions of his life.

He might still be on antidepressants; he might be forgetting to take them. Either way, the only true emotion he feels is anger. If he is on the drugs, the anger is blunted, but still present, palpable. *Those bastards stole my life. They killed my family. They took meaning from me. They took belief.* Sometimes he hears it, like this, in words. More often, his mind is a smoky blank, the anger its glowing embers.

Into this picture walks a man. A couple of men? They are at a satsang, at the Shivashakti ashram. They somehow walk out with Venkat and his sister. They strike up a conversation.

Venkat and his sister give their address, as well as quite a bit of other information. The men promise to visit, and Venkat feels eagerness in anticipation of seeing them. It's a relief to feel an emotion other than anger, though it is chiefly his anger that attracts them. When the men come, they talk in ways that make sense to him, about how the Jews have a homeland, the Muslims have a homeland, the Sikhs want a homeland. India—which they call Bharat—is the Hindus' homeland, but we are made to bow to minority rule here! The Christians, the Sikhs, even the

Muslims, who have their own goddamned country—they are allowed to make the laws! India is a democracy—the majority must rule!

Venkat subscribes. He pledges his salary to this worthy cause: purify Mother India. The men continue to visit. They talk strategy, philosophy, finance.

Seth, encountering Venkat at his mother's home, notices his renewed energy and cheer, even meets his new friends, though he mistakes them for actual friends, mistakes their interest as benign. Seth doesn't know. Venkat never tells him.

I had wormed my way into Venkat's mind. I wouldn't have thought I could. He reminded me—here is where you get the full depths of my own neurosis, but—he reminded me a little of my mother. His irrationality, the ridiculous leaps of logic. How can you put someone like that together on paper?

Fiction is the practice of "if this, then what?" For all my pages of notes on the strange things my mother said and did—from her physical roughness with us children, which she would deny; to her vanity about my father, which he might have seen as affection; to her insistence on the pogroms' non-occurrence, which became a wedge between my parents until Appa made it clear she was never to mention the subject—I could never extrapolate, or penetrate. Any guess I made as to her motivations, any prediction as to her next action, struck me as wrong. I knew her well enough to know that. I never knew her any better.

It probably helped that I didn't know Venkat very well. And however he talked, his actions, were not, I must admit, wholly illogical. What do normal people do in life? They love, they work. He gave his parakeets his love, and he gave his salary to—

I got in my car, started it, let it stall and turned the engine off again. *You must change your life.*

I am a man thrice-struck by lightning. The first strike, the pogroms, came close. The second, the bombing, struck home. Somehow I'd expected the third to come soon after and to kill me. Why think that way? It's lightning—nothing personal, even if I seemed to attract it. I waited seventeen years. Finally, the third bolt had struck, but at a distance. It didn't kill me, but it deadened me, for about fourteen months.

I was on a five-month leave from the IRDS, as a visiting professor at the Indian Institute of Management, in Ahmedabad. I had never taught before. They had sought me out, to teach on Organizational Behaviour, a leap from the work I was best known for, but not, it turned out, a long one. My lectures focused on social responsibility, corporate culture, conformity and change. The course had led me to idle musing on a new writing project, unrelated to my therapeutic practice, about the new business scene, outsourcing, globalization.

As I crossed the campus that day, following my twice-weekly seminar, the shadows made me stop. Long shadows, late afternoon. The seminar was going marvellously. I had always thought my native impatience would scupper any attempt at teaching, but this was *the* Indian Institute of Management, and my students were no dimbulbs. True, many gained admission largely on their skills with test-taking and teacher-pleasing, and so were bewildered when obsequiousness and regurgitation got nothing out of me but thunder. Underneath their eager veneers, though, real thoughts often lurked, and as they relaxed with me, these kids began to reveal the fascinations of their minds. Their company was rejuvenating.

In a couple of hours, two of my favourite students were to arrive at my on-campus quarters to talk about a joint research project, from which their theses would be drawn. Amita was brash and mouthy; she had worked two years in Bangalore, in the tech centre of an American bank, before entering grad studies with an eye toward microfinance. Jaggi, her batch-mate, was more reserved, an electrical engineer with more conventional career aspirations. I was guiding their research on a local Internet start-up, but our conversations often ballooned.

My thoughts were circling pleasantly as I crossed the campus, when the light—did I say shadows?—the majesty of the campus brought me to a halt. Particularly with the sun on the cusp of a rapid descent, the red brick arches framing views of red clay paths and green grass lawns and peacocks strutting across it all. When I started walking again, the direction of my thoughts had shifted: how little I knew of architectural magic. Were good minds attracted to beautiful places, or were the shapes of the buildings themselves conducive to deep thought? If it was the latter, what did it mean for the thinking of the poor that they so rarely lived and worked in places designed for aesthetic enrichment? What about the brains of the main run of the capitalist classes, to whom aesthetic value was typically sentimental or profitable, preferably both?

I had been given a large townhouse in professors' row, rather good. I lived here ten days at a stretch, going back to Delhi four days each fortnight to maintain my therapeutic practice, though I had reduced my client load to accommodate the leave. It was this rhythm, in combination with the relatively light load at IIM, that had let me finish a book: case studies and reflections on narrative therapies with Indian army personnel and their families. I hadn't heard back from my publisher yet, and as I turned on the TV news, was wondering whether to call him.

My students found me sitting in the dark. I had left the large sitting-room door open to the common lawns; otherwise, they said, they might have thought I was not home. They had seen the news, too, and thought to cancel our meeting, but had badly wanted to talk to me.

In Godhra, two hours west of us, a train load of Hindu pilgrims had had a rest stop, that morning, about 7:45. This much is agreed upon. They were returning from a mission that may have been devotional but was equally political: visiting the site of a proposed temple to baby Rama at the place of his apocryphal birth. The site had been cleared ten years earlier by 150,000 "volunteers." I prefer "fall-on-spears." Many of them couldn't agree even on who Lord Rama was, but reached a consensus long enough to tear down a mosque that had been on their chosen site since the time of Babur.

* * *

Pakistan or Kabristan! I heard the 150,000 squawking in chorus, as I tried again, still in front of Venkat's house, to start the car. *Pakistan, land of the pure—or Kabristan, land of the dead!*

Get out, they meant, or go to hell.

✳ ✳ ✳

Now, in 2002, ten years after the mosque's destruction, some pilgrims were returning from paying tribute to that temple yet to come. Their train paused at a station next to a neighbourhood overwhelmingly poor and Muslim.

Pilgrims stretched and peed. Pilgrims bought snacks and chai. Maybe pilgrims threw a Muslim chai-seller's tea back at him. Maybe pilgrims threw him off the train. Maybe a Muslim insulted a pilgrim. Maybe pilgrims forced him and others to profess devotion to Hindu Gods. Maybe pilgrims molested his daughter. Maybe it was the other way around.

Maybe it was a five-minute pause, maybe it was twenty-five. The train started to leave the station, then stopped, the emergency cord pulled. Maybe pilgrims pulled it themselves, inside the train, because other pilgrims had been left on the platform and Muslims were gathering there, attracted by their fellows' cries. Almost undisputed is that the fight then began in earnest. The railroad right-of-way is paved with stones and these stones began to fly.

But did the Muslims manage to dodge the stones, petrol-douse the inside of a compartment *and* throw flaming rags through the windows? Or did one of the stones, or even one of the pilgrims, knock a kerosene cookstove toward another cookstove-chiffonsari-oilynewspaper and did this domino into the conflagration that spread through the state?

Coach S-6. Fifty-eight dead by burning.

The Muslims were blamed, *post hoc ergo propter hoc*, as they say in the local lingo. A fight on the platform followed by a train-car fire—how could they not be responsible? It has since been alleged (post hoc again, but perhaps more propter hoc) that Chief Minister Narendra Modi and others mobilized, that same night, a spontaneous outpouring of grief and violence over the Hindu pilgrims' deaths. The personnel were ready to *Click!* into mob formation.

The train pulled into Ahmedabad exactly twenty-four hours late. Colonial legacies: tick-tock trains; communal riots. Relatives met the remains, carried into the station on the train: bodies heat-shrunk, faces fire-grimaced, eye sockets singed and empty.

The burning train car was merely the head of the match, struck and held to a fuse. Riots sparked, burned, sparked, burned, spread throughout the state.

I didn't leave my apartment that week. I barely left my sofa.

Some of my students organized a rally at the state legislative assembly and asked me to join. When I refused, they looked at me as though I were a coward. I did ask them not to go, it's true. I thought it dangerous for them. But I laughed when they suggested I wasn't coming because it was dangerous for me. "Me? I have nothing to live for!" I wheezed. I never saw them again.

One scattershot colleague worked up a delegation to Chief Minister Modi. He thought I might ornament his squad, me with my book on the Delhi pogroms, the one that made me famous among the few who cared. "Modi doesn't want to meet me," I informed him. "He doesn't know who I am. And if he does, he definitely doesn't want to meet me." I hung up without waiting for his counter-arguments.

It was midday, in the middle of that week. I hadn't locked the door since the last time I entered, and they walked in without knocking: Munir, a student of mine, his arm around a teenaged boy I didn't know.

"This is my brother, Sohail," Munir told me. "You have to hide us."

I liked Munir, difficult as he was in class, something hair-trigger about him. Very bright. He had to be: he was the only Gujarati Muslim on the IIM campus that year, a travesty he could classify in various ways. Still, he was not unreachable, then.

I gestured for them to sit, and brought them lime-water. The boys smelled of iron-carbon-nitrogen, blood-smoke-piss. Their eyes were flat and small. I had seen accounts of the atrocities on the news, though nothing yet like the full accounting that is still emerging: unborn children cut from bellies, systematic rape of Muslim women, throats slit and bodies burned.

"You are going to drive us to Delhi." That was the first thing Sohail said.

"You will take us, Professor Rao. I know you will, because I read that book you wrote, *Who Are the Victims?*" Munir reached for my cigarettes.

He drew one out of the pack and across his moustache-fuzz, smelling the unburnt tobacco. "Our family is dead. Killed by Hindus, Professor Rao. Like you."

* * *

I tried to drive away from Venkat's house, leaving him inside with his parakeet, mouthing the same slogans as the mobs that had killed Munir's family. My car kept stalling, starting, stalling.

I thought of my father, of how he was galvanized by the Delhi pogroms. He had been in his late sixties at the time, retired, contented. A good career, a life well lived, service to his country, his country as a cause. He had always voted for Congress. These were his beliefs.

The pogroms gave this life the lie. So he changed his life. He joined peace organizations; he helped Sikh widows fill out forms as they sought reparations; he volunteered in slum schools. If he had not seen what he had, on our street, and others, perhaps he would have, like Venkat, blamed the murders of our loved ones on "the Sikhs." Losing Kritika and the children slowed him down, it's true. But then he plunged in once more.

I have mentioned here only two books about the Delhi pogroms and their aftermath, including my own. *Who Are the Guilty?* And *Who Are the Victims?* There are practically no others—why?

Some ten years after the violence, Amitav Ghosh, a novelist of extraordinary scope, wrote a piece for an American magazine, asking the same question. He had been living in Delhi at the time. His neighbourhood was attacked, though he didn't witness the burnings. He, too, was reluctant to march, though he did, in the same protests as I. "Writers don't join crowds," he writes. "But what do you do when the constitutional authority fails to act? You join and in joining bear all the responsibilities and obligations and guilt that joining represents." And yet, he says, "Until now I have never really written about what I saw in November of 1984. Nobody, so far as I know, has written about it except in passing." Why silent for so long? "As a writer," he says, "I had only one obvious subject, the violence. From the news report, or the latest film or novel, we have come to expect the bloody detail or the elegantly staged conflagration that closes a chapter or effects a climax." He is a writer mostly of fiction; I suppose those temptations are particularly present for them.

Ghosh's article has three climaxes: a busload of people protecting a Sikh fellow commuter; a Hindu serving her Sikh neighbour tea in the muffled hush of her parlour while the mob sieges their street; and a moment I must have seen but which is effaced from my own memory: a group of thugs approached us, "brandishing knives and steel rods . . . A kind of rapture descended on us, exhilaration in anticipation of a climax . . . all the women in our group stepped out and surrounded the men; their saris and *kameezes* became a thin, fluttering barrier, a wall around us. They turned to face the approaching men, challenging them, daring them to attack. The thugs took a few more steps toward us and then faltered, confused. A moment later, they were gone."

Part of the reason he didn't write about the bloodshed is that he was spared the trauma of witnessing it. "What I saw at first hand," he said, "was not the horror of violence but the affirmation of humanity . . . the risks that perfectly ordinary people are willing to take for one another."

His representation is honest and necessary. Still, it doesn't fully unlock my understanding of that time. The key, for me, was more ephemeral, less dramatic than either the violence or the resistence. Something in the middle, something about surviving and shifting. About seeing. The critical moment, the thing I remember and want to record, was my father's transformation: one citizen awakened to his own blindness, his own complicity; my father's hands held to his eyes in pain as the scales fell.

Those who alter the course of history by being party either to violence or resistance are, in my experience, a minority. History happens *to* most people, not because of them. As for me, Ashwin Thrice-Struck. Or perhaps, more accurately, Thrice-Missed.

✳ ✳ ✳

I hid the boys for a few days, waiting for the streets to cool down. The cook, who had continued to come and go, said it was good I was eating again. I asked her to bring extra. "Making up for lost time," I told her. I didn't trust the mood on campus any more than the boys did.

I smoked and watched them eat, watched them hate themselves, their appetites, their impotence, me.

"You going to write a big book about this?" Munir asked at one point.

"No—" I said, but he stopped me before I could elaborate.

"I don't care. Why did I ask? Why am I asking why I asked? Curiosity is an old habit."

You can see why I liked him.

* * *

At the time, I was ashamed of not participating in any of the public acts of resistance, yet I continued to refuse. This was the third strike, and I had been spared. What for?

Mostly, in those days, I was musing on how limited the catalogue is of horrors people have perpetrated on one another through history. Unless they were Nazis. They, it has to be admitted, took the possibilities of ethnic warfare to a new level—managing nearly to eliminate the role of emotion from their methods. Most organizers of similar projects have not had the Nazis' resources and imagination. Fear and greed flow close to the surface and are easily tapped, but an oily slick of ignorance has greased the machines from Turkey to Nazi Germany to Bosnia to Rwanda to here.

The BJP: the Hindu nationalists' political party. The VHP: their cultural wing. The RSS: their paramilitary volunteers. Whoever you consider to be behind the Godhra attacks, whoever Venkat was supporting, did not have the Nazis' ingenuity, and they had the task of convincing an astonishingly diverse people of their essential homogeneity. But they did take the Nazis' lessons to heart. Sparky youth camps full of chanting and games; a plan of national assimilation and standards by which to judge it. They controlled education, so that school history books told a story of a past India remarkably similar to the India they wanted to create: valorous, prosperous, unitary, Hindu.

This was their plan: a consummately modern ideal of a nation-state unified by an apocryphal identity resurrected for people who didn't know the difference. A key tenet: elimination of the Muslims. The Hindu nationalists were more generous in this than others have been. The Muslims didn't have to be killed. They could convert. They could leave. But those willing to do neither had to be exterminated, which task now devolved to the mob. *Pakistan or Kabristan!*

* * *

The boys and I left around midnight on the sixth day, by which time news reports suggested that the violence was no longer constant, even in the epicentres—but why would we trust the news? I was nervous for the boys. The dew-like sweat on their high, clear brows; the dilation of their eyes—they had lost everything but their lives, and gave off an eager, reckless air.

We had to drive for twelve hours through the desert, but the hardest part of our flight to Delhi would be the first twenty minutes. The boys insisted I drive them back through their old neighbourhood. True, this was the quickest way out of town. It was also the quickest way to get us killed, which may have been a motive. Both boys were alternately inscrutable and contradictory, so I didn't ask their reasons. Perhaps I didn't want to know.

They held hands in the back of the car. The campus itself was serene and impassive as always, its architectural unity tightly walled. I drove out the gates and toward the boys' neighbourhood, as directed. The normal nocturnal rarity of human forms thickened into crowds until finally the car was surrounded by chanting Hindu hooligans.

I am stopped by a pounding on the hood and windshield of my car. I roll down my window. I argue. I show my ID. How can I be convincing when I don't care if I live or not? But I do it, for the sake of the boys. The car is rocking a little and at first I think it's the crowd, but the crowd is drifting away. It is Munir and Sohail, struggling in the back seat. Sohail has got his window down and shouts, "It's me! Your *miyabhai*! Come! I'm here for killing!"

The man talking to me looks interested. I tell him, "We don't like what you're doing. My sons are calling themselves Muslim in protest."

"Go," he tells me, as Munir wrestles Sohail back inside the car and we do as we are told.

"*Jai Shree Ram!*" we hear someone shout as we drive off.

* * *

When we got to Delhi, I asked them, *Where will you go?*

Pakistan, they said, and left me. Terrorists in the making. Suicide bombers, ready-to-use.

This was six months after 9/11. Their career options couldn't have been better advertised. I have looked for their faces ever since in newspapers, in pictures of the wanted and the dead.

How many well-intentioned colleagues urged me, back at the IRDS, *You must write about this. You were a witness.*

I wasn't, I told them. *I didn't see anything.* Though they didn't believe me, they ultimately accepted this, all except one woman, the sort of lefty who acted as though communism was her wounded lover. "Oh, you probably voted BJP," she hissed at me in the canteen, crowning days of direct and indirect harassment.

"Unlike you, I would not pretend to understand mass murder because I passed it in a moving car," I told her. She was a pathologically thin woman with thick eyeliner and rouge. I took a repulsive satisfaction in seeing her cower as I rose. "Unlike you, I don't believe I always have something of value to say."

As good as it felt, my outburst did nothing to relieve my puzzlement and shame over my inaction. I started to pull away from my work, which was all I had. No close friends, no family. No work. No love. Limbo. Drift. And then I got word of the trial, and bought a ticket to Canada. You know the rest, dear reader. Deadened and then galvanized. This was the work of the third strike.

* * *

Why had Venkat not told Seth about his support for the Hindu nationalists? Because Seth would have been appalled? Hardly: I know these Tamil Brahmins—those back home are insular and defensive; those abroad, clouded by nostalgia and misinformation. Seth would have seen the violence against Muslims in Gujarat as the work of isolated extremists, nutjobs, much the way 99.9 percent of Sikhs see the Air India bombers. Except that the Sikhs, in this regard, are right. Seth would probably not approve of Venkat sending money to the nationalists, but he would understand the impulse. His community believes itself to be under attack for its historical privilege; he would appreciate the Hindu desire to protect Bharat Mata. Up to a point.

He would have thought Venkat was being imprudent, though, that he should save his money, give it to his nephews and nieces. Better yet, give it to Shivashakti.

Or perhaps Venkat kept it secret in unseen rebellion against the way Seth infantilized him, a private proof that his decisions were still his own.

All of the above? It didn't matter. I didn't think about it even as long as it took for you to read about me thinking about it.

Why did Venkat choose me to tell? He saw in me his reflection. They wrecked his life; they wrecked mine. This is what he was doing about it. What was I doing?

I needed badly to get back to my apartment. I turned the key, again, started the car, drove.

I had laid in whisky the night before, knowing I was going to Venkat's house today. I congratulated myself on my foresight, but now hesitated at the bottom of the fire escape, knowing the fire water waited above. It was barely noon, and I thought at first that was why I stopped, feeling the gods of decorum tugging at my sleeve.

No, it wasn't that. I stopped because I didn't want to deaden my self-analysis, the way I had for nearly twenty years.

Why dredge all this up?

Because I needed to understand it. Understand what?

This: what happened to me?

This: could it have been stopped?

I didn't mount my iron stairs. I turned away, up my alley, and began to walk.

Alone. Always alone. I needed a guide, a hand-holder, a Krishna to my Arjuna. Who?

Seth would have been happy to listen as I talked this through, but I wasn't yet close enough to him to ask. My old adviser, Marie Chambord? Perhaps, had she not died. But she wouldn't have been the right person for this either.

I wanted my Appa.

A teddy bear man with a porcupine son. My prickliness, as I grew, was a disappointment to him. But whose doing was that? By the time my father came to realize what my mother's bitterness had wrought, he couldn't have done much to correct it. Or maybe the way I am is simply innate.

After the disaster, my mother's health worsened. Cancer came. Appa cared for her, fed her, his gestures almost paternal. Indian women transfer their dependence from parents to their husbands; it is encouraged. My mother had entered marriage at sixteen, much younger than my father. Lakshmi once said Seth had been like a mother to her, in their early years in Canada, when she was so young and feeling abandoned by her family. I might have characterized my father's care for my mother as maternal, except my experience of maternal care didn't include such tenderness.

I didn't look after my mother when she was dying. I looked after my father as he looked after her. I fixed his meals, went to the pharmacy, sat with him as he sat with her. I had never made her happy; Kritika was the child she would have wanted at her bedside.

When my mother died, in 1993, I asked Appa whether he wanted to move in with me, but he said he didn't want to be trapped in an apartment complex, meeting other old people who lived in their grown children's extra rooms. If I had had a wife and children, we would have made more of an effort. As it was, neither of us wanted him too close to my arid life.

He stayed in our old neighbourhood, with his old friends, and some young ones: two of the neighbours had small children he enjoyed; he even babysat, from time to time.

I visited him, once or twice a week. We would eat ice cream, take walks, drop in on his chums. He never spoke of Kritika and the children except to recall their brilliance. Once, he talked of my mother. He had first seen her bitterness when we children were young. She would criticize the flat, which was small and not nice, criticizing my father, by extension, for not yet being able to afford more, though he was still young. She went frequently to her mother's. We got our first house when I was six, and moved into the second and final one when Kritika and I were in our teens. It was large and airy. We had always had an ayah and a maid, and now there was a cook, and eventually a driver. Still, my mother only grew more bossy, and no less resentful.

"I often wished she were happier," Appa said. His voice was hoarse, in age, something obstructing its passage from the cavity of his chest. "But I could accept, at least, that her unhappiness was not my fault. It was something she couldn't identify." He had never told me this before. Would it have helped if he had? He surprised me, then. "I always thought you saw this. She was the enigma that drove you to study the human mind."

His housecleaner found him one morning, fully stiffened in a living room chair, a fatal stroke, or so the doctors told me.

* * *

Think on what you know, Ashwin, I heard now as I walked, his voice booming as though from behind the distant mountains, a voice Marlon Brando might have used to play a Bollywood don. *Not why it was you never married. You have plenty of theories on that. Not about that troll, Venkat.*

The breezes across Lohikarma's slopes were bracing. My cheeks chapped in the dry winter air.

Think back, my son. Appa's voice gained strength and intimacy in my mind, sounding increasingly like Seth's. *Not about yourself.*

Ah.

I began, tentatively:

The Air India bombing was not simply the result of some limited if collective murderous rage. That rage was fed by a larger sense of outrage, resulting from the under-noticed, under-reported Delhi pogroms.

The pogroms? The doing of overzealous party functionaries, using the Dragon Lady's assassination as an excuse to wage an intimidation campaign against Sikhs.

The assassination? A reprisal for her having ordered the invasion of the Golden Temple in Amritsar.

Keep going. Amritsar?

* * *

I had circled my neighbourhood to land at the Chinese restaurant downtown. Thirty tables at least, no more than six occupied at any given time. Red carpet, stained near the door. A tank of carp I stood and watched until a bobbing-frowning waiter reminded me that I should seat myself.

* * *

Sikhdom's holiest shrine rises as a lily from a pool; the city is named for that water—*amrit*, the Sikhs' holy nectar, drunk by the devoted when they are baptized. The generals had been told not to destroy the temple. "We entered with humility in our hearts and prayers on our lips," said one, in the true spirit of Indian secularism, which means not that the state governs without God, but rather that every god governs at once.

The Dragon Lady upturned that bowl of amrit, drowned fleeing fighters and praying pilgrims, blew fiery breath ahead of the spreading nectar, drenched Sikhs around the world. They tasted ash in it; they tasted blood. They burned the Dragon Lady in effigy, and hung her, and stomped upon her. Prominent Sikhs in India returned their government awards, resigned their parliamentary seats, and so found themselves allied with a movement whose aims and leadership they had never admired.

The government's response was to pull out the Terrorism and Disruptive Activities Act—TADA! No need to steal your neighbour's apples; if you wanted his tree, all you needed to do was accuse him of being a Khalistani sympathizer. "Suddenly there was no crime in Punjab," said a former police officer, "only terror." Thus began the long summer that led up to the Dragon's slaying.

But again, said my father, as I twirled a noodle that seemed to have no beginning and no end, *think. There comes a time to act, but . . .*

Not for me?

Do not put words in my mouth. You eventually must act, but for now you must think.

To act is to do violence.

Bullshit, my son.

That was me putting words in his mouth—Appa never would have said that. The expression suited him, though, and it made me smile to hear him use it.

You fool yourself, that your life is something done to you, that you live but don't act. You left Rosslyn.

Did I tell him about her?

You are stringing that poor Vijaya along.

I most definitely did not tell him about the widow.

You counsel people daily to change their lives. He was thundering at me. *You will act!*

I looked around the restaurant, a little unnerved, but the other patrons—two men, gazing shyly at each other as if on a second date; an Asian businessman steering noodles away from his lapels; a drab threesome of college girls—were in their own little worlds. I love that old saw: *their own little worlds.* The world in my head seemed neither small nor mine, but that was why I became a therapist.

My father was growing impatient. *Think! What came before?*

The Emergency.

✳ ✳ ✳

In 1975, a resolution was introduced by the government of Punjab—a state poor in cash but rich in resources—suggesting a devolution of power into the hands of the states. The young P.M., Indira Gandhi, did not take kindly to it. And she was having other problems: on trial for election hanky-panky. She took care of all of it by declaring a national State of Emergency.

I was in Canada, then. My father wrote me letters throughout, so that the Emergency happened, for me, in the measured, regretful voice of his reportage. At that time, he thought the prime minister did what had to be done, no more, no less.

I don't think that anymore, he interjected gruffly.

I always thought you were fooling yourself.

So you say.

* * *

Mass demonstrations followed. The first? In Amritsar. Yes, the Sikhs of Punjab were the first to raise the cry, and after twenty-one months, as protests were squashed and silence spread, the Sikhs were the last men standing, even if behind bars: 33 percent of the Emergency's nearly 150,000 detainees were said to have been Sikhs, who make up 2 percent of the Indian population.

Given this, how could some of them not start to imagine a Sikh nation?

They had taken on several strange bedfellows (are bedfellows always strange?): Hindu nationalists, who, since they oppose Congress, are natural allies for any other opposition. Thus they opposed the storming of the Golden Temple. Thus they in fact helped Sikhs during the post-assassination riots of 1984.

But they also, later, encouraged destruction of mosques and churches, professed expulsion or forced conversion. And, earlier, they encouraged the killing of that much more famous Gandhi—no dragon, no lady—in the service of this abhorrent idea: India for Hindus.

* * *

I left the restaurant pondering Venkat. *What's with that strange light in his eyes?* I asked my father. *Or the patterns on his face, like time-lapse immigration maps.*

Hardly were those words out when Venkat himself faced me on the sidewalk. The temperature was dropping and his putty-like breath mingled visibly with mine in the brief space between us. He carried a large birdcage with a couple of blankets over it, and I glanced at the door he had emerged from: a vet's office. This was one of Lohikarma's shabbier streets, studded with dormant storefronts, their windows soaped over and signs inverted.

"Ah," Venkat said. Would he ask me why I had bolted from his house a few hours earlier? But he didn't seem to have found it strange. "You must join us," he said, summoning an odd heartiness that queered my stomach. He leaned to envelop me in a thin, warm miasma of damp down-fill and vet's office. "A group of young persons, white Canadians, have asked me to lead them in learning about Vedic practices. You would have much to say. Come, this afternoon, 2 P.M., at the Lutheran church, not six blocks from here."

Say yes, say no, but walk away, my son! Walk away!

"What?" I asked.

Venkat's fleshy lips seemed isolated in his otherworldly face. "Sacrifice. Soma. A revival of our original order . . ."

I backed away from him, feeling a strange grin on my face. I waved effeminately and scurried off, slipping and sliding over icy patches in my inappropriate shoes until finally I scrambled up my fire escape, exhilarated, chuckling aloud.

I put the kettle on for tea, looking guiltily at my bottle of whisky, as we do in the presence of our parents.

Ah, what the hell, he said, *I'll join you.*

I smiled and poured two shots. We toasted. I drank.

So, carry on.

✳ ✳ ✳

The Mahatma's assassination. I was eight. The man who had killed him thought that Gandhiji and Nehru were Muslim-lovers, that this (and not the longstanding British policy of divide and rule . . .) had led to the creation of Pakistan, a Muslim state lopped off India's northwest and northeast corners, like ears on that sacred cow's face. West Pakistan was cut from the Sikhs' holy land, Punjab, with a double-edged sword. The Sikhs were balanced on the blade. Forced, they jumped toward India, a self-proclaimed secular democracy, where their rights would exist on paper, at least.

Sikhs had served in the British army through multiple generations, multiple wars, but this had become tougher as they came to realize that was all the white man wanted them for. Second-generation
Sikh Canadians, receiving Second World War conscription notices
from Ottawa, asked why they got soldiers' uniforms but not the vote.
First-class fighters; second-class citizens. Sure, we'll battle the Krauts
and Japs; let's see you open the doors to your white-collar world.

In 1919, they had endured another Amritsar massacre, when General Dyer's troops opened fire on peaceable, picnicking Punjabis, part
and parcel of the period's paranoia. After the First World War, Canada,
Australia and New Zealand gained greater sovereignty, the Empire's
thanks for so many donated lives. India? Not. There, His Majesty's
forces put themselves to much trouble quelling a nascent independence
movement. They were just wiping their brows, having publicly executed nearly a hundred such violent dreamers, supporters of the Ghadars.
This was a party started by North American Sikhs, which envisioned
a United States of India for all Indians, a free, secular, democratic nation—plainly a ridiculous notion, of which the inferior races needed to
be disabused.

We, Indians, have never given them sufficient credit for that.

As one Canadian parliamentarian put it, with quaintly rough-
hewn grammar: "The Hindoos never did one solitary thing for
humanity in the past two thousand years and will probably not in the
next two thousand."

Canada had always courted European immigrants while barring
the Brown Peril, exercising Canada's right to Keep Canada White. In
1914, under newly written (and, because of successful legal challenges, repeatedly rewritten) immigration laws, Canada famously turned a
shipload of Indians back at Vancouver harbour. "Hindoo Invasion Re-
pelled!" the headlines hollered, floating on strains of "White Canada
Forever!" an anthem sung by mobs ten thousand strong.

When the emigrés returned to India, they were fired on by the
Brits, who feared that this rejection—demonstrating that all British subjects were hardly equal within and throughout the Empire—might have
converted some of them to the Ghadars' cause.

Which it did.

Each humiliation grew the Sikhs' pride. Each galvanized a small subset into quests for purity and self-rule. Each formed a rough link on history's rattling chains.

Once upon a time—

No, be specific.

Punjab, the Land of Five Rivers, at the dawn of the sixteenth century. *Better.*

There was a Hindu who was bothered by empty ritual and hierarchy. His name was Nanak. He founded a cult devoted to humility, service, and meditation on the word of God. Its adherents were called Sikhs, which means, I think, only "disciple." His fame spread; his following grew.

On his deathbed, Guru Nanak appointed a successor from among his disciples, who begat another guru in the same manner, until this lineage culminated in the *Guru Granth*: a book composed of centuries of wisdom from the Sikh Gurus and from others: devotees, mystics and saints professing Hinduism, Islam, and shades of belief in between. The final guru: a perfect admixture, a true immortal, a book.

Was there persecution, over these years? There was. Martyrs were made. Sikhs believe in valour. But I recall a young Sikh telling me the story of the ninth guru, who was killed while defending Hindus. "Sikhs are in the world not for Sikhs alone, but for anybody who needs a Sikh," he said, eyes shining.

And yet.

By the time I came back to India, Sikhs were no longer seen as defenders of any interests but their own. "It used to be that if we were riding on a train and saw a Sikh in our carriage, we would feel safer," my mother told me, in the midst of the riots. "Nowadays if we see one, we feel scared."

When I repeated to a Sikh colleague what my mother had said, he grew heartsick. "They are tarring us all with the same brush," he said. "Khalistan, land of the pure!" Disgusted, he had become tempted to shave his beard and yank off his turban. Others had been convinced, by repeated acts of oppression and discrimination in India, England, Canada, the USA, that self-determination was the only way, but most of them still would not follow the self-appointed guardians of orthodoxy, so the purists were attacking them. The terrorist's dilemma: acting on behalf of constituencies who cannot be convinced except by their own deaths. Purity: the old lie.

When I think on the Air India disaster, I hear the chain of history rattle. Its links are loops. Loops have holes. Was the bombing a Canadian or an Indian tragedy? Why pose this false division? Canada was colonized when India was, and their fates were ever linked. There is no expiation. The declaration of any single truth is itself an act of violence.

Once upon a time—here, I cannot be specific—Hinduism arose, perhaps on the soil south of the Indus; perhaps brought by Northern invaders. Without Hinduism, there would not have been Sikhism. Without India, could there be Empire? Without Empire, could there be radicalizing? Without Canada, could there have been a bomb?

Once upon a time: poetry, syncretism, mysticism, death.

Once upon a time: evolution, matter, being.

Once upon a time: time.

* * *

Night had fallen early beyond my Canadian windows. I had a message on my phone from Seth. Would I tell him what Venkat had told me?

Don't you think it's important that Seth be made aware?

I'm not sure.

Maybe you are not sure you are the one to do it.

I doubt my telling him will do anything but anger me.

So why lay these links out, in order, as you have?

You tell me.

I can. Firstly, for you, my son, thinking is action.

(No reply. I was thinking.)

At least insofar as you write down your thoughts.

This causal chain must frame my book?

It must.

New links on the chain are still being forged.

Yes, that is why.

And what else?

Think.

I had what I needed and now I wanted to leave Lohikarma: I wasn't ready to see Seth and it would be too hard to avoid him if I stayed. I would perhaps call him from Winnipeg to say I could do nothing for Venkat, promise to return in winter. Would Brinda come home for a winter break? *Pang!* Excellent word: from the beginning of pain to the beginning of anger, the sound replicates the feeling, of being snapped in the heart. Would I ever see her again? How was she? I thought of her not only because I regularly thought of her, but because I felt now a little of what she might have felt on leaving me: a tenuous, suspicious sense of peace.

That's it—that's the other thing, my son.

You felt that a little, after my mother died.

Come now! I always felt it.

Seth was so like my father—*gracious forbearance*—how had I not seen it before?

On my visits with Appa, toward the end of his life, I would go into his room to say good night, and sit beside his bed until he slept, practising for his death, worried he would die awake and alone. He did, anyway.

And yet. Here I am, old boy, like it or not.

I crossed to the dining table, opened my computer, and wrote an e-mail to Vijaya, a response to a dull, polite note of inquiry she had written to me months earlier. I was cordial and distant and, without saying so, made it clear that there was nothing to be hoped for between us. I was vague on when I would return to India. I said I hoped she and her children were well, but asked nothing about any of them. I did ask about the cat.

Did I let myself think about whether I would contact Rosslyn when I got to Ottawa? Likely I did. Think about it, that is.

I drank a final drink. I slept alone, as always. The next morning, I drove east.

WINTER 2004/05

If you want to play this game of love.
Bring me your head in the palm of your hand.

—Guru Nanak

$\mathcal{B}$rinda drove west. No one knew she had gone. No one thought to expect her. She drove over frozen Canadian roads, hairpinning up and up then down, up and up then down, through blinding Kootenay snow. She had not expected to drive her car this winter, and her snow tires languished in the storage room of an Edmonton apartment building. She wasn't seeing the edge of the road so much as intuiting it. If she saw anything, it was the home and future she was abandoning, floating in her mind's eye. She drove slowly, aware in some dim and peevish way of her vulnerability. Her face was stony; it was wet with tears. She was alone with the sound of her breathing. It was hard to get the radio here, inside the mountains' cradles.

A bounding shape coalesced out of the snow, curled horns and shaggy bearing. Brinda heard a whistle, as if from a flute, and swerved. A mountain goat, it must have been, grinning and unaware, caught by the headlights but not in them. If she had swung the lights back, it would have been gone, the teasing snow drawing aside to reveal nothing but darkness and more darkness behind. But she was sliding, now turning the wheel the opposite way, feeling the crunch that was the edge of the road, the rear of the car dipping toward the precipice.

She put the car in neutral, remembering vaguely some prescription of that sort, though whether it applied in this situation, she didn't know. She tapped the brake pedal, then pushed hard. Nothing happened. That was a first. The car was spinning, very slowly, turning her away from where the view would have been. She knew there were mountains hovering out there in the darkness, and in daylight she would have trusted they touched the earth, but she couldn't see the mountains nor where they touched, and so, for her, all that was behind her was snow falling through space and time without end. She slid toward endless falling, some version of herself endlessly falling.

Then the back wheels of the car slipped off the road and the nose tipped up: space and time were infinite, but not for her, not tonight. She forehanded the gearshift into drive, depressed the accelerator and rose up out of death's jaw, braking as soon as the car was horizontal. It didn't stop her from hitting the cliff walling the other side of the road, but stopped her from hitting it too hard. She reversed very slowly back into her own lane and started, again, to drive.

A semi-trailer passed her going the other way, a motorhome appeared behind her, and she saw them crossing each other where the ghost of her car might have sat ruminating on the fate it had escaped. Each vehicle had half her ghost-car stuck to its nose; the blood on their bumpers was hers. *Exit ghost.*

At 8 p.m. on a snowy night in mid-December 2004, the Sethuratnams' doorbell rang. Lakshmi, on the treadmill in front of the TV, started. She would never answer the door alone at night, however, and only interrupted her exercise under duress, so she did nothing but wait for Seth. Seth was in the bathroom and so expected Lakshmi to go. The doorbell rang again. They met at the door, each looking annoyed as Seth undid the dead bolt and Lakshmi opened the door.

It was Brinda, whom they weren't expecting for another ten days. "Sweetheart!"

She endured their embraces, then unzipped her down-filled jacket. Her hair fell in her face as she took off her boots. Even when she straightened, though, she didn't look her parents in the eye. She hadn't said anything yet, and didn't seem overjoyed to have surprised them. She looked strange and had some strange mark on her face, and when Seth took a last look outside before closing the door, he saw that the front of her little Honda was pugged, with one headlight smashed.

"You drove here in that car?"

Brinda looked at him, grey and weary. "I had a little accident, a bighorn. It's fine, I'm not hurt. I need to— I'm leaving Dev."

"Oh, oh, oh." Lakshmi folded their girl into her arms and Brinda's tears started up. "Of course you need to," the mother said, and Seth thought, *She does?*

It must be something only a mother could see. Lakshmi could be critical of her daughters but her claws came out at the first sign that anyone else might have hurt them. And neither she nor Seth loved Dev.

But Brinda had never told them anything before this, before saying she was . . . *oh God*, it couldn't be true. What had happened to her? What had happened to her car? What had he failed to protect her from?

They shuffled to the family room, Lakshmi's arms still wrapped around her daughter. She gestured at him as he sat. "Seth. Get her a glass of water." He went.

"I hadn't—" Brinda paused, not exactly waiting for her father to return, but not wanting to repeat herself in case she said something he needed to hear. She was herself curious to hear what she would say. She hadn't known she was certain about leaving Dev until she made her announcement at the door. The idea was six months old and the marriage was in tatters. But still she hadn't decided. Seth gave her the water, she sipped and tried again, "I wasn't . . ." She realized now that she had in fact been certain only since escaping death in dark and snow, since backing away from the mountain, hands up.

Her mother sat, holding Brinda's hand and looking down tactfully so that her daughter wouldn't see in her eyes the distress and anxiety that she was communicating, anyhow, through her fingers. Seth sat on her other side. Brinda felt an ancient surge of impatience—even now, when she needed them, when she was breaking their hearts—impatience with her parents' love and worry. Prompted by this familiar inner storm, she lied.

"He's been seeing someone else for awhile." She pulled her hand out of Lakshmi's. She had loved her mother's hands as a child, soft skin, ridged nails, ropy veins she played with in moments when her mother couldn't pay attention to her. She wished she could play with them now; she wished her mother were distracted and she were small again. She moved to an armchair, where they couldn't crowd her.

"It wasn't the first time, though it was the first time I threatened to leave him. He came to visit me in Baltimore, but when I got back for Christmas, I could see there's no way anything's changing. So yesterday, while he was at work, I jumped in the car and drove." She waved vaguely toward the great darkness without, began to cry again, and moved back to the sofa, where her mother put her arms around her. They had not left Seth quite enough room, but he perched where he could and put a hand on Brinda's back.

She wiped her cheeks hard, felt her parents' hands warm and heavy on her back and wished she could shrug them away. "I'll be fine."
Rage clawed at Seth as he went to the meditation corner, at one side of

the hearth in their family room. He bent to take up his rudraksha mala, his hands shaking. Canada! What ever possessed them to come here? His mother had had it right when she said her greatest regret was letting him emigrate. It opened up the flood, in their family. Now half of his siblings' children also were located abroad—oh God, what would his brothers and sisters say when they heard?

He began the concatenation of syllables his God had prescribed for him when they'd met: *Jai Shivashakti Jai, Jai Shivashakti Jai, Shiva Shivashakti, Jai Shivashakti, Jai Shivashakti Jai.* The prayer was just under his breath, holding up that bridge of air between him and the outside world, barely loud and hard and real enough to drown out the sounds of his wife getting his daughter settled in her old bedroom upstairs.

His mother had said that once you let your child leave India, you lose him. He comes back every four years, she said, with loving smiles and Cadbury's chocolate, talking about all he misses, but then he fades away again to eat meat and speak English with white people in cold lands. He promised you he wouldn't eat meat, he says he isn't eating it, but you can smell it on him. If you let your child go, she warned the neighbours, you will never know him again and you will lose command of his children and his wife.

Lakshmi loved it in Canada. Seth had heard her talk about the freedoms she had here: not to participate in the oppression of ritual; not to justify her choices for her children to all the relatives; not to attend every wedding of the season; to dress as she liked; to be alone when she needed. She had contrasted herself with Sita in this regard, whom Venkat had held to specific standards. Seth hadn't had the strength, apparently.

Lakshmi had not suffered Seth's level of anxiety when their daughters came of marriageable age. It wasn't *her* dharma at stake. *Kanyadanam*. He had asked his wife, when the inquiries started to arrive from other parents in their community, from out east, from California, one from India, to talk to Brinda and Ranjani, to ask if they would consider one of their boys—promising young professionals from good families. Seth found them, at least superficially, suitable. *But, no.* Even though neither girl had any other prospect at that point, they demurred: they had been raised Canadian, they said. They couldn't agree to a marriage with someone they didn't know. They could get to know the boy before the marriage, Seth said. What they meant, they said, is that they would have to get to know the boy and then decide whether to marry him; they couldn't agree to marry him and then get to know him. That, they said, would be too weird.

Jai Shivashakti Jai, Jai Shivashakti Jai, Shiva Shivashakti, Jai Shivashakti, Jai Shivashakti Jai.

Being Canadian meant being fussy and then settling after all for second-best. Would Brinda be in this situation now if she had married into one of the families on offer? No, she would have finished her doctorate, gotten a job and had two babies by now. She would be happy, like everyone else.

There had always been something a little funny about Dev. Sure, he and Lakshmi had been happy at first: a PhD, Indian. Okay, the mother was uneducated, and Christian—not ideal. The father, not so communicative. Not Tamil. But overall, promising. Seth had been glad to be wrong in not trusting the young to choose for themselves. Now, look.

And Ranjani. His nostrils flared.

When she called to tell them she was pregnant, he had been enthusiastic. A baby is never wrong. They always liked Greg. Respectful to Seth and Lakshmi. Good to Ranjani, and good for her. But when Seth had asked when they were going to get married, she had said, "Dad." Her tone: practised and ungentle. "We've been living together for eight years. In the eyes of the law, we're married whether we want to be or not." And what were he and Lakshmi supposed to say to their friends? Their mothers?

Lakshmi's solution: when they announced the pregnancy, they said Ranjani and Greg had married a few years earlier in a civil ceremony without telling anyone, that the young couple didn't believe in the spectacle and waste of weddings.

"You're right that's one reason I don't want to get married," Ranjani retorted, impatience humming up the wires. "Why say *I am* married at the same time?"

Lakshmi told her that unless she wanted to explain to each and every one of their friends why she wasn't married, she should let her parents say what they want.

Seth hadn't liked the strategy any better. "Why would anyone get married like that?" *Preposterous.*

"Seth! Remember that's what Brinda's friend Colleen did? She didn't want to deal with the family politics, who to invite, this and that. I thought it was a great idea."

"Who would do that?" he asked, and Lakshmi threw up her hands.

He felt his eyebrows dampen and wiped them with his thumb. His mother had been right. And now it was too late.

Jai Shivashakti Jai, Jai Shivashakti Jai, Shiva Shivashakti, Jai Shivashakti, Jai Shivashakti Jai.

What was he praying for? Peace? But he didn't want peace. He wanted to be angry. He wanted his daughters to be happy. Goddammit, why couldn't he make them listen to him? Well, Ranjani did seem happy, so maybe Seth didn't have a leg to stand on there. But Brinda: No husband. No job. No proper degree. It was his fault, for not being firmer. This country robbed parents of their dharma. He heard Lakshmi enter the family room behind him. It was her fault. She was always disagreeing with him. And now Brinda was paying the price. He heard her sit on the sofa, but as though from a great distance. A heat in his ears was obliterating the sound of his prayers.

Lakshmi waited a time, and when he didn't stop or turn, came to sit beside him. She waited again, and then put a hand on his thigh. "Seth?"

His rage concentrated at the point of her touch. He was inside the head of Shiva, as the Lord sat deep in stone-cold meditation atop Mount Kailash. And here was Kama, now disguised as his wife, approaching as if innocently even while taking aim with a flowery arrow. Don't look, Seth! The eye of your enlightenment will open and the cold beam of knowledge burn her to ash.

Seth fixed his gaze on the engraved-silver vessel of *vibhuti* on the hearth. Shivashakti materialized holy ash after each address, and Seth had replenished his supply on his last trip to India, standing in line as a devotee scraped portions into bits of paper torn from *The Hindu* newspaper. He had carried it home in his breast pocket.

Jai Shivashakti Jai, Jai Shivashakti Jai, Shiva Shivashakti, Jai Shivashakti, Jai Shivashakti Jai.

Lakshmi withdrew.

And from inside the mind of his Lord, Seth now heard Him speak, the silence of the everynowhere voice, so that the hiss in his ears dissolved.

Yes, my son, Kama is an arrogant imp—Desire, the great disruptor. If not for him, the cycles of creation and destruction would halt! And well might your thoughts be disrupted! Please, sir, ask Vanity and Illusion to stand aside. All you have suffered, Lakshmi has suffered too. Every decision she has taken was also yours. This crisis has tipped your rajas out of balance, and so you show your flank to anger and desire. Think again. You can slow time by speeding motion, but you cannot reverse it. Right your rajas. Slow yourself. Open to your other half.

Seth put his rudraksha mala down and took up a pinch of vibhuti in a single gesture, smearing it on his forehead and neck as he rose. He found Lakshmi upstairs in her own meditation corner, in Ranjani's old room.

Ranjani had fled to Vancouver straight after high school. He and Lakshmi could never understand. Brinda was still living at home, going to Harbord. She seemed happy. Ranjani made it clear she would never move back—took all her albums, posters, knick-knacks and doo-dads. By contrast, when Brinda left, she said she wanted to return, and so took only the bare essentials.

The first few years, he and Lakshmi left the girls' bedrooms as they were. They hoped Ranjani might at least come home for summers; she didn't. They hoped Brinda might find a job at Harbord after finishing her PhD. She didn't finish her PhD. And when she married, Lakshmi helped her pack up her sentimental items to take to Edmonton, since they could all now finally accept that she would never again move back home. Seth thought of her now, in the queen bed they installed so that she and Dev could use it together when they came for holidays.

Gradually, too, they had made changes in Ranjani's room. She told them not to wait for a wedding. She told them, a few years after she met Greg, that she was living with him and that she wouldn't come home for holidays unless he could come too, and stay in the same room with her. Seth and Lakshmi meekly got a larger bed for her room also. There were other guests, from time to time, they reasoned, for whom it would come in handy.

And Lakshmi, increasingly serious about a certain Godless, soundless, structureless and yet (to Seth's way of thinking) horribly demanding school of meditation, had chosen to practise it in Ranjani's former bedroom, saying the relative isolation and lack of decor helped her focus. Seeing her there now, he chose not to disturb her, but hearing him, she rose and followed him, past Brinda's closed door, each of their hearts crumpling like a damp tissue in the palm.

In their bedroom, she told him, "I was angry, that you went first to pray to Shivashakti instead of coming to talk to me." Was it in the nature of a confession? She held her head and neck stiffly. "And then I thought I should calm down and realized you were probably trying to find a way to calm down also, and that you would come to me when you were ready."

He nodded. Let her think that he was trying to calm down. She would not believe the truth, that it was Shivashakti who bade him be reasonable and return to her.

"We have to be calm. No one has died, after all," she said, and he saw in her liquid eyes all his own terror and disbelief.

He moved to take her into his arms, be taken into hers. "What does it mean?" he asked into her hair.

"I don't know, I don't know." She held his arm around her neck as she would a buoy. "These things happen, these days. Not in our family, okay. Not among our friends . . . But even back home, young people are choosing not to marry."

"She did marry, unlike Ranjani."

"Ranjani may as well be married."

"Fine." He could admit now that he wasn't worried about Ranjani. If she was happy, he was happy. And she *was* happy, while Brinda—oh, his poor little girl. "Divorce?" (He pronounced it "die—." Distasteful foreign word, yet another his daughters had tried to teach him to pronounce correctly: "'Div,' Dad. As in *div-ide*.") "Perhaps I'll talk to Ashwin Rao about it," he said. "He is unmarried. And he has seen how things have changed, in India, in the last twenty years."

"Brinda is not living in India, Seth." She backed out of his arms, got her nightclothes from the back of the bathroom door and began changing. "And I don't know that I'm interested in telling that Ashwin Rao much about our family life."

"He's very highly thought-of in his field," Seth said, but under the exasperation at her quick judgements, his pleasure tinkled minutely. She liked him best. Even if Ashwin was like her—iconoclastic, reclusive, skeptical—Lakshmi liked Seth best. She was Seth's other half.

Ashwin didn't have one.

And now, neither did Brinda.

* * *

In bed, at last.

Nearly asleep, then *gasp*, *thump*, and the image came back—naked, clifftop, night, falling into the void—once a year the nightmare returned with an eerie familiarity. Oh, how his heart thumped, still.

He remembered: this is what drove him into the arms of his Lord. The bhajan songs: *An aged man is but a paltry thing /Unless soul clap its hands and sing, and louder sing / For every tatter in its mortal dress . . .* The sound, filling the void: nothing that would stop you from falling, but maybe stop you from being so afraid.

*I*t wasn't entirely true that no one knew Brinda was coming.

When I left Lohikarma in November, I had continued east across the country. I had thought to stay and work in Montreal, except that Suresh and Lisette were insisting on putting me up, for months, if needed. They had the room and were away all day, they said, but I wasn't positive of my capacity to live with others for that long a stretch.

All right. It wasn't only that.

On my way to Montreal, I had stopped in Ottawa. After my single interview, I drove again to Rosslyn's neighbourhood. A sunny Wednesday, four o'clock, early for a commuter to be home, unless she worked in schools.

She was in her front yard. I drove past, no more than five metres away, but she didn't see me; she had eyes only for the chainsaw she held with both hands, her lips clamped as she severed a massive tree branch. She looked just the same—at that distance, from a moving car, through the veil of my shock—just the same. Papery skin; mild freckles; determined eyes. Scrunching her face as she used to do twenty years ago, when she manoeuvred an eighty-pound manure sack on a wheelbarrow through the community garden, or showed her nephew how to do chinups. She wore unflattering jeans and a sweatshirt, but she was still lithe as she strained with and against the chainsaw.

I drove around the block, assuming I would pull up short to park and watch her some more, but instead I veered off, out of her neighborhood, and kept going, and kept going, until I surprised Suresh by showing up at his house that same night.

Where was her husband? Suresh asked me, when I told him. *Surely she wouldn't be doing that if she were married.*

Maybe her husband hadn't returned home yet? I couldn't remember what line of work he was in. Her husband. It could have been me. She hadn't wanted to live together before getting married, her reasons more romantic than moral. Why rush the courtship? She wanted marriage eventually, but said cohabitation was nearly as tough to revoke, and equally mundane.

I felt the same about the marital institution as I do now. She should have agreed to move in with me. Perhaps then I might have given in and married—she was right that it would hardly have been different. Certainly, I thought, I would not have left. Even as I thought it, I felt how partial was that sentiment: I could no longer feel whatever drove my decisions of twenty years ago. The past has as few certainties as the present. Who knew?

Where was her husband?

Suresh encouraged me to return to Ottawa. I did, and spent a month working there, dining at our old haunts, driving down her street every few days, and did not see her again. I had begun playing with the notion of staying on, through the holiday season, at least. There was nowhere I had to be. No one expecting me, though I had seen a couple of old friends and colleagues in Ottawa, and might be asked to join them. Suresh did not insist I return to Montreal: Christmas is not our thing—in India, it tends to be strictly for Christians, and a bit dour— and I think he didn't want to be reminded of how we used to celebrate with Asha and Anand. He and Lisette surely had plans, maybe with her family, maybe not. Lisette had her own memories to avoid.

But then Brinda lit my cell phone.

"I'm in Calgary," she told me. I hadn't heard from her since our parting last June. Her voice sounded as though she were shivering. "I decided I'm not staying in Edmonton. I'm going home for the holidays. Where are you now?"

"I'm in . . . it doesn't matter. Do you want me to meet you in Lohikarma?"

"Not if . . . Can you?"

"Yes, yes. I was planning to be there soon, anyway." I had not planned on travelling west again for another six weeks, had planned on doing another set of interviews as I drove west and arriving in Vancouver for the verdict. Oh well. "I will see you in three or four days."

It's what I would have done for Asha.

I reassembled toiletries, bundled laundry, coiled computer cords.

Packing took me less than twelve minutes. *What I would have done*: even in my mind, this sounded forced. I would have done this for Asha, yes, but I wasn't doing it for her. I would do it for Brinda too, apparently.

This was, what, early afternoon? First stop, Sudbury, a seven-hour scramble at ninety-five clicks per, up the Canadian Shield: hard over the country's snowy breast, under which beat its riddled heart, *en garde* for thee! The sunset? I glanced and it was gone. Six further hours to go in darkness. I turned on the radio: all snow, but for two country-and-western stations, and one smug CBC voice, whose plummy tones were soon blizzarded into obscurity. Sudbury, I recalled vaguely, was the kind of place Brinda would want to epidemiologize: nickel mining, acid rain. Astronauts came here for basic training, a moonscape-on-earth.

My own pathetic fallacy might have seemed funny, as the desolation went on and on and on, had my pride not been both slightly inflated by my mission and also damped by my cowardice. I was skimming Canada's vast armoured plates toward Brinda, but, despite my vow to act, I had failed to see Rosslyn, failed to stop, failed to knock, failed to stay, failed.

I recalled my one glimpse of my one true love, as I had so many times that month that the image had become cartoonish in my mind's eye: a gallant maiden defeating an evil tree with her chainsaw. I checked into the Moonlight Inn by moonlight; installed myself at the Tim Hortons with a bowl of chili; I found Rosslyn McAllister in my phone and pressed.

She picked up before I heard a ring, saying, "Hi, honey. Sorry about that. Where were we?"

Honestly. Twenty years: a wrinkle in the fabric of time, neatly mended shut. Where were we, indeed? You were pregnant by someone else and I was half a world away, that's where we were. I'm sorry, too.

Except she couldn't be talking to me. "Hello?" she repeated. Just before I pressed "end," I heard "Alistair?"

Alistair: her husband? But why would he be calling her, this time of night, for a long conversation? I flushed: a lover. Wait: the birth announcement. The baby got his father's surname, while his given name evoked his mother's. He would be nineteen now, away at university, in all likelihood.

I dialled her again. She didn't pick up. I had spooked her. It went to voice-mail. No leaving a message.

Spooked her. Hardly. She was on the phone with Alistair. Girlfriend problems. Trying to choose classes. Their conversation must have lasted as long as my dinner. I was about to go to my room when my phone rang.

Rosslyn McAllister

I had to pick up. Letting it go to my voice-mail would be worse than my leaving a message for her. "Hello, Rosslyn?"

"Oh. Hi? Who is this?"

* * *

It would be cheesy (is that the word? It has the right sound, but I have fooled myself before) to give every detail here, which, anyway, I would have to invent: I was at such a pitch of anxiety that I have no memory of the conversation until it was nearly done. When had I ever been so anxious? Not at first sex: by the time I realized the opportunity was upon me, so was the girl. Not at my dissertation defence: cocky to a fault, that way. Not on first meeting Rosslyn: I noticed her, when she sat beside me at a conference keynote. Citrusy-smelling, sea-green dress, aloof. Audrey Hepburn-ish, with russety hair. The speaker was a blowhard, an idiot. Within minutes, I was in fear my head would explode. I was holding it together, elbows to knees, fingertips to temples, when I looked sideways and saw Rosslyn in the same posture. Same fear? Or mocking yours truly?

She, from beneath the columns of her hands, caught my eye. Who started laughing first? We were both helpless, within minutes, and beat an exit through the sparse crowd; rude, yes, but it would have been ruder to stay.

The highlights of our phone conversation:

She was no longer married. She and her husband had separated, some three years before (his instigation, a potential affair that fizzled, she said, her tone unclear), but then, a year later, he was killed by a car as he cycled to work.

Two boys, Alistair and Griffin, the elder now at McGill ("Your alma mater," she remembered), the younger struggling a little with some subjects. ("Amazing with math, physics and industrial arts," she said. "Reading not so much.") I remembered then that she had sent me a holiday card with a family picture, once, when the boys were young, and she said, "Yes, you never acknowledged it." I apologized. No need to mention that I had put it straight in the rubbish.

How long did we talk? It might have been an hour. Or longer. Not without awkward pauses, but also evident interest, on both sides. And, yes, I told her I would be coming to Ottawa (I mentioned that I had been through town already, though I omitted some stalker-ish details) and that I would call again to let her know when. It wasn't only that I wanted another excuse to call; I needed to recalculate my research plan now that I was sacrificing a set of interviews to drive straight across the country.

* * *

How could I have thought to do the trip in three days? Five driving days later, some of them very long, I pulled into the parking lot beneath my little apartment, available through the holidays, miraculously, despite Lohikarma's skiing, its pubs, its unhurried jollity. Snow-blind, lumbago in full flare, I bumped my roll-aboard up the stairs, blowing through the knife-thin ridge of snow atop each iron slat, and extracted the key from its combo-lock safe. I was in bed in 30 minutes, and slept on my back, exuding avuncular exhaustion in snores so loud they woke me.

Brinda came to see me next morning, bringing an Italian-style coffee for me (very nice), and full of news. Her hip points jutted beneath her jeans—she had lost weight she couldn't afford—and her skin was shiny and blotchy. I smelled insomnia on her—a musty scent, as of slept-in clothes or sheets. It was magnified by the crystalline scent of snow that blew in with her entrance.

"Not sleeping?" I asked her.

She started and looked back at me as she made her way onto my sofa. "Not much, no." Her hair looked lank, and she wore at least two bulky sweaters. And yet there was also something frantically cheerful there.

"Tell me." I took the armchair, my hand warming on my paper-cup cappuccino.

"Yeah." She exhaled through her lips, not a long pause. "Now that I've decided I'm leaving Dev, I can't understand how I stuck with him for so long."

Had she said this last summer? Our minds often work cyclically.

"He'll never change. We tried counselling when I went back last summer, but he never properly admitted a thing. It was all still unresolved when I left, and then he came to see me in October, and it was terrible. I didn't want to be anywhere near him. As soon as he left Baltimore, I started—I, like, fell into an affair." Her mouth crept up, an involuntary smile.

"Good," I said, more emphatically even than I had intended.

"It's . . . friendly. A French guy. Nothing that will last."

"Sounds perfect." I let caution ring in my voice.

"I think so. You can't totally control your emotions in these things, but I would be surprised if we ended up anything more, or less, than friends. He's a, you might say, a libertine." She looked amused at the term, but perhaps was trying to gauge if I was shocked.

"French, you say?"

"Half. He grew up in Brazil."

"A finishing school for libertines."

She snorted. "Yeah. It's not as though I would want to be rebounding to, say, Adrian." She crumbled into tears.

"Oh, dear girl." Where were the tissues? Dear, dear girl. "Are you in touch with Adrian?"

"He's sticking it out with his girlfriend, for now. His father died, in October, right when the worst hit me with Dev." She blew her nose. "I think he was back and forth quite a bit, through the fall. I e-mailed him, after I arrived, a couple of days ago, wondering if he'd be here for the holidays. We hadn't been in touch for a couple of months."

"And?"

"He's in Vancouver, meeting his mother at his sister's house."

"Ah."

"The wierdest part is how terrifying it is. Dev never made me feel all that secure—he was always threatening to leave his job for God knows what, and spent most of what he earned on music and films and eating out. We didn't own a house. But we had a home, a life. Now I have no home, no job, no real relationship. It's like the earth cracked open under me."

And yet, she was having a wonderful year, in all other ways. She talked to me: the thesis, hard but exhilarating; Baltimore, different from anywhere she'd lived; new friends, their writing, their escapades; her professors, their opinions, their mannerisms—she was on fire with it all. And yet. The doubt and insecurity were real, and justified. She would get over it, but now, she was shuffling one foot forward through very interesting terrain while the other toed a crevasse so deep she was scared to look down. (Yet another laboured metaphor, but surely you are accustomed to them by now?)

I rubbed my neck as she spoke, and tried to hide the stiffness in my back. She would be here some four or five weeks; Johns Hopkins had a long winter break, lots of time to work on her thesis. Her sister, about whom Brinda had spoken little, would be home in a week. I couldn't tell how Brinda felt about her, but had grown too tired to ask. I walked her out—we would meet again in a few days—and bought a paper across the street. The trial was back in the news: it had ended. Everyone, including me, had nearly stopped paying attention. The justice, one Josephson, had announced his intention to reveal his verdict on March 16. I would have to return to Vancouver to hear it.

Back in the flat, I lay down. I had called Seth the day I left Ottawa, and we had an afternoon appointment. Would he ask any further about my abrupt departure in the fall? Would I be able to avoid Venkat? I realized I didn't care much whether I did or not. My last thought, before I snoozed, was how asinine, how ridiculous, I was still to be so excited, four days later, at having talked to Rosslyn.

S eth's skin was greyish. Surely, he couldn't have developed wrinkles in six weeks, but I had not seen before this downward-pointing pattern in the lines of his face. His eyebrows, particularly, seemed on a collision course, as though destined to squeeze shut the third eye. He rose to greet me, then sat again behind his desk.

All I could think to ask was "How are you?"

"I am—we're fine," he replied. The Newton's cradle was on his desk and he set the balls a-clack. "Brinda, my elder daughter—you met her? Last summer."

I indicated that I had.

"She has come home for the holidays, earlier than expected. Her husband has not come with her. My second daughter will come next week, with her, er, her husband. She is expecting." The steelies swung in two-two time. He watched them for a long time, then spoke while still looking at them. "One of many mysteries, in physics, is why it is that all the atoms of any given substance configure identically. Their size, their weight, their behaviour—at least in limited circumstances—will be uniform. And if we try to change them, they will act so as to return to their initial state. Conservation of momentum, static states, conservation of energy—resistance to change seems to be a universal law."

"Even with people?"

"Feynman—you ever read Richard Feynman? Genius. He said, 'what animals do, atoms do.' We are a mass of interlocked systems, from our atoms to our organs. No system wants to break or change, so when you seem to see such a break, you look for what else changes to accommodate it, so that the overall effect is still equilibrium."

"Or you examine the laws to see how your theory fails." All this was equally applicable to therapy.

"Exactly. You know anything about quantum theory?"

Oh God. I searched my recollections but quickly realized I wanted only to hear what he had to say. "No," I answered.

He settled back in his chair, knees and elbows spreading slightly. "It's the most elegant set of developments in physics since classical times." His eyebrows had crept back into positions of repose. "Essentially, quantum theory is based on Heisenberg's uncertainty principle, which says we can't know where an atom is and how it is moving at the same time. We can only know one or the other. Yes?"

I gave an ambiguous nod.

"Either way, the existence of the atom, at a place, or at a speed, is confirmed only via the observation. Until it is observed, in other words, it effectively does not exist, except as a possibility, a sort of ghost. I take much longer to develop this in my classes, you understand."

Some mechanism clicked or whirred in the recesses of my mind. "Schrödinger's cat," I said.

He beamed and slapped his knee. "Excellent! What is the paradox?"

I had gotten myself into this. I worked in hopes of another smile. "That, uh, the cat is neither, or both, alive or dead?"

"Very good. And this is not the cat's experience, obviously."

"But how is the paradox resolved?"

"This continues to be an area of exploration. Niels Bohr speculated that, in a sense, reality occurs at the point of observation, that many related possibilities remain equally real or unreal until observation separates one from the others, causing the others to vanish or fall away. Me, I like to think about the multi-verse proposition, that each time an observation is made, the universe splits. So that in one universe, Schrodinger's cat lives; in the other, it is dead."

In one ramified universe, Sundar and Sita are alive; in this one, they have died. In one universe, the Sikh pogroms happened; in another, the rule of law prevailed. In some universes, humans never evolved, while elsewhere in time and space I sit on branch of a branch of a branch of reality, playing Monopoly with Asha's children and talking John Coltrane with her Bosnian-émigré husband.

Whereas in this one, I talk to Seth.

"Physics supports this?" I asked, then. "You believe this?" This theory seemed wildly improbable and unproveable and simplistic. And it wasn't even comforting.

"Science, I think, need not prove anything," he said. "At times it has appeared to, but some say a theory's value is in its usefulness: if it can describe or explain a set of phenomena, it is good as far as that goes."

I thought I was catching on. "As one Canadian therapist put it, stories used to be considered true because they were meaningful, not meaningful because they were true."

"Precisely. This eliminates dualism, just as in Hinduism we are trying to eliminate the separation between self and God, matter and consciousness. We understand the world to be an illusion. Heisenberg said, 'The division of the world into body and soul, inner world and outer world, is no longer adequate.' In observing the world, we create it."

I have read that once people didn't speak of belief in God so much as behave in a way consistent with such a belief. When I was young, when my parents wanted to go to the temple, I went, I bent, I prayed as needed. No one asked whether I believed. Was Seth saying that every thinking person is an agnostic? Bring God into being through worship; no need to try to prove God's existence. The best lack all conviction, while the worst are full of passionate intensity.

"I am not a scientist, however," he said. "I am merely a teacher, parroting laws, like Mandy. '$E=mc^2$!' '$E=mc^2$!' Bloody smart, for a bird!" He chuckled, a sound more like a hiccup, with the pressure of his distress.

Unlike most people, Seth is most himself when joking, and the room let its breath out. But then he gave me a different smile, and started again to age, the lines in his face unsmoothing and pointing once again in accusation at his elongating nose and drooping mouth. The transformation—from professor alight with the beauty of ideas to man bent under a burden of worry—was profound and touching.

We said our farewells. He turned, reaching into his jacket pocket, turned back. "Where are you spending the holidays?"

"I—here in Lohikarma, in fact." Caught off guard. "I have a lot of work and I thought I might have the peace and solitude here to get it done."

He appeared to accept this, then to remember something. "Our daughter's *velaikappu*, bangle ceremony. Does your community do this? The ceremony for a pregnant woman."

I nodded vaguely. I might have heard of such a thing.

"Traditionally only women attend. But our daughter refused to have a proper wedding. They married in a secret civil ceremony, no guests, totally private. Ridiculous," he said apologetically, even though my reaction was to admire her. "But finally we have a chance to celebrate the marriage, the baby! You must come. December thirtieth. Most of the Indians in town will be there!"

To anyone else I would have said this was the best reason to avoid it, but how, when one daughter's future weighed so heavily on him, could I refuse the opportunity to celebrate the other's?

"Thank you," I said.

"You have a mailing address here? I'll send you an invitation."

His hand had slipped back into his pocket as I wrote it on a Post-it on his desk. I left, Seth's loop of rudraksha beads clicking softly through his fingers as he counted time in units of God's name, the door clicking softly shut behind me.

’*T*was the night before Christmas when Ranjani and Greg arrived. Seth and Lakshmi went together to fetch them from the Castlegar airport, so that all four tumbled into the house a bit giddy, what with Ranjani flying barely under the pregnancy wire and the incipient holiday-party atmosphere generated on the hour-long drive. Brinda, who had spent their absence on the couch, curled around the cat, let them in.

She had called Ranjani a week earlier, to break her news, get it over with and spare her parents, who talked to Ranjani every couple of days, the agony of concealing it. They would start telling relatives and friends across the globe after the holidays.

Ranjani had been rigidly thin since late adolescence, never having recovered from the rigours of losing her baby fat. Now she looked cheeky and appetizing as she twinkled in on shiny boots. Earrings fanning her face like excited maids. Her beach ball, as she called it, draped in black. Handsome, solicitous Greg followed her in with the baggage.

The sight of them made Brinda want to stab someone, any anonymous person randomly passing behind her. *Turn, slash, turn back. Don party face.*

They greeted with hugs. Greg carried the bags up to their room and descended to receive a beer from Seth's outstretched hand, while Ranjani arranged herself on the sofa with ginger ale.

Seth offered Greg his recliner, but Greg sat instead beside Ranjani, a hand on her knee.

"I'm nervous about you flying." Seth pointed at Ranjani. "And I said you shouldn't be driving in Vancouver."

She rolled her eyes. "Is this just while I'm pregnant? Or d'you want to come out and chauffeur us till the baby's, what, twenty-five? Or maybe forever?"

Seth tinkled his ice. It would take three lifetimes to learn how not to offend his daughters, mostly because he didn't see why he should learn such a thing. What did it matter? Ranjani was so much warmer these days, calling to chat about fetal development and delivery options, sounding happier and acting more open toward them than she had since she was a child. In truth, he could feel he was becoming reconciled to it, her refusal to marry. As Lakshmi pointed out, they themselves might not ever have gotten legally married, had he not had to bring her to Canada. He wondered if Hindu priests back home were now legal officiants. He and Lakshmi had never even had birth certificates, but that didn't mean they weren't born.

Ranjani said she and Greg were legally joined, common-law, emphasis on "law," saying it made no legal difference. Seth didn't quite trust that—if it was true, why were there separate categories?—but he trusted Greg. He and Ranjani were settled. That was the important thing. *A child, a child*, Seth chorused to himself. Long, warm fingers encircled his rib cage and he glanced over at Brinda, who looked as though similar tentacles gripped her, less affectionately. He and Lakshmi had longed for a grandchild ever since Brinda's marriage. Why had it not occurred to them that they would have one from Ranjani? Mostly because Ranjani, through the long years of never quite becoming the film artist she had aimed to be, had never mentioned motherhood. Brinda had. Brinda married. And then she rolled off the rails of stability, even while Ranjani's bile and disillusion turned some corner and receded. Ranjani found a steady job, as a videographer with a consulting company. Greg's work schedule, though still erratically freelance, became full, as did his wallet. They were no longer struggling artists; they were yuppies.

He looked again at Brinda, the daughter he had thought he understood. No house, no husband, no babies. What had happened to her?

The sound of his mantra filled his ears as though he were holding conch shells to his head on a crowded beach, shutting out the holiday chatter to pretend to listen to the sound of the inexorable ocean. *Jai Shivashakti Jai, Jai Shivashakti Jai, Shiva Shivashakti, Jai Shivashakti, Jai Shivashakti Jai.*

When Brinda had showed up in distress, Seth called in sick, missing his last classes of the semester, since Lakshmi had already used up her holiday time for the year. He put off his grading, as well as piled-up duties for the Shivashakti Centre of the Kootenays, on whose board he served (now Past President), to show Brinda he had all the time in the world for her. After a few days, though, she made it clear that wasn't what she wanted.

His wife had been the one to speak with their daughters when they were upset. She would then tell Seth what was wrong. The arrangement suited them all. This time, when Lakshmi asked Brinda to tell her more about what had happened, Brinda had said she was still working it out herself. Lakshmi had pressed a little—she wanted to know, as he did, about the affairs—*who how long when such a shock*—but Brinda had reacted badly, saying it wasn't her responsibility to mitigate that shock. Lakshmi told him later, pressing her thumb and forefinger into her eyelids, "She's right, of course. What difference does it make?"

After that, they tiptoed. At dinner, they would talk about the news, about family friends—others' weddings, others' babies, subjects that fizzled quickly—and about Brinda's thesis, the only topic on which she grew animated and assured.

Given that there was practically nothing, nothing practical, that Seth could do to help Brinda or to assuage her pain, he had filled every spare moment with prayer, sitting at the shrine whenever possible and, otherwise—at traffic lights, at the photocopier, at the kitchen sink—filling his thoughts with the name of the Eternal One.

Which was practical in one sense: it kept his head from popping off in a mortal scream, and so meant that if ever there was anything his family needed, he was still alive to do it. When he was distracted from both prayer and worry, say, in a student conference, it was the worry that returned first, in a fist-biting rush, a million tiny pickaxes.

"I can very well see that I'm in a fix," Brinda yelled at them in a rare moment of open discussion. "Thirty-five, no job, home, marriage. I don't need you to worry. I'm doing plenty of that."

She was asking them to buoy her up with faith in her abilities, her decisions, her future. But that's exactly what they had done her whole life. They hadn't opposed any of her decisions. And she seemed no more pleased than they were at the result.

Was he praying for Shivashakti to help his daughter? He had never prayed in that way before. Could Brinda be helped by a god she didn't believe in? Seth believed: perhaps Shivashakti would show him once again which course of action to take.

Thinking that he might, Seth grew irrationally afraid, once more reminded of Arjuna, in the Bhagavad Gita, in the moment when Krishna, to convince the warrior of his own puniness, reveals himself in his full divinity. He thought about it now, that almost too-familiar passage, as he watched his women talk and ran his palm along the family cat's bony back. It was the passage that J. Robert Oppenheimer quoted, or misquoted, or was said to have misquoted, even mentally, at the moment when he saw his bomb explode.

Seth used a 1965 video clip in his Intro Physics classes, of Oppenheimer, looking like a heavy-browed elf with his bald head and pointy ears, his eyes aimed away from the camera, recalling that moment twenty years before. "I remembered the line from the Hindu scripture, the Bhagavad Gita. Vishnu is trying to persuade the Prince that he should do his duty and to impress him takes on his multi-armed form and says, 'Now, I am become Death, the destroyer of worlds.' I suppose we all thought that one way or another."

Of course, one can quibble. The god in the Bhagavad Gita is never called Vishnu, but rather Krishna—one of Vishnu's incarnations, Prince Arjuna's charioteer. The god doesn't merely "take on his multi-armed form" but reveals the full radiance of his divinity—containing multitudes, not only of arms, but heads, bodies, consciousnesses. It is more than mortal sight, mortal understanding, can bear. And he doesn't do it merely "to impress" Arjuna, he does it because it seems the only way to make Arjuna understand that whatever he does or doesn't do, everyone on that battlefield is destined to die—as is the Prince himself.

Most importantly, though, the word in Sanskrit that Oppenheimer translates as "Death" is also "Time." The translation Seth and Lakshmi used to read with the kids says, "I am the mighty world-destroying Time . . ." Seth would use this in his class for an anecdotal break in the sessions on fusion and fission, but would return to it at the end of the course, when he talked about time as perceived by the average person— inexorable, linear, constantly vanishing—then as conceived by most physicists—as another dimension, as with space, and subject to all those limits and freedoms, an elastic and explorable territory of existence.

And anyway, according to Oppenheimer's brother, whatever Oppenheimer may have thought, all he actually said when the bomb exploded was, "It worked."

*A*n aside. I had thought, on this visit to Lohikarma, of telling Seth what Venkat was doing. On our first meeting, I was prevented by his distress. The longer I waited, the harder it was, but it wasn't only that. I feared that Seth somehow knew, and, worse, that he would approve.

This is what I think: Oppenheimer believed he had usurped God. With the bomb, he and his co-creators could control Death—Time, the destroyer of worlds. They had moved outside of history. Oppenheimer was not without humility and public sentiment, but I believe this is what he thought. Seth may have understood that moment in the Gita as the one in which Arjuna sees he is powerless to affect the course of history, but I don't think he thought beyond that to question the hubris of those who would wage war in God's name or America's.

My guess is that Seth, like practically all of our countrymen, felt proud that in Oppenheimer's moment of great glory, when he had a vision of what the world might become as a result of his genius—*I am become Death*—the scripture that best served this self-awe was Hindu. I have known many who have wanted to use this as evidence that Kaliyug, the destruction of the known world, will culminate in a Hindu raj.

The Turkish novelist Orhan Pamuk has an essay, "The Anger of the Damned," concerning the fact that most of us in poor countries know we are condemned to shorter and harder lives than people in the developed world, that our countries are not as wealthy or as well run, and that we feel this is, in some way, our own fault. Colonialism is now almost three generations past, we say, in our conferences and coffee shops. What is wrong with us? Pamuk speaks of the "overwhelming feeling of humiliation that is experienced by most of the world's population." What he doesn't mention is that this feeling is not limited to the poorest strata of these vertiginously vertical societies. My country of billions is as steep as it is broad, and those teetering at the top also feel a rage-making shame at our national poverty.

This is how Sudhir Kakar (the writer and psychoanalyst I would be if Kakar weren't that person already) puts it in his groundbreaking analysis of Hindu–Muslim violence in India: "For the elites of the non-western world, there is an additional humiliation in their greater consciousness of the defeat of their civilizations in the colonial encounter with the West. This defeat is not merely an abstraction or a historical memory, but one which is confirmed by the peripheral role of their countries in the international economic and political order of the post-colonial world."

The governing classes' ongoing failure to provide for their poor is held up to them at meetings of the UN–OPEC–IMF. It is a blade idly and perpetually scratching their testicles. And this is why I worried that Seth, even if he would never profess a politics of sectarian violence, was not likely to disagree with it. How could he be a devotee of Shivashakti's for so long and not know that Hindu nationalist groups recruited on the ashram grounds, insinuating themselves into conversations with the vulnerable, particularly those with connections to Western money? I could only think that he must know that, even if he didn't know—or didn't want to know—that Venkat had succumbed.

What if I revealed Venkat's secret and Seth was not disillusioned, not even disapproving? Could I love him anymore? Perhaps. I could not yet risk it.

Christmas morning, after presents and brunch, Seth showered and made one more cup of coffee for the road. His daughters loitered in the kitchen. "Are you coming, Brinda?" Seth jingled his keys in his pocket.

"Time to go, already?" She rose from her chair and stretched.

"I like to be there by eleven fifteen."

As Seth backed down the steep driveway to the equally steep road, Brinda said, "And how is Venkat Uncle?"

Seth raised his eyebrows and grimaced. "My guess is that he's lying in bed with the goddamn birds flying around. He's going to catch avian flu. When I was there yesterday, one of them . . ." He stumbled into the trap of his daughter's amusement. "It went . . . potty. On the table, while he was eating. While he was feeding it from his plate." He shuddered.

"You've been complaining about that for over fifteen years, Dad." Brinda's voice bounced back to her from the car window, her breath dimming the pane, the cold taking it back. "It didn't go in his food, did it?"

"It could have. Scary."

Venkat didn't deserve to be smitten by anything so protracted—and ironic—as avian flu, Brinda thought. A nice fat lightning bolt, though, or a quadruple-ventricle cardiac arrest—picture the fist of his heart unfurling as his mottled soul ascends—might offer him deliverance.

"Scary." She mimicked her father's tone almost without thought. "It could have gone in yours."

"I don't eat anything there, unless I've taken it out of the box and microwaved it myself."

"I've seen that on microwaveable boxes: Full Complement of Daily Vitamins, and Neutralizes Bird Poop!" Brinda grinned in adolescent triumph, but then the cheer and normalcy of the moment made her self-conscious, her depression rising again, a veil between her and life.

They reached downtown within five minutes of leaving their house. Seth turned left along High Street, her hometown's heart, six short blocks hammocked between low purple mountains. So different from when she was growing up: brick sidewalks now curved up to fudge shop doors; scrawny young trees guarded wrought-iron benches to host tired tourists' bottoms. Historic buildings had been restored, though almost none for its original purpose.

Brinda did miss the ratty Dairy Queen, the saggy-ceilinged Catholic bookstore where she bought votive candles for self-consciously kitsch undergrad parties. But tourism was insurance that her hometown wouldn't disappear. So many other boom towns became ghost towns. Even her parents' villages in India were returning to dust: a few old people on verandas grinned through betel-blotched teeth as their houses literally crumbled behind them, walls pitted for lack of whitewash, bricks washing away in the rain, kids and money washing away to the cities.

There was a new WELCOME TO LOHIKARMA sign at the edge of town, with the ouroboros, a dragon biting its own tail. When she was little, the town logo had frightened her. It looked like self-obliteration.

Then, when she left for Edmonton, she had a tiny ouroboros tattooed around her navel. Friends, and Dev, had thought it was an expression of loyalty to her hometown. She didn't correct them. To her, it was about Sundar, but how or why wasn't clear. She never told her parents.

Her father was still talking about Venkat. "He's on leave, because of that breakdown, or whatever it was. Terrible. No teaching for the rest of this academic year." Seth rolled his head from side to side. His winter coat was new, looked stiff. "The Dean told me they're going to ask him to retire."

"Does he still come on Fridays?" Brinda realized he hadn't come last night.

"Oh, sure. We postponed yesterday. He'll come tonight." He gave her an uncertain smile and then found a spot and began to parallel park.

Brinda stared ahead as he bounced the car forward and back a few times—unnecessarily, in her view. "I'm not looking forward to seeing him."

"Tch." He finally put the car in park and got out, put his hands to his lower back and stretched, then bent to squint at the meter. "Poor fellow."

She followed her father to the entrance, each of them cradling a large bag of tomatoes. Mealy though tomatoes were at this time of year, the chronically vitamin-C-deprived homeless would relish them.

The Welcome Centre was located in the old Hudson's Bay building, vacated when the chain's stores across the country went down, the economy a giant game of Whac-A-Mole. The homelessness advocacy organization, a strong one with branches throughout the lower mainland, had signed a cheap lease, with the condition that this would not be a shelter but rather a place to provide a meal, counselling, and other daylight-hour resources to the region's homeless, a population that had always been large but burgeoned during exceptionally bad or good times. The soup kitchen was set up in the old cafeteria. Various community groups and individuals provided volunteer assistance, but the Shivashakti devotees were a mainstay, staffing lunch every Saturday and donating much of the food they served.

Seth and Brinda signed in at a desk manned by a security guard with a crewcut who was densely highlighting a battered paperback. Brinda checked the multi-creased spine: *The Fountainhead*. The Welcome Centre door opened behind them, blowing in the fragrance of spices heated in oil.

"Oh, Brinda, you have come! To help also." Mrs. Arora, the wife of Seth's colleague in the physics department, waddled toward her. She had lost a two-year-old grandchild, a swimming accident, as Brinda recalled, about five years ago. "Hello, Dr. Sethuratnam. All right?"

In the kitchen, they put on long, white aprons. Mrs. Arora surveyed the lunch counter and got bread out of the fridge. Seth greeted the cook with familiarity—he was the kitchen's only full-time employee, and they took their orders from him—and put a colander in the industrial sink to rinse the tomatoes. Brinda shuffled along beside him, unsure of what to do, until the cook gave her some wilting heads of iceberg lettuce to slice.

There were two other volunteers already there, both of whom Brinda knew slightly. One was a nervously energetic academic—an Indian man with a high voice, younger than her parents. He had arrived a couple of years back, a new hire in Chemistry, but a Shivashakti devotee since childhood. He didn't do conversations, only harangues, mostly non sequiturs on Western immorality. Lakshmi couldn't stand him, but still, he had come to their memorial last June.

The other familiar face was that of a white man in his fifties, soft-spoken, with a beard—Bill? Jim? Hmm. He had struck Brinda as intelligent, compared to the general run of Shivashakti adherents. She had even heard him crack a mild joke once. Her dad told her that Bill? Jim?—Ah: Nick!—owned a graphic design company and printed the organic food co-op's newsletter.

Two new volunteers crept into the kitchen as the chatter of clients intruded from the dining room. One was a young woman with stringy brown hair, a pilly black sweater and fabulous boots of parti-coloured suede. She was called Addie, followed instructions quickly, said nothing, and smiled only, briefly, at Mrs. Arora. Anytime her trembly hands were not occupied, they would fly to her mouth so she could bite her cuticles with unselfconscious violence, as though trying to reach the bone. Though it was a habit Brinda shared, the biting struck her as unhygienic in this context.

The other new volunteer was quasi-useless, which was fine, since six in the kitchen was too many. They always scheduled one extra, Seth had told her, in case someone couldn't make it. *Or was useless*, Brinda imagined saying to him after, when they might laugh about this guy: in his early forties, shaped like a Weeble. A meandering cloud of beard divided the slope of his cheek from his neck. Told to portion cheesecake into small bowls, he did, but only as long, apparently, as the instruction reverberated in his head. He decelerated through the filling of eight bowls before taking up his meditation wheel to stand, spinning it, a conspicuously still centre amid the increasing activity. *As though he's superior to the work he volunteered for*, Brinda thought, *as though he's teaching us how to live*. The harried cook got him back on task twice, and then finally assigned the cheesecake to Addie and asked the Buddhist to go stand on the far side of the industrial freezer.

In the minutes before the cook declared that lunch was served, he ran pots to the lunch counter. Brinda peered at the alternative universe dimly sighted through the Sterno-scented steam now rising from lentil soup, pasta, egg fried-rice: the haphazard vegetarian menu negotiated when the Shivashakti-ites offered to do the Saturday meal on the one condition that they not be asked to serve meat. This was the only thing about her father's faith that impressed her: that it had led him into regular, friendly contact with the dispossessed, now lined up, joking through missing teeth.

Brinda dished up rice and smiled timidly, conscious of trying to show how non-judgemental she was, and feeling falser for it. Her dad knew many of them by name. A grubby white man with Down's syndrome reached awkwardly beneath the glass hood to shake his hand. A native man with a merlot scar bisecting his face, forehead to nose-tip, leaned toward Seth and muttered something that sounded threatening. Seth pointed a ladle as though it were a gun, and said, "Hey, who's the real Indian here?" The two of them laughed, holding their guts in an oddly similar way.

The clients were perhaps 60 percent native. There was one Sikh man, in a turban and beard, who nodded solemnly to the servers and ate by himself. Two men looked Chinese—or Vietnamese? Migrant workers who somehow got shut out of their own communities? The rest were white. There was a couple who only reluctantly stopped embracing to join the back of the lunch line, though the woman held onto her man's ski jacket at the back while he got a tray of food. When they sat at one of the long tables, they locked their legs together and hunched protectively over their single tray. They ate from the same plate and drank Hawaiian Punch from the same cup.

As Brinda speculated on all that couple might have lost and on what had brought the others to this pass, she felt a familiar awareness of the futility of wanting to know them, of knowing anyone. She had been given so many clues to Dev's character, and still had no idea who he was or what he thought. So, essentially, there was no true intimacy, or not for her. It might be different for those who were better at extracting information or who were less trusting, or whose judgements were more accurate . . . No, in this mood, she would have to believe it was the same for everyone. You could only know what a person told you or what you witnessed, and the person could deny what they said, and you could completely misinterpret what you saw.

The thing Dev seemed not to understand was the currency of confession, the way weakness could endear you to someone. Until it made them despise you for all you could not give.

The soup kitchen line was through. Apart from a minimum of clean-up, the servers were done their shift. The cook told them to help themselves to lunch, but none of them did. Mrs. Arora and the young professor said their goodbyes. The Buddhist stood and spun his wheel in the doorway between the kitchen and dining room, as if alerting the others to a portal between worlds. Seth and Nick, who liked to get a cup of coffee and hang out among the lunchers, had to squeeze past him, as did Brinda. Addie of the harlequin boots, who looked panicked when Mrs. Arora left, followed them, middle finger to mouth. Although the kitchen was then empty, the cook came and whacked the wheel-spinner's shoulder with the back of his hand. "Buddy. Get outta the way?"

Seth sat down at a table with a few empty chairs, pulling one out for Brinda as she watched Addie and the Buddhist leave. "That guy was unbelievable," she said to her father, *sotto voce*, as someone came up to him with a chessboard.

Seth looked at her and back at his chess partner, who was setting up the board on the table in front of him. "What?"

"The Buddhist? Spinning his little wheel like it was a party favour?"

"It's a form of meditation," Seth said.

"I know. Why did he have to do it when he was supposed to be working?" The clatter in the dining room was like a sound screen, and anyone close to them was interested only in the chess game.

Seth shrugged. "Maybe he needed to. You can't know."

Brinda gave him a look of undisguised exasperation. "Why did he sign up to volunteer if he needed to meditate?"

"You can't know." Seth realized yet again, with pity, that Brinda had no idea what he felt, all the time, in and out of Shivashakti's presence. His faith was not monolithic, but even his doubts sustained him. Her arrogance, and Ranjani's, was almost impressive.

Brinda sighed. "It felt holier-than-thou. Literally."

He sighed, too, and frowned at the chessboard.

"It looked," she went on, and he so wished that she wouldn't, "as though he signed up to serve poor people because he felt he should, so he would get dharma credit or whatever, but then was double-timing it with public prayer to be on the safe side."

"Why are you concerned with how it looked?" Seth asked.

"Isn't that kind of what it's about? Doing this for the service of God, instead of simply for your fellow human beings?"

"It's the same thing, *kanna*," Seth said softly. It was so obvious that it was more meaningful, not less, to serve God by serving those whose lives were hard. Such an intelligent girl, with so little grasp of an inexpressible, private truth.

"How do you think they feel about it?" Brinda gestured at milling lunchers with her eyes, but Seth didn't look up from the board. "Some of them might not believe in God."

Seth snorted. "They get lunch. They don't care."

"It's about your motivations, all of you, I mean. I don't get it."

Seth agreed, but didn't say so.

"You're looking at people with real problems, but you're only thinking of God."

"Oh?" Seth said. He moved a knight.

Perhaps (Seth would suggest to me later) she got frustrated that he wouldn't agree or (my interpretation) that he wouldn't take the bait, or perhaps (this was Brinda's own thinking, after she cooled off) she was too full of her own confusion to stop herself.

"What about real life? I can tell you think I shouldn't have left Dev."

Seth stood and took her elbow, saying nothing to anyone as he guided her outside. "I never said that."

"You never said one way or another. I feel your accusations, about my failure."

"No, *kanna*, it's my failure." His chess partner came to the glass door, cupping his hands against the glare to see father and daughter on the sidewalk, then turned around and went back inside.

"Mine." She was his height, matched him eye to eye. "I'm an adult. I can take responsibility for my mistakes."

"Okay!" Nothing he could say would make this better.

"You infantilize me. That's why I didn't try to talk to you and Mom about our problems, beforehand."

"Did you talk to anyone about it?" he asked, trying to look concerned but not, what, not paternal? She was his child. She needed to get real.

"I saw a therapist, in Edmonton. And Ashwin, last summer, was a huge help."

"Ashwin?" *Ashwin?*

"Yeah." Her eyes got big, and she covered her mouth with her hands but spoke through them. "Ashwin Rao."

"Ashwin Rao. You talked to him about your marriage?"

"Yeah. Um. I told him not to tell you that we were talking about it. He's a psychologist, a good one."

"I know damn well he's a psychologist, but he was pretty high and mighty about not helping Venkat, lack of licence or some such, even though Venkat needed it, and then on the other side, he's meeting you and coaching you to leave Dev? To get divorced? Who the hell is this guy?"

Brinda, arms crossed, gestured toward the car with a hunched shoulder. "Could we get off the street, please?"

Seth stalked over to unlock it, and they both got in.

"Look, Dad, he said he couldn't be my therapist, like you said. And he never coached me to leave Dev. I asked him if I could talk to him, because I trusted him."

"I encouraged you to go and meet with him." So stupid, so trusting. "Machiavellian."

"You've got it wrong. He told me he shouldn't, but I made him. He didn't charge me, and I made him promise not to tell you."

"And he agreed."

"I am an adult, in case you forgot!"

"I am your father, in case you forgot! You're talking to some stranger, and not to me?"

"It was easier to talk to someone who didn't have a stake! Everything that hurts me seems to hurt you twice as much."

"It was highly inappropriate of Ashwin Rao."

"Are you going to tell Mom?"

He gave her a look that she thought she should understand, but she didn't, and no further answer was forthcoming.

✳ ✳ ✳

Mid-afternoon, Seth called Venkat to ask when he was coming.

"Ah? Oh! Friday, is it?"

Seth cleared his throat and tried to talk so that the others couldn't hear. "No. It's Christmas." He had mentioned it only yesterday.

There was a short pause at the other end.

"Ah, okay, yes, thank you. We'll see you at suppertime."

We. Venkat had, for years now, brought Mandy with him when he came to dinner at Seth's house. The first couple of times, Lakshmi was disgusted and wanted Seth to say something, but Seth couldn't. Then, one time, Ranjani and Brinda were there and Venkat took Mandy out of his cage to entertain them. They all had to admit he was a well-adjusted bird. That evening was the most fun they had ever had with Venkat—the only time, Ranjani and Brinda said, that they had ever actually enjoyed his presence, as they fed Mandy apple pieces and tried to teach him to sing Bob and Doug McKenzie's theme song: "*Coo roo coo coo, coo roo coo coo!*" It might have been too long a sequence for a parakeet, but Venkat, who wasn't familiar with the tune, shortened it, so that Mandy now said, "Cuckoo! Cuckoo!" proficiently, particularly when cued by a doorbell.

So that tonight, when Venkat rang the doorbell, Mandy chorused along from under his polar-fleece cage-cover, "Cuckoo! Cuckoo!" When Brinda opened the door, it was as though some unseen guardian angel was warning her that a crazy man cometh.

But she let him in and they all wished him Merry Christmas.

("Was that just to spike him?" Seth would later ask his women.

"*Spite*, Dad," Brinda would respond absent-mindedly, while Seth waited for an answer that never came.)

"To you all, I say Happy *Pongal*," Venkat said with a note of warning. "You can call it solstice." He turned his baggy glare on their raggedy tinsel tree. "The lunar calendar has drifted such that the established day doesn't arrive until what we call mid-January, but this is the festival you are meaning to celebrate. " Ranjani made a comic face at Seth as she took Venkat's coat. Brinda had already escaped to the kitchen. "It is a pagan festival, and we, as members of an agricultural society, can and should observe it."

"Agriculture. The Pentiction Peach Festival, you mean?" Lakshmi asked, gesturing toward the living room as Venkat stopped Seth from picking the cage up, despite the cat's approach.

"Lakshmi, our roots!" Venkat threw his hands in the air. "Our roots!"

Seth watched his women suppress their laughter. He hadn't had a chance to tell Lakshmi about Ashwin Rao, but would have to, tonight. She was going to hit the roof.

He brooded. How he loved their faces: Lakshmi's mother's eyes replicated in Ranjani; Brinda furrowing his own sister's brow. Lakshmi bore little resemblance to any relative. He imagined that she resembled some long-ago people whose delicate phenotypics, buried in genetic codes, surfaced only in the rarest of their descendants.

Venkat poked the cat away with his toe, set the cage on the coffee table, bent to lift the fleece drape over his own head and chirped at his bird. Three years after he first got the birds, four years after the bombing, the thing Seth and Lakshmi had feared came to pass: one of the birds, half of a mating pair, sickened and died. Venkat had four at the time: Mandy; a female with whom Mandy had refused to mate; and the couple. The other male started pulling his feathers out when his mate got ill. Venkat, too, lost hair, beside himself with the effort to save her. His teaching suffered, but it didn't have far to fall. Seth and Lakshmi went on high alert, calling the hospital's psychiatric wing and the animal shelter to check on space availability and warn them of the possible arrival of sudden guests.

When the bird's death came, however, Venkat received it with unexpected grace. Seth and Lakshmi returned home from work to a voice-mail announcement from Venkat, who sounded grave but hardly distraught. They met him an hour later at a pet crematorium and then accompanied him to a nook of the Kootenay River he had apparently decided on in advance as the spot to spread the ashes.

The place was beautiful: half an hour from town, deep in birch woods, among moss-softened rocks and fallen timber out of whose crevices shelved huge, mustard-hued fungi. It was late fall. Clearly no one had been along the path in some time. Seth himself never would have known it was there. He wondered how often Venkat came and what else he did in the times when Seth was not with him. It struck him as marvellous and frightening how little we can know of the lives of others, even the closest, hours and hours in each day when they are out of our sight and we are out of their minds, leaving them to wander in mind and spirit to lonely places.

Om . . . Venkat began chanting the Mahamrityunjaya Mantra . . . *Tryambakam Yajamahe Sugandhim Pushtivardhanam Urvarukamiva* . . . Lakshmi joined, then Seth, clearing his throat. *Bandhanan Mrityor Mukshiya Maamritat* . . . They prayed to Shiva, the three-eyed, omniscient, omnipresent, omnipotent, to deliver them from ignorance into understanding and acceptance, of life, of death.

After scattering the ashes, Venkat came to the Sethuratnams' house for a bite of supper. Lakshmi asked him how it was he seemed so calm.

Venkat was nonplussed but quickly warmed to his answer. "I nursed her all through her sickness, I cared for her, and when she died, in my own hand" —he held out his hands as he said this, cupped as if to hold a quivering green knot of life—"it was a relief. It was a good death, a natural death. Who are we to fight the will of God?"

"We're relieved to see you handling it so well," Lakshmi said warmly.

Venkat gave her an odd look. "I lost my wife and child, Lakshmi. How could any other death seriously affect me?" More pensively, he added, "But I have not lost the ability to grieve."

It convinced them that he had settled, emotionally. He was still strange, but not volatile, teaching on a schedule, looking after the parakeets. Then came the trial, and then the outburst in class, and now they were all living once more with that long-ago fear of what he might do to himself. The verdict—whatever it was—couldn't come soon enough.

Mandy climbed Venkat's arm to perch on his shoulder. The bird would stay there throughout the meal, accepting snacks of cucumbers or nuts. It had never mated, though Venkat now had three other pairs and had tried each of the new females first with Mandarin before giving her as a wife to a lesser, dumber husband. Venkat said Mandy was too full of filial devotion to love a mate, that he was a *sannyasin*, an ascetic and celibate, though Brinda and Ranjani delighted in e-mailing Seth articles on homosexuality in the animal world. *Told you: Venkat Uncle needs to try Mandy with one of the males!* ★

"But where is your husband, Brinda?" Venkat asked, as they helped themselves to dinner from the buffet.

Brinda looked at her parents and then at Venkat, who glanced at her without evident interest. She noticed that the stippling in his face was configured at present into a Rorschach vase, his forehead, nose and chin darker than the rest of his face, the lower end blending into uneven stubble.

"He's spending the holiday with his own family," she mumbled.

"Is his family not your own?" he asked, not ungently, but he was preparing for one of his set-piece speeches. "I understand this kind of thinking is becoming common even in India today, but we have always understood the Hindu woman to be the core of the family. That is strength, not weakness! These Westerners."

Brinda had argued with Venkat once or twice as a hot-headed feminist-progressive teen, but since then, she had chosen to steer the conversation elsewhere and preserve her self-esteem with an occasional choice riposte that she was never sure he caught. Today, she felt as though she had handed him the hot pan of her humiliation so he could shake it and watch her fry.

Ranjani usually left when Venkat went into this mode. Tonight, her blood a swollen torrent of maternal hormones, she came to her sister's defence. "You are living in, like, the sixteenth century. Maybe she has her reasons for being here on her own, like, maybe she wasn't being treated very well? It's none of your business. I don't see what Hindu identity has to do with preaching and meddling."

Venkat had started when she began speaking. They would say later that he had gotten used to hearing no voices but birdy echoes of his own. "But no, but, dear girl," he said, with puzzlement, "why do you . . . We are talking only, nothing to take so seriously."

Ranjani's fury was not abating, and Venkat looked at Brinda, seated at the next edge of the table, closest to him. Her eyes were stretched wide, to contain her tears. "Is it true?" He reached a hand toward her shoulder, distress in his voice even though his face, with its odd stillness, looked stern and impassive. "You are a very good girl. *Chamathu*. Please don't cry. Everything will be all right."

Brinda got up and walked stiffly out of the dining room.

"*Paavum*, the poor thing. Tch, tch, tch." Venkat looked from Brinda's retreating back to Seth. "Such good girls. Like daughters to me."

Seth looked at Lakshmi. *Note to selves*: if this was how their most judgemental friend reacted to the separation, maybe they didn't need to fear the judgements of others.

"Greg," he said, waving for his son-in-law's empty wineglass. "Refill." As he passed the full glass back, Ranjani intercepted and took a swig. She winked at her dad across Venkat's shiny bald head, bowed over his plate.

Why didn't Seth feel relieved? Oh, right: he still had to tell Lakshmi about Ashwin.

nd my Christmas day, mere blocks away from all this subtle drama? As peaceful as any I ever had.

I had work, glorious work, oodles of it. I was planning an interdisciplinary conference at the IRDS, and considering taking over the centre's directorship for a two-year term; on a side table was a colleague's manuscript I'd been asked to read. And *The Art of Losing*, my study based on this year's interviews, was taking shape. My new plan was to stay in Lohikarma until early March, when I would go to Vancouver to hear the verdict, which would, whatever it was, provide some sort of epilogue or capstone to my interviewees' story. I organized my transcripts, noting patterns, exceptions, potential explanations, whatever the interviews thus far could yield, and planned for a final set of interviews to follow the verdict.

I had bought rather a good port, the day before, and that evening, took two different Stiltons from paper wrappings, one blue-veined, the other studded with bits of fig and orange. Did I mention I had planned to call Rosslyn again, on Boxing Day evening? Wouldn't want to interfere with her Christmas. I arranged my food into a still life with some items I kept on the coffee table, a bird-skull and some stones lustered by the steady thoughtlessness of the lake. And a book: Auden's Christmas Oratorio, *For the Time Being*.

My intention had been to read it aloud, but when I heard myself speak the opening lines, "Darkness and snow descend; The clock on the mantelpiece / Has nothing to recommend," I sounded comical. "Winter completes an age . . ."—so true it was ridiculous. I tossed it aside and turned on the boob tube. *It's a Wonderful Life*. Unironic, sentimental cheer, made available at an ironic, artificial distance. That was more like it.

*S*unday, the 26th, the Sethuratnams began the final phase of preparation for Ranjani's bangle ceremony, her velaikappu, to take place on the 30th. She had shyly confessed to them that although she hated weddings, once she learned she was pregnant, she knew she wanted this ceremony for the baby. Thrilled, Seth and Lakshmi displaced all their thwarted wedding energy onto this event, violating tradition to include men in the celebration, broadening the circle so that it genuinely, not only symbolically, included everyone who might be part of the baby's life. Only the women would actually perform the ritual, though: bangles were not for guys, and one should only push tradition so far.

They had booked a lakeside community hall, owned by a church. Seth had favoured having it at the Shivashakti ashram in the centre of town, but Ranjani had said, "Sorry, Dad," before he even finished the suggestion. He didn't nurse the hurt for long. Friends were coming from Vancouver; Lakshmi's brother and mother from Toronto. The morning of the 26th, Ranjani and Seth arrived in the kitchen to find Lakshmi stewing over lists assigning friends to duties and duties to friends, lists of items to buy and items to bring, lists of calls, lists of lists. As Ranjani fixed coffee, Greg descended the stairs and asked to turn on the TV.

A tsunami had hit Asia the previous night, and now was breaking over and over, on-screen, in fragmentary amateur footage. "Where is this?" Seth kept asking, "Where is this?" as the footage switched to newcasters in front of a smoothly digital, cerulean ocean jagged by the red edges of shifting tectonic plates and cartoon-yellow seismic tremors. Two beaches in Chennai had been hit. Seth's brother lived near one, in Adyar, where he and his wife walked daily. They couldn't get through to him, the phone lines jammed. They didn't know anyone living near the other, Marina Beach, although it was possible at any time that someone they knew might be there. It was a popular urban beach full of their fond holiday memories: Seth dunking his sari-wrapped younger sisters; two-rupee peeps into the freak-booths; tooth-rattling gallops on a malnourished nag; black-roasted corn rubbed with lime juice and salt.

Late morning, an e-mail reached them from Seth's brother, saying he and his wife had felt the tremors as they returned from their morning walk perhaps an hour before the waves hit. Their guess was that a number of the fisher-families whose huts lined the shore would have been devastated, but it increasingly appeared that no one close to them had been taken.

As soon as he had heard from his brother, Seth called Kaj Halonen, the current vice-president of the Shivashakti Centre, and turned on his computer. His browser was set for Shivashakti's website, to which their own centre's site was linked. There was already a message on the guru's homepage, of consolation and guidance for the tsunami victims and those who would help them.

"*Jai Guru*. We're watching the news," said Kaj. "Tamil Nadu. Have you talked to your family?"

"*Jai Guru*. All fine."

"Oh, good, good, good. We can give relief money. It's in the coffers. We'll hold an emergency vote to release it. And the members'll give more."

"I know it. But the suggestion should come from you. Indian adepts will be shy to bring it up."

Talking with Kaj reminded Seth that he had, in his briefcase, a video he had been meaning to watch since the start of the holidays. A colleague had left it in his box sometime during exam week, a BBC piece on Shivashakti, taped off the TV, it seemed. Seth had been surprised at the gesture; that colleague, though Indian and a recent arrival, had never acted particularly warmly toward him. Seth didn't even know how he knew about Seth's own interest in Shivashakti. It came with a note: *Something you should see.*

There were other documentaries on Shivashakti, but produced by devotees. It was nice to see interest from the mainstream media. If they could do lives of Gandhi and Nehru, Bill Gates and the Pope, it wasn't surprising that they would eventually want to tell Shivashakti's story. He had suggested watching it to Brinda and Lakshmi a few nights ago but . . . what had happened? Brinda had brought home some Italian film, *Bread and Tulips*. They had enjoyed it.

Now there would be no time until the velaikappu was done. He could watch it alone, but he wanted to watch it with his family. Even if they continued to disagree with him, it was important that they understand Shivashakti's stature in the world.

By the evening, the tsunami was relegated to number of dead, number of dollars, anecdotes of elsewhere. Seth imagined that this was what other households might have felt like in the days after the Air India bombing: there but for the grace of name-your-deity; and then the newspeople make as much hay as they can until some other disaster drives it off the front pages.

Seth recalled Bantry Bay, the sea calm as surely the Indian ocean now was, lapping at its own debris, the way their cat ate its own vomit.

* * *

They drove to the caterer's the next morning, with the car radio blaring news, still *all-tsunami, all the time*. Seth switched it off as they arrived. Inside, at one of the three tables, an old man buttoned into a brown cardigan sat playing a game of Chinese checkers with a boy of nine or ten, who bore some resemblance to Sundar. Twenty years. Sundar might have been coming to the velaikappu with his own children. Or not: Brinda had none. Seth had to stop thinking in the old terms. Sundar was dead and nothing ever turned out the way you expected.

Ah, why not dream? That maybe someday, ten years from now on an afternoon much like this, he would be sitting across a Chinese checkerboard with his own grandchild, watching that hidden girl or boy wrinkle Seth's own eyebrows, still too large on the child's serious, heart-shaped face.

$\mathcal{M}$ onday, the 27th, I went to the High Street post office to send back my colleague's manuscript. The weather had turned foul. Clumps of snow, like hairballs, criss-crossed the air as if borne on competing winds. I marched along miserably, a scarf wrapped about my head, my eyelashes freezing together. Driving would have been worse. En route, I passed an outdoor-wear shop doing brisk business, and stopped to get a Gulag-guard hat: nylon shell and earflaps lined in fake fur. My eyelashes still froze on the way back.

I was surprised when Brinda kept our four o'clock appointment.

"Why didn't you postpone?" I asked, as she stamped and shook outside, then entered and gingerly removed her thawing things on the mat.

She twisted her lips and bit a cuticle.

"Something happened?" I asked.

The kettle called. She moved to sit on the sofa, but then rose again and came to where I was making tea.

"I . . ." She looked away and then back at me. "You've been great, about all this, meeting, talking."

She didn't want to meet anymore? Melancholy lines from yesterday's book, Chekhov stories, rose in my mind: *Don't leave me, my darling. I'm afraid to be alone.*

"I somehow, accidentally, mentioned to my dad that I had talked to you, last summer, about my problems. He took it wrong."

They would both leave me. I would have no one. Again.

"I told him I had twisted your arm, and that I needed to speak to someone who wasn't a friend or relative. I said I trusted you. I think that was right. But he just—he's still in shock about all this."

I was having some trouble breathing. I focused on not letting her see.

"I thought I should tell you. Because you see him, right?"

I nodded, but still couldn't speak.

"So I had to tell you. But I don't think it matters much. He'll come around. I told him how helpful you've been. So generous."

"Nothing like that," I said. My mouth was dry. I poured two cups, added milk and sugar, sipped. Hot tea: why don't doctors prescribe it?

We moved on: she had much to tell. Her pain at seeing Ranjani, who was supposed to have been the lost one, afloat on all the satisfactions Brinda herself had wanted. The self-hate her jealousy brought on. Christmas morning; the soup kitchen; the fight with her father, partly about me (again, the stab of fear); Christmas dinner with Venkat.

"My dad said he asked you to treat Venkat Uncle, after his breakdown or whatever that was, in October?"

"He did." I would have said more—to hell with confidentiality— but she was rising, donning her coat.

"I don't know what my dad thinks you should have done for him. Can't imagine Venkat Uncle's big on introspection."

"Mm-hmm."

I was filling with panic again and took deep breaths through my nose.

"I saw your name on the velaikappu guest list." She pulled on a turquoise wool hat, waterproof gloves, an improbably long scarf. "So we'll see you Thursday?"

What could I say to that?

"Come!" she said.

I remembered last summer, when I told her I was coming to the memorial, and she had wanted me to stay away.

"If you need to talk in the meantime, do not hesitate," I said, with difficulty. "Call me."

She raised the edge of her scarf, beneath smiling eyes, to cover her mouth–nose–cheeks, and turned out into the blizzard.

Oh, what was Seth thinking now? I poured a small draft of port and took it to the window seat. The outlines of Trismegistus—those lines where the layered mountains bumped the sky and footed the lake—were faint enough to make me think I was imagining them. Was all this to be lost to me?

My journal lay on the window seat. I took it up, but couldn't bring myself to open it. The last entry recorded my last meeting with Seth. Naturally, he felt betrayed: I had known all along what he was not telling me, all of it, and more—much more than he knew. I knew intimate details about his daughter. What man would not feel invaded?

When I picked up my journal, I uncovered my phone. I had spent three quarters of an hour in this same nook last night, hearing about Rosslyn's recent work, telling her a little about mine. Telling her how it would bring me back through Ottawa late in spring. "You should time it to see the tulips," she said.

I flipped my phone open. Her number, first of the Recent Calls. I shouldn't, I knew. Two calls in two weeks was fine, all things considered. But two calls in two days?

I pressed "redial."

"Ashwin?" She sounded guarded.

Last night, I had lapped up the happy surprise in her voice as if it were a sweet splash of port.

"I wouldn't have called, Rosslyn, but . . ." The phone heated the brain cells beneath my throbbing ear. I could kill myself this way, with absence and longing. "Maybe I shouldn't have called." She was waiting, wondering. "Did you have a good day?"

"Yes, sure. The boys and I took my mother for lunch. They're out seeing friends now. I'm finishing my Sunday book."

"You still do that." We could suture up the lost time. I could be with her again.

"I do. Ashwin. I need to tell you something. Listen. I am seeing someone."

I won't describe how that felt.

Now that she had got the information out, her voice gentled a little. "Just for the last three or four months. My first relationship since John and I split up, and since he died."

"I see," I said.

"A roller coaster," she said at the same time. "It's not that . . . Okay, you and I are too old for games. Life is way shorter than I ever realized. So let me lay it out. I am excited to see you. Even though you live in India and I don't imagine twenty years of living alone— You said you never married, right?"

"Yes."

"I don't imagine all these years of single life have made you any easier to be with."

"No." I was seized with an urge to protect her, particularly from me. "I am very difficult."

"I know. Better than anyone. I'm an authority."

"I shouldn't come."

"Let me decide that. I'm not the naïf you once knew. And I am *really* looking forward to seeing you again. I don't know where things are going with Henri. Maybe not anywhere. But I didn't want to be dishonest. You have hopes, clearly. But let's both be sensible enough not to have expectations."

"*Henri?*"

She laughed. "Got a problem with that?"

"With 'John' maybe I could compete. But ooh-la-la, zis Henri, avec 'is champagne and pâté de foie gras et *je ne sais quoi. Oui ou non?* Pop goes the Indian."

I thought, not for the first time, of the last time we met, when she was pregnant and full of her future, and how she looked at me like I was a brother, a brother's friend. Compassion, no eros. I couldn't settle for that now, but her voice didn't sound like that now either. I had been brought into many marriages in these years, even if I never had one of my own. They contain shades of feeling, phases of being, informed by all the other kinds of love—fraternal, paternal. *He was like a mother to me*, Lakshmi had said of Seth.

Rosslyn and I talked. Of what? Barbara Gowdy, the tsunami, the weather in Canada, her kids. My brain simmered in the phone-heat. The snow continued to fall.

✳ ✳ ✳

The next morning, I woke late. The Canadian darkness had thrown me off, but it wasn't only that. The chat with Rosslyn had been everything I wanted and needed, without my having told her why I called. She would have wanted to know. Did I need to tell her? But how to begin, to tell her what Seth was to me, the loneliness I feared falling back into, the way Brinda had drawn me out, the potential significance of this year and her place in it, how? How?

And if I couldn't tell her, why call at all?

There was to be no work that day. For twenty years, I had hidden in my work. The lives of others, indeed. I took up my journal, intending to write what Brinda had told me. Should I attend the velaikappu? I wanted to, badly, but was simultaneously dreading it. Where had I heard that before? I flipped back in my journal: I had said the same about the memorial, and about the trial. And I'd written, *I seem to learn as much about myself through my writing as I do about others.*

Rosslyn's voice, in my head, said, *Write it!* Not just events, briefly noted in your journal. Try to tell the story. Why you left, what happened. Who you are.

*T*hursday, December 30, velaikappu day, was bright and unseasonably warm, so that green and yellow tufts of the gardens around the pavilion showed through melting snow by the time we guests gathered, mid-afternoon. The paths were shovelled but slippery. Slush-puddles meant many of the women entered with dark rings edging the borders of their saris. The guests segregated themselves naturally, men gravitating toward the back, where hot and cold beverages were available throughout the ceremony, at Seth's insistence, while the women came toward the front.

I had so many sound reasons to flee. Instead, I forced myself to enter, organic baby-gift box in hand. Seth, greeting guests at the door, extended a hand robotically to shake mine. No smile. Nothing from the eyebrows. I could have fallen at his feet.

"Welcome," he said.

"Seth. I would like to meet you to talk, soon."

He looked past me, and his eyebrows moved for someone else.

"I understand Brinda told you she saw me, last summer, about her situation. I would like to explain—she had me pledge confidentiality—but I would like to tell you in what spirit I let her talk to me."

He wasn't thawing, but he assented. "Next week. After Ranjani leaves."

"Brinda's a wonderful child," I blurted. His eyes narrowed a little. "She will be fine. I predict this," I went on. Now it was as though a warm breeze melted the lines of his face. "A wonderful girl," I repeated.

Lakshmi approached from behind him, and I put my palms together. Why I would do this now, when we had greeted one another much more informally in the past, I'm not sure, except that the gesture is one of worship. She wore an amethyst sari in that thick, lush South Indian silk I remember from my childhood. She greeted me, warmer than Seth, if a little self-conscious, and gestured me into the hall.

Brinda was beside her sister, positioned to receive gifts and otherwise run interference as needed. I gave my box to her and she granted me the gift of a smile, before introducing me to her sister. The ceremony began, and I moved to one side.

* * *

Lakshmi was the first to give the blessing, taking a selection of bangles from the tray Brinda held out to her and pushing them onto each of Ranjani's wrists before pinching a dab of vermilion from a silver cup on the tray and rubbing it into the part of her pregnant daughter's hair. Brinda imagined it gave her mother more than a little satisfaction to do so: the vermilion signalled a married woman. Brinda's own scalp felt naked. She watched her mother kiss Ranjani and whisper something, and Ranjani whisper back, "Thank you." Lakshmi wiped her eyes.

Next was Lakshmi's mother, who, though widowed, had been included. Among Brahmins back home, widows were disqualified from wishing happiness to young couples and families. Lakshmi overrode custom's dictates, to her mother's pleasure, though both were also a bit anguished. She smoothed Ranjani's hair with trembling hands and cracked her knuckles against her own head, defences against the evil eye. She embraced Brinda too, and said, "You will be next!" before she turned away.

No one had asked Brinda, *You don't want a baby?* but the omission was almost as bad as the question. Their concern was evident, brightened with curiosity, as though each person had reassuringly patted her face until it was stinging and raw, as good as slapped.

She herself entered the line next, biting back her own emotion as she put the bangles on her sister, willing herself only to acknowledge the genuine love and good will she felt toward Ranjani and her future niece or nephew, not the rancid jealousy and lip-chewing fears rubbing hot, prickly flanks against the better emotions. She didn't believe in *drishti*, the evil eye, but she knew it was most often cast inadvertently. Anyway, her mother, who lived to deny all such superstitions, had broken down and waved a fistful of salt around Ranjani's glowing visage that morning, muttering the ancient incantations to make them safe from all they didn't believe in, and then flushing the danger down the toilet to the Kootenay River. Brinda laid a hand on her little sister's cheek and kissed the other, saying, "I'm so proud and excited for you."

The rest of the Tamil Brahmin ladies came forward, and then the other academic wives behind them. The smell of each woman, as she bent over the tray, her perfume–breath–aura, brought back the smell of each house, which Brinda now realized she knew as well as her own, even though she hadn't been in their houses for ten years or more. Despite her glued-on smile, she felt real affection for them, and for her complicated history with them, with their kids, adventures and dramas in their kitchens and basements, while adults were occupied elsewhere.

Next, their neighbours, the Aidallberrys. He was a classics prof; his wife, Thomasin, a poet who wrote in a garret at the top of their dilapidated house. Then a small raft of Shivashakti devotees, Indian and white, who had become Seth's friends over the years. Several of Seth's colleagues, one or two of Lakshmi's, three of Brinda's friends who were still based here, hippies and academics, also with families in tow, and, finally, friends of Ranjani's who had come from Vancouver—women in their thirties, several with men at their sides holding toddlers. She didn't seem to have any friends left in Lohikarma.

One after another, they ascended to bless Ranjani and her baby. Brinda watched them approach, clink-clack the bracelets she offered from the tray, ching-chuck them onto Ranjani's heavy-growing wrists, smear her scalp blessed red and kiss her glowing cheeks, the brush of aging lips telling their own disappointments and desires and the thrill of their role in this renewal, while Brinda felt herself to be a wraith at Ranjani's side. Exit ghost.

✳ ✳ ✳

Seth watched from within the masculine rank, with his son-in-common-law and his friends. He was aflood in sentiment, watching the infinite ascension of the women's backs, curved-straight-old-young-wide-narrow, in bright silks and pastel sweaters: the women. Without them, there is no continuity, no ceremony, no courage.

And, receiving the women, his daughters. His daughters!

$\mathcal{N}$ew Year's Eve, at noon, Seth and Lakshmi were arrayed on the sectional, waiting for Brinda to join them—ready, finally, to watch the Shivashakti documentary. They had put him off for days. No longer.

In front of each of them, on a floral TV tray, was a full thali. It was a Sunday-and-holiday tradition that had evolved since their kids left home: a rice-meal at noon, two side dishes, no cutlery, accompanied by daytime television (Oprah, if she was available), followed by a nap. Seth had learned to sous-chef in response to Lakshmi's objections that the meal was too much work for midday.

Brinda crossed in front of them to sit, cushion-cocooned, in the sofa's corner.

"We left your food on the stove," Lakshmi told her.

"Thanks. I'll eat after."

"Ready?" Seth asked, and pressed "start" on the remote, before handing it over to Lakshmi, who always controlled the volume.

Ranjani and Greg had left that morning, after gift-opening and packing into the wee hours. They had New Year's Eve plans back in Vancouver, a party with some of the friends who had come for the velaikappu, which made Seth suggest they all stay and celebrate here, but no one had responded.

Lakshmi's mother and brother had left, also—the brother was on-call New Year's Day, and the mother would not fly alone. The Sethuratnams had broken the divorce news to her the prior evening. She took it much better than they had feared. "You are a good girl," she told Brinda, gathering her in with hands that trembled, not from weakness, just from age. "Focus on your studies. *Chamathu*. Don't be afraid." It had felt like the blessing they all needed to go forward.

Seth scooped and mashed rice into okra sambar. The texture—crumbling lentils imbued with tamarind, cumin, coriander, coconut—against his fingers was an inoculation of sorts. It felt like stability, timelessness, a time before snow, before distance, before "divorce" and "my daughter" could ever be spoken together. The second inoculation was the taste. A recipe for time travel.

In the days after Brinda told them her news, he had been unable to eat. Lakshmi had made her peerless idlis, but for the first time in his life, the steamed dumplings tasted, to Seth, exactly like what they were: fermented paste. Rancid, gluey, no transformational magic, as though, in the West, their food was exposed as inferior, as though it should never have left India. But as he had digested the news, food and its illusions began to work on him again.

Were they illusions? He was revising his lectures for the spring and finding himself particularly interested in the ones on time and perception. He considered now whether to insert something about the physics of memory and imagination, how it is that a smell or taste can transport us to a different time, so that we are living simultaneously in our imagined past and in a present that is what we call reality.

Images of Shivashakti appeared on the television screen as the narration commenced, a woman speaking in a nasal South London accent. "Man and woman, God and human, Shivashakti is a religious leader with power that many think will someday rival the Pope's." Seth indicated the screen with his eyebrows, but his wife and daughter looked unimpressed, if carefully neutral. "Born into poverty in rural India, Shivashakti has long since transformed the village of his birth into a bustling town, eventually renamed Shivashaktipurum, with a clinic, schools, and a large ashram where his followers live and worship. All were built on donations from this guru's devotees. It is rumoured that he is in the top ten Indian charitable organizations for receipt of foreign funds. But the rumours don't stop there. In the wake of an attempted suicide by a teenage follower, stories have begun circulating that, for years, Shivashakti has habitually forced young devotees to participate in clandestine sexual activities."

Seth's ears began to ring. *He is God.* In temples *back home*, in the moment when the priest did the *arathi*, circling the god's features with a lamp of burning camphor, another priest would ring a bell as worshippers bowed to the deity. The space would empty of all sound save the ringing, in the silence of worship. Was Shivashakti ringing a bell now to drown out the documentary's harangue, to create a corridor through which Seth could return to him? *Tat Tvam Asi. That thou art.* His wife and daughter appeared frozen, either genuinely attentive to the TV or permitting him to nurse his humiliation in private. On Seth's plate, sticky okra seeds glistened as if with thwarted sexual will; flecks of spices corroded slickly congealed peaks of rice. He stared at the TV, willing his God, Shivashakti, who had sustained him all these years, to give him *darshan. My lord. Look at me. I am here.*

It seemed an eternity before Shivashakti looked out at the viewers. It was old footage—the guru twenty years younger, the age he was when Seth first went to the ashram—but still, his glance appeared to Seth not to be the blessing gaze of divine upliftment that he knew so well. It was now the hollow look of a hunted man.

Whatever the accusations, true or untrue, they changed nothing. Shivashakti's wisdom, which was your own. His strength, which was your own. The good he brought into the lives of his followers.

He couldn't look at his wife and daughter. They were saying nothing, but their thoughts—"We knew it! We knew it all along!"—radiated toward him like a stink. They knew nothing. Which used to be fine. Now they would never know.

He rose. "I need to go out."

Lakshmi asked, "Where? You don't want to see the rest?"

Not with you, he wanted to say. "No."

"Do you want us to stop it?"

"As you like," he said. "The office, I'm going to work."

Lakshmi looked at Brinda, who asked her father, "Do you want me to drive you?"

He shook his head and was gone.

✳ ✳ ✳

"What do you think?" Lakshmi asked. Her lower lip was always chapped in winter and she chewed on it now.

"I guess it's probably fine," Brinda said slowly. "Let him go. I feel bad for him."

"Yes. Poor thing. Do you want to keep watching? I don't know if I need to."

"No, let's finish, maybe . . . all we've learned about are the accusations. Let's find out what actually happened and then we can tell Dad if he wants to know."

Lakshmi restarted the video. The BBC had found three people, two men and one woman, who testified that as young people living in or around the ashram, they had been brought to their guru for a semi-private audience. Together with the one or two other young people present, they had been encouraged, by Shivashakti, to engage in sexual touching. Some eventually had intercourse, also in the presence of the guru. Condoms were provided, and instruction given—hands-on, if necessary—in how to use them. On camera, their faces obscured and voices distorted for the tape, all of the young people denied that they had had sex with the guru, but they agreed that he was present and watching at all times. When they were asked whether he touched himself or otherwise showed arousal as he was watching them, one mumbled in the affirmative, one emphatically denied it, and one said he couldn't say. When asked why they didn't refuse, none of them responded. When asked if they enjoyed it or felt humiliated, one man broke down in tears. The other man said he did enjoy it, but that the girl he was with seemed reluctant and shy, and he felt sorry for her, which spoiled his enjoyment somewhat. Another time, though, he was with a boy and a girl, and he didn't enjoy that as much. Brinda had to keep reminding herself that their voices were deliberately altered; the effect was to make them sound deaf or otherwise disabled.

The third interviewee, a woman, said she enjoyed it very much and was grateful to her guru for having introduced her to sex, for making her understand that the act was sacred in and of itself. When she was married, she said, she would have much more to offer her husband. But she didn't want anyone to know who she was, because that would jeopardize her chances at marriage. Once, he had invited her into his chambers alone and encouraged her to touch herself. "He taught me the pleasure of my body," she said.

"Is that what you believe he meant to do?" asked the interviewer.

Brinda said, "That's not a fair question."

The woman paused. "I don't know."

"Bizarre, bizarre." Brinda put both hands on her head. "What was he doing?"

The interviews were interspersed with others asking the same question.

"First of all, it is not true," said a smiling young man the documentary identified as an Official Spokesperson for the guru. Despite contradicting the BBC's suppositions, he wagged his head in the Indian affirmative, as though to pacify the detractors. "And then, whatever Shivashakti does, it is for the good. It cannot be for the bad, even when we cannot see the good result."

"So why do you think he did it?" asked the unseen interviewer.

"He just said he didn't do it," Brinda muttered.

"Am I God?" the Spokesperson responded, smiling still more broadly, leaning in a little toward the camera, teasing. "I cannot know what is in the mind of God." He threw his hands up, lightly. "Maybe he wants us to question."

Brinda wanted to resent his smugness, but there was something so enviable about his certainty in the midst of chaos—she wished she could feel it too.

"Sure, it could be true," said another devotee, an American in a raw silk blazer, the head of a well-known pop-music recording label. His jaw jutted pugilistically, and Brinda recalled that he had had some scandals of his own. "It doesn't matter to me. This man turned my life around. I would be wandering in the darkness right now if it weren't for Shivashakti." Brinda and Ranjani used to joke that Westerners' pronunciation put the "shock" in "shakti." It made their dad laugh. Never again. "He might have done it, whatever you say he did. I don't know and it doesn't make any difference." He brushed thinning hair out of his eyes. "I know myself because of him."

Over footage of Shivashaktipurum—clean, broad boulevards lined with airy-looking concrete buildings; young people doing exercises in formation in the schoolyard, kitted out in uniforms of the hand-loomed red cloth traditional to that area; devotees at work in the ashram kitchens and at prayer in the ashram galleries—the narrator spoke of two young people, called to one of these unconventional sessions, who had gone on to marry, overcoming their parents' objections by telling them that their guru had, effectively, married them already.

Every commentator the BBC spoke to had a wildly different interpretation of the swami's actions. A Western academic who wrote about contemporary Indian religious movements suggested that he might have been trying to encourage Indian young people in greater sexual freedom. "He may have felt he couldn't do so openly without alienating Indian parents. Why he had to *watch* them, though . . ." She looked uncomfortable. "Maybe to make sure they did what he said?"

An Indian activist with a salt-and-pepper beard who called himself a "guru-buster" dispassionately offered alternatives. "It could be that he is sexually perverted. An old story: the guru uses power to get sex. But it could also be that he is using it to get more power. He is a worm in the heart and mind." He looked as though he had saddened himself. "He is not a soul-healer. He is a soul-stealer."

The father of the boy who had attempted suicide bared his teeth at the camera as it caught him mid-accusation. "Western money has corruped this so-called godman, to turn our Indian boys into homosexuals and make our country weak." The camera lingered on his face for a few seconds after he finished speaking, bewilderment between his brows, disgust in the crow's feet at the corners of his eyes.

Brinda knew that expression: she had seen it on Venkat. It was the face of a man who had lost a son to a nebulous evil, one that wasn't targeting his son specifically, just people like his son, anyone who happened, like a minnow, to drift into its net.

* * *

There were many routes Seth could take to his office, none long, though some were longer than others. In his first years of teaching, he had always taken the quickest way, since he was always short of time and since he hadn't yet developed the subtle, binding affection that he now felt for the place. He had not chosen Lohikarma any more than he had chosen where he would be born or to whom. That inevitability was, for him, the start of love. He hadn't chosen whom he would marry or what nature of kids they would have: male or female, tall or short, peaceful or agitated or furious. People and places came to you and you came to love them.

He drove, the houses he passed as familiar as the words of a mantra. In past crises, the Air India bomb of twenty years ago, the Brinda bomb of two weeks ago, he had turned to God. How would he get through this one?

The corner houses on their street teetered in his peripheral vision as he got his bearings and chose which way to turn. The blue ranch house on the south was strung with an exuberance of lights in uneven patterns. The house on the northern corner was beige and sedate. Professor and Mrs. Aidallbery: a menorah in their picture window. Seth wondered, when he and Jake toasted the New Year with their annual brandy tomorrow afternoon, whether he would be able to confess his sadness, or would hide it.

He turned north, toward the lake, toward the house of an art collector, specializing in west coast tribes. They had known him as Pasha Essad Bey, until he was unmasked as a Nazi war criminal and deported. That had been a shock: did the Pasha collect marvels of native art as a recompense for his past evils, or did he acquire the artifacts while denying their makers' humanity? It didn't matter now. Seth slowed to get a glimpse of his favourite among the more than forty totem poles on the lawns. It was Salish, topped with an enormous eagle, wings outspread, painted in rich red, yellow, green and black. Though the palette was different, it reminded him of the Dravidian deities that guarded the temples of his childhood, with their wide-open eyes and snarling mouths.

He had always thought, semi-jestingly, of his peek through the shrubbery as a *darshan*-on-the-go, like those they would take at roadside shrines back home: bending and peering to get a glimpse of the god within and reciprocally receive the god's blessing glance. Today, though, when he made eye contact with the eagle, he recalled one of the many proofs of Shivashakti's divinity, his unblinking gaze, and an unexpected curtain of tears cut him off from the great bird's sight.

He turned his attention to the road, breathing hard through his nose, slowing at the corner by a house with a storefront on the ground floor. He used to take the children here to buy Mojo candies and Double Bubble gum, and Number 7 cigarettes for himself. It was run by a Chinese family, the man about Seth's age. His father, who sat in the back, had worked in the mines. *His* father had worked on the railroad. The daughter had graduated with Brinda.

Turning right, he gained a magnificent view of the mountains before his car started down a precipitous decline toward the centere of town.

* * *

The video said that a few people had been calling for the allegations to be investigated, but the police seemed not to be responding. A police spokesperson said that there was insufficient evidence of wrongdoing and no evidence of criminality. When asked whether Shivashakti would be investigated, the officer said, "We must protect the rights of all our people, madam."

"Which means . . . ?" Brinda asked the set, but no one answered.

The BBC speculated that given the number of high-ranking politicians who had visited the ashram, there would be no pressure from any official direction for the guru to explain his actions.

"And devotees have closed ranks, saying, effectively, that God works in mysterious ways," the narrator concluded.

"No kidding," Brinda said, as the credits rolled. She thought of Sundar, who had spent a summer doing *sewa* in Shivashaktipurum. Was Shivashakti doing this sort of thing back then?

"Disgusting," Lakshmi said, getting up and gathering plates. "Those poor kids."

Brinda's hadn't felt quite so ready to judge. "So you believe it?"

Lakshmi hesitated. "It never surprises me when one of these gurus is unmasked."

"What do you think Dad thinks?" Brinda followed her mother to the kitchen to get her own lunch.

"He couldn't have seen or heard anything like this before, or he never would have continued on as a devotee. I imagine he doesn't know what to think." Lakshmi finished washing her hands, dried them on a tea towel. "I'll phone him or go by his office in a little while. Let's give him some space."

*　*　*

Seth drove through downtown and arrived at the Phys-Chem building, but arced through the empty parking lot and out again without slowing down, turning the car back toward the town centre. He had been at home in India, and now he was at home here. There had been a limbo: After college, he taught school for a year, in India but far from home. Then Indiana, which had hit him hard, but he had made friends and even dated a couple of girls. One was a physics office secretary who went on a date with every foreign grad student in the department. The other was an undergraduate, Anna Gradeless, a farm girl. He hadn't thought of her in years! The longer he spent with her, the more fraternal his feelings became—something anti-erotic in getting to know a girl before marriage.

He aimed west of High Street, toward one of the mixed commercial blocks that rimmed the downtown. It happened to be the street with the old Hudson's Bay Co. building, now the soup kitchen where he volunteered on Saturdays—tomorrow.

The other devotees. *Did they know?* The video had been broadcast some months ago, in the U.K. How could he not have heard about its awful accusations? But there were always detractors, naysayers. Such as those in his own family. If Seth sensed the criticism coming, he turned off, tuned out, as they used to say. Why would none of the other devotees have told him? He would have listened if it had come from Nick or Kaj. Kaj would have said something. He must not have heard either.

He drove the dragging belly of the old town. In front of The Minter's Arms, he saw a hepatitis sufferer he knew from the soup kitchen, bloated and alone, either waiting for the bar to open or not permitted to enter. Seth hoped it was the latter. What time did the bars open? He would have liked a drink himself except that it would mean stopping the car. His native buddy from the soup kitchen, the one with the cloven face, was across the street, his arm around a woman. All his years in Canada and, with a couple of exceptions on Harbord U committees, the only Natives he had met were on the other side of the Sterno divide.

Ah, no, wait. A memory undimmed. He turned east, toward it, toward their second apartment, the one they had moved to when Lakshmi was pregnant. They lived on the ground floor, a two-bedroom flat. At the very top was a tiny attic suite inhabited by a quiet girl with long brown hair and glasses, in nursing school. Francine. She spoke another language—Kutenai? Why was Seth remembering such trivia now? He drove past the house, which had been dilapidated when they lived there, split up, propped up, carpeted. Now its gingerbread was repaired and repainted in stately plum and beige, of a piece with all the other historic homes reclaimed from the students and itinerant workers, fancy landscaping burying the stories of their recent past.

Had Francine been in the residential schools? He hadn't given her a thought when all the news was breaking on these generations-old traumas, dating to when government officials seized children from their homes, putting them in the care of lecherous priests who beat them for speaking their mother tongues. Francine spoke English with a lilting accent, when she spoke at all.

Seth's only experience of Catholic priests was at St. Joseph's. Horrors must have happened, there as elsewhere, at some point, he was forced to admit. But systematically? Surely he would have known. Had Father O'Sullivan, beloved of all, heard of such things? How could he not? Seth tasted something bitter on his lips, but couldn't feel his mouth. He couldn't feel his fingertips, either, though it wasn't that cold. He turned the heat up and spiralled, north again, toward their first apartment.

Consume my heart away; sick with desire / And fastened to a dying animal . . .

Seth remembered Venkat's long-ago warning, in the wake of his suicide attempt: *Attachment is pain*, he had said. Perhaps Shivashakti had orchestrated this: given Seth his mantra; cultivated his love; put him in the midst of a crisis so he could save himself with prayer and then, when Seth's attachment and gratitude were at their heights, look him in the eye and show him his folly. Was it folly? He was not sure. Speak to me, Lord!

. . . and gather me / Into the artifice of eternity.

His very first apartment here. A basement studio. The house looked neglected now: foundation cracked; stucco patchy; walk unshovelled and icing over, ready to crack the hip of whatever ancient resident had been abandoned inside. Surely not his old landlady? She had been in her sixties at the time, thirty-five, no, thirty-seven years ago. Dr. Shiner, a history prof, no family that they ever saw, though there was an old photo on the mantel: a woman that could have been her, in a dark shin-length dress and small hat; a confident smile dividing sharp, hooded eyes from a jutting chin, posed with a man and two children.

Dr. Shiner had doted on Seth to the point of imposition. Fortunately, he had been raised to accept the controlling attention of elders, surely one reason she loved renting to him. Then Lakshmi arrived. He recalled that first year of marriage as a sex-addled haze with occasional breaks for teaching. Dr. Shiner transferred her affections to Lakshmi, who was home more. Pregnancy gave them an excuse to move.

Perhaps Shivashakti, incarnate, was as fallible, as prey to the same blind desires and bad judgements, as any other mortal? Plausible. But insufficient.

Seth turned again. He saw a hawk wheeling up as he descended.

Turning and turning in the widening gyre / The falcon cannot hear the falconer.

This time he drove farther north, past the university, before turning west to enclose Willard Park in the counter-clockwise loop. *Things fall apart . . .*

If Sita and Sundar had not been killed, he would never have found God. The old game: what would he have done instead? Maybe he would have had a hobby. Model trains. Birdwatching. Perhaps with Venkat? But Venkat would never have become interested in birds if his family had lived. Most of the condo residents had given the parakeets back. Moe got an aviary for the lobby, but when residents reported there had been a bird dead in the cage for three days, he set the rest free. The parakeets went feral for the summer, flashing among the trees in Willard Park. Winter was another thing: when bright corpses started appearing in the snow, the SPCA rounded up the survivors and adopted them out to a local cult, which erected a parakeet shrine in the park. Now, a lone Steller's jay mocked the crows hopping under barren trees, strange and flat against the grey air, and little brown birds rustled berries in the bushes.

The spiral grew wider and looser, past his children's schools, past the plant nursery where Sita had worked, and then out of Lohikarma along the lake. The road bowed away from the water to make room for parklands but the lake was never fully out of sight. Crafty Canadians: they knew which side their bread was buttered on. These days, clear-cutting was allowed only on mountainsides facing away from the highways, so that the only people who could see the ugly bald patches were ones who had already made their commitment to the place. It was a principle he admired. His kids could call him cynical, but everyone was out to make a buck. In India, they didn't care what they spoiled. Beautiful spots became cesspools, hill stations trashed and unrecognizable. It was possible Canadians truly respected and valued nature, but even the ones who didn't had to act as though they did. Made life easier for everyone. Another hawk circled trees and lake, then another.

He turned onto a country highway. Trees closed in, but beyond them was pastureland. He was out in Canada now. *Out in Canada*. It sounded like a TV show. It sounded like one of his kids' jokes, something they might invent to pass the time on a road trip. Bungling Indian FOB drives around the Kootenay countryside asking real Canadians dumb questions about things that seem obvious. The kind of thing he would laugh at, particularly now that he, too, was Canadian. But in the early years, that was him.

Out in Canada, an untended field to one side and what might have been an ancient orchard on the other. Fragments of Shivashakti's lectures drifted up before him. They were always there, favoured phrases and arguments. For twenty years, Seth had steered his life by them. He looked out at the gnarled trees bent with phantom fruit and remembered, *The worm is happy in the apple's core, and knows no other home*. Why an apple, not a jackfruit or mango? He had thought perhaps the reference had become universal, or thought it was evidence of how effortlessly international were the workings of Shivashakti's mind: universal mind. Now he wondered if it was a deliberate attempt to reach out to Western devotees. Would that be so bad?

The lake made him recall the guru's words on the tsunami: *The calmest water has within it this power to take the life it also gives. Let your mind be the ocean, calm and accepting. Reserve your power to rise up and conquer weakness and temptation.*

Something about this had troubled him but he had not had time this week to think about it. Now, he understood it to be the hint that nature had intention. If Lakshmi or his daughters had raised this objection, he would have resented their literalism. Asked if they had ever heard of metaphor. Pointed out that there was nothing untrue in the words, if you read closely, which they hadn't. To say the ocean is calm is correct: this is a physical state, not only an emotional one. Perhaps he had been infected by their view, over time. They were hard to resist. Perhaps Shivashakti had driven him into their arms. Perhaps that was his intention.

The country highway had turned to gravel at some point. Up ahead was a a turn that led into the woods, very like one he and the kids took, a couple of times, to a campsite they loved. You drove through the woods to the site, fifty metres from a cliff with a huge view of the sky. He would feel better if he could see that view.

The barren landscape brought to mind Shivashakti's talks on death, especially what he said in the wake of the bombing: *Krishna said to Arjuna, I am death, shatterer of worlds. Your world has been shattered. But death comes, by human hand or divine will. This loss makes you want to kill. If you must strive, strive against this. Think, what else can I give? All is karma. These matters are not within your control. But the actions of this life are. If you must strive, strive to do good and be humble. Then strive to cease striving.*

Strive to cease striving. Renounce even renunciation. Seth had found himself, in recent years, thinking more and more on such prescriptions, perhaps particularly as Lakshmi became more and more committed to the new form of meditation she had found, without gods, mantras or other trappings; perhaps particularly as they both aged toward the phase of life when their own traditions prescribed that they begin withdrawing from the push and pull of material life, toward asceticism. Maybe they would move out into the country, he thought with a vague glance at the enfolded mountains, the well-made fields. But no, they should do it gradually, with few outward alterations. Shivashakti talked about how strictness in asceticism can itself become a distraction, a source of vanity. *The goal is not the goal*, he would say. It put Seth, smugly, in mind of Bala and his boasts on the many things he could live without. Poor Bala: his son seemed to be struggling. Their daughter was doing well, though: a medical professor, married to an investment banker, two kids. He thought of Brinda. His throat grew tight.

The goal is not the goal. Strive to cease striving. He'd always liked the sound of that. Strive to cease striving.

Drive to cease driving. His accelerator felt loose. It seemed he was on a logging road, a couple of ruts through the trees, scrubby grass between them, made for and by Jeeps and trucks. How long had the gas indicator light been on? It was hard to see in daylight but all too visible in the off-road shade. He remembered now that he had meant to fill up on returning from the airport this morning. The car rolled to a halt as the motor died into the silence of the vast Canadian winter.

After yesterday's warm spell, the temperature was dropping again. He always overheated the car; it began cooling quickly now in the evergreen shade. He was wearing gloves and a winter coat but had forgotten hat and scarf. Thin socks. Oxfords, with thick rubber soles, so he wouldn't fall, but he still could freeze. What could he do? He had to walk. Where? He got out of the car and regretted it as the cold clapped his cheeks and boxed his ears, which started ringing again—panic. Where the hell was he and which way should he go?

He turned toward the nose of the car, pointing deeper into the woods. How far would he have gone if he'd had more gas? How far would a full tank have taken him? Maybe it was a blessing—maybe he was closer to civilization than he otherwise would have been. And still it was only mid-afternoon. Winter, though: only a few hours till sunset. The road curved off ahead and disappeared, nothing familiar about it, and there was little chance of finding anyone at the end of it who could help.

He started to retrace his way. How long had it been since he had passed a house or anyplace that looked even vaguely tended? How long had he been driving? He looked at his watch. Three o'clock. What time had he left home?

His coat was bulky and inelegant, with sturdy snaps and zippers; it looked as though it were made for this weather and it had served him well from home to car to office, but now he felt the difference between it and its more expensive counterparts. A hood, for one thing. He pulled the puffy collar up close to his ears. He balanced among the heavy-truck treads, fossilized in the frozen mud, stiff as the soles of his shoes. Glancing behind, he found his car had already disappeared. Progress! The trees around him were not huge but they were indistinguishable. He presumed his car was still back there. His eyes stung. It wasn't that cold. Maybe a couple degrees below freezing. No wind. Why were his eyes watering? Not that cold compared to what? Most of Canada. He was thinking fast but it wasn't helping him. Mind racing; car stalled. Sounded like a fortune cookie. Fate don't fail me now—ha! Jokes no help. Cold hands; warm heart. What was he supposed to do, pray? Ha, and ha again!

The trees were different now. Everything changes. They weren't all evergreens anymore. Birches, he thought, *bent to left and right*. Frost! Last thing he needed was more frost: what about a poem called "Nice Warm Fire?" Or "Gas Station." Ha again. More light coming through. His daughters had told him about this, how trees tell you the age of the woods. Back when they went out in the woods together. Not often, long long ago. Evergreen woods are older. *Straighter, darker trees.* He thought so anyway. Younger woods let in more light. It was warmer, by a tint, he could feel it. Splashes of sun on his face. Younger woods, more recently cleared. Old growth long gone. Old farms grown over? Or land cleared for some other reason. Or land where no trees had grown before.

Now there were almost no evergreens. And he was walking fast and faster. He was almost warm. Why the sudden sense of optimism? He could still be miles from anyone who could help. Any second now, he would trip over the body of the last guy abandoned by God in the middle of a crisis. It probably happened all the time. His eyes were still watering. His cheeks were wet. The woods thinned. He was at a crossroads.

The road he had climbed—he only now noticed that he had been walking uphill—plateaued and continued through the intersection and beyond, flatter now, no longer an undulation underfoot. It stretched ahead, as far as Seth could see, toward a vanishing point. But what if it actually vanished at that point? It looked so unused that he could easily imagine it terminating in a field, thinning and running aground, sliding under the floating wreck of a pioneer cabin. You still saw them sometimes, roof beams rotted and caved, mysterious holes in the log walls. He imagined taking that road, and living out his days in the ghost cabin, combing wheat seeds out of hulls with his teeth and chewing them raw, drinking the nectar of wildflowers, beard long and soft across his naked chest as he trance-huddled against the one standing wall of his shelter. But what if he couldn't grow a long beard? He had never tried.

The crossing road delineated a wilder from a tamer place, woods from field, overgrown from overcleared. *Two roads diverged in a wood . . .* He had walked out of the wild and had to choose: walk into the tame or take the road that straddled these ways of being? *Way leads on to way . . .*

To his left, west. He took a couple of experimental steps, shoes crunching gravel, and it felt so good he kept going, up hill and down dale until he came to the ocean. And kept going and discovered he could breathe underwater. He had simply never tried. Perhaps it only worked in salt water. Sundar and Sita were there. The water had pieced them back together and there they lived, swimming with the fishes. Sita couldn't swim before. But necessity is the mother of mothers.

Then there was the appeal of the east. He looked back over his shoulder at it. The vast expanse of where he came from. He jumped and was pulled back there, legs and arms flung from the force of the vortex that funnelled along the road. *The widening gyre*. He spun, he tumbled, he flew, miming in reverse the actions that had brought him to the crossroads, till he was shocked back into the darkness of the womb.

East or west: it was his choice.

But he always chose badly. He was not trained for choice; he didn't like it. The only things that made sense in his life were the things he had not chosen. His wife, his kids, his nations, his job. His God? Was that a choice? Or had Shivashakti chosen him? It felt as though Seth had chosen freely. He had overcome the resistance of his wife and kids to do it. Had he chosen badly? His department chose his courses; his students chose him. His parents chose his wife. When they went to a restaurant, Lakshmi's food was always better, unless he let her order for him. He could always be happy with a choice someone else had made. He should not be given such responsibility as this. He turned to face each direction one more time. *Sorry I could not travel both and be one traveler* . . .

He sank to his knees and wept at the crossroads. He wept and could not choose and could not move.

"Sir?" A man's voice, uneasy. "Could you stand please? Slowly. What you feel is a gun in your back. No sudden moves."

Seth continued to kneel, looking down at the mixed dirt and gravel where the roads entwined, and saw boots, brown hiking boots, to one side. Beyond them, if he shot his eyes as far to the side as they would go without turning his head, he could see the tires of a truck resting quite ordinarily on the western road. He became aware, as he had been so politely informed he might, of an iron nubbin of pressure on the bend of his spine. He took his hands off his chest, slowly put them to his thighs, and then pressed his fingertips to the chapped skin of the winter ground as he tried to straighten his legs. One didn't work. He tried the other. That one failed as well and he fell over.

"Shit." This voice was different from the other and came from behind him. "Pat him down."

Seth, on his side on the sloping ground, shook his feet to try to get the feeling back into them and his legs. As the tingles started, so did the fear. He looked up at the first man who had spoken to him, wearing a ski jacket and a nylon balaclava.

"I'm checking for weapons and your wallet, understand?" There was fear in his voice, but still his intentions could be violent and godless. "Hold your feet still. Cut that out." He zipped open Seth's jacket without helping him up, kneeled awkwardly to check where his pockets should be, and, finding Seth's wallet, stood back and opened it. "What are you doing out here?" he asked, pulling out Seth's driver's licence, credit card, Harbord ID card. "Faculty? You're a professor?"

Seth nodded and tried to roll himself to his feet.

"Let me help you," the man with his wallet said, and gestured with his head to the other man, leaner and taller than the first, also in a ski mask.

They got Seth to his feet. His legs would support him now but he couldn't feel much below his knees. "Which department do you teach in?"

"Physics," Seth said, and his voice was hoarse as if long unused. He coughed. They dusted him off a little. He did the same.

They waited. His knees buckled as if they'd been waiting to do so. Both men leapt to catch him.

"Goddammit," said the shorter man, looking at the other, and then at Seth. "Maybe you had better sit down for a few minutes. We need to talk."

They started to lower Seth back onto the ground and then reconsidered. "You may as well get in the truck." When they had hoisted him into the cab, they withdrew, conferred, then returned to stand at the open door.

The shorter man asked, "Do you have any idea what you're doing out here?"

Seth sensed concern. "Praying?"

The taller man looked away, then back at Seth. "Can we drive you home? Your address is on your licence."

"I'm wondering, should we take him to a hospital," said the shorter one.

"No, actually, I'm fine," Seth said, rubbing his cheeks. "I was driving. I ran out of gas. My car is down that road, in the woods." That's what it was. He ran out of gas.

"Down there? You sure?"

"Is there any way you could take me to a gas station? Then I could call a tow truck to bring me back here."

They looked at each other. The taller one gestured to the shorter with his head and they walked away again, leaving the truck doors open. They stood out of earshot, the dark thickening around them. The taller one scooped up a snowball and threw it away. As they walked back, they peeled off their masks. They were in their late twenties, tidy-looking, a couple of well-groomed white men in the prime of youth coming upon him in the middle of nowhere.

The skinny one had dark hair and was clean-shaven. He got into the driver's seat. "Okay . . . what's your name again?" he asked.

"Seth. Rhymes with 'faith.'"

"Seth. Um, pleased to meet you." He grinned a bit, not a smile, and held out his hand. "I'm Brian."

The other, shorter, blonder, with a bit of a beard, was called Jeff. He hoisted himself into the passenger seat. "So, listen. We were on our way home. What we think is, you come with us. It's not too far. Have a bowl of soup, wash your face."

Seth put his hand to his face and then checked it in the rear-view mirror.

"Then we need to go to town anyway for some errands, and so we'll take you, get your gas, and then drive you back here to your car. Sound all right?"

"You're very kind," Seth said. "But that's a lot of trouble for you."

"Nah, it's fine. But . . ." Brian looked at Jeff and Jeff looked out the window. "I hate to have to say this, but, I think you can trust us—well, no, what I mean to say is that you can totally trust us, but I think it would be better for us if—well, we don't want you to know where we live."

Huh, Seth thought.

"I don't really think you know where you are at this point, do you?"

Seth smiled. "No clue, no sir."

"Do you have a hat?"

"I don't. I . . . wasn't thinking."

"Uh, yeah, so here's my toque." Brian handed Seth his cap, started the engine and spoke over Seth's thanks. "Just put it on backward and pull it down over your eyes. That oughta do it."

Seth obeyed. His brain was working again. The cloak of darkness made it impossible to ask the usual polite questions: *What do you do? Tell me about the area.* In the absence of appropriate niceties, he breathed shallowly in the knit cap, smelling another man's scalp, and waited. Were they undercover cops? But then they wouldn't live together. Were they gay? But many gay people lived quite openly these days. Illegal immigrants? No: Canadian accents. Where was the gun, by the way? By the way! Was it a gun? Finger? Too hard to be a finger.

In time, the truck stopped. "All right, here we are."

Seth hesitated, but Brian said, "You can give my toque back now. You're good."

They had arrived at a farmhouse, dilapidated but with renovation work in progress on the wraparound porch. Toddler toys were strewn in the yard and there was a chicken house and a plastic-sheet greenhouse visible around the side.

Jeff walked backward a few steps, saying, "Let me let them know what's up." He gave Seth an apologetic look. "Cell phones don't work out here." He wiggled his fingers in the air. "Black hole." The screen door banged behind him as Seth was still dismounting from the heights of the truck.

Brian went around to the truck bed, let down the back and jumped up to drag sacks of soil to the edge, moving a couple of snowboards to do it. Hopping down again—his agility was impressive to Seth, but that's what it is to be young—he hoisted one onto his shoulder as Jeff came back out. Behind him were two young women, one of whom carried a baby. The other was significantly pregnant, with a toddler around one leg.

"Come on up," said Jeff. "This is Karen, and my little boy, Lucan." He took the hairless child from the blond woman, while the pregnant woman, who had toasted-almond hair, eyes and freckles, said, "I'm Eiko, Brian's wife." Her little girl swung the ball of her wooden cup toy at Eiko's knee and she winced.

Eiko and Karen were tidy, pretty, dressed in mismatched woollens over a dress or jeans, like hippies, or so was Seth's vague impression. The children were equally pretty if dishevelled.

Jeff said, "I'm going to help Brian unload. Karen and Eiko'll get you a cup of tea or something, eh?"

Seth followed the women and children through an old-fashioned foyer to the kitchen in the back of the house, where Eiko put a kettle on the stove and said, "Please, have a seat."

Seth accepted but then again sat in the awkward silence that his every instinct militated against. It was only the girls, though, so what could be the harm in attempting to be polite? What if they were being held here against their will? Stockholm syndrome! A cult!

He cleared his throat as tea was set before him with some kind of syrup—*agave*, he read on the label—and honey and a bottle of organic milk.

Karen sat the baby on her lap. "Jeff said you ran out of gas?"

"Yes, yes, carelessness." He chose honey. "In such a remote place! Stupid. You have lived here for a long time?" Of course, they might not be remote—for all he knew they had driven back toward town. Did they know he had been brought here blindfolded? They may have been brought here the same way.

"Maybe a year or so?" Karen looked at Eiko, who shrugged. "A few months before Lucan was born, I guess."

They sat a few more minutes, Seth trying to get Eiko's daughter to show him her toy, until Brian and Jeff came back.

"We gotta skedaddle." Jeff opened the fridge. "New Year's Eve. Seth, when was the last time you ate?"

"No, no, I . . ." Seth began, but Jeff stared him down over the top of the fridge door, and Seth turned his hands up in a gesture that may as well have said, *Feed me*.

"We have some leftover dal and rice," Eiko said. "It won't take a sec to warm up."

The dal was bland and unfamiliar, but with yogourt and brown rice, it was close enough to what he needed. They walked out again and got in the truck. The dark had sealed the chill and Jeff gave Seth a wool cap, politely asking him to pull it down over his eyes while they left.

"First stop the longhouse?" Jeff asked. He was driving this time, his voice to Seth's left.

Seth heard the rustle of paper, to his right.

"Yep. Seth, we have to make a couple stop-offs on our way to town. Hope you're all right with that."

"Yes, yes, of course." He was a small, old man with a toque pulled over his eyes. Who was he to make demands?

"Customer appreciation night," Jeff said, and cackled a little. It must have been a witty remark.

After ten minutes of winding and bumping, the truck came to a halt. Jeff cut the motor while Brian hopped out, leaving the door open.

"Are you cool, Seth?" Jeff asked after a minute or two.

There was some cold air coming in from the open door, but again, Seth wasn't one to complain. And his face was nicely protected. "No, I'm fine."

"No, I mean, are you cool with . . ."

Seth felt the seat dip to his right and Brian closed the truck door.

"Bri, you think we can let Seth take the hat off?" Jeff asked over the ignition.

"Are you uncomfortable, Seth?" Brian asked.

"No, no, no. Fine, fine." There was comfort in passivity, even despite an abnormally high blink-rate and cheap wool chafing his eyelids.

"He's gonna have to hang with us at the bar," Jeff said. "Nothing between here and there's any worse."

"Y'okay. Pull the hat up, Seth, or take it off if you want."

He obeyed and they granted him friendly grins as he smoothed his hair. A waning moon lit the Kootenay countryside. He recalled that they had driven for spells on proper roads, but mostly travelled on gravel, as they were doing now. They turned out onto a single-lane road bordering a sheer cliff, making Seth wish they had let him keep the toque over his eyes. They crested and then rolled down off the mountain and along a road covered with undisturbed snow. Perhaps snow had fallen more recently here—*Where on earth are we?*—but it had been five days since it last snowed in Lohikarma—*And what the hell are we here for?*

A short drive to a bumpy stop in front of a shack of raw, warping boards, a tin chimney protruding to exhale a thin line of smoke.

"You or me?" Brian asked, not looking at Jeff.

"Aw, d'you mind? I think I did it last time. Just, say hi for me."

Brian opened the cab and jumped down, then took something from a knapsack on the footboard. He approached the door and knocked, then waited what seemed a very long time. Jeff leaned over the wheel, stretching his back and watching Brian.

"Dude has cancer. It's, like, got his whole body now. His wife maybe goes to the store once every couple of weeks but apart from that, they're just up here. Alone. They used to be totally self-sufficient, I heard." No one had yet opened the door and Brian knocked again. When the door at last swung out, pushing the snow off the step onto the snow-covered yard, Seth saw a large person, with a bloated, hairless face, long iron-black hair and a dark robe. Man or woman, he couldn't tell. Brian handed over the item from the bag. "C'mon, Brian," Jeff said softly. "Sometimes they make us come in. I get it, they're isolated. But the place smells like death."

"They don't want to move into town?" He didn't even know what town he might be speaking of. Maybe it was only the idea of a town.

"Wants to die in his own place, his own bed. Docs can't do anything for him now and he thinks the cities are poison."

They drove back along the cliffside and out of the snow, to a little apartment complex with no apparent reason for being where it was. Brian got out.

"Crackhouse," said Jeff, opening his door to spit onto the ground and slamming it shut again. "It's the thing I hate about this job," he told

Seth. "You're lumped in with the lowlifes. Bottom feeders"—Jeff indicated the door, where a small, backlit man in a T-shirt and sticking-up hair was talking to Brian—"but also organized crime, you know. It's all up and down the coast. Vancouver. Roll down Brian's window, would you?" Jeff peered out past him. "We grow a high-quality product. Totally organic. We work for it and we guarantee it and we believe in it. Free access, man. Mayor Owens said it himself—grow it, sell it, tax the hell out of it. Why not? But it's the drug war."

There was some shouting now from the apartment complex and Brian was backing away, holding up his hands.

"Cross this dump off our list." Brian climbed in. "Asshole."

The next drop was in a thickly settled suburb, the clients a Mountie and her husband. Brian laughed at Seth's confusion. "She's cool. She's fighting those huge, disgusting grow-ops too. Illegals, smuggled in to work up here, using chemical fertilizers and selling that mass-produced shit on the streets."

Seth recalled having read that marijuana now accounted for 60 percent of British Columbia's sagging provincial economy. When they first arrived in Lohikarma, he had, once or twice, seen a joint passed at a party. Earlier, back home, he used to see ganja-smoking sadhus drifting in the vicinity of some holy places. But those were different times, simpler, more innocent. Then again, Brian and Jeff seemed as simple and innocent as anyone. He looked at their faces. He liked them. Good eggs.

"But can I ask, I think there are official suppliers of medical marijuana now. I saw something on the news. You can't apply?"

Both men were shaking their heads. "First of all, unless you're employed by some mega-secret-underground government-owned lab in the frozen prairies, you can't get certified to supply to more than one person." They had arrived in a tiny hamlet (was there any other kind?) and pulled up to a hospice, pink stucco, indeterminately institutional. "All the trouble to get certified, and you get to help one person!"

"Apart from which," Brian chimed in drily, "we believe in helping people who just want to get stoned. Apart from which, even, a person's gotta make a living."

Seth elected to wait in the foyer. He jingled change up out of his pockets for a machine-vended coffee and spun a white-wire rack filled with leaflets, mostly on "Living with AIDS" and "Letting Your Loved One Go." The door opened and he felt a bluster of chatter blow in on a cold breeze. A well-dressed man and a couple of very tall women clattered over the tiled floors toward the elevator. One of the women glanced at him impersonally as the doors closed: she was a man. False eyelashes. Evening dress. Wig?

His first thought was of a group of *aravanis*, eunuchs who disrupted his sister's wedding, dancing, clapping, tweaking the men's dhotis, until they were paid off and left. Everyone hated them, but they were said to be good luck. His second was of the New Year's Party he and Lakshmi were to have attended tonight, over the mountain and far away. Maybe he would get home in time to join it.

The elevator opened again and Jeff and Brian stepped out. They held the door for a gaunt man in a bathrobe. He shuffled out, no word of thanks or anything else, toward the vinyl-covered armchairs.

"Ready, man?" Brian asked Seth. As they went through the vestibule, Seth looked back at the man, now sitting and looking where Seth could find nothing to see.

Their final stop was a pub—worn carpet on the floor, worn felt on the pool table, worn faces on the clientele. A board advertised *Mac-n-Cheez* and *Pikled Eggs*. The latter seemed unnecessary given the quantity of such eggs displayed on the bar, enbrined in a jar large enough to be an aquarium. They went to a booth, and a waitress, her hair recently tunnelled by curlers, slopped six-ounce glasses down, three per person, on the table.

"Numerous and pale, like the patrons," Brian said, lifting a glass.

Seth laughed, but Jeff looked mortified. "Except Seth, of course," he said.

Seth stood the drinks, eighty-five cents a glass, against the men's protests. "It's the least I can do. I'm just glad I have cash. I'm usually a little short." They gave him a look he was used to: students on the first day of his class, not sure when he was joking. "Get it?" He put a hand above his head. "A little short."

"Badoom-ching," Jeff said, and they clinked glasses.

From across the room, an untidy fellow otherwise dressed like Seth's companions nodded a greeting at them. They nodded back, and he joined them at their table. The waitress sped over but he waved her away.

Jeff slid one of his glasses over. "Happy New Year."

The man inclined his head and raised the glass. "Dude," he said, and sipped.

Brian was rummaging under the table in his knapsack. The man fidgeted with his gloves in his lap. He nodded at Seth. Brian nodded at him. He finished his beer and left.

A few other similar encounters ensued: people, singly or in pairs, came and sat, made small talk and kept their hands under the table. The waitress was permitted to lay another round down. Seth wondered at the social rituals of the young. On his way back from the restroom, he noticed the cigarette machine. A fixture of his younger years. It had been so long since he had used one. He bought a pack of Number 7, for old times' sake, and got matches off the bar.

Brian gave the cigarettes a sour look as he rejoined them at the table. "Things'll kill you, Seth."

Yes, he wanted to say, *things will kill me and things will kill you. And probably not the things you expect.* He laid the cigarette package on the table as he realized marijuana was being sold beneath it, under his very nose, slightly above his very knees. *Look at these two babies*, selling the stuff of life: soma, bliss, an end to pain. He shook his head, snorting with laughter. *Things'll kill you. Oh, yes. Oh, oh, yes.*

Brian and Jeff were starting to look concerned. Seth waved his hand at them, wiped his eyes, but couldn't quite stop. *Ayoh-yoh-yoh. The kind of thing Shivashakti would have laughed at.*

That at last dampened his mirth. He pictured his god, seized with delight, and was himself seized with drunken longing. Was he all alone? For twenty years, he had carried his god, or his god had carried him. He looked around the bar, looked at his new friends, finished another beer, and remembered the injunction against drinking alone. Was everyone in here drinking alone? Or had they chosen their gods more wisely? If they had, it was because they had been raised to choose: Westerners. Even if they chose badly, they understood this to be part of the risk. *Brinda.* Why had he not been content with the gods of his childhood? They had not betrayed him. Lord Shiva, passionate and generative; the goddess Shakti, grounding and generative; they quarrelled and united, danced and fought, their mutually encircling arms holding and elevating one another. They were fractious, faulty. Above all: inaccessible. *Above all . . .* He smiled again. They were above all, while Shivashakti moved among men. What if Shivashakti wasn't so different from them, though?

All the bad decisions Seth would have taken had he not had Lakshmi. Which left only the bad decisions he still managed to make with her. Lakshmi, too: without him, she would be anxious, even sharper-tongued, possibly friendless. *I should phone home*, he thought, but the pay phone by the door was in use.

Shivashakti was both man and woman, self-regenerating, the dragon biting its own tail. Maybe the problem was celibacy. Seth pictured Shivashakti torn from himself, flung out along some infinite trajectory.

He sat up. Brian and Jeff seemed ready to go.

They were quiet as they drove to the gas station, where Seth purchased a plastic canister and filled it. It was late. He glanced around for a pay phone, but didn't see one.

The crossroads by moonlight had an air of abandonment more serene than its mood by day, the snow in the fields like guttering flames, the woods like a crowd come to pray. "This way?" Brian asked, turning down the logging road, but neither of them expected Seth to answer. They had led him a merry dance off his path of grief, but time was leading him back to the tapering end of the spiral.

Time.

In the temples of his childhood, one way to worship was by walking clockwise around the deity, or even around the temple, each worshipper a human shadow on a divine sundial, marking time. Had he intended to go the wrong way, the direction of undoing, the demon's march? Was his god undone?

He poured the gas into his tank and his new friends pointed him toward the highway.

Brian handed him a joint. "Happy New Year, my friend." Seth accepted it without thought.

"You take care," Jeff said, as both men shook his hand.

Seth made a straight shot through the spiral and past its centre—coasted past his home, elbows on the wheel, while he put the joint in his mouth and lit it, then drove downtown and stopped across from the Shivashakti Centre.

The joint had gone out. He lit it again. There was no charge for any municipal parking spots tonight, and the cab tabs were on the city. DON'T DRIVE DRUNK! billboards had shouted for weeks now. A few minutes to midnight, according to his car clock. He dragged, held, coughed.

Shivashakti, undone. He was dizzy as he left the car. *She's come undone*, that voice in his head sang, the one that loved to sing him songs he didn't feel like hearing. Brinda, undone. *She didn't know what she was headed for / And when she found what she was headed for / It was too late.*

The keys jangled on his finger. Images of tottering revellers behind him swung and wobbled in the glass door and then he was through the looking glass and up the stairs. *We're off to see the Wizard!* For twenty years, the wizard had lived in him, made it possible for him to live.

* * *

Seth stepped into the ashram's darkness. Disappointment came at him. What? Had he thought Shivashakti would be here, waiting, the way he had when they met twenty years ago, all ready to explain?

Vertiginous, he touched the walls. At one end of the meditation hall, a photo of the guru presided. Seth's eyes began to adjust. The room was lit by a misty glow from beyond the cheap white blinds on the windows. Windows high up, office style: natural light but no distractions. Good for meditation as well as the business of the world. Street lights refracted through falling snow dulled by dirty window panes and edited again by the blinds, but still, the resulting low haze was enough. The room was empty but for Seth and . . . God? The spirit of God? The likeness of the guru? He looked at Shivashakti's picture on the shrine, but couldn't tell whether it was becoming clearer in the low light or less so.

Should he sit, as usual? Stand, as he would for a confrontation? He approached the shrine and struck a match, as if to light the candles, but instead re-lit his joint. *Out, out brief candle.*

The only way Seth had ever invoked Shivashakti was by use of a mantra, given to Seth by the guru himself—he called Shivashakti by praying to Shivashakti. Seth didn't think that was what he had come here to do.

He felt the floor shove against his bottom, as though some aggressive host had popped his knees with a chair. So: he would sit, then.

Seated, he felt habit press him to begin prayer, but as he resisted that, he heard instead, clattering in the cavity of his frightened mind, a rising wave: clatter-clatter—time and matter—chatter-chatter—daughter-daughter—double daughter—doppelgänger—Oppenheimer—double-couple—toil and trouble—now uncouple—all undone—*it was too late*—Ah, Sita—Oh, Sundar—*Ah—Oh—M—Om—Ommm.*

The ear-ringing resolved into one sound. *Om.* Then dissolved again into three parts. *Ah. Oh. M.* The strands separated and joined. *Like cloves of mangosteen,* Shivashakti had said, instructing them on the universal syllable. Picture the sweet white heart, the spongy purple flesh.

Om expands and its parts join. A geodesic d-*om*-e. The last syllable of recorded time.

Om. Seth ached as he chanted, louder and surer now. *Speak to me, Shivashakti. But no words, please, I'm sick of them.*

Sick with desire… Gather me into the artifice of eternity.

Om. This, too, was a mantra, but from a time before his god. There were others, from childhood. *Hare Krishna, Hare Krishna, Krishna, Krishna, Hare, Hare.* Seth would chant it on his way to school, or while playing, back when he loved Krishna. All children did. "Hurray, Krishna!" Ranjani used to say. As a child, he had perfect confidence in his gods' distant heroism, despite their flaws. When had he lost the ability to believe like that?

A time before his god—he never even would have thought such a thing before seeing the video today. An absurd thought. There is no time before the eternal.

Om.

Did Shivashakti exist before Seth knew him or did Seth bring him to life by way of his devotion? He could think that as a scientist, but not as a devotee.

Om.

From the street, he heard shouts and the thunder of fireworks. *Darkness drops again.*

Midnight sun. Sun invocation.

"Om *bhur bhuvah suvahah. Tat savitur varenyam. Bhargo devasya dhimahi. Diyo yo nah prachodayat . . .*"

Oh, universe—heaven, earth, and all that rotates between and beyond.

I bow to your infinite centre, You, Sun. I bathe in your infinite rays.

I dissolve in the radiance of the all-mind.

Draw me in to your centre. Drive me out to your borders.

Not-I, all-we, and the infinite plane.

* * *

And then, He came.

Whether by the grace of the mantra, or by the way that it pro-pelled Seth into an attitude of receptiveness, Shivashakti appeared.

Appeared might be too strong a word, but there is no weaker one that works. The god was watery and faint as one might expect an ap-parition to be—*I am the ghost of Christmas past!* Despite all the promises, and all it had achieved, Seth's mind was no more still or controlled than it had ever been.

. . . I am with you and within you . . .

No words, Seth pleaded, peeking around the edge of his mind, which seemed determined, now that the moment had arrived, to obstruct. In fact, he realized—his third eye was adjusting now—that Shivashakti was, in this form, nothing like his form in life. Or perhaps he was ini-tially some ghost-twin of his known and remembered form, but he was dismembering now, changing rapidly. Expanding and merging in some terrifying way with Seth and the air and the light and not-light.

Without form, was this still Shivashakti? *I am not here to say I am God. I am here to prove that you are God. Tat Tvam Asi.*

Seth dimly recalled his initial intention—confrontation, right? the big question: why?—but then it spun out of him and away, caught in a tornado . . . *We're off to see the Wiz* . . . Then the words were gone, what a relief, all the words, disappearing faster and faster now, sucked away from him faster than they could appear, flung out steadily and with in-tention to the farthest reaches of the cosmos, where they continued on, and on, and on.

The divine quakes before creation, just as Seth was quaking now, just as he and Lakshmi created babies and then were terrified by their myster-ies and wildness. You can *only* love what you cannot understand because only the fool believes he understands, so that only the wise—the bewil-dered—truly love. Bewilder: to lead into the wild unknown. This what Shivashakti had done for him. Brought him to the precipice of unknow-ing. The wild sharp cliffs, the wide grey wilderness, the vast green sea.

* * *

New Year's morning, 2005. Seth felt a rustling, under his head. He started up from what he thought must be the earth and some small creature trying to nest in his ear, but looked down at the blue carpet and then up into Kaj's blue eyes.

"Uh, trying to put this, under, uh . . ." Kaj smiled a faint, hard smile and tossed the meditation cushion he was holding back against the wall from where he would have got it. He rose ponderously to his feet—bulky man—and offered Seth a hand.

Seth reached to take it, then waved it away and got to his feet on his own, shaky, the second time in twenty-four hours his legs seemed not to want to hold him, even under an unwelcome gaze of concern.

"I'm . . ." Kaj sighed. "Going to put a pot of coffee on. Came by to get some copies of, uh, last week's lecture."

"Lakshmi asked you to come?" Seth said.

Kaj held his palms up, with a delicate wave of his head. "She . . . she didn't have a key. I think she's on her way over. Let me put on some coffee, eh?"

Lakshmi must not have told him about the video. Kaj thought it was a marital issue. As well it might become. Seth noticed, on the carpet, the burnt end of the joint, flattened from his lying on it. He went to the bathroom to flush it away. When he came out, teeth brushed with a finger, hair smoothed with water, it was to the smell of coffee.

"What time is it?" Seth asked his friend.

"Wouldja look at that? Twenty to."

Lakshmi and Brinda appeared in the stairwell. "Oh, thank God," Lakshmi said, starting to cry.

"I'm . . ." Seth stood. He was what? Fine? Sorry? He was both and neither.

Kaj pointed out past them. "On my way to the soup kitchen." He raised a hand and descended the stairs.

"Dad, listen," said Brinda. Seth waved them into the kitchen, where Lakshmi, her eyes drying, poured coffee. "I know the opening to the video was pretty sensationalistic, but the rest of it is, well, not that you'll feel great about it, but . . ." She looked at her mother. "I don't think it implies Shivashakti is evil. Misguided, maybe, or, well, I don't know. Mahatma Gandhi is supposed to have done some pretty strange things, also, apart from all the great things. I don't know if those aspects can necessarily be separated, in charismatic people. Maybe in anyone. I'm not sure it takes away from Gandhi's accomplishments, and maybe you'll feel the same about Shivashakti. You know how I feel about him, so believe me when I say this! You should make up your own mind." She looked around. "Feels weird to be talking about this here."

Seth wanted to get out of the ashram, but didn't feel quite ready to respond to Brinda. "Why don't we all go volunteer at the soup kitchen?" This felt right: something they liked to do together.

""I can take your place," Brinda said. "Don't you and Mom ...?"

Seth looked at Lakshmi, who narrowed her eyes a tiny bit and shook her head. "Let's talk later." She sighed, quick and hard. "I was worried sick."

Seth pinched the bridge of his nose. "I am sorry. I, I meant to call."

"Mom and I are going to horn in on your brandy at Dr. Aidall-berry's." Brinda said. "You're not the only one who needs a drink."

Seth, smiling, descended the stairs with a hand on each of their napes.

* * *

"*Jai Shivashakti*," the others all said to Seth and his family when they got to the soup kitchen.

"*Jai* . . ." he tried. He mumbled, he faltered. Did they notice? "*Jai Guru*," he eventually responded. Glory to the teacher. Which?

Physical work, familiar activity—the comforts of routine. As Seth served, Seth recalled Brinda's objection to his serving his god by serving these people. What had he said? *They get fed, they don't care.*

Namaskaram, he thought now. Lakshmi had dragged him to a yoga class one time, where the teacher had translated this into English, the greeting that looks like a prayer. Palms together, at the heart: *I salute the divine in you.* He never would have thought to put it in words, this idea, but she wasn't wrong. Still, he never went back.

He thought it as he ladled out minestrone. If Seth loved his kids, he loved God in his kids. He loved God in his wife. He repeated it for each scoop of soup—*namaskaram*—his head throbbing lightly so that he was aware of the beat of his heart—*namaskaram*—as he sifted vaguely and painfully through splintered recollections of the long night before.

*B*rinda stayed in Lohikarma some two or three weeks longer. I saw her several times, and when she left, made her promise this time to stay in touch.

Seth made himself harder to see. I called him, but the dull chill in his voice froze out even something so simple as *Could we meet, a coffee?*

I persisted. We met. I did my best to explain.

He listened, his eyebrows slightly furrowed and, significantly, motionless. His tone was unencouraging when he said, "Lakshmi seemed to think it was a good thing that Brinda talked to you." Another of his women had allied with me—how they pulled the rugs out from under him! It must have enraged him, not that it would have gone any better for me had she taken his side.

I was oddly reconciled to our estrangement, though. He was displacing his anger and anxiety about Brinda's divorce onto me. Okay. He needed to do that. And my guess was that, as those feelings ebbed, he might come to agree with his wife. My initial frantic fears and self-recrimination—I had, as always, paved the way for my own loss—had also ebbed, enabling me to see this was likely a temporary loss, the kind normal people dealt with, in normal life, where one has friends and lovers and differs with them and reconciles, where life goes on.

Writing it was helping. I cautiously let myself see some coherence in the story I had begun composing. The longest-ago sections were most digested; I must have thought about all that much more in the intervening time than I had realized. The Lohikarma sections drew on the narratives I had been writing for *The Art of Losing*, but inserting myself helped me to understand them better. Narrative Therapy. Physician, heal thyself.

It also helped that Rosslyn and I had continued to speak, every week or so at first, and then with increasing frequency, until we were on the phone several nights a week, for hours on end.

When was it that she said she would come to Vancouver, to meet me?

"My sister lives there now, and—you said the verdict is going to be announced March 16?"

"That's right," I said, shivering with old fears, old hopes, the anticipatory delight of old habits.

"Spring break. Griffin's going on a class trip to Russia."

"Russia!"

"I know." She laughed. "I'm going to be so anxious. It will be good for me to go away too. Otherwise, when you come through Ottawa in May, you're on your way back to India, right?"

"Yes, that's right."

"I don't want that to be the first time we meet. I'll see you in Vancouver."

"That would be so . . . yes, I would love that." But I had to specify. "Just don't—you don't mean you'll come to hear the verdict, do you?"

A long pause. "Yes, that was what I meant." Icy. "You don't want me to come?"

"I very much, very much want you to come. But not that day." Oh, Rosslyn. How to explain? "Give me . . . a few days' grace."

As I fished around in my inchoate resistance, you spoke. "Grace," you repeated. "I always thought that part of what justified your leaving me, in your mind, was that I couldn't properly understand what you had been through."

"That may be true."

"I didn't think *you* fully understood it either, though."

I concurred.

"So—*write it*." You actually said it, just as I had imagined you saying it. "Your story. And then let me read it. Maybe I'll be slightly more convinced that the same thing won't happen again."

"I am!" I shouted. "I have been writing it, for weeks already." I had thought I was writing it for myself, but I am not my ideal reader. You are, Rosslyn. You are. "I will give it to you," I said. "It cannot be finished, until the verdict. There is so much, not just the story of back then, but of this year—so much you need to know."

"I do."

You weren't done. Much as my father had told me to include the complex of prior causes in *The Art of Losing*, you further advised me to frame it with my own loss, to preface it by saying that while it is an analytic study of how twelve families came through the disaster, I didn't come to it strictly as a psychologist. You also told me to make an accounting of my omission to the families, in the course of my final interviews.

You were right. I did.

* * *

And so—forward. Into the final chapters, in which Seth does, as I foretold, forgive me, though it does not happen in the way I expected. He and his family held and healed my heart and so, unknowingly, bore it back to you, dear reader. Dearest Rosslyn.

Ready to write the book? Just about.

SPRING 2005

The art of losing isn't hard to master.
so many things seem filled with the intent
to be lost that their loss is no disaster.
                                        —Elizabeth Bishop

MARCH 16, VERDICT DAY.

*M*y brain skittered all that morning, causing me to make coffee I forgot to drink, shave the same patch three times, until blood-drops bloomed like a field of poppies. I was filled with sick anxiety simply in anticipation of the verdict, but also, Seth had called me that morning, the first time he had initiated contact since our falling-out.

"Ashwin," he said, "we'll see you at the courthouse today?"

My heart hummed. Spring: the frost had melted! I could hear it in his voice. I was welcome in his life again.

"I need to talk to you," he said. "Look for us?"

Sometimes relief and the state one wants relief from feel approximately the same. Which is how I expected the verdict to go as well.

* * *

There is a courtyard that, appropriately, runs alongside the courthouse. I arrived nearly an hour before the verdict, sat on the stone benches, watched the plants suffocating in the urban air, unable, at first, to go in. Should I have let you come, Rosslyn? But my pitch of anxiety—particularly since it was, to my way of thinking, so unjustifiable—made me testy. I would have been resistant to touch, unwilling to talk. We might have fought. That would have been agonizing. I wanted you there, but it was better that I had resisted.

I felt your presence, though. Was that wrong—preferring the luminous clarity of a general idea to your flesh-and-blood challenges? No: we would meet, in real life, in a few days. So I let myself invoke you: the joking voice, a gesture I loved, a concentration of something fresh, almost unbearably alive, warm and cool and citron-scented, there among the hard stones and blurring trees. You see? Even though I could not let you come, you helped, as you knew you would.

Inside, I pushed through a crowd to find Seth, with Lakshmi at his side. He reached to shake my hand; I steadied both of mine by clasping his.

Lakshmi gave me her usual brief acknowledgement, then shushed Seth, who had grasped my elbow and pulled me close in the bustle. "There is someone else you must speak to," he began, with an urgent air, but Lakshmi tugged his sport coat sleeve decisively and frowned.

"Later."

He made a questioning gesture at her with a hand—*what?*— as we heard a shout. Some man, pushing through the crowd, was yelling, "Go back home to the Dark Age! We don't want your problems in Canada." Venkat and Bala found us just then, but we were too humiliated for eye contact. The crowd moved and we were swept inside.

*　*　*

It is hard to remember the only thing worth remembering: the difference, if any, between before and after the verdict. Not guilty. Unlike most others, I was not devastated. I was hardly even disappointed. Who Are the Guilty? Only they and their Maker know.

The bombers were not forced to admit personal responsibility. Okay. They could never, to my way of thinking, be so guilty as an elected government perpetrating violence and death on its own people. Whatever terrorists claim, they never represent the will of a majority. Popular governments, by contrast, are supposed to. Those five or ten Khalistani fools who engineered the bomb plot: they killed some hundreds of people, and I'm willing to wager no more than that many people cheered their actions. Perhaps the same is true in the cases of the Vancouver anti-Asian demonstrations, the Brits' anti-Independence brutality, the Delhi pogroms, the Godhra massacre. But that's not how it looks. All those originated in the centres of power, not the margins, which is why I was moved to anatomize them, while those turbaned sadsacks on the dock in Vancouver moved me little, if at all.

Others felt differently. Many were crushed. Not least by reading this as the all-too-predictable result of a majoritarian government's longstanding failure to countenance a visible minority's concerns.

We milled in the glass-vaulted atrium of the courthouse. All around us, people stood in stunned silence and yet the noise of chatter rose and rose. Where was it coming from?

"Not guilty," Venkat said, his face eerie and motionless, as usual, his eyes dull, red and hurt. "I'm going back home."

"Yes, of course," said Bala, beside him.

"You want us to take you, right now?" Seth asked. He and Lakshmi were on their way back from a vacation. They had gone with their daughters and new grandson to Malcolm Island, that same place off the west coast where they had holidayed with Sita and Sundar thirty years earlier. Venkat had flown in to Vancouver yesterday, and they had planned to drive him back to Lohikarma after a day or two.

"No," Venkat said.

I stared, thinking I saw the stormy blue-black pixels of his complexion receding or merging. His face seemed to have no shape of its own.

"I am going *home*. Canada is dead to me."

This was the last time I saw him.

As the others worked themselves into a flutter trying to figure out what he wanted and how either to give it to him or to dissuade him, I took my leave. Seth said he would call me.

✳ ✳ ✳

We met the next afternoon. Venkat had made Bala drive him to the airport, where he boarded the next plane for India. "Must have cost a fortune. But what else has he got to spend his money on?"

Did Seth want to know? I was no longer afraid his reaction would change my feelings for him, even though our recent estrangement was still fresh, making me fear a confrontation.

"We're going to have to do something with the birds," Seth went on, "but his leaving spared Lakshmi and me a lot of agony, let me tell you."

To hell with it, I thought, *I'll tell you.* The Canadian government was rejecting calls for an inquiry into the mishandling of the Air India disaster, rejecting any imputation that race had been a factor. *Fertilizing home-grown terrorists.*

But as I opened my mouth, Seth held up a hand.

"Let me tell you," he repeated, and I shut up and listened.

$\mathcal{M}$ arch 5, eleven days before the verdict, Seth picked Brinda up from the airport in Vancouver about noon and they drove to Malcolm Island. Lakshmi and Ranjani awaited them in a cabin there: they had accompanied Greg on a shoot in the area, since Ranjani hadn't wanted him to be away from the baby for too long, and Lakshmi had gone along to help her daughter. But Greg was going to be bushwhacking for the week following, so Ranjani had proposed her father and sister come. Brinda was on spring break from Johns Hopkins and hadn't met the baby yet. And they had wanted to return to Malcolm Island ever since that long-ago holiday—Ranjani because she had been too young to remember it, and the others because they remembered it fondly—but they had never gotten close.

It was remote: a tiny island several hundred kilometres up the coast, colonized by utopian Finns a hundred years earlier. The dream hadn't lasted but the settlers had stayed, integrating into local industries, eking out a subsistence living. Kaj Halonen, of Finnish origin himself, passed on to Seth a tidbit: it was on Malcolm Island that John Harbord had come up with Lohikarma's name.

Brinda and Seth pulled in a little after eight that night. The cabin was on a quiet beach road. As they unfolded themselves, a briny chill sluiced the stale car air from their clothes and nostrils. Holiday melancholy seized them, Seth gently—*it's cold!*—and Brinda violently—*have I packed enough books?*—in anticipation of aimless strolling and curio-'n'-fudge shops and eventual boredom. When they opened the cabin door, though, all those feelings fled. A faint milkiness to the atmosphere, small flannel blankets dropped on the sofa, a bramble of rattles above a black-and-white play mat. "Where's the baby?" The first words out of both of their mouths.

Ranjani emerged, holding him, from some other room. "Who wants him?" Kieran squinted in his aunt's direction, his chin bumping out from a yellow terry sleeper, forehead outlined by an uneven scraggle of black hair, thinning at the top. "Baby-pattern baldness." Ranjani grinned as she handed him to Brinda.

"What's that about?" Brinda asked.

"They go through a phase in the womb where they're covered with lanugo, monkey fur." Ranjani reached to stroke his head. "They're supposed to lose it in the ninth month of gestation, but my theory is he's still losing his."

Brinda was relieved. He wasn't beautiful, not yet. But he felt-good-smelled-good, the little parcel, and was already more appetizing by multiples than his repulsive newborn pictures. She could only hope that as he grew cuter, her ability to withstand it would grow commensurately.

"Don't you love it? He's still becoming human."

"Aren't we all. Eh, baby?" Brinda searched his hooded eyes, and rotated him to kiss the nape-fringe of his weird tonsure.

✳ ✳ ✳

The next morning, a lazy one. Ranjani went back to bed after breakfast while the others played idly on the floor with Kieran's small fists, wound his fuzzy-buzzy bee, read his *Goodnight Moon*. At lunchtime, Ranjani and Brinda suggested they all walk down to Sointula's main strip, but it was chilly and blustery. "The baby could get an ear infection," Seth told them irritably. They got in the car.

Their first stop was a café, homey and a bit shabby, much like the town. Seth was more amenable to strolling a few blocks in the centre, so, after lunch, they walked to the local museum, full of historic photos and artifacts telling the Sointula story: injustice and hardship, utopian failure and more hardship, soldiering on . . . to more hardship. The docent, an old-timer descended from the original Finnish settlers, gave them a tour. "In the sixties, the hippies started arriving," she said, pointing to pictures of grubby but well-nourished people holding banjos and wooden flutes. "Draft dodgers from the States, and others. They took to our culture, though. Learned how to bake bread and build saunas."

"Saunas, eh?" said Seth.

They learned a new word: *sisu*, a Finnish word for maritime stick-to-it-iveness. *Sisu* mingled with desperation and hope in the windblown streets as they passed galleries and storefronts, buildings of weather-worn candy-green or peeling melon-pink, and others that had been permitted to silver into age, a more dignified option, perhaps, but also sadly final. Ranjani carried Kieran in a long strip of fabric, knotted around her waist and shoulders, and Seth walked with one arm always half outstretched toward them, in case she should trip, or need a hand up a curb or a cloak thrown over a puddle. Their final destination was THE SOINTULA CO-OPERATIVE STORE ASSOCIATION EST. 1909.

Seth came in, but when the groceries mounted, left to bring the car to the parking lot of the co-op. He entered again, holding the door for a woman behind him, who an over-the-shoulder glance revealed possibly to be Indian. He nodded as he always did, didn't smile, exactly, but showed some slight recognition, perceptible only in the contact of eyes, the mirrored intention of the other Indian in the store, theatre, airport. The woman made reciprocal eye contact, perhaps unintentionally, a blink of distracted thanks for the door-holding. As Seth tussled with Brinda over who should carry the bags and their party of five—five!—bundled toward the door, he saw that the woman still stood there, a hand over her mouth, so he nodded again, more slightly, as one does on passing a stranger twice. Her hair was so short it looked shaven.

The others may not have nodded. They weren't as inclined as Seth to act as though every Indian were someone they should know. In the car, though, Lakshmi said, "Did you see that woman?"

Seth grunted agreement through a mild frown, a lip-shrug. He glanced in his rear-view mirror before turning the car. The woman had come out and was watching them depart. "I didn't expect to see an Indian up here."

"I wasn't sure she was Indian," Brinda said from the back. "Hispanic? Native, maybe."

"She looked like Sita," said Lakshmi.

"You're thinking that because we were here with her and Sundar last time," Seth said. They had all, without yet having spoken of it, thought more than once of Sundar and Sita since their arrival.

Lakshmi sighed and leaned her head back in her seat. "I suppose."

They were back at the cabin within minutes, and unaccountably sleepy. Even the baby slept.

Late afternoon there came a knock on the thin front door. Who in the world? "Can someone get it?" Lakshmi called, her hands wet with onions. Ranjani was staring down a diaper, and Seth put down his newspaper, but it was Brinda, on her way to make tea, who answered the knock.

The strange-looking woman from the co-op. A buzz-cut of silvering hair, deep eye sockets, hollow cheeks, a wide brown mouth held tight. A dark coat with frayed wrists, wrinkled pants, boots whose creases slashed deep the toes. As she stepped inside, Brinda smelled her: woodsmoke, earth, breezes, but above and beneath it all a large, pervasive sourness, not unpleasant until it filled the room, not a smell she would want to live with. The woman looked famished, and gazed at them as though she would eat them. Ranjani hung back with the baby.

"You don't know me?" the woman asked, sounding breathless. Was that a smile or a grimace? "You don't know me."

Seth came to the front of his family, the man of the household, to face the stranger. Strange and stranger: that voice, with a little more force; that face, with a little more flesh. "Sita," he said, not meaning to, and felt it catch at his throat.

Ghost doubles. Schrödinger's wife. Dead until they opened the box to find her alive.

* * *

Her story first: Years of profound unhappiness with Venkat, no surprise there, though she had never exactly said as much in life. *In life.* Was she in their life now? Or in another one?

Until that drive from Lohikarma to Vancouver twenty years earlier, when she confessed her desperation to Sundar. He understood what she didn't say, how it had worsened since he had left for university. She no longer had her joy morning and night. "It wasn't his job, to cheer me up. But he did. I lived for him."

Her nostrils flared and her mouth re-tightened, and Lakshmi put a hand over Sita's. Seth saw his wife's sympathy as a foregone conclusion, saw it as though from a distant, imperious height, his wife's hand over that other one's.

That drive wasn't the first time Sita and Sundar had talked in this vein. Her son had, a couple of times, tried to address Venkat's dominance, his failure to listen, all that Sita could demand and didn't. "But Sundar's feelings, about me and how I was wronged, these were too mixed up. He was still an adolescent. I didn't see what I could do." She had at times defended Venkat to him, at other times promised to try harder to defend herself; she had also tried to intercede with Venkat on Sundar's behalf. She met with no success. "He was a wonderful boy, a perfect boy. He never gave us one single thing to complain about and still Venkat complained. Fought with him. Why? Why could he not enjoy, not appreciate, Sundar?" To Sundar, she would say that Venkat's advice was not bad; engineering school was a practical choice; Venkat was reliable, steady, "a good man," but she believed this less and less with time. She started to feel instead that Venkat's behaviour was governed not by love, but by abstract convictions or some fidelity to a noble self-image that had little to do with them, more to do with a monstrous, narcissistic pride. Not that he was monstrous, he loved his wife and child, but abstractly—he didn't feel any obligation to know them in their particulars.

"He used to criticize me for not being harder on Sundar. Those days, when his father was criticizing him for not working harder, not being more serious, those were the only days my son had on this earth." Her voice cracked and she rubbed her face with a practised-seeming motion, up the cheeks to the forehead, down and across the mouth, too many times, a gesture that looked obsessive. (I asked her about it, later, when I met her and saw her do it. She said she felt tears stinging her face from inside, so she rubbed until the surface burned. No tears fell. "I don't get to cry," she said.)

"I was dreading the trip to India, three weeks in his mother's house. His sister was very sweet, though tiring. I pitied her. Is she still alive?"

"Yes," said Seth. "Not the mother, though."

"The brother's wife was frightful. And his mother, too. She would pinch me, sometimes. Hard." She took hold of her upper arm to show how and where her mother-in-law would abuse her. "I screamed the first couple of times, and then I learned no one, not even his sister, believed me.

"Sundar told me, on the way to the airport, don't come. He had once already been to India by himself, two years earlier. You know, he was planning to go to film school, after engineering. He wanted to finish his engineering degree. He was not rash. But he was going to apply, not only UBC but UCLA and NYU. He had a new video camera with him. He liked his cousins, enjoyed his grandmother, he was excited, but he told me, 'Don't come, *amma*. There's no need.'"

She hadn't thought of this until he suggested it: *don't come*. She could never have defied Venkat so completely in his presence, but there, on the road, far away, without him there to challenge her—even though the aftertones of his voice rang in her head, the aftersmell of him, the after-feel—the idea began to gain plausibility. But where would she go instead?

"'A hotel,' Sundar told me. He didn't seem to think it was so hard. *Find someplace nice. Maybe on the waterfront.* And how long would I stay there? I asked. *Until you feel ready to go home, I guess.* I thought about it. As we approached the airport, I noticed how many hotels there were, so cheap, so close. Shuttle buses from the airport. We checked in for our flight. I hadn't quite got the courage up. I didn't know where to stop, or when, when to tell Sundar goodbye. So I kept going, right onto the plane. I don't remember exactly when I decided. There wasn't a moment when I thought, *yes, this is right*. There were factors. Sundar could tell his relatives I had had a last-minute crisis at work, and by the time they called Venkat, I would already have called him. I think that made me hesitate, that I would have to call him to tell him what I had done. But I would have twenty-four hours of solitude first."

That seemed as much the reason as any other: a full day and night of solitude, when she would not be accountable or self-conscious. She would be invisible and Sundar well looked-after. "I got him settled on the plane. He wanted me to have the window seat. That's when I turned to him and said, *I'm not coming. I'm going now. You'll be all right?*" Her voice cracked, her face cracked, she started rubbing-scrubbing-scouring her visage again. A hoarse whisper, "That's what I asked him."

Lakshmi got her a glass of water and she sipped. Her tea, which she had been given despite refusing the offer, sat cooling.

"*Okay, kanna*, I said. *I'm going. I'll call Daddy tomorrow so that I know you have arrived.* He said, *Great, Mom. Go for it.* He moved into the window seat. The aisle was crowded, last-minute passengers. I must have kissed him but there was no particular moment, nothing memorable. They were checking the passageway, wanting to close the door, and I was suddenly—I got very afraid that I would change my mind, so I picked up my handbag and ran out the door, down that tunnel, I remember it seemed very long, and they perhaps shouted, but I didn't stop. Took the first shuttle. Took the first hotel. It was a strange . . . euphoria."

The euphoria might have wobbled, as she slept and woke through dreams, nightmares and the thrill of unsettlement, but it didn't desert her till morning, in the hotel coffee shop, where people were eating and staff swabbing tables to the accompaniment of breakfast-hour TV news.

"Terrible, about that plane, eh?" said her waitress, nodding stiff curls at the ceiling-mounted screen as she licked a finger and turned a page on her pad.

* * *

"*That's* how you found out?" Brinda asked, and Lakshmi put her hand over Sita's again.

"They never took you off the passenger list," Seth said.

"No?" Sita asked.

Had she never thought about this? Seth wondered.

"They probably would have done it at Heathrow," said Lakshmi.

"You could never get away with that now," said Ranjani, jiggling the baby from one arm to the other. "They would ground the plane, locate your luggage and make sure it left with you."

"Sure, it was because of this bomb that they started doing all that," Brinda pointed out.

"We have been living twenty years with your death," said Seth.

Sita looked around at them, opened her mouth, closed it again. Apologetic? "I didn't know," she said. Helpless. "And . . . Venkat? How is he?"

Seth thought of Venkat, pottering among his stinking, chattering birds, his clothes hanging off his shrunken frame. His house overheated to keep the birds comfortable; his bare feet, his toenails yellow, thick and curving, beak-like. Once, Seth himself had trimmed them. "He's pathetic."

Sita blinked at the blow but trembled her head, *yes*.

Twenty years they had looked after Venkat, worried for him, the worry a fixture of their lives. Accompanied him to Ireland. Seth didn't even like the man! They were barely related! And she had been alive the whole time. *Monstrous*—she said that about Venkat? Her selfishness was monstrous.

"Why did I not call? This is what you want to know. Why did I not come back?" Sita said.

Seth sat, arms crossed, and the women of his life, for once, looked to him. He said nothing.

"I don't remember much of those first days, months. I thought I would kill myself. Except it wasn't exactly thinking. I was alive by accident. Sundar was dead. I had left him. But then I thought, God kept me alive to punish me."

"It might have been a better punishment for you to return to Venkat." Seth heard himself say this, as if from another room, as though he were eavesdropping on some other branch of his multi-furcated life. He had never been so harsh and confident.

"I tried to call, one time." Sita wiped a gleam of sweat from the cup of each eye. "After I got here. Maybe around . . . it was winter. November? There was no answer at home and when I called his office, they said he was on leave."

They all waited but Seth said nothing.

Lakshmi wiped tears from her own lashes with the palms of her hands and explained, "He would have been in India then. He, he did try to kill himself."

She didn't touch Sita as she said this, Seth noticed. Nothing to soften this news. In this branch of his life, it appeared that Lakshmi and his daughters allied themselves with him, followed his lead. It was what he'd always wanted and yet now it discomfited him.

"By the time I stopped believing in God," said Sita, "I had started believing life was a kind of penance, set by, maybe by the force of life itself."

She might so easily have slipped through history's cracks, were it not for this chance occurrence: her favourite people from her past life, practically on her doorstep.

"And how do you live here, Sita?" Lakshmi asked.

She told them about the ATM card and chequebook she carried, for an account she had established secretly when Sundar was six, when she began working outside of the home, so she could afford small things for him—swim goggles, comic books—that Venkat wouldn't allow. At first she put in only a few dollars weekly; she was working part time and was wary of detection. But over time, her contributions grew, so that, when the disaster struck, she had enough to sustain her for months. "Especially since I wasn't really eating and didn't care where I slept. I just walked and kept walking, north, I suppose."

She was unclear exactly how she came to Malcolm Island, but thought she must have landed there about the time her money ran low, when she took on seasonal work in the fish processing plant. (A fish-works must have been an advanced circle of hell for a Tamil Brahmin, with their fastidious vegetarian genetics. And it would have held a par-ticular sting for her, looking death-by-air in the face a thousand times a day.) "When I got here, I remembered our holiday. Remember that?" They all nodded. "It was so nice, that week here, with Sundar. He en-joyed it so much. So did I."

Her second winter here, she was working as a cashier at the co-op. One day, a local named George Sinclair struck up a conversation with her. An ex-American, the sort they had heard of, he had recently moved onto a single acre of his own. He recognized her from the fish plant. "He offered to let me garden a patch on his land. The first week that I worked on it, I walked six kilometres each way from my rented room, an hour and a half each way, with the gardening work in between. Sinclair had a truck, so he started to pick me up and drop me, but I felt I was a burden. A burden to people, a burden to the earth. That felt wrong. I must only give, now: a ghost should not take. So he asked and I moved in to his cabin." She sounded impersonal, but looked somehow dreamy. "No shock, no shame." She gestured at her torso. "This is not even a body to me, anymore."

Then she seemed to awaken slightly, and told Lakshmi, "So this is how we get along. I sell my vegetables and flowers, late spring, sum-mer, fall. Sinclair teaches yoga, does odd repairs here and there. He has kayaks and sometimes he takes tourists out. Can you come and see me there? Our home?" Her manner grew slightly frantic. "How long are you here? And how are all of you? Ranjani, with a baby," she crooned a little, the volubility and animation seeming strange on her.

"Yes," Seth said, trying to seize the lead. "Ranjani's husband's work brought us up this way again." *Ranjani's husband*. There is no truth. *Ev-ery one is 99 percent secret*, he thought. What had Sita not told them? What was untellable? What was Venkat doing now?

"I went—" Seth began. It seemed important to tell her this. "—with Venkat to Ireland, to look for, to claim . . ." Your bodies? His bodies? "Sundar's body was found. We identified it. Venkat took the ashes to India, to the Kaveri."

Sita had brought a hand to her mouth, her gesture, perhaps, to greet the dead or long-gone, and her eyes looked more like her eyes than ever. "He saw him."

"His body, yes."

"He saw him last. And took his ashes back home, to scatter, in the Kaveri."

Seth—*boom*—was blinded by another bludgeon of fury. "You could have seen him too."

"Not with *him*!" she said, vehement, dismissive, clubbing him with her words, thought Seth—*boom*, how he disliked her, *boom*, what kind of woman was she?

Sita looked around at them, at a spectrum of reactions that she read or misread as misunderstanding, or understanding too well. "It wasn't my fault alone that I wasn't on that plane. How could I—I couldn't have stood beside him, to collect my Sundar's, my Sundar's . . ." She made a noise, guttural, desperate; and again, the rubbing of the face. "It wasn't only God that gave me this hell."

"Why didn't you call us?" Lakshmi asked then, her voice gentle, her hand extended once more.

"Back then? I'm not sure." Another sip of water. "I didn't want to involve you?"

"But why did you pursue us here, if that was how you felt?" Seth sounded softer but felt no softening. Why did he feel no softening?

"How could I have lived with myself if I had let you go? I don't always understand myself too well. That holiday, here, with all of you. It might have been the best week of my life." In a yet-softer voice, she asked Ranjani, "What is your baby called?"

"Kieran." Ranjani pulled his blanket a little higher, cupping his head so that he couldn't be seen. "Kieran Sundar."

Sita made a startled, lateral movement with a small noise of pain, as though someone had slipped a knife in beneath her shoulder blade. Seth felt it, too, and felt his petty moral ire drain, burst, from his own wound. Whatever she had done or failed to do, he and Lakshmi sat before her now with their girls and their grandson. Sundar had died.

"We're so sorry." His tears came, finally, with grand force. "Such a wonderful boy. And you—such a good mother to him." He went outside to cry alone.

* * *

They agreed that they would come to see her at home.

"Anytime," Sita said. "I won't be coming into town again for a week or so, I'll be home preparing the beds for planting. Bring towels. We have a sauna. I'll build a fire. There's a beach. Ocean view. I'll make tea." She sounded like an only child planning a make-believe party. "We don't have a phone, so if you want to send a message to me, just ask at the co-op if anyone is coming out our way. Sinclair, and Karma—that is what I'm called now, here."

They talked, in the days that followed, as they walked shores of stone and shores of sand; scrutinized wall-hung weavings and photos of the dead, a new kind of family discussion, where daughters talked directly to father and anyone might take any side. No three females giggling in secret, cynical rightness; no Seth stewing in solitary silence. Most often, the women felt Sita had had the right to leave Venkat, especially after Sundar was grown. And Seth had little trouble saying he wouldn't want to be married to Venkat. He had not chosen his mate, but if fate had chosen a Venkat for him, he might have been forced to tinker.

The women were no more convinced than Sita herself had been that she was right not to show herself after the crash. Or however that went. They got tangled in the double-negatives; language failed them. They all resented that their family had been, for twenty years—twenty years!—burdened with Venkat. But Sita had been burdened with him for twenty-five years before that. And she hadn't chosen him or that responsibility any more than they had; in fact, they might say she had less choice—so how could they say she was remiss?

Finally, Seth asked, "What do we say to Venkat?"

"Nothing," said Brinda, and her father nodded and said, "That's right."

* * *

They were over the midline hump of their holiday already, and a day dawned bright for their trip to the island's northwest flank. Ranjani

opted to stay back, because of the baby—Sita had no running water and
only a wood stove for heat—so the other three went, mid-afternoon.
Sita had drawn them a map and it proved itself. They exited the car
"in the middle of nowhere," except for a scarf Sita had tied to mark the
path. The forest scraggled out onto a narrow strip of beach, as though a
curtain had been pulled back before they were quite ready, to show them
the grey-green sea.

To their left was a cabin whose walls were made of fitted and mud-
ded wood, seven feet high at one end, slanting under large tar-coated
shingles to a terminal wall of five feet or so. Seventy, eighty square feet?
At most. A small chimney poked out the top of the low end. It kept its
hunched back to the woods, and they walked around the front to find
the garden patch on its other side. The brush had been hacked back
there and Sita was turning soil in full sun, the bones of her arms all jags
and points under a billowing T-shirt. Her jeans were bunched at the
hips. She let her shovel drop, and dusted her hands on her pants to reach
toward them, face eerie, joy-animated skin over a still-frozen skull, sunlight filling some hollows so that the others seemed darker than ever.
She clutched their sleeves and showed them around.

She gardened some flowers now, but mostly vegetables. Brinda
asked about her one-time dream, to create a Linnean clock out of flowers that would open in sequence to show the hours. Seth had pressed
her, back in the day, to propose it to the City of Lohikarma, do it in
Harbord Park.

Sita twisted her lips to one side. "Vanity," she said.

Brinda remembered that the Air India Memorial in Bantry Bay was
a sundial, but didn't ask if Sita knew about it.

The cabin, it turned out, was made of driftwood. "Logging, you
know. Incredible what washes up. No need to cut any more down." Sinclair had just left, she said, to teach a yoga class in town. That might
have been his truck they passed. He would be back in a couple of hours.
She had had a feeling they would come today. She had scraped out the
fire pit at the edge of the beach and built within it a teepee-frame of
sticks filled with brush. A blackened kettle sat on the ground, ringed by
chipped enamelled-tin cups.

They peeked inside the house, whose door opened to the woods:

a bunk and a bench, the width of each implying that Sinclair must be nearly as skinny as Sita, trestle table, chair for a guest, pot-bellied stove. Pot-hooks screwed into the walls, a two-foot shelf of dishes and books, another of dry goods. A window to the sea and an oil lamp.

"You cook here?" Lakshmi asked, trying to see the contents of the Mason jars on the dry goods shelf.

"We mostly eat raw food. One of us might make a dal from time to time. We have a root cellar for, for *thayir.*"

It was the first Tamil word they had heard from her, the woman who had been made to speak only English to her husband, only Tamil to her son. *Thayir*: the homemade yogourt they all had craved in their early years far from home. Some made poor attempts with commercial brands, but it wasn't worth it; they lacked the taste, the spirit of home. Finally, in the seventies, someone brought—smuggled?—some culture over and it grew and spread from home to home across Canada in preciously Tupperwared tablespoons, to every Tamil Brahmin in the land. Sita had been cut off from all that.

The sauna was a more sophisticated building, with a tiny adorable antechamber and connected hot-room. "Sinclair knew better what he was doing by this point. He built the house first," Sita said, seeming not to see anything but them, but wanting them to see it all.

She does have a life, Brinda thought, watching her. *And it gives her, if not joy, then pride; if not pride, then satisfaction.*

Sinclair's latest project was a yoga studio, usable already if not complete, with a sea-view picture window to match the sauna's. They irrigated the garden from a bore well.

"So simple," said Lakshmi, her highest compliment.

Seth remembered then that his wife said once, in response to a question from the kids: *What would you be or do if you didn't have a family?* "A monastic," she had replied. No hesitation. She sounded almost surprised that they didn't already know. It fit perfectly. What else, with her silent meditation and retreats? The nunnery: what she would have done in Venkat's place. No paralytic fear for her—she had a backup plan, an imagined life in parallel.

"So you garden through the summer?" she asked Sita. "And in the winter?"

Sita wanted to please, but didn't seem to get the question. Ah, how does she occupy her time, in the winter.

"Time," she said, as though it were a puzzle.

It was, the family agreed later. They didn't think enough about how to solve the question of time. They thought, as did most people, about how best to spend it.

"Time passes. I walk the shore. Winter days are short." A strange smile shape-shifted Sita's hollows. "I remember Sundar. I remember all he said, his feel and weight and scent"—the brown-cereal aroma of his little-boy time, the must of adolescence, the sulphury power of growing manhood—"what he liked, what he didn't like, what hurt his feelings, all he knew, what he hid from me. I think of him, when I wake in the night, when I sit at the shore. Time passes." She took a deep breath, salt air. "Let me get the fire started. Tea. I've heated the sauna, already. You must try it."

Seth still had some hard questions to ask. "And, your boyfriend, you told him about us?"

"Yes, I told him about you." She had a smudge of charcoal on her nose. The fire kindled.

"Does he know of your life before?"

"I told him I lost my husband and son in the disaster."

The truth, in other words, thought Seth. Sita shrugged brightly at him as though he had spoken it aloud. "You said, about Venkat, *He loved us but he never knew us.* It made me wonder if my wife and daughters should leave me: I freely admit that *I* don't understand them."

She gave him a very small smile, no reassurance, no condemnation. "It's time for a sauna. You should go first."

He resisted. "No, ladies first." Lakshmi was also a little reticent, so it was decided that the two of them would go for a stroll while Sita and Brinda went first.

"We will yell when we come out," said Sita, "so that you can cover your eyes if you don't want to see us naked when we run out for our ocean dip."

This was distasteful to him. Their hostess: if she hadn't known so many details of their past, their shared lives, he never would have believed her to be the same Sita, that demure paragon, excellent cook, shapely, soft, unassuming. She really had died.

And yet . . .

"Ocean dip?" Brinda asked Sita as he and Lakshmi walked away.

And yet: there was something familiar in his feelings for her, perhaps because of how she had changed. She had been so opaque before, treated him as a respected older relative, kept herself masked. And in any case, the wife of a relative—what did Seth need to know? But now she seemed as though, for all she had been hiding for twenty years, she had nothing to hide. She perhaps feared nothing. She positively invited the direct question! What was familiar? She reminded him more of his daughters now, and his way of relating, even perhaps his actual feelings, had obediently merged with her shift, into an affectionate sense of familial discord.

* * *

It was very strange for Brinda to undress with Sita. Women of her mother's time and place were exceedingly if inconsistently shy about nudity. She remembered her Toronto aunt telling her once that she couldn't stand the gym locker room because it embarrassed her to see other women naked. Yet every Indian river had women standing in its flow, their thin, wet saris hiding practically nothing.

Sita pulled off her T-shirt, dropped her jeans, picked up a towel without hiding herself in it. "Ready?" she asked. In the hot-room, Sita spread her towel untidily on a bench, scooped water onto the stones, her movements completely unselfconscious. *This is not a body to me anymore*, she had told Brinda's dad. *No shock, no shame.* As though she were crone or child, or, as she put it, ghost.

* * *

"So different, eh?" Lakshmi said, picking up a piece of driftwood as they neared the water.

"Huh? Oh, yes."

"Really makes me question how we live, our values."

No surprise for Seth there. "For her, her life seems not to have any value."

"I'm not sure of that."

"She said it, didn't she?" He picked up a rock and threw it into the water. "She has nothing to live for, now that Sundar is gone."

"I guess that's what I'm asking: why do we have to live *for* something?" Now she sounded defensive, irritable. "Why can't we simply live?"

Before, he had lived for his family. He thought Shivashakti had saved him from that. He was learning.

"Okay. You win," he said. "But I didn't come to Canada and live here forty years to give up flush toilets."

She snorted and slapped his arm. They walked on.

* * *

Sita was emaciated, but still, when she sat, there were those few inches of below-the-navel shirring, the body's graffiti: *Baby Wuz Here*. Ex-skinny Ranjani had it now, a muffin-top above the chic jeans. But she would get back to exercising. And then she would have it all, wouldn't she? Envy can become a way of life. It's why Brinda had to try to avoid her sister until she had a life of her own.

"You are not married, no babies," Sita said.

Brinda couldn't decide whether the steam intensified the burn in her nostrils or mitigated it, just as she had never been sure that she liked saunas. She looked down at her own smooth belly, up and out to the ocean. "Divorced."

"Oh-oh-oh." Sita shook her head. "I could feel it."

"I wish I were like you," Brinda cried then with the force of a realization. "I *want* so much. You're so self-contained. If I didn't want, I could have stayed with Dev. Or I could be happy divorced. Or if not happy, then . . . then whatever you are."

"What I am: this is natural?"

"How do you mean?"

"Sinclair is happy. Whatever he has renounced"—she made scales with her hands—"he has gained just as much. He has his projects. His days are structured by small goals."

"But not yours."

"I didn't renounce desire, or ambition." Sita shuddered, quick, like a cat. "I lost them. I have broken with nature. I live outside of its circle. I am a stranger to all. But what happened, child? Why could you not stay with your husband, and, now, what?"

Brinda took a breath and told Sita what had happened with Dev. The truth, quickly, in summary. It had gotten easier to tell, and she found better ways to thread it, with each repetition. *No shock, no shame.*

"Dev was furious at me for ending the marriage. 'Ten years!' he said. 'Doesn't that mean anything to you?' The most painful thing I've ever been through. Since, that is, since Sundar's death. It changed our lives. Changed our dad."

Sita was very still. "Venkat liked sex with me when I was sleeping. Sleeping! Even when Sundar was small and waking me twice every night, this man liked it best when I was asleep. How did he manage to catch me asleep, even? Then I would wake up, while he was, you know, but I would pretend, because I knew he wanted that and because that way I wouldn't have to look at him. After, he would go back to sleep and I would lie awake." She stacked tight fists on her knees. "I would be so angry! I thought I would go nuts. I did, a little bit," she said, sounding almost clinical. "I've had enough sauna. You?"

"Definitely." Brinda had been wondering whether to tell her parents the truth about her marriage. Now she knew she wouldn't.

"Okay, I'll shout so your father isn't embarrassed! Run!"

✳ ✳ ✳

Seth and Lakshmi heard the shouts from where they were: a quarter-mile down the shore where they sat on a big chilly boulder, watching the waves. Lakshmi saw them enter the water; Seth looked the other way.

He had been telling Lakshmi, for the first time, about Ireland. The sight of waves always cast back at him images of Bantry Bay: a woman in a pink sari, a man in a utility vest, days of staring out at the water only to see a rock, a seal.

Sundar's body. The young mother's roses.

"You never told me," said his wife.

"I didn't?" He sounded like Sita. "No, I suppose not. I couldn't, when I first returned. I couldn't do that to you."

"You should have trusted me." Undeniable accusation, if blunted by time.

He felt a violent wonder at her presence: her miraculous profile, the apple of her cheek, its profound, dusky curve. Waylaid by beauty.

She patted his knee, mocking a little, *why so serious*? Pressed her face to his shoulder.

They rose, returned. Sita was putting the kettle on. Lakshmi confessed she had no interest in the sauna. Seth confessed he did. Brinda arrived, dressed, shivering-grinning-bright, hair damp at the temples. Seth hugged her, rubbing her back as she huddled into him.

"How was it?"

"You'll love it, Dad. Do it. You have to."

"Go, Seth." Lakshmi held her hands out to the fire.

"And I have to jump in the ocean after?"

Sita nodded

"Cold?"

"What do you think?" asked Brinda.

Sita sat with a sigh. "Just shout. We'll look away."

The stones hissed in the silence. Seth dribbled on another dipper of water just to hear it. Nothing permeated, not the incessant tree-whisper, not the women's chat, not the roar of the surf . . . oh, wait. Maybe the roar was the hush? The water beat-beat-beating out all other sounds.

He settled on his towel to watch it, across the grey Canadian shore, and his mind turned not to Ireland and the terrible things thrown up or swallowed by its sea, but rather, almost idly, to spiritual progress and the contents of betrayal, and, more actively, to Shivashakti. He had recently, tentatively, started again to attend satsang at the ashram, after a break of several months. He didn't know that he would continue, but for the moment it felt truer than isolating himself from the community.

He thought, as he had so many times, of his ashram encounter on New Year's Eve. At first, he had been able to recall very little, but, with time, the memory had filled in and taken shape, until it seemed he wasn't merely remembering the event, but creating it. The mystery had not lessened, though. You can only love what you cannot understand.

Om, he began now, though only in his mind, so the silence was still unbroken. *Om*, a syllable of silence billowing out over the precipice of unknowing. *Om*.

And Seth, sweating-shouting-loving-naked, ran, his furry belly bouncing, he ran, his shrivelled jewels swinging, he ran to the salty water on his stiff old legs, he ran, by God, and he jumped.

ACKNOWLEDGEMENTS

I owe a huge debt to others' writing on the topics of this novel. They not only enhanced my thinking, but supplied quotes and anecdotes. Any factual accuracy owes to these works, while factual errors, deliberate and otherwise, are mine alone. Foremost among them:

Christian Beels, *A Different Story: The Rise of Narrative in Psychotherapy*

Kim Bolan, *Loss of Faith: How the Air India Bombers Got Away with Murder*

Norman Buchignani and Doreen M. Indra, with Ram Srivastava, *Continuous Journey: A Social History of South Asians in Canada*

Veena Das, *Mirrors of Violence: Communities, Riots and Survivors in South Asia*, particularly her essay, "Our Work to Cry: Your Work to Listen."

Paul Davies, *God and the New Physics*

Richard Feynman, *Six Easy Pieces*

Amitav Ghosh, "The Ghosts of Mrs. Gandhi," from *The New Yorker*, July 17, 1995

Sturla Gunnarsson, *Air India 182* (DVD)

Sudhir Kakar, *The Colors of Violence: Cultural Identities, Religion and Conflict, The Analyst and the Mystic*; and others

Ali Kazimi, *Continuous Journey* (DVD) and *Undesirables*

David Ludden, ed., *Making India Hindu: Religion, Community, and the Politics of Democracy in India*

Cynthia Mahmood, *Fighting for Faith and Nation: Dialogues with Sikh Militants*

Manoj Mitta and H S Phoolka, *When a Tree Shook Delhi: The 1984 Carnage and Its Aftermath*

Bharati Mukherjee and Clarke Blaise, *The Sorrow and the Terror*

Martha C. Nussbaum, *The Clash Within: Democracy, Religious Violence, and India's Future*

Alan Parry and Robert E. Doan, *Story Re-Visions: Narrative Therapy in the Postmodern World*

Sumit Sarkar, *Beyond Nationalist Frames*

Amartya Sen, *The Argumentative Indian: Writings on Indian History, Culture, and Identity*

Articles by Cassel Busse, Amber Dean, Angela Failler, Maya Seshia, Raja Singh Soni and Asha Varadharajan, in a feature section on the bombing of AI 182, edited by Chandrima Chakraborty, in *TOPIA: Canadian Journal of Cultural Studies*, 2012.

The writing of this book received generous support from The Canada Council for the Arts, the US National Endowment for the Arts, The Arkansas Arts Council, and The Writers Colony at Dairy Hollow.

The manuscript benefited from expert readings by generous friends: Deena Aziz, Kirstin Erickson, Andy McCord, Alan Parry, Surendra Singh and Reeta Vyas. Kim Bolan talked to me about Khalistani extremism, the bombing and the trial. Colin Soskolne talked to me about epidemiology. Dhanam Kochoi, Ravi Kumar, Shoba Kumar and Thara Kumar kept my family warm and entertained when I left to do research. Bhuvana Viswanathan, S. P. Viswanathan, Van Brock and Frances Brock contributed manuscript-readings, child care, and 1,001 loving encouragements. Bruce Westwood and Carolyn Forde, agents extraordinaires, pledged enthusiasm through multiple drafts. Anne Collins, gift from the editor gods, sculpted the book with years of assiduous notes. Mira Brock and Ravi Brock gave daily—hours of peace for writing; means of recovery from writing; a bright poetic heat that I reached for as I wrote. And Geoff Brock, believe it or not (I barely can), gave *all* of the above.